Sadomasochism for Accountants

Published in Great Britain and the United States in 2009 by
MARION BOYARS PUBLISHERS LTD
24 Lacy Road London SW15 1NL

www.marionboyars.co.uk

Distributed in Australia by Tower Books Pty Ltd,
Unit 2, 17 Rodborough Road, Frenchs Forest, NSW 2086, Australia

Printed in 2009
10 9 8 7 6 5 4 3 2 1

A CIP catalogue record for this book is available from the British Library.
A CIP catalog record for this book is available from the Library of Congress.

ISBN 978-0-7145-3181-6

Set in Bembo 11/14pt

Printed in England by J.H. Haynes & Co. Ltd., Sparkford

To Jess for teaching me about hedonism
The Geek for teaching me about discipline (ooo err)
And Mum. Because she knows where I live.

by Rosy Barnes

MARION BOYARS
LONDON • NEW YORK

Part One: MAY

Part Two: OCTOBER

Part Three: NOVEMBER

Part Four: JANUARY

Part One: MAY

Chapter One | PAULA

Paula did not really consider herself to be a stalker.

It was just one of those cruel ironies of fate that the flat her ex-boyfriend shared with his new fiancée – the lovely Belinda – happened to be en route to the local supermarket, forcing her to walk right past his front door every day.

Still more unfortunate that it happened to be situated between the bedsit where she was living and all the local amenities at the heart of Clapham, including the launderette, library, hairdressers and swimming pool.

That Paula lived in Finsbury Park, a mere fifty minutes away, was no reason to stop shopping in Clapham. She couldn't *not* shop in Clapham just because Alan lived there: it was vitally important she did not let him affect her life. (The group therapy sessions had been very strong on this.) It was nothing to do with Alan.

And so, it follows, that if she *just so* happens to be passing after a late night tipple in one of Lavender Hill's trendy drinkeries and *just so* happens to glimpse Alan's lit sitting room window through her 90mm portable refractor telescope from up a large tree in his back garden… Well, what could she do? The fact that Alan insisted on transparent Japanese paper blinds on the garden side of his flat was surely tantamount to blatant provocation and absolved her of all responsibility for anything she might – completely inadvertently – happen to see.

Paula shifted her weight uncomfortably to prevent her bottom being impaled on a particularly spiny twig and raised the telescope up to her face.

Her stomach lurched as the indistinct pink blob jumped into view, resolving itself into the familiar, beloved, shimmering circumference of Alan's balding pate, levitating over the top of the back of a cream leather sofa. It was bobbing. Paula swivelled the scope to catch sight of a comedian on the television. The pate paused for a second and then started bobbing again, like a ping-pong ball on the surface of a pond.

Alan.

Paula felt a stab, as she always did, faced with the changes to her former home. Belinda did not sit around. Gone were the familiar magnolia walls, replaced by a muted palette in a greyish colour Paula found out was known as 'taupe'. Gone were the faded green sofas; gone the throws and rugs, the moth-eaten posters of Janis Joplin and Jimi Hendrix, the reproduction Durer's rabbit, the flea market sampler; the familiar clutter collected over eight years of cohabitation and car boot sales.

Instead, two predatory sleek leather cream sofas prowled a laminate Serengeti plain, whilst above, cool as vultures, arty black and white photographs hovered in brushed metal frames: a nice-looking man in the foetal position, a nice-looking woman in the foetal position, and – for a bit of variety – a nice-looking man *with* a nice-looking woman. In the foetal position.

Nothing remained of the home she once knew but the ornate egg and dart cornice that had once curled around her cosy life with Alan like a sleeping cat, now warily stalking a reproduction regency chandelier.

She absently raked her telescope over the rest of the flat – kitchenette: monstrous granite breakfast bar like a misplaced ocean liner, American diner-style coffee maker, designer lemon squeezer with legs. Master bedroom (a pang): more taupe. Or was it mushroom? – before returning to the hall in time to catch a tanned, tailored woman with paper-straight highlighted hair letting herself in through the front door.

There she was. Bitch.

The woman carefully hung up her tailored jacket and handbag, running a caressing hand over the latter before making her way to the sitting room. She stood over the bald pate momentarily, hands on hips, before taking the remote control and changing channels. The bald patch stopped bobbing and jerked round. The woman thrust out her neat breasts with a pout. He reached out a hand but her sharp heels were already stinging their way across the laminate towards the window.

Paula jumped to find the tanned face staring straight at her and dropped the telescope in surprise. It hurtled down into the bushes at the base of the tree, sending a marmalade cat yowling across the lawn. *Shit.*

The apartment window opened with a shriek of swollen wood.

'Who's there?' the woman demanded in a high-pitched bark, craning her neck below. 'Declare yourself!'

Paula sat as rigid as the novelty owl perched on the roof above

Belinda's head.

'Alan, there's a burglar out there!'

'Don't be silly darling, it's just cats.'

'Cats my arse, I tell you Alan, there's somebody out there!'

'Come on, come back.' Then, in fruity tones, 'I know a way to relax you.'

The figure at the window hesitated before withdrawing her head and rolling the window down with a resolute bang. Desperately, Paula reached for her emergency binoculars in time to see Belinda's plucked and pinched face vanishing underneath the designer Japanese blind. Bugger. The lights dimmed. Paula's eyes were just acclimatising to the light, and beginning to make out the dim shapes through the screen in a way she did not like at all, when the lights went out. Shit shit shit. What was she going to do now? Her mind raced with scenes of impossible acrobatics unfolding behind those paper-thin barriers. Still glued to the binoculars, she sat back on her branch and reached one hand into the small khaki rucksack dangling from a leafy branch above her head.

'Hello? Prugg and Cartwright's residence,' said a female voice; harsh, irritated and suspiciously out of breath.

Paula said nothing.

'Hello? Hello? I'm afraid I can't hear you.' There was a '*tsk*' of annoyance.

'Hello?' Paula said quickly before Belinda could hang up on her. She instantly regretted it.

'Who's this?' Belinda's voice was sharp.

'I am...' Paula hedged, casting around for a suitable identity. She cupped her hand over her mobile speaker and lowered her voice. '…your worst nightmare…'

'Alan! It's that crazy cow again!'

Alan's voice came onto the line. 'Paula, is that you?'

'No,' she said.

'Look, Paula, how many times…?'

But his voice was snatched away to be replaced by the other, harsh and shrill.

'Do you know what time it is, you freaky bitch?'

'I want to talk to Alan.'

'He's not here.'

'I just spoke to him.'

'Well he doesn't want to speak to you.'

'Tell him – '

'No, I bloody won't!' And she hung up.

Paula sat for a moment, teary-eyed, looking at the reflection of the street lights in the black pools of the windows across the way, and fiddled with her phone.

This time, it was Alan's voice that answered; she had to make it quick.

'I love you. Alan. I love you, so much…can't live without you, I – '

There was a sigh. 'Look,' he mumbled under his breath, trailing off as Belinda's voice in the background demanded, 'Is it that bloody lunatic again?'

The harsh voice zoomed into focus, spitting down the receiver, 'Look, you pathetic little woman. Alan is not yours anymore, okay? He's mine. Mine. You hear that? Right. Now fuck-the-fuck off!'

The phone went dead.

Paula sat back, winded, staring at the mobile in her hand.

Belinda was going to regret that last statement.

It started to drizzle.

The idea of a warming bite to eat from a nearby takeaway threatened to erode her resolve, but Belinda's parting pleasantry was enough to ignite a fire in her stomach worthy of any chicken vindaloo.

The faded khaki rucksack circled slowly in a gust of breeze. Inside: her notebook, thermos, some pieces of chicken wrapped in foil and a waterproof sleeping bag, which she now removed and carefully unfurled.

Manoeuvring herself inside with some difficulty, Paula wiggled about until she finally found a relatively comfortable position wedged between the trunk of the tree and one of its thicker branches. She reached for her thermos and poured herself a lidful of hot black tea. The drizzle worsened and she cupped her freezing fingers around the lid, steam rising, allowing the feeling in her fingers to gradually return – at first painful with pins and needles, then mellowing to a dull, be-splintered ache. And there she sat, sipping tea, blowing on her hands and gazing out at the windows across the way.

It was going to be a long, uncomfortable night.

Chapter Two | HIDDEN AGENDA

Alan and Paula had been together for eight years when he announced he was going to leave her.

If Paula closes her eyes she can see the scene vividly, like an out-of-body experience – a floating ghost watching from above.

Alan is sitting, swinging back on one of the dining chairs, a small cigar in one hand. They had been relaxing together after their weekend meal – venison she remembers; Alan liked to eat well.

She sees the slightly overweight, balding man in his freshly pressed suit taking a casual sip from his glass; she sees the anxious pale woman standing.

There is nothing to signal it is New Year's Eve save the occasional pop of a firework and the drooping party hat on Alan's head.

Dusty and faded like an old photograph, with the drawn look of many on the fast road to nowhere in particular, she stands gripping a tea towel, tightly, too tightly. Nobody speaks.

Alan replaces his half-glass of port carefully on the table, before saying, slowly and carefully, 'Paula, I have something to tell you. I…umm…met a woman in the office disabled toilets. No…I mean I didn't *meet* her there obviously. I met her at the training seminar last month. But we were given a tour of the building and… Well, to cut a long story short I've asked her to marry me. I wanted you to be the first to know.'

He takes a long drag of his cigar. He appears lost in contemplation, as though considering the strange beauty of the slowly spiralling smoke before adding, 'Don't get me wrong, it's been a fine eight years, but I'm afraid you bore me, Paula. I hope you understand.'

Paula sees her past self, standing, immobile. She seems to have stopped breathing. Is she going to say something? Come on! Say something, anything. There are so many things Paula wants her to say. *You bastard. How can you do this to me? How dare you? After all I've done. All I've…* Go on. Say it. Tell him he's a fucking, *fucking…*

A firework crackles.

The pale woman opens her mouth. 'But I thought…maybe *we'd* get married one day.'

Alan's chair comes down to earth with a bang.

'Married? Oh Paula!'

'But I thought you wanted…? And children. We talked of…'

'Paula, Paula, Paula, what are we to do with you, eh?' He shakes his head in sorrow. 'We have to face facts. You're not getting any younger.'

'I'm younger than you.'

Alan tut-tuts benevolently. 'I'm sorry, but it is a simple fact that at forty I am, and will remain, perfectly fit to father children for years to come, whereas a woman of thirty-eight… Well, we can't be selfish now, can we? One has to consider the quality of the gene pool.'

He looks at her, kindly. 'Belinda,' he adds, 'is thirty-two.'

The tea towel trembles in Paula's hands.

'And from such a distinguished family too. Her father is a summer pudding magnate you know. He was recently awarded an OBE for his services to frozen foods.' He sighs in rapture. 'We're just made for each other, Belinda and I. She's an accountant too so, you see, we have a lot in common. Like…accountancy for instance.' He nods thoughtfully. 'Besides, she's great in the sack. That time she spent in Thailand *really* paid off. So, you see…?'

'Yes,' the faded woman whispers, in a faded voice.

'You do? Oh good.'

The angry ghost of Floating Paula watches as he gets up and walks over to her past self. The apparition circles restlessly, desperately, looking for clues.

Is that a bead of sweat glistening on his bald patch, or just the reflection of a stray firework at the window? Do his lips tremble, or is it just the effect of standing on a wobbly floorboard with traffic rumbling past?

She wills herself to say something – *tell him, now!* But, as he opens his arms, the faded woman rushes into them, clinging and sobbing.

He holds her for a second before carefully disentangling himself – her fingers prised from around his neck, back duly patted in paternal fashion – and pushes her away.

Outside the cheering erupts as the New Year rushes in.

'So, you'll understand that I need you out by the end of the month.'

*****

Paula is the kind of woman that people tend to describe as 'pale and interesting'. Sadly, these people are wrong. There is nothing remotely interesting about Paula's appearance. Her hair is less blonde or brunette than characterised by a complete absence of colour; even the term 'mousy' would be pushing it a bit on the interesting front. Her eyes are watery, her features non-descript. Does she have eyelashes? Does anyone bother to check? Her diminutive stature, combined with sadly sloping eyebrows and trigger-happy shoulders, that fly to her ears at the slightest suggestion of embarrassment or nervousness, all conspire to give her the startled appearance of the proverbial rabbit in headlights. Or perhaps, more accurately, the horrified yet resigned expression of a philosophically-minded tortoise finding himself – too late – in the path of a rocket-propelled tar-spreader.

The most memorable thing about Paula's appearance is its striking lack of memorableness, sliding from the senses like an extra mild cheddar or a wall painted white with a hint of beige.

Take, for example, the young man in the climbing shop, World of Rock. Never would he normally have noticed the unbelievably pale and uninteresting woman who, at ten to one exactly, pushed open the double ice-axed doors and started heading determinedly towards the rope display.

Raising his eyes across at Jim, he went back to cashing up the till and doing his best to look unhelpful.

However, when she came over to ask his advice a few minutes later, there was something about this washed-out looking housewife with an apparently insatiable fascination for the subtle technicalities of wedging and rappelling that ignited a faint curiosity – in his trouser region mainly.

She certainly showed more interest in what he was saying than most women did. Than any woman, come to think of it.

Had his girlfriend ever shown any understanding of the passion of achievement, the poetry of a delicately-handled ascent, the near orgasmic release as one finally overcomes the treacherous adversary that is the hard, unyielding rock-face? No, she merely spent her time griping about the dirty gear cluttering up the flat and the weekends he spent away with his rock-climbing chums. *Women had no soul.*

Yet, the small pale woman before him now getting tangled up in climbing ropes and waving a pair of aluminium carabiners in his face demanding, 'What's this?' and 'Could you use it in a domestic interior perhaps?' had the look of a real fanatic.

Could it be that serendipity had cast this stranger into his path with some hitherto as yet unknown dark and secret motive (sex hopefully) where, for the first time in his stunted adolescent-minded existence, he would find nirvana in the arms of a true soul mate?

Paula, of course, was unaware of all of this. She was too distracted by picking out buckles and manhandling chunky harnesses, all the time recording busily in her scratched and tattered notebook. The attendant seemed helpful enough in a gormless sort of way. He spoke the jargon – in fact seemed to enjoy flinging a lot of that at her – but it proved difficult to pin him down without giving the game away. She decided it was time to leave.

As he held open the door for her to struggle out obscured by her purchases (a jumbled mountain of ropes, ice-axes and spring-loaded canning devices), she unexpectedly cast him such a sudden and radiant smile that the attendant wondered, fleetingly, if he was making a mistake in letting her go.

His entire life kaleidoscoped into that one moment and

he found himself questioning everything: his emotions, his expectations, how good he was in bed... Was he hopelessly shallow? Did he view women as useless sex objects rather than thinking, feeling, separate, sentient beings like himself? Was he part of the unconscious patriarchy that mirrored colonial ideas of imperialism where women were perpetually symbolised as 'other'? Was he gay? Who was he anyway?

They were questions considered for at least two, maybe even three, profound and thoughtful seconds before a quick recce revealed the superiority (at least two cup sizes worth) of his girlfriend's tits, and the mysterious workings of fate were quickly consigned to the delete file of his compartmentalised male brain.

He turned back into the room and nodded across at his colleague Jim, shop attendant by weekday, uncrowned Tiverton freestyle snowboarding champion by weekend.

'Could have had her.'

Jim just sniffed.

'One more thing,' said the woman's disembodied head, suddenly reappearing around the doorframe. 'Does this stuff hold on plaster?'

Back in the office, Paula stowed her acquisitions carefully under her desk so that, by the time the others came in from lunch she was inconspicuously tapping away as normal.

Her colleagues in the Human Resources Department of the Smith, Smith-Brown and Smith office had no idea that behind the dusty façade of their overlooked assistant lay the mind, talent and surveillance expertise of a criminal mastermind. They wouldn't have cared anyway. Instead, they ignored her completely, which suited Paula fine.

'I just went mad this morning, mad,' Tanya said, untangling her model-like legs: legs women would die for, legs men would pay money for, legs that would make a flamingo look frumpy. 'Had two bowls of Kellogg's Special K – I feel *sooo* disgusting. Look how bloated I am.' She smoothed her skirt over her extraordinarily flat stomach and poked at it a bit.

'Tell me about it,' Sonya agreed readily, 'I went on a total Slimfast bender this weekend. I'm going to be drying out for months.'

Tanya swung her minuscule hips across the room and helped herself to some water from the cooler. 'Don't forget your seven pints a day, babe. Flush away those toxins, girl.'

'How does that work then?' Sonya asked.

'Your body gets filled up with these toxins, right? Like chemicals, like? And water, like, it's pure, yeah? So it, you know, fights with the toxins? And they come out in your pee, yeah? Great for the skin. Cos you know when you're in the womb, right, you're swimming about in water? Well, you can't get much younger-looking than that, can you?'

Paula bit into her wilting tuna mayo sandwich and stared out of the window remembering that horrible scene all those months before. Boring. Boring? Of all the things he might have said, this had been the least expected. She bored him. And worse, she was boring in the bedroom.

Okay, perhaps they weren't exactly hanging from the chandeliers, but their sex life had been average. *Exactly* average, to be precise. (A copy of a leading women's magazine had been purchased for the sole purpose of verifying this fact.) Two and a half times a week: Thursday night, Saturday morning and one half effort on Wednesday, when Alan would invariably roll off panting and complaining of a headache. Two and a half times a week. Perfectly normal, perfectly average, perfectly respectable statistics.

The odd sentence of office gossip drifted across her consciousness.

'She just couldn't work out why her underwear was getting too big for her – and she's no stick insect, know what I mean…'

Paula pressed a key and in a flash, the evaluation form disappeared from her screen to be replaced by a large close-up of Alan's bedroom window.

'I mean she walked in and there he was – in her hold-ups. She couldn't wear them after that.'
'Too stretched?'
'Too disgusted.'
'Oh!'

Paula switched to a large spreadsheet and typed 'quiet' in the 2pm slot. She checked out Camera 2: sitting room. Nothing. (Not totally unexpected, as Alan was, at that moment, busily accounting away on the other side of the Smith, Smith-Brown and Smith building.)

'Wanna go for a fag?' Tanya said.
'Are they rollies?'
'Yeah. They're organic, so they don't have any chemicals in.'
'Really? So they're like good for you then?'

'Yeah. It's the multinational companies what puts the chemicals in. It's all the fault of globalisation.'

'I don't know anything about politics, Tanya. I'm not up on these things, like you.'

'I don't put anything unorganic in my body, Sonya, you just don't know where its been. '

'You're so politically aware, Tanya.'

'When it comes to my body, Sonya, no sacrifice is too big.'

They left the room without so much as a glance at the hunched figure in front of the window. Paula wasted no time in opening up another file on her desktop – a large chart – which, although she could have recited it by heart, she proceeded to study carefully.

Alan
• **Rises: 6am.**
• **Breakfast: bowl of crunchy nut cornflakes with semi-skimmed milk (part of his ongoing paunch reduction campaign). Large jug of coffee – Colombian – which he drinks weak but in vast quantities.**
• **Goes back to bed for twenty minutes. Gets out of bed.**
• **Goes into bathroom for 10 minutes. Emerges in suit, tie and shaved. Leaves approx 7.30am.**

Belinda
• **Rises: 5am.**
• **Breakfast: five strong espressos (two in kitchen and three in her personal gym on, variously: cross-treader, exercise bike and rowing machine. (No spillage.)**

- **6.10am enters the bathroom. 45 minutes later emerges with make-up, suit, hair straightened with cast-iron precision.**
- **7am, leaves for work: sixth espresso in hand.**

Weekly Routine

Alan
- **Mon–Fri: evening in front of the television.**

(Except for Thurs, when he liked to take advantage of the late night opening hours to add to his collection of electronic gadgetry.)

- **Weekend: occasional visit to the opera or a restaurant. More television.**

Belinda
- **Tues and Sat: wedding meetings.**
- **Mon, Weds, Thurs, Fri: gym.**

(This was different from her home gym, providing Belinda with the opportunity to see and to be seen. She could often be observed through the floor-length windows, slogging it out on the cross-trainer whilst talking to the department secretary on her mobile phone.)

- **Regularly stays late at work resulting in a return as late as 10.30 or 11pm.**

Paula rolled her sandwich cellophane into a tiny ball and

pondered the precious little time Alan and Belinda spent together. Belinda was often out, otherwise in a flurry of summits with her planner, caterer, dressmaker, florist or personal hairdresser. All were frequent visitors to the house, along with various relations and two bridesmaids ('friends' from primary school cemented to Belinda through a mutual need to believe they had not *always* been so unpopular) fine-tuning their harmonious combinations of hats and bags, going over their on-the-day schedule and practising their communal high-heeled-walking skills.

By contrast, Alan had not, during the time Paula had spent observing them (which was considerable), attended even *one* wedding meeting. If you factored in the time 'doing culture' at the weekends it came to approximately – Paula did a quick calculation on the side of her pad – 2.5 waking hours a week spent alone in each other's company. And, as often as not, Belinda spent that time on the telephone. What an uncaring bitch she was! Paula felt a hot rage well in her chest. Poor Alan. *How did you get yourself in this situation, my lamb?* He was obviously out of his depth, she could see that now.

For her plan to have a chance of success, he had to be alone: at the time of least expectation and maximum potential excitement. It was no good springing it on him straight after he came in, for example, or following a big meal or too much wine. In fact, it was hardly worth springing anything on him in the evening, his tendency being to conk out from the moment he fell zombie-like through the front door, briefcase dropping like a stone, until he collapsed like a corpse in his bed. But then, he was scarcely more alive in the mornings, when there was the added obstacle of exercise-biking Belinda to contend with. Belinda – acting as she did with inhuman predictability – would no doubt be safely peddling away in the second bedroom until 6.55am exactly. Paula considered this for a second...no no no! What if he cried out? Or worse, dropped dead of a heart attack?

It *had* to be an evening – at a time when Alan wasn't completely comatose and with Belinda safely out of the picture.

That ruled out Monday. And Friday. Tuesday was Belinda's wedding summit evening and Wednesday was *Celebrity Gardening Challenge,* in front of which Alan routinely slept, which left Thursday. His wife-to-be would have left for her exercise class and wouldn't be back for hours. This did not leave a huge window of opportunity, but as far as Paula was concerned, it was the only opportunity.

A sudden gale of laughter shocked Paula out of her reverie.

'I think it was when he suggested she leave her armpits unshaved that was the final straw,' Tanya said from the doorway.

'That is seriously disgusting!' Sonya flicked her asymmetrical hairdo. 'A woman must always maintain an air of mystique. No man should see a girl's pits *au naturale.*'

They traversed the room. Paula seamlessly hit a key and the evaluation sheet she had been working on to evaluate the recruitment evaluation process took over her screen.

Thank you for filling out this form so we can continue to make our evaluation process as satisfying for you as it is for us.

How would you evaluate this evaluation process?

1. Fantastically wonderful, sublime and superb ☐
2. Great, I'd recommend this process to everyone I know ☐
3. Very very good ☐
4. Pretty good ☐
5. Near as dammit to pretty good ☐

Then a very odd thing happened.

Remembering vaguely that there was supposed to be someone else in the room, Tanya suddenly looked up from where she was leaning over Sonya's desk showing off her new bosoms ('It was a choice between paying off some of the mortgage or a new pair of tits – and I think you'll agree – I made the right decision') and, to Paula's surprise, addressed a question in her direction.

'What do you think…' she groped for a name, '…Thingie?'

Two pairs of eyes wandered vaguely over to Paula's side of the room.

Paula froze.

Their twinned sets of orbs roamed around her computer terminal – to her left, to her right, above her left ear, below her right ankle – but, discovering nothing more interesting than an unremarkable magnolia wall, glazed over in a collective veil of unseeingness and promptly forgot why they had travelled over there in the first place. Their owners returned to their conversation.

Paula let her shoulders fall in relief.

Voices rose and fell around her, but she wasn't listening. She was too busy scouring the hallway and entrance from Camera 3. Yes,

Thursday was the day... Thursday. Thursday the 15th of May was the day that would change the rest of their lives. Forever.

Chapter Three | **ALAN**

Alan had no idea how significant Thursday the 15th of May would prove to be, although he was cultivating certain modest hopes for that day. For, as it happened, this was the date on which he planned to hold a drinks party for some of his work colleagues, whom he was anxious to impress.

It was true that, left to his own devices, Alan would probably not have bothered too hard to try and impress them much at all or, at least, would not necessarily have thought of inviting them round with the *specific* purpose of impressing them. For whilst Alan, being a city accountant, enjoyed impressing his fellow man as much as the next city accountant (which is rather more than your average person, who hopefully does not view every social interaction as an opportunity to show off one's latest acquisition of electronic goods or to chunder on about one's terribly fascinating skiing trip with the managing director), he preferred to do this from behind the safety of a restaurant table or the wheel of an expensive little sports car. To invite people to his home, into his bolthole, as it were, seemed to him to put the pressure somewhat on *himself* to be impressive, about which he felt considerable less certainty.

Belinda, however, was adamant. 'I am taking every opportunity to be seen staying on late at the office – much good it does me – but at least I'm making a sodding effort,' she hissed. 'How, may I ask, is vegging out in front of the television going to further your career?' Before throwing out her bottom lip in sultry pose and adding a subtly menacing, 'We ARE getting married, remember.'

And so it was, with some reluctance, that Alan decided to sacrifice a precious evening's potatoing in favour of a spot of social climbing, to please his wife-to-be. Which is why he finds himself, one Saturday afternoon, driving back from Bang and Olufsen with two brand new state-of-the-art speakers strapped safely into the passenger seat, poking proudly through his sunroof. ('You can entertain them with sparkling conversation about the opera, you've got some intelligent things to say about that, haven't you? And make sure you mention our opera season tickets!') He's not exactly hurrying home.

He shakes his head at the wonder of women. One minute they are shagging you like some prostitute-stroke-contortionist in the office disabled toilets, the next thing you know, you are being told that you are to be wed in a stately home in Surrey in front of friends and relations you never knew you had and that your beloved 70s MG Roadster is not 'child-friendly' and is to be replaced by something resembling an armour-plated tank.

What invariably provokes this transformation and why men never notice, he thinks, is one of life's great mysteries – one certainly beyond his limited imagination and experience.

But one thing is clear. There is no choice. He can see that now.

He puts the Roadster into fourth, swearing affectionately at the stubbornness of the ancient gear stick, and accelerates up a narrow street, to the accompaniment of Beethoven's 'Ode to Joy'. He is, after all, a sophisticated connoisseur of the arts, dutifully doing his time with monthly visits to the theatre and the opera. As the music reaches its joyous crescendo, he joins in with a couple of blasts of the horn aimed at the two idling pedestrians who fail to get out of his way. Dreadlocked-Rastafarian-in-Large-Woolly-Hat quickens across, but Archetypal-Little-Old-Lady-with-Stick, striking out in vain from the small traffic island where she had taken refuge, is not quite quick enough. The vanquishing bray of the triumphal horn sends her scurrying in desperation for the safety of the opposite bank, before she abandons her support altogether and hurls her frail body onto the pavement.

Alan smiles to himself, knowingly. Didn't need it for walking, then.

Alan likes driving.

He loves the reactions of pedestrians and his passengers as he expertly negotiates yet another close shave for some unsuspecting victim. Close shaves, in Alan's view, are the real measure of a driver: the greater number of shaves, the more closely shaved, the better a driver you are.

Window rolled down, arm resting casually on the frame, he drives one-handed – often with a mobile crooked importantly in the cradle of his shoulder. In this manner, he likes to career through the babbling hustle of all the different communities, letting the colours, tastes and smells cascade around him. And as he passes the crowds, the streets, the markets, the colour and bustle of the city, he feels – as he always does at these moments – part of the scene, part of the hurry and hum of England's great capital, the wide panorama of possibility that is London.

Of course, as he speeds past the sellers and wanderers, he would never have dreamed of stopping and having a wander himself. It is not a world he intends to encounter close-hand. He's a man with a mission. Always on the move. Going somewhere. Doing something urgent. He likes to imagine himself in these moments as the James Bond of accountancy: a suave devil behind the wheel and a stallion between the spreadsheets.

'Look out!'

With a shriek of brakes, the little yellow car swerves violently, narrowly escaping collision with Large-Woman-in-Tweed-Skirt-and-Heels.

Alan casts a glance over his shoulder.

'Nice car!' she yells as she hits the ground, her bulky shoulder bag exploding dramatically, raining its contents in a shower all around her.

'Shame about the small dick driving it!'

Alan glances back in his mirror, irritated. Obviously has an axe to grind against men. Probably because no man would have her. Probably a lesbian ('Lesbian!' he yells out the window) forced to take the Sapphic option ('Lesbian!' he yells again, in case she had not heard him the first time) because no red-blooded male would stop to give her one. He sits back smugly. That was probably it: too ugly to get a man.

Yes, he reassures himself, as he expertly negotiates another near-death experience for Mother-With-Three-Scampering-Offspring-plus-Dog, he may not know much about women, but he knows what he likes. Women should be petite. Blonde hair, dark hair – no particular preference – so long as it's nicely brushed and kept tidy and hygienic. Breasts, small and compact. (Disliking too much sign of sexual ostentation in his women, Alan prides himself, instead, on being the sort of man who can look at page three with a yawn and a shrug and profess a predilection for someone more sophisticated and preferably French. Juliette Binoche always tended to impress. Or Isabelle Huppert. Both getting on a bit now, though. He frowns; he really should research someone new.)

In Alan's view, all things have their place: breasts to be brought out when required and then put away back where they belong, slotted neatly under the lapels of an expensive tailored trouser suit or suitably pressed blouse.

Neatness, tidiness, smallness, that's what he likes. A woman who needs looking after.

The memory of his collision with the Woman-in-Tweed returns, along with her painful remark. What does she know? Little Alan wouldn't touch her with a leper's crutch. Yes, it's not a case of her rejecting Little Alan; it's a case of Little Alan rejecting her!

Finding himself feeling inexplicably horny, Alan looks at his watch. About time Belinda's mother was buggering off. Maybe time for a quick one-two before the opera.

With a bellow of exhaust, a shriek of tyres and a blast of Tchaikovsky, the sunshine yellow Roadster makes a last bid for notice as it roars up the narrow street, before being swallowed by London's all-consuming empyrean roar.

★★★★★

Alan let himself into the small two-bedroomed flat in Clapham to find Belinda pouring over several swatches of shiny material.

'They're out of fuchsia, fucking typical,' she said, not looking up. 'Bridesmaids,' she added by way of explanation.

Alan wandered over to the sideboard and poured himself a glass of port. It looked like this was probably not the moment to introduce frisky ideas into the conversation. Unsure of what to do next, he eventually parked himself in a somewhat unbalanced, but what he hoped might appear casual, debonair pose against the sideboard, one leg crossed. He glanced idly out of the window.

The one tree, a large lime, rather too big for the narrow strip of lawn it terminated, waved and groaned in the wind, in blissful ignorance of its fate.

'A garden,' Belinda had told him, 'is an extension of our house and therefore an extension of our personality. You wouldn't keep someone's old kitchen units would you?' she had demanded. 'No of course you wouldn't, so why keep a mouldy old tree?'

Strictly speaking, the garden was supposed to be communal, so, as far as Alan could see, not the most appropriate place to start extending one's personality. Belinda, however, had other ideas. Within a week of moving in she was at daggers drawn with the elderly Miss Kennedy on the ground floor about the old woman's unfortunate taste (or lack of) in bizzy lizzies.

Miss Kennedy made her feelings forcibly known by attempting to impede their access to the garden through the judicious placement of cast-iron leg-mutilating garden furniture. But the advantage was Belinda's when she discovered that Miss Kennedy's conservatory had neither been granted planning permission nor conformed to fire safety regulations: out went the bizzie lizzies and in came Belinda's Grand Plan.

Low-growing expensive Japanese acers, she said. Controllable and elegant. With a paved dining area and decking. To entertain guests. And the tree: the tree had to go.

Alan had initially expected more opposition to this idea, but it was a walk-over. Miss Kennedy – short and curlies well and truly caught in the conservatory doors – put up little in the way of resistance; whilst the hippies who lived above, after offering some wishy-washy avowals of tree-love, were easily bought off with a spot of creative accountancy on the books of their lucrative chain of 'Save the Rain Forest' juice-bars. It seemed as though no one cared about an ordinary old tree.

Except, that is, for Alan.

For now, in the warm evening light, Alan could not help but feel a twinge of conscience as he marvelled at the tree's monstrous growth and luxurious branches laden with their napkin-like leaves, its sheer aliveness.

'I mean if I'd wanted cerise for the bridesmaids I'd have said cerise.' Belinda said. 'Do I look like a fucking cerise kind of person? Am I the kind of person who walks down the street with everyone going, "Look there's that tasteless woman wearing cerise"?'

Alan's eye was distracted by a sudden movement at the tree's base. He trained his eyes on the spot but there was nothing. Bloody cats.

'Do I?'

'Absolutely not, darling.'

She looked up, briefly, offering a narrow window of opportunity for him to expand his chest and lower his lids seductively, which he duly did. She flashed him a joyless grimace before returning to studying her fabrics.

'And I've had an awful day. I dropped into the office because I knew David had a lunchtime meeting with a client – it *had* to be a celebrity because I can't see him breaking his no weekend rule for just *anyone*. Anyway I thought I'd just pop in, you know, and finish off that report...stayed there three and a half hours, UNPAID. Doesn't even come out of his bloody office. Finally at three o'clock I knock on his door just to see if he and his guest could do with a cup of tea...and can you believe it? There's nobody bloody there! Transpires the meeting was cancelled yesterday. Did anyone tell me? No. Bunch of bloody bitches. Had to find out from the bloody cleaner.'

Alan clucked sympathetically and returned to gazing out of the window. There it was again – a sudden flurry at the base of the tree, he was sure... His eyes hurt from straining. He was desperately short-sighted but too squeamish for contacts. He had some prescription lenses somewhere in a drawer that he refused to wear. It wasn't vanity; if they suited him he'd wear them. He was just not a spectacles kind of person. Some people were spectacles people. Like librarians. Or plain women. Or plain librarians. Not him.

Finally admitting defeat, he shook his head. His eyes must be playing tricks on him. He directed his attention back into the room. Belinda was shaking a piece of fabric in her fist. Alan felt an inexplicable prickling in his testicles, imagining her grabbing his scrotum with as much enthusiasm.

'I tell you there's too much oestrogen in that office. A whole three and a half hours wasted. And I bet Pat was there yesterday when he left – all smiley and oh-can-do. Then out the door at 5.30.

How's that for commitment?'

'Oh darling!'

'Look, I know what you're going to say and I have every sympathy for Pat but that shouldn't get in the way of fairness. The truth is that woman hasn't lifted a *finger* since the accident.'

'To be fair, she hasn't been *able* to lift a finger since the accident.'

'That's beside the point! I'm sorry but I'm not going to pander to the political-correctness-gone-mad-brigade. Basically, the woman's had nothing but advantages dealt out to her – everyone gushing on about how hardworking she is and how she's a sure-fire candidate for promotion. But I ask you – how hard can it really be sitting there poking a keyboard with a forehead probe all day?'

Alan tried a shrug. Wrong response.

He shook his head. 'Such a tragedy. And with everything ahead of her too. They were predicting she'd make partner in five years. Before, you know....' He shook his head in wonder. 'Such lousy luck – I mean, what were the chances of being mowed down by a hit'n'run milk float?'

'Yes, well, she was always overrated if you ask me,' Belinda said, throwing open another book of materials with some force. 'I just can't believe she's carrying on. I think in the circumstances resignation is the only honourable course of action. It's just not fair! I tell you, Alan, if she gets promoted over me I'm going to sue!' She let out a wail of bitter indignation. 'After all the extra hours I've put in – I ask you, what's the point – what's the bloody point, if nobody *sees* me?'

On balance, Alan thought, maybe now was not a good time to suggest a shag.

'Fancy a shag?'

'Alan, we're getting sodding married. Is this really the time to be thinking about sex?'

'Do you want to see my new hi-fi?'

'No.'

Alan poured himself another drink and gazed out across the lawn – if you could call it a lawn – at the majestic tree. No, he really wasn't very happy about Belinda's plan now he came to think of it. He had a lot in common with that tree, he thought sadly. Large, broad-shouldered, disregarded... *Be damned*! His eyes watered with alcohol but he was sure he could see something moving – a large something – on the second branch on the left...

'And then to top it all they mess up on the fuchsia! And I'm stuck with cerise bridesmaids. Cerise! What with the wedding dress more peach than parchment, I'm going to look like a dollop of ice-cream surrounded by a mob of glacier cherries. The whole wedding's turning into a fucking fruit salad.'

His eyes had cleared, but whatever it was was no longer there. Probably just kids, messing about. He'd have to get some barbed wire. Or maybe broken glass for the top of the wall, like they did in the grander houses down the street.

'Sure you don't fancy a shag?'

'Alan!'

'I'll be quick.'

She flung angrily out of the room.

Alan gazed ruminatively back out of the window. 'I'll take that as a no then.'

Chapter Four | **NOT SO BORING NOW**

The morning of Thursday the 15th of May opened unceremoniously enough at 5am with the alarm, leaving Alan lying immobile, only vaguely aware of Belinda's leaping form charging off to commence her daily caffeine-fuelled workout.

The morning of Thursday the 15th May was heralded for the second time an hour later with Alan's alarm. Its owner turned over sleepily and hit the snooze button.

The executive boardroom is intimidating, lined with dark wood and even darker Victorian portraits. He enters, in his best suit, single-breasted. Crisp, white shirt. Polka-dot tie (he was no ordinary accountant). Ahead of him, stretching to the left and the right as far as he can see…

Five minutes later, the morning of Thursday the 15th of May made yet another unwelcome appearance. Alan swore loudly and knocked the clock to the floor.

Ahead of him, stretching to the left and the right as far as he can see, the gleaming surface of the mahogany table behind which the serried ranks of Smith, Smith-Brown and Smith have been summoned. And there, at their axis, on his padded leather throne, is the man himself.

'Sit down.'

Alan sits, forcing himself to raise his reluctant gaze and place it captive in the saggy brown stare of his mentor, his master, his messiah… Eyes that have seen life, eyes that have triumphed, suffered, felt the pain of all mankind. (Alan's sleeping form shuddered in ecstasy.) *Those eyes are now on Alan, stripping him bare, searching out every weakness, seeing through to his very soul!*

The alarm clock crashed in again from under the bed. Alan forced an eyelid up. Then let it fall.

Sir Alan Smith-Brown looks at Alan and heaves a great sigh. 'Alan,' he said in his gruff, grave, yet strangely virile voice. 'You and I share more than just a name. I see a lot of myself in you when I was younger…' He takes a breath and Alan breaks out in a cold sweat (sleeping Alan likewise).

'You're the man I want standing beside me when it comes to the audit. You're hired!'

The alarm clock blasted once more into his consciousness.

'Aaaghh.' Alan placed a pillow over his head.

Ten minutes later he was scurrying to the shower in his underpants, swearing loudly.

*****

Across the city, in her Finsbury Park bedsit, Paula opened her eyes and lay there peacefully in a streak of morning sun. She put a sleepy hand under her bed and pulled out a crowbar.

*****

Up until the smoking ban, The Smelly Ferret had been one of those old men's pubs that perpetually smelt of old men, urine and stale cigars. Now, it just smelt of old men and urine.

At 4pm that afternoon, Alan threw open the damp and slightly sticky door and took a deep breath of pungent air.

'Ahhhh! Authentic eh lads?'

At the traditional bar in gleaming dark wood – with an impressive array of pumps, bottles and murky-looking beers called things like 'Old Goat' and 'Compost Heap' – sat a row of sunken-faced men over sixty, spaced out at intervals of four feet or so, faces buried in muddy pints. Snowy visions of *Deal or No Deal* floated just above the barman's left ear from the flickering face of an ancient television set. It was eerily quiet.

'Great atmosphere, great atmosphere. Really…genuine,' Alan said, throwing his jacket over the back of a worm-eaten wooden chair and having second thoughts about whether this was the best venue to highlight his managerial potential but determined to make the best of things. 'So, what's it to be boys?'

His companions comprised, in reverse order: Mr. Malcolm Sergeant, a lowly trainee; Mr Anthony Hossier, who had joined Smith, Smith-Brown and Smith on secondment as Insolvency Compliance Officer; and Mr. Geoffrey Pike, a partner from a neighbouring department, or, as he was otherwise known by those in the know, 'Mr Tax'.

'Let me,' said Geoffrey, pulling a fat wallet from his suit pocket.

'A round of Porridge-Growers?'

The others assented happily and sat down.

Alan was slightly disappointed by the low turnout. The unexpected news that one of their clients, a major distribution company, had just gone belly-up – piles of unsold stock, creditors in disarray – had led to the whole Bankruptcy and Liquidation department knocking off early in celebration.

Most of the trendier element had gone home to prepare for hitting Bar Zeus later. But, as Bar Zeus was miles away from his flat, Alan knew it was well-nigh impossible for him to lure them back to his for wine and nibbles. And as, on the one occasion he had ventured there, he had been refused admittance on grounds of age and lack of fashion-sense, he was not keen to repeat this humiliation – certainly not in front of the very colleagues he was seeking to impress.

Perhaps, thought Alan, it had been too much to hope for that Mr Smith-Brown himself should have put in an appearance. But at least Geoffrey had deigned to come along.

His enthusiasm extended rather less towards Malcolm, who did not count, in Alan's view, as a person impressive enough to be worth impressing, although Alan noticed he was sporting a rather fetching sheepskin jacket over the top of his sober grey suit and tie. As Geoffrey set off to fetch a round of Porridge-Growers, Alan leant over and took a quick gauge of the material.

'Nice jacket.'

'Thanks,' said Malcolm.

'I suppose you are aware it is May. It's twenty-two degrees. And we're inside.'

Malcolm blushed. That is, his already red and sweating face

turned an even darker, shinier shade of crimson.

'Going all crusty on us, eh Malc?' said Anthony Hossier.

Alan simultaneously loathed and revered Anthony Hossier, both for his smooth confident upper-classness and the fact he had gone to Eton, of which Alan was eternally jealous. As far as Alan was concerned no amount of social climbing was ever going to compete with the invaluable networking opportunity of being buggered at an early age by the sons of people of influence.

'Watch out or you'll be wearing sandals, growing your hair and turning vegan next,' Hossier said cheerfully.

They all guffawed loudly and shot simultaneous dirty looks at the neighbouring table where a scruffy long-haired sandal-wearing bloke was sitting wearing a T-shirt that read, 'My body is Not a Charnel House for Dead Animals.' He raised his glass of Old Goat and they turned away in disgust.

'Actually, my friend Samantha advised I wear it,' Malcolm said.

There was a tense, impressed silence: *Malcolm was friends with a woman?*

'She did a makeover on me. Said it made me look manly.'

Alan looked at Malcolm. Now, there was no denying he was a nice guy – not very competitive maybe and generally considered a bit on the dim side, yet nice nonetheless. But *manly*?

'Choosing clothes for you, eh?' said Geoffrey, pleasantly, setting down the drinks with precision. 'Must have her eye on you.'

Alan felt a hot rash of irritation spread across his body.

'You think so?' Malcolm was saying, self-consciously...

'Don't be ridiculous!' Alan burst out. 'She's treating you like a toy, a doll. She obviously feels *maternal* towards you. And whatever she said, I'm sure she didn't mean you to wear the damn thing all year round.'

Malcolm hunched over his pint.

'Well, bravo, anyway,' Geoffrey said, taking his seat beside Malcolm. 'Whatever her motivation, you make the best of it, my lad.'

*****

The trouble was, Alan thought, as he went up to the bar for Round No. 6, it was difficult to impress people with one's knowledge of the opera and one's taste in interior décor when those subjects never came up.

So far, in the course of the last two hours, they had talked of nothing but mobile phones. Mind you, he had done pretty well in that department. Anthony may have been the victor on the size stakes with a model that fitted in the heel of his shoe ('you never know when you might be naked in the desert with only your shoes for storage') but Alan had whipped his ass in the coolness stakes with his untouchably trendy 3G affair complete with digital camera, PDA, wi-fi, camcorder, projector, cigarette lighter, bottle-opener and condom-dispenser combined. ('You never know when you might need a ho,' followed by much uproarious laughter at own wittiness.) He had also managed to squeeze in a mention of his new MP3 player with room for over 500,000 tracks with automatic chooser that combined songs according to the fourth letter of the artist's name.

But he still hadn't ticked off half the subjects on Belinda's list. Carefully negotiating the drinks back from the bar, he quickly ran it through his mind: opera season tickets, art, the new chandelier, taupe…

As soon as he sat down, he decided, he would say something about chandeliers; he prepared his first line. But when he took his place, he found the others were deep into a discussion about pulling birds (at least Malcolm and Anthony were; Geoffrey was engrossed in a free supplement listing the top ten delicatessens). More specifically, Anthony was enthusiastically outlining his involvement with what he called the 'online seduction circle' – as far as Alan could make out a group of blokes who liked to compare pulling tips on the Internet.

Unfortunately this was a subject about which Alan knew precisely nothing, having never actively pulled a woman in his life. Nobody could have been more surprised than he when, dawdling behind the Accessible Facilities Tour to tie a shoelace, he found himself shoved into the office Disabled toilets with Belinda attached like a plunger to his mouth. As for Paula… He handed round the drinks and relived the exquisite pain of that night: the pair of them side-by-side on the sofa, too terrified to touch each other. He could not even be sure who made the first move in the end; perhaps it had been the sofa that had finally got fed up with the tedium of it all and impatiently snapped them into each other's arms like a Venus flytrap.

'According to that esteemed repository of pulling advice, www.getinherpants.com,' Anthony was saying with confidence, 'women possess a deep-rooted pre-evolutionary compulsion to spread their legs for the alpha male. They can't help it, you know. One whiff of your general..err…alpha-ness and she secretes a special hormone that makes her so overcome with lust that she'll practically keel over with her legs in the air.'

'Really?' Malcolm blushed.

'It's a scientifically proven fact: they tested it out on water shrews.'

'Oh! Well in that case –'

Geoffrey smiled non-committally.

Anthony continued, 'In the words of ManWolf – he's very famous in America,' he added defensively.

The others stared back blankly.

'Well according to him, we men have become oppressed. We have become desexualised, emasculated, disempowered. That's why ManWolf developed the Ten Basic Rules, The ManWolf Method, to help us fight back and become the proud predatory pulling beasts of our forefathers. I went to one of his seminars. The man's a visionary.'

'Oh *ManWolf*,' said Alan airily.

'You heard of him?' Anthony said.

Alan was taken off-guard. He had been waiting for an opportunity to link what Anthony was saying to taupe, or chandeliers. Unable to think of anything, he decided to play it laid back and ambiguous.

'Heard of him?' (Knowing chuckle.)

Anthony's glass hit the table with a thump. 'You're kidding me.' He laughed round at the others and shot out a hand.

Alan took it with a faint embarrassment.

'PM or PG?'

'Huh?'

'Are you a Pulling Master or a Pulling Guru?'

Alan escaped into his pint for a while and stared at the bottom of his glass. 'More of a Pulling Semi-Senior, I'd say.'

'Wow, I've never heard that term before.'

Even at this point, there was still an opportunity for a quick backtrack with an 'only joking' or an 'in my dreams!' but, as he looked around at his audience, it dawned on Alan suddenly that, with the possible exception of Geoffrey who was looking almost impossibly mild, this was the most impressed he had yet seen them. There was no choice but to wade in deeper.

'Yes, I'm afraid I haven't been completely upfront with you guys. I am not who you think I am.'

'You're not Alan Prugg?' said Geoffrey.

'Well, ye-es… I am, but –' He looked round their expectant faces. The attention was beginning to go to his head, along with the Porridge-Grower. 'I am also known by another name.' He stood up. 'I am *Enigma, seducer of women, envy of men!*'

He looked round in triumph. Anthony shook his head, dumbstruck with awe; Malcolm's shiny face glowed pink with excitement; if Paula's lack of distinctiveness could be described as an extra mild cheddar, Geoffrey's expression, in that moment, was purest cottage.

Alan was just about to add something even more impressive when, over the tops of their heads, he saw the door of the pub open and a *woman* walk in.

Now, The Smelly Ferret was the kind of 'authentic' old man's pub where the inhabitants would notice if any woman were to walk into the bar. When an extremely attractive woman walked in, as one now proceeded to do, you could have heard a pin drop.

As it was, the only sound was the deafening scrape of Alan's chair as he hastily sat down again.

Geoffrey and Anthony sat paused, pints mid-mouthful. Malcolm shrunk down inside his sheepskin jacket. The old men at the bar swivelled silently and said nothing. The room was alive with the unspoken tension of everyone feeling they should be availing themselves of the situation in some way, but all secretly willing her to leave so they wouldn't have to do anything about it.

The attractive woman passed across to the bar and ordered herself a drink.

'So, Alan, here's your chance.'

'What do you mean?' Alan squinted across at Anthony. He had the feeling he wasn't going to like the answer.

'To demonstrate *The Enigma Method*.'

'Oh. I don't think – that's – well, it's not – you know, there's no *need*. Actually,' he said in a stronger tone of voice, 'I'm not sure I can be bothered, to tell you the truth – another chick. Chicks here, chicks there, they're all the same at the end of the day.' Then, trying another tack, 'Obviously I would love to oblige normally, but I'm an almost-married man, Anthony – can I call you Tony? – Another story if I were single…' He took a hasty glug and lapsed into silence.

'You don't have to take her home with you,' Anthony said. 'Just show us how it's done.'

Alan looked slowly from face to face: so much faith, so much trust.

'For old Malcolm here.'

Alan gave Geoffrey a look as if to say 'young people, eh?' but Geoffrey just smiled back mildly.

'How about some chanting – get you in the mood,' said Anthony.

'Chanting?' *Oh god what was he on about now?*

'Now repeat after me: all women are bitches.'

'All women are bitches,' Malcolm chanted obediently.

'All women are bitches,' mumbled Alan.

'We refuse to give in to their scheming demands.'

'We refuse to give in to their scheming demands.'

'We are men.'

'Hoo!'

'Alpha men.'

'Haa!'

'If she asks us to do the washing up we say?'

'No! Bitch! Get back in the kitchen, get your rubber gloves on while we put our feet up and watch telly!'

Alan was starting to enjoy himself. Perhaps Anthony was right. He *was* emasculated, disempowered. Here was a chance to prove his worth and impress his colleagues. Yes! He downed the rest of his pint and felt the deluded strength of drunkenness sweep across his body. He leapt to his feet. He was going to pull that woman! For *Belinda*'s sake.

'Good man,' Anthony said. 'Now remember – act mysterious.'

'What?'

'Mysterious. ManWolf says if you get her hot with curiosity, you'll find other things getting hot as well, know what I mean.'

'Of course I know that, rudimentary stuff,' Alan said impatiently. He smoothed down his hair and pulled in his paunch. Mysterious, he could do that. How hard could it be?

'OK Ladies, watch and learn…'

From their vantage point in the corner, Anthony, Malcolm and Geoffrey watched Alan saunter towards the bar. The attractive

51

woman looked up briefly before returning to her Tia Maria; Alan turned towards them, smirked, before sending a thumbs up.

'He's in there,' Malcolm said in an awed whisper. 'You don't just ignore people like that unless you're *really* interested.'

As they watched, Alan leaned in unsteadily towards his potential conquest, said something, patted the side of his nose knowingly, and sauntered back to regain his seat with a loud 'Aaaah!'.

'Just wait, boys,' he said, smugly.

Fifteen minutes later they were still waiting.

'What did you say to her?' said a breathless Malcolm.

'Maybe she didn't hear you,' said Anthony.

Alan frowned. 'My overwhelming display of dominance has made her nervous that's all. That's evolutionary biology for you. She'll be over in a minute.'

A minute passed. And then another. Followed by a few more.

'Maybe some women take longer to secrete that…err… particular hormone than others,' Malcolm offered helpfully.

'Perhaps she doesn't speak English,' Geoffrey said.

'We hadn't thought of that,' Anthony said. 'I mean one shouldn't let a complete inability to communicate get in the way. It's not like you're intending to discuss Shakespeare with her, know what I mean?'

This time, as he leaned nonchalantly on the bar beside her, Alan decided to play it cool.

'DO YOU UNDERSTAND ENGLISH?' he boomed loudly, in a foreign accent.

The woman stared at him. 'Yes.'

'Good good, just checking. Now – let's see… So what do you

do? No, hang on, you should be asking me questions. Mysterious, mysterious, that's right. Ummm,' He lowered his voice urgently. 'Ask me what I do.'

'Why?'

'Please?'

She paused for a second, then, with a slight shake of the head said, 'Well, what *do* you do?'

This was the opportunity Alan had been waiting for. 'Aha!' he said triumphantly.

As she did not respond, he said 'Aha' again a couple of times, just to make sure she'd heard him properly (it was becoming increasingly obvious she had some kind of hearing problem) and added in a wink for good measure.

'Wouldn't you like to know?' he prompted, after a while.

'Not particularly,' said the object of his infallible seduction technique.

'You'll never believe it if I told you…' he continued manfully.

She was showing no signs of playing along, so he probed a bit further. 'I bet you can't guess, can you? Can you guess?'

She looked him up and down. 'An accountant?'

Alan stood up straight. 'Oh you think you're so clever, don't you?'

'Not really,' she said.

'Well, I'll have you know you're wrong. Liquidation Semi-Senior, actually.'

'No good,' he said to his colleagues as he sat down. 'Sits on the other side of the Church.'

'Oh. Bad luck,' Geoffrey said.

'What?' That was Malcolm.

'Kicks with the other foot, bats for the other side. You know. Likes to sip from the furry cup. Muff-muncher,' explained Anthony.

'Blinking hippies with their funny diets,' said Malcolm crossly, glaring across at both the woman and Mr I'm-Not-A-Charnel-House in turn. They all looked at him.

As no one knew what to say to this they lapsed into an unsteady silence.

'How about some more chanting?' Anthony said. 'Regroup.'

'Let's not,' Alan said.

'It'll cheer you up.'

'After all, you weren't to know she had an eating disorder,' Malcolm said kindly, if somewhat cryptically.

Alan was getting fed up of being a pulling guru now. 'I tell you what,' he said. 'You two go ahead and I'll just have a chat to Geoffrey here.'

Anthony and Malcolm were in full-flow and Alan and Geoffrey had only started getting to grips with the first two of Geoffrey's top ten delicatessens, when Alan's mobile burst into a lively rendition of the Brandenburg concertos on the steel drums. Six pints of 'Porridge Grower' mixed with a couple of 'Compost Heaps' were doing nothing for Alan's co-ordination and he managed to play Def Leppard followed by LL Cool J, followed by the first menacing bars of Orff's 'Carmina Burana' before, finally, Belinda's cross voice sounded in his ear.

'Have you mentioned the opera season tickets yet?'

'Oh hello darling.'

'Women are bitches!' Malcolm yelled excitedly.

'What?'

'Nothing, darling. You were saying?'

'The fucking season tickets, Alan! We agreed. To prove you're management material. We don't want them to think we're just suburban middle-brow.'

'Get back in the kitchen!' shouted Malcolm, happily.

'*What?*'

'Don't worry about that. Just some hooligans. Yes,' Alan said, sending Malcolm a meaningful look. 'The bouncers are removing them now.'

'You're not on your way? Bloody hell, what are you doing?'

'Having a few jars.'

'Well, hurry up and get back or the crudités will be soft.'

'Aye aye captain.'

'And remember – season tickets.'

'I have a penis!' shrilled Malcolm.

'Love you,' Alan said hastily and turned off his phone.

'Problem at home there, Alan?' Anthony asked.

'No no no,' said Alan, glaring at Malcolm. 'At it like rabbits, actually. As you asked.'

'Did we?' enquired Geoffrey, although he did not seem to be looking for an answer.

Alan took another cloudy mouthful and cast around for a subtle way of working opera season tickets into the conversation, but eight pints of murk were doing nothing for his powers of imagination either.

'We have opera season tickets, you know,' he said.

'Oh my god,' Malcolm said in a small voice.

'And I think you'll find they were extremely expensive.'

'Ohmygodohmygodohmygod!'

Alan was a little surprised at the strength of this reaction; he hadn't realised Malcolm was such an ardent opera fan.

'It must be the jacket, it must be!' Malcolm squeaked before disappearing into his pint.

Alan followed Malcolm's terrified gaze to see the attractive woman from the bar unfurling her lovely long legs from her barstool. She stood up, drink in hand, her long auburn tresses caressing her shoulders, and started moving towards them: magnificently, magnetically, untouchably, unattainably...

'OhmyGodohmyGod,' muttered Malcolm. 'Ohmygodohmygo dohmy – makehergoaway!–OhmyGodomy Godohmy–'

Alan felt himself flushing with impatience. 'Come on – ' he said with an easy laugh, reaching out a hand. 'Just take it off. You must be roasting.'

'No!' Malcolm hung on desperately.

Alan tightened his grip but was met with surprisingly intractable resistance. 'You're being unreasonable, man!' he hollered, unreasonably.

'I don't care!' Malcolm's voice came out in a high-pitched squeak.

A peculiar tussle took place, amidst the various eyebrow exchanges of Geoffrey and Anthony.

'Get off!' yelled Malcolm, as the two fell to the floor. The bump was enough to bring Alan to his senses and he realised that perhaps Old Porridge-Grower was stronger than he had thought.

'Can I buy you a drink?' purred a beautiful husky voice, deep as burnished mahogany: the voice of a siren.

'Yes!' Malcolm cried. 'Yes! Yes! You can, yes!'

'Tomato juice, cheers,' said a deep crusty vegan-sounding voice.

Malcolm's head snapped round to see Mr I'm–Not–a–Charnel–House stick his 'V's up, cheerfully.

'Coming up.' And she turned back to the bar, hips swinging in the slipstream of her glorious wake.

Alan put a bracing hand on Malcolm's shoulder and felt the unmistakable sensation of beer trickling off the table onto his trouser leg. He suddenly felt totally depressed. What an evening. The way things were going, perhaps it was just as well Sir Alan hadn't turned up, after all.

'Aha! Thought I'd find you boys here!' said a voice – rich as gravy, gravelly as pumice, and as virile as the voice of Alan's dreams. Shit, it *was* the voice of Alan's dreams.

'Sir Alan! Sir!'

Alan scrambled to his feet, hastily working a twenty-pence out of his pocket as he did so.

'There you go, Malcolm,' he said sternly, handing him the coin and helping him to his feet. 'I think you'll find that's what you were looking for. Be more careful next time, eh?'

He turned to Sir Alan Smith-Brown who gazed back at him with his trademark mournful shaggy stare. There was a tense pause. Then, to everyone's enormous surprise, Sir Alan shot out a paternal arm and punched Alan hard on the shoulder. 'That's what I like to see, that's what I like to see.' Sir Alan turned to the others. 'See this man here?'

Alan smiled weakly under the force of their envy.

'This is what I call good accountancy material. Every coin accounted for. Look after the pennies and the pounds will look after themselves, eh Alan?'

'Yes, Sir.'

'This man will go far! Eh?' He eyeballed them each individually. 'Eh? Eh? Eh? Now,' He clapped his hands together. 'Where's this drinks do Geoffrey was on about?'

*****

…Little did they know, but at that moment a black-clad figure, silhouetted against the evening sky, passed noiselessly along the Clapham rooftops. Moving as rapidly as a tight-rope-walker along the spine of the buildings, it traverses like a ghost across the tiles. Pausing only once to side-step a strange bird-shaped obstacle, it gathers like a barely perceptible shadow at the gable end of number eleven and peers perilously over the edge…

*****

Blissfully unaware of all this, Alan and his pals continued to roll their way through the small intestine of London's underground, heatedly discussing everything from Good Practice in Asset Disposal (Sir Alan, Geoffrey and Alan) to the pros and cons of Jordan's Breasts (Anthony and Malcolm), assessing their potential life-saving qualities (keeping you afloat in the North Sea for example) versus the danger of them putting you there in the first place (by exploding on an aeroplane).

Alan could hardly contain his excitement at his good fortune. Not only had he wowed Anthony and Malcolm with his pulling expertise, but he had managed to impress his boss with his miserly penny-pinching attitude and now here was the great man himself on the way to admire Alan's new hi-fi.

If you had told the Alan of last week, the Alan of yesterday – nay, the Alan of this morning even! – that life could turn out like this, he would have never have believed you.

*****

…The black-clad figure carefully lowers itself with a rope attached to the chimney above and begins to abseil down the back of the terrace; a small dark clot, the fly at the end of the cast line, a small black spider spinning its thread in its wake. The spider sails effortlessly downwards past the serried ranks of windows and comes to a silent swinging halt outside one of their number on the second floor. Looking once left, then right, it reaches round to extract a large jemmy from its backpack and sets to, levering it under the frame…

*****

'Welcome to my abode,' Alan cried, sweeping a grand arm across the hall in pursuit of the over-enthusiastically thrown front door, slamming itself into the wall with a kamikaze smack. 'Or, rather, *our* abode I should say.' He leaned forward conspiratorially. 'We're getting married you know.'

'Yes, we know. Jolly well done,' said Geoffrey, warmly.

'Congratulations,' added Anthony, overly-warmly.

'We'll have to see about sorting you out a little something,' said Sir Alan Smith-Brown, throwing his suit jacket at Alan.

'Oh my goodness,' oozed Alan, 'that's so kind, we didn't expect…'

Sir Alan waved him to silence, loosened his tie and started down the corridor.

Alan cast out his other arm. 'Coats?'

Malcolm hugged his jacket to his breast. At the last minute Alan's arm decided to just leave it and delivered a friendly thump to Malcolm's back instead. He flung the coats hastily into the second bedroom and darted after Sir Alan's substantial form which was poised at the door of the kitchen. He didn't want the head of Smith, Smith-Brown and Smith to see the Rothschild – not just yet.

'This way, please,' he said hastily, steering his wayward boss towards the sitting room. He opened the door with a flourish, standing back to let them go first.

'Come in, come in to our humble sitting room. Please note the new chandelier – in keeping with the period features, we thought, and do cast your eye over the Art. We thought it added a certain Bohemian air…'

He carefully did not mention his new hi-fi. He would let them discover its full glory for themselves.

His guests wandered past him into the room.

'Good lad,' said Sir Alan, delivering another shoulder-numbing thump to Alan's arm.

Alan did not linger to bask in the inevitable remarks about the unspoilt quality of the cornices but trotted off to the kitchen, rubbing his hands (and his arm) in delight. Wait until he told Belinda about this. *Sir Alan. Sir Alan Smith-Brown, actually here, in their flat. Looking at his hi-fi.* He hummed to himself as he fussed about with the glasses and positioned plates of nibbles on a tray. Everything was going so well.

'I take it no one has any objection to Rothschild?' he called out merrily as he reversed into the room with the drinks tray.

He was gratified to be greeted by an awe-struck silence.

'Oh you've discovered my guilty secret,' he heard himself trilling. 'Belinda was against my blowing so much money – and I mean *so much* money – on just another of my toys but – '

He peered round at his rapt audience, who were standing rigid, mouths agog, staring at the opposite wall.

They were obviously impressed. Alan's eyes danced happily across to take in his new integrated home theatre system with Dolby 5.1 surround-sound and 32 bit DVD audio. They lost themselves briefly in the silken surface of his new 50 inch floating plasma screen (Anthony certainly didn't have one of those); bounced happily across his new 802.11G wireless media player ('I know it's a bit naughty,' he heard himself saying oh-so-casually, 'but I just couldn't resist the wi-fi hi-fi, it really *is* the latest thing.'); skipped lightly across the naked ex-girlfriend, attached to the wall just above the mantelpiece, with two-way carabiners, adjustable leather wrist-straps, funky stripey knee-guards and a large sign saying, 'Not so boring now, am I?', and positively tap-danced across his new Bang and Olufsen speakers. ('Yes,' he imagined himself expounding knowledgeably, 'I hate to admit to being a closet audiophile but, I think you'll have to admit there's no contest once you've heard these babies.') Oh the unremitting darkness of those sheer black cases! The mesmeric beauty of their taught skins, dusky as the bloom on a grape! The way their tall, thin, contemporary lines sliced through the stylish interior with the precision of a surgeon's blade, the faint hum of sexuality implicit in two tall, sheer, black, contemporary forms: erect and potent symbols of pulsating manhood *thrusting* towards the ceiling!...

...And shot back in horror to the naked ex-girlfriend above the mantelpiece, who waved slightly, with an apologetic wince.

In one smooth movement, Alan reeled around over one of Belinda's antique coffee tables and dropped his tray with a crash.

There was a long and horrible silence.

And then some.

The naked ex-girlfriend was just beginning to wonder if she should attempt an escape by abseiling down one of the Bang and Olufsens when the lull was finally broken by Anthony Hossier's braying voice.

'Good God, Alan, you dark horse.' He took a step forward and said to Paula, 'Haven't I seen you somewhere before? – I take it I'm allowed to talk to the Art, am I, Alan?'

Alan – still flailing over the antique side-table – appeared to be struggling to retain consciousness, leaving Paula no choice but to try and distract attention. This wasn't difficult. No one was looking at Alan.

'That's fine. I'm – an interactive piece,' she said. 'About… about…umm relationships, the oppression of the patriarchy… that sort of thing.'

Malcolm, who was staying well back, shrunk inside his sheepskin jacket and said nothing whilst Geoffrey moved in for a better look. 'Brave,' he mused, scrutinising her closely. 'Very brave.'

'I remember!' said Anthony, suddenly. 'Serpentine, wasn't it? You were the one who writhed around in lion poo to change our preconceptions about conservation. God I love contemporary art!' He ducked his head and put out a closed fist disconcertingly. 'Total respect. Huge fan.'

'Thanks.'

The three accountants stood politely for a while, looking her up and down, then, one by one, they all turned to Sir Alan, who still had not uttered a single word and was standing, apparently transfixed, by the vision before him.

Sir Alan inhaled deeply: his copious chest becoming even more copious.

'No,' he said at last. 'Wouldn't hang that in my wife's bathroom. More of a Constable man, myself. Always know where you are with Constable.'

'Suffolk, normally,' Geoffrey said.

But Sir Alan ignored him. 'Now, did my ears deceive me or did someone say something about a Rothschild? Good grief, Alan, what *are* you doing to that coffee table?'

Part Two: OCTOBER

Chapter Five | THE IMPORTANCE OF PENGUINS

If he could count to three, Fred thought, then to five, then to ten, the urge, the bodily craving, the desperate need would pass over.

One – Two – Three –

Fred stood, the sweat beading his forehead, muscles standing out on his neck (impressive for someone who spent the majority of his life immobile in a swivel chair).

Four – Five –

That's what they said. He had to hold strong until it passed.

Six –

The bodily urge. The need…

Seven – Eight

The desperate pull…

Nine

The need.

With relief, he felt it passing.

Ten –

His body, wrung out, teetered beneath him and collapsed to the ground, where he lay panting; a thin veil of sweat congealing on his forehead.

He shouldn't be surprised, he thought, that the desire should be clinging on so desperately, tightening its grip at the very moment he tried to let go. Withdrawal symptoms, that's all it was. To be expected. Totally normal and natural in the circumstances.

He let his head fall back to look up at the underside of his wash cupboard, dirty and toothpaste-spattered. A small roll of chewing-gum nestled in one of the grimy joins. His feeble body felt the pull, like an insignificant iron filing in the face of a powerful magnet, pulled up towards what he knew lurked in that cupboard, between his *Star Wars* mug and the soap shaped like a spaceship... Waiting for him... Calling to him...

He had thought long and hard about his motivations: about his background, his past, his early formative experiences and (of course) his mother.

It seemed obvious she was to blame just by *being* his mother: the large pile of self-help literature, stacked at the side of his bed, agreed that it was her fault.

Was she the reason for his painful addiction? His shameful secret?

They had fostered a competitive relationship, his ambitious parents, each vying to overtake the other on the slippery ascent through the higher echelons of academia. When his father won, gaining his professorship first, his mother, being the good Feminist she was, had run off with her Lesbian Separatist PhD student to live in a commune in Hebden Bridge. He had never seen her again.

The young Fred took refuge in a world of trains, engines and spaceships; airmen and aliens; goblins and dragons; battleships and bazookas and facts; lots and lots of clean, hard facts.

Facts did not do incomprehensible things like running off to Hebden Bridge. Facts, the young Fred decided, did not let you down.

As he lay naked on the floor, gasping like a stranded fish, Fred tried to push these uncomfortable memories from his mind. He took to studying his genitalia instead. What a strange-looking cluster of oddments they were. From this angle, he fancied, his bore more than a passing resemblance to one of his heroes, the great George Melly. Fred liked to imagine that they too, one day, might be so mysteriously popular with women.

So far, his sole 'relationship' – if you could call it that – had been a disaster, with a woman he knew from his Bicycle Maintenance evening class (Advanced). Needless to say she was the only woman studying Bicycle Maintenance (Advanced) and, as far as Fred was concerned, showed an insufficient interest in the mechanics of bipedular modes of transport. (Which, had he thought harder about it, might have primed him for being less utterly gob-smacked when, after a few weeks of silent dinners and frigid visits to the cinema, an end-of-term pub lunch, five rounds of drinks followed by cocktails at The Cavendish Wine Bar, he found himself back at her place wrestling on the sofa with his trousers round his ankles.) She was considerably older than him and had been married, twice. He had hoped that this greater level of experience, plus her obvious hidden agenda for joining Bicycle Maintenance (Advanced) in the first place, might have suggested a greater level of sympathy and a nurturing spirit; instead of her bitter announcement: 'Oh God, you're a virgin. It had to be me, didn't it? It's always bloody me.'

It was after this that he had started to develop his painful habit...

Life would be so much simpler, thought Fred, eyes fixated on the underside of the wash cupboard, if women were like facts. As predictable, as knowable. (How did that piece of chewing gum end up there?) No equivocation, no room for emotion or subjectivity. (The urge to stand up and open the mirrored front of the cupboard washed over him.) There was a certain comfort in... (His hands itched, he placed them under his bottom. He was definitely safer here on the floor.) Facts were facts: solid, pure, dependable.

Breathless, he started to run through some old friends: the breeding seasons of his top ten favourite birds, the moths of the UK, Europe, Africa – his top ten favourite equations: he felt himself calming again, his pulse slowing, his body melting into the carpet.

A quick examination of his living quarters is revealing. Two clapped out computers, three crates of robot Lego, a poster of butterflies and moths along with its partner, *A Guide to British Fungi*.

A roll of the head leads to a face to face encounter with the glassy quizzical stare of a stuffed partridge in full winter plumage. The six-foot glass museum case contains another five, accompanied by a crouching hare in its glorious white winter fur-coat. Together with its companion-piece – six stuffed partridges in summer plumage posed against a meticulously painted Highland backdrop – they dominate the small room, forcing his sleeping arrangements to take futon-form, squashed in underneath his washbasin.

The cases were the only things he had saved from his parents' house, an old Georgian Edinburgh townhouse that had previously belonged to a centenarian vicar with a not inconsiderable interest in natural history. Fred's parents, being academic and strange, had seen little reason to make any changes and it had remained completely unaltered since it was decorated in the height of Victorian fashion in 1878.

His only reminder of his childhood home.

Partridges, books and abandonment: he was a psychologist's wet dream.

But all that was about to change. No more would he be the tongue-tied loner with the social skills of one of his pre-human hominid ancestors (one without the flexible tongue). No more would he have to put up with the ridicule of his male peers in the face of his shameful ignorance about football. Or the blank stares of members of the opposite sex, as they recoiled in horror from his stammering attempts to engage them on subjects such as the philosophical subtext of *Star Trek* or the difference, both from a historical and mythological perspective, between goblins, hobgoblins and orcs. He was going to be strong. He had made a decision…

He felt the sweat break out between his shoulder blades, still cold and damp from the last time. *No! Resist! Breathe.* (One…. Two… Three…)

'What – what – what – what…? What brings you –' he improvised aloud from the floor. He closed his eyes, but could see the contempt in her face already.

'W-w-w-what b-b-b-b-rings – ? '

(Five… Six…) Arggggggghhhhhh.

He must resist…

(Seven… Eight…)

He was going to change, change his life – he didn't need it. He didn't need…

(Nine…)

'What-what-what b-b-b-brings…?' A hissing sound escaped his dry lips like a steam kettle. With a lunge, Fred swung out a knobbly leg and launched himself up onto his feet. Face to face with the mirrored front of the wash cupboard, he paused, hand on the glass.

Looking straight into his own eyes, he stared at himself anxiously. His reflection staring back just as anxiously made him feel worse. *Oh shit.*

…Ten!

Trembling, Fred wrenched open the cupboard door and came face-to-face with his *Star Wars* cup, toothbrush poking out in defiance, one razor; a pot of shaving cream and a soap in the shape of a spaceship. Fingers, sticky with fear, searched desperately behind the cup, to emerge grasping a small piece of folded black material.

Lying there, limp in his hands, it was nothing much to write home about. Humble and homemade – nothing swish, shiny or PVC. A moral objection to leather could not explain his fondness for this very ordinary piece of black cotton which he now unfolded carefully, feeling the long silk laces as they tumbled through his fingers. Taking a breath, he held it up to his face, deftly tying the laces around his head.

This time the eyes that looked back at him from the wash cupboard mirror were neither anxious nor cowed; but twinkled sharply and intelligently from behind an intriguing black mask. What had looked drab and homemade in his hands, was transformed on his face into something altogether more risqué, more dangerous, its frayed edges lent an air of rawness, of unpredictability. In one smooth movement Fred swirled round to face himself in the floor-length mirror strapped to the back of the bedsit door.

'Well – hello,' said the Naked Man in the Mask, 'I must say you are looking very lovely tonight. You seem to me to be a woman of the world. Would you be very offended if I offered to buy you a drink?' The Masked Man laughed warmly. 'Oh what? This old thing? I've had this since…' He looked down, 'I call him George, don't I George? Would he like to go out with you? Well, I'm afraid we come as a package…George and I. Ha ha ha. Sorry? What was that? My name, you say? My name… My name is – '

Fred let his arms fall with an agitated flop. *What was he doing?* He wrenched the mask off and flung it across the room. The sight of himself naked and unmasked in the full-length mirror sent horror and shame washing over him with a sickening familiarity. What a pale maggoty creature.

He reeled over the sink and stood, head in his hands.

He could do this thing. On his own. He didn't *need*…

He had made his decision. He just needed a game plan, a couple of anchors in the conversation to hold onto when the going got tough. Small talk. That's what other people used. He started pulling on some clothes. What did other people small talk about? The weather, fashion… He looked around his room for inspiration. The partridges gazed back at him, their blank glassy stares horribly reminiscent of the expression of his partner on every date he had ever been on. Partridges, no. Fungi, no. He stared about, increasingly desperate: computers, Lego? The serried rows of science fiction spines stared back at him…no, no, no! Women did not go in for that kind of stuff. They wanted pink, they wanted fluffy, they wanted *feelings*. His desperate eyes fell upon a smaller poster half-hidden by the mountain of old monitors. A snowy landscape in the beautiful dawn light. A small cute furry face of a baby penguin peered out from between his father's stalwart legs, protecting him from the slanting sleet. The title, in a sloping fancy font, said '*Family Life in the Antarctic*'. Perfect. The beating in his chest began to subside as a sudden thought sent him hunting through a mound of dirty clothes. He held up a wilted T-shirt. Yes, it was going to be fine. Taking one last hesitant look in the mirror, he grabbed his keys and cast himself out of the door to set out confidently down the street in his 'I ♥ PENGUINS' T-shirt.

After all, *everyone* loved penguins.

Most nights at this time he would have dropped in on his local chippie for a bag of chips and two pickled eggs. But tonight was different. Tonight he did not want to smell of pickled egg.

He ate his chips en route, pretending to himself as he did so that he had not, before leaving, stooped to retrieve the small droop of black material from the bedsit floor, nor that it was now residing, carefully folded, in the right back pocket of his jeans.

*****

The front of the old church was grey and somewhat forbidding; until you lowered your gaze and let it fall upon a cheerful painted sign over the arching door that read, 'R&B, funky grooves and garage beats. Why not hire us for your next party?'

Underneath, clutching a tartan tin with a large roll of tickets balanced on top, stood a little old lady sporting the kind of unflattering pleated skirt beloved only of senior citizens and Scottish country dancers. 'Here for the dating, love?' she asked in motherly tones. Fred could not bring himself to speak but nodded, too vigorously.

'Don't be nervous,' she said, kindly. 'Have a shortbread.' She passed him the tin. Fred dubiously considered its enamelled invitation to '*Och go on! Taste a wee piece of Scottish heaven.*'

'Thanks.'

'You're welcome, love. Here –' and she reached over and violently stamped his hand leaving him branded with the smudgy slogan: I have a date with the Lord.

'Think about it,' she said significantly as he passed into the main chamber.

The vaulting interior of the church still showed signs of decoration from the last Harvest Festival, including a large pumpkin display on top of the old upright piano. At the centre, ten small tables had been erected and were covered in jolly check picnic cloths. At the other end of the room five apparently identical little old ladies stood behind a long trestle table selling fairy-cakes and tea. Fred had never been speed-dating before, but he was certain that tea and fairy cakes were not normally part of the bargain. They smiled across at him knowingly and waved. He gave a weak smile and turned away to nibble self-consciously on his shortbread.

It was alright. He could do this. This was good. He liked this. He felt the familiar flush of rising panic and his hand crept to his back pocket. No! He was not going to give in. Sweating, he looked around him. Various nervous individuals stood around clutching shortbread, trying to look like they were not burningly conscious of their conspicuously unaccompanied state. Fred felt a pressure behind his eyes: his head seemed muffled by cotton wool. He had made his decision and was sticking by it. He was going to be completely normal from now on. He was going to do normal things like normal people, date a normal woman, have a normal child or two and look forward to a thoroughly bog-standard, normal life. His hand crept inexorably towards the pocket of his jeans. The desire, the desire to just reach in. To feel the relaxation wash across his body… No! What was he thinking of? People would know. People would see. No no no! Look at these people. Nice – ordinary – people. Nice – ordinary – *female* people, some of them. Single – available – female - people…

Choking, he clutched at the neck of his T-shirt. Single, available, female people who would laugh at him. Who would see straight through him (he started to cough) to his dark, sordid secret…

'You alright, love?'

He came to, strangely weak and gasping.

'Sh-sh-shortbread –'

'Drink this. Wash it down.' The old lady in the pleated skirt smiled kindly, passing him a glass of water. 'Or do you think maybe you need a bit of watering by God, maybe?' she added knowingly. 'Think about it.'

He stared after her.

But she was already striding purposely towards the middle of the room where she surreptitiously managed to gain everyone's attention by thumping a large gong. Everyone jumped and looked round. She lowered her eyelids modestly and coughed.

'Excuse me ladies and gentlemen. Now, this is the first speed-dating event we've held here at St John's. As you will know, the upkeep of this historic building is considerable, and so we have entered into a spot of – err – outreach work, in order to pay for repairs. As well as speed-dating we hold regular "discothèques".' She pulled out a little piece of paper from her shortbread tin. 'On Saturday the 13th DJ Daddy-oh will be mixing his reggae grooves with his – err – beatbox beats to give us the wonderful sounding evening: *Sex it Up, Mother-Fucker*. After that, on Friday the 19th DJ Bitch–Juice will be treating us to a very interesting evening of Garage and Techno styles while on Saturday the 27th Rapper Snoop-Droopy-Droop gives us some hot tunes from his underground album "*Give it Up like the Ho you Are, Mama-Girl-Sister-Lover*".'

Right. Now. As you know, tonight is speed-dating. For some of our young people. As I stressed earlier, this is not a religious event. But we have vetted the young – err – persons and they are all very nice and clean. So if any of the nice and clean-looking young people would like to enter into a discussion about God at any point in the evening – perhaps you may find Mr or should I say Mzzz Right and want to know where God fits into your blossoming relationship? Just a thought – anyway, any of the ladies here would be delighted to have a little chat. Just ask anyone over there behind the fairy-cakes. Okay. Now, you know the rules: Three minutes each, then the men move on to the next table.

Ladies remain seated. Paper and pens are on the tables. Oh – and before we start, I would just like to stress that we do consider ourselves to be a modern, forward-looking church so for those who think they might get lucky tonight there's a condom-machine in the toilet. Although we feel it is our moral duty to point out that you will go to hell. But, no pressure. Right. Any questions?'

Strangely, there were none.

'Then, let the dating commence!' And she struck the gong again so hard that the church eaves continued to vibrate long after she had left the floor and retired behind the fairy cakes with a large hunk of sponge and a cup of tea.

In a daze, Fred approached the first table. The woman, who had nice red hair, was sitting rather stiffly, he noticed, and did not look too thrilled to see him. However, he gathered his courage, plonked himself down, and took a deep breath.

'Hello, I'm Penelope,' she said eventually.

And then, after some seconds, 'And you are…?'

'F-F-F-F-Fred.'

'Nice to meet you, Fred.'

Penelope fiddled with her lovely red hair. She seemed to be waiting for something. Fred waited to see what she was waiting for.

'So, Fred,' she tried again, valiantly. 'Tell me what you're into. Do you have any hobbies or interests?'

'I – I like penguins.'

'P-p-p-p-p-p-p-p-penguins,' she trilled in delight, 'you remember, the advert?… Sorry. That was… Ummm. Maybe I should tell you about me. I like going out, staying in, going to the cinema, not going to the cinema, going to the pub with my friends, staying in and watching a DVD –'

'D–d–do you like penguins?'

'Well, I prefer Hobnobs, myself. Especially the chocolate variety.'

'No! N–n–not…'

'Oh, you mean the bird? They are cute, aren't they?' Her tone changed disturbingly. 'And I've always thought the North Pole is very romantic, don't you?' She was fiddling with her hair a lot now. 'Apart from the weather maybe.' She laughed, tinklingly.

Fred felt his irritation rising. Couldn't the woman get her facts straight?

'P–p–p–p–enguins don't live at the North Pole,' he said, somewhat heatedly.

'Don't they?'

'No. They live at the South Pole.'

He clenched his hands and stared at the table. How had he got himself in this situation? It was a disaster. Calm down. So, she didn't know about penguins? Disappointing but not the end of the world, she could have other qualities – he couldn't for the life of him think what they could possibly be just now but it surely wasn't beyond the realms of possibility. His cheeks burned.

'Are you alright?' Her large brown eyes were staring into his with obvious concern and he felt himself melting slightly. Perhaps she did have some other qualities after all…

'I–I–I… '

She reached out a hand. 'It doesn't matter one way or the other really, does it? North Pole, South Pole…' and she laughed her tinkling laugh.

Her hair suddenly looked less becoming. He glared at her.

'Doesn't matter? ' He was speechless for a moment. 'It may not matter to you, but it's a matter of life and death to a penguin! If they lived at the North Pole the p-polar bears would eat them. Everyone knows that.'

'Time's up!' yelled the shortbread lady, banging her gong with abandon.

'I mean it doesn't take a rocket scientist –' Fred was saying, impatiently.

'TIME'S UPPPP!' the shortbread lady bellowed, adding perkily, 'Don't want to give you an unfair advantage, do we?'

Fred and Penelope sat glaring at each other. He was breathing hard.

'Nice to meet you, Fred,' said Penelope, less than friendly.

Fred stood up and pulled a face at the replacement hovering to take his place. 'Got a right one here.' He muttered out of the corner of his mouth as he passed. 'Thinks penguins live at the North Pole.'

The man shrugged doltishly.

'Well don't say I didn't warn you.' Fred left, shaking his head in disbelief.

The rest of the session did not go too well:

'Hiya, I'm Karen and my interests are celebrity hairstyles and Ceroc dancing.'

'Where do penguins live?'

'Uh, in the zoo?'

*****

'Hello, I'm Marjorie.'

'D-do you like penguins?'

'Well, yes, in their place…'

'And where's that?'

'I don't think I quite understand –'

'Y-you said you liked them in their place, implying you knew where that place was. All I'm asking for is the exact whereabouts of that place, the p-p-place you were talking about that is.'

'Look I don't know what you are going on about? If this is something to do with my divorce settlement, I'll have you know he totally deserved it. It's lucky he has a roof over his head!'

'I j-just want to know where penguins live.'

'Jesus! How should I know? They can live at Buckingham-fucking-palace for all I care. And you can tell him that from me!'

*****

'F-F-Fred.'

'Janice.'

'Okay Janice, so if I said to you s-small s-s-slow-moving flightless bird, large fast-moving vicious c-c-carnivore – would you say they could share an iceberg together?'

'Are you calling me fat?'

*****

It was no good. Ten available women in the room. Some of them even passably attractive. Not ONE of them knew where penguins lived. Or realised how crucial this was to a penguin's well-being. It was a disaster. By the time the shortbread lady struck the final gong Fred knew what he had to do. He strode over purposely with his paper.

'Have a shortbread,' she said kindly.

'Uh th-th-th – ' He took a shortbread and stood there stupidly, holding his *wee piece of Scottish heaven* and shifting from foot to foot.

'While we're on the subject,' she said nimbly. 'Have you ever considered letting God into your heart at all?'

'N-n-n-not really.'

'You should try it.'

'I'm s-s-sorry,' Fred said, suddenly. 'Some might say I'm s-super-ficial, judging a book by its cover. But everyone has their st-standards…'

The shortbread lady sighed, contented. 'Ah and yet God has the highest standards of all and still he forgives –'

'P-p-penguins happen to be very important to me.'

'Penguins.'

'Penguins.'

He looked intently into her face for a glimmer of fellow feeling.

'You don't like shortbread, then?'

Fred struggled to contain himself, but instead took a deep breath and carefully and politely replaced his piece of shortbread in the tin. His hand was shaking.

'*Not the bis-cuit.* The b-bird.'

'Oh. I see.'

'You do?' He studied her face closely.

'Err. Yes,' she said, backing off slightly.

'Then you will see that I have no choice but to – ?' and ceremoniously held out his blank sheet of paper and pen.

'Oh. Yes, of course,' she said, somewhat stunned.

'Are you going to take these?'

'Oh, oh yes.' She put out her hand in a daze.

'Cheers for the sh-shortbread.'

'You're welcome,' she said, automatically.

He turned and left while she continued to stand, wondering what had just happened.

He was halfway out the door before she managed to rouse herself sufficiently to call after him, 'Do you like acid house at all? Think about it…'

But Fred did not hear her. He hiked up the collar of his jacket around his ears and ran off into the rain. He'd tried. He'd given it his best shot. And he had promised himself, promised… But it was no good. Even God had it in for him. Perhaps it was a sign. At least he knew he'd done everything he could. He was left with no choice. He knew where he was going.

Two hundred yards up the road he took a right turn into a small cobbled lane meandering under an archway. He felt his heart expand with joy as he saw the line of familiar faces, casually queuing outside the familiar peeling red entrance.

Fred's hand reached for his back pocket and pulled out the small dark object, darkening further in the rain. He unfolded it lovingly and lifted the small black mask up to his face…

Chapter Six | GORGEOUS GEORGE

A well kept secret from the street, an idle passer-by would never have known the club was there – only an unassuming cobbled lane and a pair of plain, red-painted double doors.

Even inside, the draughty stone foyer, though a little inhospitable when empty, could have been bright and innocent enough by day to pass as a gallery, if it were not for the kinky clothes stall next to the loos (for those needing to change) complete with rubber-clad gothic totty showing off her rail of wares.

As a newcomer, this is the place where you might linger a while to build up some confidence, have a quick rake through the fetish-wear or just hang out by the cloakroom exchanging pleasantries with the gothic totty, before, unable to delay the inevitable any longer, you turn to face the curtained archway immediately ahead. You might stand, staring at it for a while, before suddenly pushing through into the heart of the club beyond.

Draped in crimson velvet, in what might be described as a gothic/bordello style: dripping with decadence; awash with candelabra, gilded mirrors and faux-gold accessories, the lavish décor is not totally successful in obscuring the building's less glamorous past as a disused warehouse. A bar curves off to the left, impractically carpeted in cherry pile. Some nights there might be a DJ and decks here. To the right; a dance floor, with enough room to seat spectators at small round tables on cabaret nights. But on nights such as these, the tables are pushed back for maximum dancing space.

To the far right, piled high with cushions in red and gold, something that resembles an oversized, luxurious bed – as though designed for a giant – reclines invitingly against the wall.

At the back of the room there is a series of seating booths with padded leather seats such as might be found in an old-fashioned pub. Some nights these might be used for fortune telling, others they just provide intimate spaces for those not yet bold enough to take that first step into the playrooms. On other occasions they turn into stalls housing dubious healers and masseurs, or fetish merchandisers flogging their novelty sex-aids and other accessories.

From here a short corridor veers off to the right, leading to a smaller bar. Before reaching this destination, you pass a number of small individual rooms followed by some loos, then a curtained off space; an adult play area, couples only.

The end of the corridor is framed by another set of curtains (plus various gilt mirrors and a naked statue or two; the club is nothing if not tasteful) – tied back to reveal a large room stretching languidly off. This room, book-ended by another bar, is smaller but cosier than the previous one, the style a cross between *Barbarella* and a *Red Dwarf* set: aiming for a hi-tech, glittery effect but somehow still managing to look like it has been entirely constructed out of cardboard.

A glitter ball spins idly above the silver stools that gather around the small bar like groupies, swivelling on their long single stems. Against the side wall, a fragile mobile of retro bubble chairs swings gently from the ceiling, faced by an army of hard plastic shapes from the 70s – seats apparently – and a couple of beanbags: the only relatively comfortable place in the room for people to drink and chat and pass out (from exhaustion rather than alcohol). Dimmer than the main bar in here, with coloured lighting for that lascivious feel, it is still light enough to check the bill.

And what of the people?

Men in black leather trousers, chests bare, funky industrial boots and an abundance of buckles and chains. (It is clear they go to the same shops.) Whilst the women show off their assets in dramatic basques and revealing PVC dresses, skin-tight gothic numbers or see-through fetish-wear. But this is just your average punter. On nights such as these everyone is welcome and everyone is here: the trannies, the slaves, the masters, the mistresses, the middle-aged swingers, the gothic dancers and those who had obviously watched too much *Blue Peter* in their youth and made their own outfits with anything that came to hand. Here they all are. Ready for the road less travelled.

Welcome to Club Liscious!

On this particular night, two transvestites sat in the foyer at a makeshift cash desk constructed from a foldaway table with a metal cashbox on top.

Luda, a club regular, had volunteered herself for door-duty partly out of loyalty to Betsy and Ron, the club owners; partly because she generally enjoyed bossing people about and refusing entry to those who, in her expert opinion, had not made enough effort; but mainly because she knew the management would overlook her sneaking the odd puff on her cigarette, without her having to brave the October night air.

Dave had volunteered because Luda had.

A queue of people snaked its way from the desk out through the red painted front doors. As Dave dispensed the tickets, Luda leisurely lit another Gauloise and went back to what she liked doing best: eyeing up the clientele as they walked in the door and throwing all-too-audible comments over her shoulder at Dave.

'What *is* she wearing?'

'I don't think red is your colour darling.'

'Has Brian taken a look at herself in the mirror lately? She looks like a member of The Village People who's stumbled into a Victoria's Secret ad.'

One might suppose, from this running commentary, that Luda had some respect for Dave's opinion on these things. Suppose not. Luda had no more respect for Dave than for any other tranny in need of her sartorial guidance, it merely being that Dave's dog-like devotion provided a permanently available set of ears, listening attentively to their mistress's voice as it raged against the poorly cross-dressed of London.

'You would have thought she could have found something more flattering than her grandmother's curtains. She's obviously not comfortable with her sexuality.'

Dave, for his part, stood quietly, exuding the steady magnanimity of a police-horse puffing quietly in the cold air. He did not pay much attention to Luda's diatribes, content merely to be tolerated at such close quarters, warming himself on the slight, agitated heat that came off her body as she raved.

'Round-toe? Round-toe? You might as well wear your hairnet and curlers with a sign on saying 'about as sexy as scrambled eggs.'

Or, spotting a particularly disappointing Liscious Fashionista:

'Well really! She could have made a bit more of an effort. Doesn't even look like she's *shaved*. I don't understand these girls, I really don't. Lazy, that's what it is. They simply don't have my will power. Do you think it's easy to stay looking this good? If I don't bother my arse to shave three times a day it's a case of smooth as a baby's bottom at lunchtime, Osama-bin-bloody-laden by 4 o'clock. Of course, not everyone has my fine attention to detail. Very feminine trait that – attention to detail. It's my innate femininity, see. The smallest thing sets me off. *Lassie, Coronation Street*. People don't get that about me. Because I don't let on, not in my day job at any rate. I'm not fucking blubbing in front of that bunch of bananas! Do you think it's easy shaving with a face rubbed RAW with tears? But do I let that stop me?' She widened her kohl-laden eyes at Dave.

'No,' guessed Dave, correctly.

'NO I BLOODY DON'T! Attention to detail, Dave. It's the

woman in me. And I'm a very feminine person, Dave. Which is why I don't like to do things FUCKING HALF-ARSED, know what I mean?'

Dave nodded sympathetically. Oh how marvellous she was. Those eyes, that passion, the rugged weather-beaten jaw (Dave felt a forbidden thrill tremble through his body), the wiry copper-dyed hair, those thick muscular arms and strong chunky legs honed by years of work in the building trade. Not that Luda liked to admit to this part of her life. If only Dave could feel those arms tightening about him. If only she would throw him onto one of the club's floor-mats in muscular abandon and criticise his clothing with the same thrilling flash in her eyes.

'How're things going out here?' said a voice. 'I'll pretend I haven't noticed that, shall I?'

Luda hastily stubbed out her Gauloise and looked up guiltily.

'Hi Betsy,' said Dave.

The woman before him was huge. Lush, luxuriant flesh oozed out from under a savage studded strap crossing her midriff, whilst two voluptuous breasts – an opulent Rococo fountain – spilt lavishly over the top of a red PVC bustier, bubbling, rippling then finally giving up and cascading down toward the eddying fleshy pools of her voluminous stomach.

The woman laughed; a delightful full-throated gurgle, like water rushing down a plughole: the sound of possibility, the sound of life itself. Her undulating chins tremored and wobbled invitingly.

'Hi Ron.'

The small figure, sheltering hitherto unnoticed under the eaves of Betsy's munificent bust, nodded anxiously. A dull-coloured sparrow to her corpulent peacock, Betsy's husband, Ron, was dressed immaculately in a shirt, tie and trousers. As far as anyone knew Ron had never shown much interest in the goings on at the Club and no one really knew why he turned up week in, week out, with such unfaltering regularity – except for the small fact of owning it, of course. Yet he had survived thirteen years of marriage to Betsy, apparently without accident or mishap, and for this he was held in the highest esteem. It had been rumoured that many a lesser erotic adventurer had confidently set sail across Betsy's vast plains, only to plunge fatally into the ravine of her commodious cleavage (out of which during the course of an evening it was not unknown for her to extract a pair of handcuffs and a small spanking paddle) never to re-emerge. It was a fate talked of with awe and not a little fear within the club confines, and yet each man privately yearned for that dark cosseted place, shuddering secretly to himself at the appalling ecstasy of such a death – unable to stop the thought, unbidden and unspoken: '*But what a way to go*'.

'Looks like a busy night,' Betsy said. 'Make sure you don't let any unknown men in, ok? We had a couple of complaints last week about that idiot trying to grope the girls by the condom-machine. Any newcomers – couples and women only, got it?'

'Got it,' Luda said, trying to obscure the overflowing ashtray with her body.

'And if I catch you smoking that thing the other side of that curtain I'll have your guts for garters.'

The woman laughed again and Luda lowered her head, humbly.

Dave watched as Betsy pushed aside the heavy velvet curtains before passing into the inner sanctum, Ron momentarily rolling his eyes before being whipped up and swept along in her wake. *What a wonderful woman.*

'One please.'

Dave turned back into the foyer. He hadn't seen the speaker come in. His hair was still spiky with rain. He must have darted straight through the door and into the foyer toilets to change. Not that he had changed into anything, more a case of remove. For the man before them was completely naked, save for a small black mask behind which his bright eyes twinkled wickedly.

'Sorry, pal. Couples and women only,' said Dave sternly.

'Oh fuck off, Dave,' said Luda, through a cloud of re-ignited cigarette. 'Those rules don't apply to George. Good to see you, George,' she said. 'Get a ticket out, would you Dave? How's it hanging, mate? Umm, I mean… Oh fucksake, you know what I mean.'

The Man in the Mask smiled and held out a note. Luda was just about to take it when she was interrupted by a kafuffle at the back of the queue, near the exit.

'Oi! What's going on back there?'

'She's pushing in.'

'Stolen my place. Hey – who do you think you are, Missus?'

Dave craned round to try and see what was happening.

As they watched, a small woman was pushing and shoving her way towards them – much to the annoyance of her fellow queuees.

Luda whistled angrily through her teeth.

The woman ploughed on, past the hip, the young and the skin-tight; the 'experimenting' couples and the beautiful black-clad girls who just 'liked the music'; blind to Neil, the office clerk, dressed in his tight PVC cat suit, his pale oh-so-British bumcheeks peeking hopefully out from where the seat had been cut away; shoving past Miriam the fifty-year old bodybuilder, looking very glamorous in her yellow silk bikini, a single ostrich plume rising magnificently from between two clenched muscular buttocks; on past Gretchen the Dominatrix ('Ooo look where you're going, love') and the Big Hairy Bearded Bloke in the tartan dress; to arrive breathless and impatient in front of Luda, to whom she proffered a crumpled twenty pound note with all the intensity of a drug addict about to buy her last fix.

'I need a ticket.'

Dave winced and exchanged a glance with The Man in the Mask.

Luda shifted her gaze to look the woman up and down with a crude and painful slowness and took a drag of her Gauloise. Unfortunately, all efforts to render this gesture elegant – the 1920s cigarette holder, the insouciant set of the shoulders, the casually floating pinky – were belied by the gulping impatience of her inhalation and the aggressive puff which supplanted it.

Dave knew that, as far as Luda was concerned, this pale mousy figure was hardly up to standard. Yes, she was wearing stilettos, it was true. And some attempt had been made to add some spice to her flagging mousy hair by tying it up in 'risqué' schoolgirl bunches. But no amount of bared shoulder was going to make that black dress any less baggy and unflattering. In fact, her whole demeanour was more of the vicar's wife at a coffee-morning than up-for-it new addition to the Club Liscious elite. Dave looked across at The Man in the Mask. He appeared unmoved, though Dave wondered if for a second he detected a slight sparkle in the eyes behind his disguise.

Luda, still looking the newcomer up and down (she was enjoying this), took another violent suck at her Gauloise, waited one, two, three long seconds before allowing an angry expulsion of smoke to explode out of her mouth and directly into the small intense face before her. The small intense face gave nothing away, but the woman's bony shoulders flew to her ears and her pale knuckles became even paler and knucklier as she tightened her grip on her twenty pound note.

'I said, one please,' she repeated, somewhat shrilly.

'Oh?' Luda's one ascending eyebrow spoke volumes. 'And what makes you think I'm going to let you in? I hardly think that meets the dress code.'

The pale woman's gaze never faltered. 'You have to let me in. I've come all the way from Finsbury Park.'

'Well in *that* case…' Luda's voice dripped sarcasm. 'Why?'

The woman looked down a second as though weighing up how much to divulge, twisting the twenty pound note in her hands. 'It's complicated,' she said at last.

The twenty pound note was coming in for some serious punishment now. 'I'm not the police,' she added reassuringly. 'I am here to learn.'

Luda's eyebrow shot up and lost itself somewhere under her coquettishly-angled beret. She opened her mouth as though to deliver a devastatingly bitchy put-down, but inspiration did not strike and she shut it again. Then, much to Dave's surprise, she looked away.

Dave scrutinised the newcomer with renewed interest. The twenty pound note was now a screwed up ball – nearly as small and screwed up as its owner. But there was something in her look of determination, even desperation, that made even Dave feel slightly ashamed. He looked round at The Man in the Mask who was still standing immobile, money in hand. He returned his gaze to Luda, noting the muscle twitching in the side of her face – oh how he yearned to run a finger across that rugged square jaw…

'I've fucking gone soft,' Luda muttered to herself.

'It's your feminine side,' Dave happily reassured her, earning nothing but a withering look for his pains.

Luda made up her mind and snatched the screwed up note from Paula. She had the uneasy feeling that she had somehow been made a fool of, but was not quite sure how. To regain her dignity she contented herself with drawing up to her full height – a not particularly impressive five foot six and a half (Luda's physique being more imposing in the horizontal than the vertical plane).

'Easy tiger,' she drawled, unnecessarily, in her most irritatingly drawly voice: the one designed to go with the French cabaret artiste look she was cultivating that evening.

The pale woman stared at her.

'Well go on then!' Luda yelled, starting the woman into life, who looked round wildly, before charging up to the velveteen curtains and stopping short as if in indecision. Then, just as abruptly, she pushed past them, her hunched shoulders flashing suddenly white before being swallowed by blood red drapes.

'*Grrrrr*,' Luda growled after her, self-consciously, clawing an elegantly manicured hand through the air.

'Are you going to cry?' asked Dave.

Luda shot him an irritated look. 'I may be ultra-feminine but I'm not totally pathetic.'

Dave rolled his eyes at The Man in the Mask but found, to his surprise, that he was staring at the still-waving curtains with a curious look on the bottom half of his face.

'Oh hurry up and get him his fucking ticket, would you Dave?' Luda turned back towards the queue, now shuffling and restless. 'I don't know what you're all looking at. Show's over. Come on! Roll up, oh roll up, you fuckers!'

Chapter Seven | FALL-OUT

You may be wondering how Paula progressed from being spread-eagled naked above Alan's mantelpiece to putting in an appearance at a notorious fetish establishment at the heart of South London.

Interestingly, this happened to be exactly what Paula herself was wondering as she let the curtains fall heavily behind her, muffling the sounds of the foyer and the rattling rain beyond, and took that first long, slow look at her new surroundings.

Needless to say, the fall-out from her plan had not been quite as she had hoped.

True, it had not been without result, including a lively write-up in her local paper, a dinner invitation from Anthony Hossier and the offer of a one-woman-show at the Empty Space Gallery in Soho. But, despite all this, she had spectacularly failed in her overriding objective: to win back the love of one man, Alan.

Everywhere she looked, she saw him: in every puddle, every paving stone, reflected off the shining head of every bald, slightly overweight man waddling down the street... When would she once again be able to lay her swooning head on his manly well-padded bosom? Kiss his shining forehead? Blow a raspberry on his plump cherubim's peaches? Alan, oh Alan! Had a woman ever suffered such agonies over an accountant?

'You bloody fool,' Alan had hissed at her at the hearing. 'Don't you realise that you have completely scuppered my chances of promotion?'

'I'm sorry – I didn't think – I –'

'Didn't *think*?'

'Can't you just tell him it's all my fault? That I'm mad. Certifiable?'

'I tried that already. No. He's got it firmly in his head that you're the new Tracy Emin or something.'

'Really? But surely that's a good thing?'

'Don't be ridiculous. If there's one thing Sir Alan loathes more than impropriety it's conceptual art! He's never going to promote me now.'

Belinda did not attend the hearing, it happened to coincide with an important wedding summit concerning placemats. But she obligingly submitted a statement to be read out in her absence that, in unsurprising and unimaginative terms, requested the 'lunatic bitch' be locked up and the key duly discarded.

As it was, Paula was issued with a restraining order preventing her from coming within a 100 metres of Alan at all times. This had been considerably reduced from 300 metres to accommodate the fact that they worked in the same building. The Smith, Smith-Brown and Smith building was so inhumanly immense that this order could be accommodated quite easily, so long as Paula took care to watch that their paths did not cross to and from the unisex toilets. To avoid this, she was issued with a convenient tracking device so that she could be aware of Alan's whereabouts at all times. (All in all, Paula was not unduly displeased with this outcome.)

Still, tracking device or not, there was no denying the fact that the restraining order left her with a lot of time on her hands. Every night her mother would phone with the latest 'helpful' suggestion to mend a broken heart.

'Have you thought about joining a crochet circle? Very therapeutic: all the stars are doing it'.

Or:

'Have you thought about belly dancing, my love? Apparently it's wonderful for toning up those problem areas.'

And:

'I was just looking through the local adult education courses and there's a great one here teaching you how to make Christmas decorations out of household rubbish – I know it's a bit early but…'

Paula hated to admit it, but her mother was right. She did need to pull herself together, get out there, get in amongst it. (Even Tanya told her kindly to 'fucking get a life'.) She had not been dumped; she had been mercifully released to pursue her own voyage of self-discovery through…'Tantric Knitting' for example or 'Aromatherapy for Dogs'. ('All the celebrities swear by it.')

She had two choices: either she could grow up, get a grip and take control; or she could allow herself to become a sad neurotic obsessive, who was allowing her life to be overtaken by the need to win back the love of a rather mediocre man. Without hesitation, she plumped for the latter.

Which is where the club came in.

Paula had an inkling joining a fetish club was not quite the kind of hobby her mother had in mind. But with Alan's accusation of boredom still ringing in her ears, it seemed the perfect way of getting over him (and at him) and moving on. She couldn't wait for him to find out.

Thinking back, Paula could not be certain where she had first heard of Club Liscious. In the office, probably, although exactly when she could never remember – one of those little gusts of gossip that passed unknowingly into her subconscious as she sat at work one day, studying her webcams. Somebody's wedding – tasteless – somebody's love child – a terrible shock. The exact details of the Liscious story she could not swear to, but to judge by Tanya's usual style it probably went something along the lines of:

'Apparently *you-know-who*'s split up with her husband.'

'Not *you-know-who*, Tanya?'

'Mmmm-hmmm. Thought the hubby was having a bit of a *you-know-what*.'

'No!'

'Silent calls. Inexplicable credit card bills. Suspicious forays into the land of the washing machine.'

'You're kidding!'

'So one night she set off to her pilates class leaving him happily watching *Dragon's Den*, when something didn't feel right and she decided to turn back. And of course who should be setting out the door?'

'Who?'

'For God's sake Sonya, *Him* of course. Who else would it be? Do keep up. Anyway. So. She decides to follow him.'

'No!'

'Yes!'

'No!'

'This could go on all night, Sonya.'

'Sorry.'

'To cut a long story short – you'll never guess where she found him,'

'*Where?*'

'Club Liscious, Sonya!'

'Omigod, Tanya! Club *Liscious* – is that that R&B place by the river?'

'No it's not! Don't you read the papers?'

'I'm not political like you, Tanya. It's not Techno, is it?'

'It's sex, Sonya.'

'What, like prostitution?'

'No, Sonya. This is specialist stuff. This is kinky.'

'*Really?*'

'When she found him,' Tanya takes a deep breath and sucks in her cheeks in the manner of a priest about to deliver the last rites. 'He was wearing a lime green minidress being spanked by a woman in a nurse's uniform.'

'Ugh, that's disgusting!'

'Yes it is, Sonya.'

'Lime green is sooo last year.'

'That's exactly what *I* said.'

From this tiny germ of information, a seed of possibility planted itself in the dark fertile soil of Paula's subconscious mind. Over the following days and weeks it began to germinate, its fragile roots burrowing deeper into her psyche, whilst a small white shoot began its tentative ascent into the lower layers of Paula's consciousness. Then, one night, as she tossed and turned in fitful sleep after a particularly emotionally gruelling session of 'Find Yourself Through Cake Decoration', there it was. A huge neon weed of a thought – flowers, leaves, thorns, the lot – glowing with radioactive intensity: Club Liscious! Club Liscious!

And, as with the most insidious intruders of its kind, once it had arrived, no amount of digging, ignoring or flagrant weed-killering, could dislodge it. In truth, she did not even try, but then and there leapt out of bed and headed for the huge and ancient computer, crouched miserably upon a bowed IKEA desk in the small kitchen/utility room, provided for communal purposes. Not that she had seen any of the other tenants doing any communing there. Her only impression of them was as darting figures on the stair, disappearing into their rooms clutching their stash of microwave ready meals. However she still felt nervous as she perched, flighty as a flea, before the enormous screen ready to leap away at the slightest noise.

It did not take her long to find what she was looking for.

'Club Liscious. An exclusive establishment for those who want to go down the road less travelled and explore the enchanted realms of lust and desire,' said the tag-line, followed by the friendly encourager, *'wrinklies welcome'.'*

Underneath were some photographs of exotic-looking people sporting the odd strategically-positioned ostrich feather and a man with a tattoo doing something very peculiar with a mango.

Paula navigated her way through the dizzying corridors of the Club Liscious website, unable to tear herself away. She had no idea how many seriously disturbing things could be done with feet for example. *And what was he doing? Disgusting!* She rotated her head through 90 degrees. *Disgusting!*

But if Paula had been in any doubt, at that moment, where her future was heading, this was finally and resoundingly quashed by the eruption of the phone, bursting into life like an angry bee. She lurched over to the kitchen counter – the one with, '*Leave me fresh and clean and I will greet you with a beam*' pinned above it – and heaved herself onto an incredibly uncomfortable high stool.

'Paula?'

'Alan!'

'Shhh. I know I shouldn't but –'

'You phoned me!'

'Don't. I'm only –'

'Oh Alan!'

'– concerned about you.'

'Alan.'

'About how you are struggling to cope. Without me.'

'Oh,' she cast around the kitchen counter for a pen to doodle with. 'I'm okay.'

'You are?' he sounded a little disappointed. 'It's just, I was concerned – not having seen you around for a while.'

'You *did* take me to court.'

'Yes, I know.'

'And slapped a restraining order on me.'

'There is that.'

'So it shouldn't be so surprising that I'm not popping over for the odd cup of tea…'

'Okay, okay. You've made your point.'

There was a brief silence and then he said, 'Paula, I just want to know one thing.'

'Yes?'

'Do you still want me back?'

Paula's heart flew. 'Yes, yes, more than anything. Oh Alan!'

There was brief expulsion of breath. 'I thought so. Paula?'

'Yes?'

'I just want to say…'

'Yes?'

'…want you to know…'

'Yes, yes?'

'…That I understand how difficult it is for you.'

'Oh.'

'I know you believe you will never get over me. That you will never find anyone to compare.' He paused as if waiting for something. 'But one day, one day – unbelievable though it seems at the moment – you *will* move on. You won't always be thinking about me, pining for me, wanting me, *yearning* for me –'

'Well, thanks for that, Alan,' she interrupted him. 'I'll bear that in mind.'

'Oh. Yes. Do.' He seemed a bit put out. Then, in the tones of a teacher re-establishing boundaries for the sake of an attractive but out-of-bounds pupil, he asked, 'How are you coping with all the bills? You *are* remembering to open the official-looking envelopes, aren't you?'

'I suppose.'

'And not leaving them to turn red?'

'I –'

'Paula! How many times do I have to tell you? If you look after your money, your money will look after you.'

'Alan, it's very late and –'

'Look, Paula, I don't have time to talk now. Belinda's back any minute and Friday night is rumpy-pumpy night so –'

'I'm going to a fetish club!'

She did not know why she said that.

'Don't be ridiculous, Paula.'

'I mean it. It's called Club Liscious. Tanya was telling me about it and –'

'You're just being silly now.'

'No I'm not.'

'Yes you are.'

'No I'm not!'

But she felt distinctly silly. What was a dull middle-aged woman like her doing, pathetically flinging herself at anything kinky or erotic like some sex-starved Stepford wife?

'What's a dull middle-aged woman like you doing, pathetically flinging yourself at anything kinky or erotic like some sex-starved Stepford wife?' Alan said.

'Fuck off, Alan.'

'Alright, I will.'

She sat and stared at the mobile in her hand for a long time after he rang off. How dare he, how dare he tell her how to live her life? If she wanted to experiment, take drugs, have sex with the entire western hemisphere, she would. She picked up a rack of post and plucked out a couple of letters, red writing winking at her, unmistakably. Alan might think the road to excitement consisted of carefully scheduled romps in the hay with a woman who looked like one half of a pair of garden shears, but Paula was altogether more spontaneous. She twirled round the kitchen, shreds of gas and electricity bills corkscrewing to the floor in her wake. That felt good. She plucked a particularly intimidating council tax reminder and tore that up too, laughing manically as she did so. Take that, you bastard! (As she ground her council tax reminder underfoot.) And that! (As the telephone bill bit the dust.) As for you, irritating laminated notes around the kitchen…

She stood in the middle of the linoleum letting the new sense of female empowerment surge through her breathless body.

A new chapter of her life was beginning. Alan was behind her, completely and utterly. She was heading into the future, alone, independent, ready for what life had in store. The universe spread its legs to reveal a cornucopia of dizzying aphrodisiacal possibilities: the world was her oyster and she the catcher, a ripe avocado with herself as the knife: a snort of powdered rhino-horn to Paula's rhino-horn snorter. She was all-woman, abundant and glorious, about to embark on her own sexual odyssey, a journey of self-discovery. Touch me, touch me, baby, squeeze my inverted female lemon, until the hot acidic juice runs down my shapely feminine leg, yeah.

Move over world. Paula's out to play.

With that, she made her herself a cup of cocoa, picked up all the little torn bits of paper, sellotaped them all together, put them tidily back in the bill rack and went upstairs to bed.

Chapter Eight | FIRST IMPRESSIONS

Paula passed through the club in a rapture. She idled a hand across a velvet drape, drank in the heady perfumed air and stood beneath the circling glitterballs letting the flecks of light caress her body; *if Alan could see her now*!

However, unknown to her, mumbles of discontent were ominously beginning to rumble.

Unsure how to react to the small intense woman with her peculiar hairdo and ill-fitting outfit, the clubgoers began to suspect that the unbearably nosy newcomer was a local reporter, or even worse, a plant from the neighbouring St John's Church Association, who had been campaigning to have Liscious closed down for the last five years.

'She looks like bloody orphan Annie,' Luda said crossly. 'What's she doing here, anyway?'

Her familiar coterie surrounded her: Dave, The Man in the Mask, leaning rakishly against the wall, and Gretchen, the goth dominatrix, whose shoe was presently being 'shined' by the tongue of her abject bald-headed disciple, affectionately known to one and all as SlaveBoy.

'Oh, I don't know,' The Man in the Mask murmured.

Luda shot him an angry look. It was hard to tell what he was thinking behind his mysterious mask, but so far he had not taken his eyes off the newcomer. Luda felt a surge of something uncomfortable cross her chest and tried to lean back further in a failed attempt at ostentatious elegance.

'She doesn't seem to be doing any harm,' said Gretchen, kindly. 'I want to see my face in it!' she added, to SlaveBoy, with a snarl.

'She's about as sexually sophisticated as Miss Marple,' spat Luda, with close attention to The Man in the Mask. 'You know what she said to Peter? She asked whether he'd just been to a party and when he said "No, why?" she said "because you're carrying a balloon!"'

They all collapsed about in giggles. All, that is, except for The Man in the Mask who, failing to acknowledge the hilariousness of this comment, continued to gaze across the room. Luda, irritated, shot out an arm and jabbed Dave, whose lumpen presence had been shifting infinitesimally closer in particularly irksome fashion, sharply in the ribs. He obediently removed himself to an acceptable distance; although, as soon as she looked away, he placed a proprietorial arm against the wall behind her.

Gretchen said, 'Well. Wendy told me she went up to her and asked, "How come so many people have hankies in here? Is there a cold going round?"'

They all collapsed again.

'What *is* she doing here?' Luda said again.

'She just looks like a bored housewife to me,' said Gretchen, absent-mindedly crushing SlaveBoy's face into the floor.

'The last thing we want are suburban snoopers,' Luda said,

'Liscious is a high-class outfit. We have a reputation to uphold.'

'Hmmm,' Gretchen agreed, over the gurgling sounds of SlaveBoy under her boot.

'Right, that's it,' said Luda. 'I'm going to find out.'

'Ow!' yelped Slaveboy.

'Oh, shhh,' Gretchen soothed. 'You know you like it really.'

Paula emerged from the ladies toilets and paused in the corridor. Heady music pulsed from the speakers above her head. Here, apart from the odd couple opposite – him: bunny ears and PVC shorts, her: silver basque, stockings, suspenders and slicked back hair – she was alone.

She peered down the corridor to her right where a series of doors led off. She stood for a while and watched people entering and leaving the private rooms. Some were couples, laughing, kissing; others furtive, watchful and alone.

What did people do in there?

Fear prickled around her neck, but there was something else too. She was excited.

Quickly, Paula passed down the corridor, ignoring the entreating smile of the woman in the suit jacket leering round to meet her. Hesitating outside one of the doors, she held her notebook before her as a shield, pen poised like a lance, before gently, tentatively pushing open the door.

Paula didn't know what she had expected to see. A couple indulging in full-on sadomasochistic activity, a crowd of half-dressed middle-aged swingers having an orgy, at the very least she expected a spot of spanking…

What she didn't expect was a rather ordinary-looking man sitting alone under the requisite glitterball with a box of multi-coloured tissues at his side. He patted the seat next to him. At least, she assumed it was a seat; it resembled something between a dentist's chair and an operating table. It even had stirrups.

Paula looked at him, slightly horrified now, but the prickle in her neck was still there. What was he going to do to her? Everything she had been taught about avoiding strange men in darkened rooms with restraining straps and stirrups flooded into her mind. What had she been thinking?

She licked her lips and looked nervously towards the door. Then she thought of Alan, stiffened her back, dropped her shoulders, walked to the dentist's chair and sat down. Trembling, she turned to her new companion, arms akimbo, ready to offer herself up to his deepest darkest desires.

'Tissue?' he said, offering her the box.

Paula had not even realised there was such a thing as a nose fetishist before. Not only did her new companion, ('Call me Trevor'), like to talk about noses (and his knowledge on all things olfactory was frightening) but he liked photographs of noses, short stories on noses and was a member of several online nose chat-forums – not to mention having a bit of a funny thing about used handkerchiefs.

But most of all he liked to kiss and caress noses.

When he asked Paula if he could touch her nose she was strangely flattered if slightly uncertain. After all, it was not like he was asking for sex. Or even a snog. She had never even considered the nose to be a potential G-spot before – maybe she would find out something new about herself.

She did.

As she squinted uncomfortably across at him through the fringe of his fingers, middle digit sensually exploring her right nostril, she discovered she did not like people sticking their fingers up her nose.

As he progressed to nuzzling, a questing tongue making the odd flickering foray into her nasal passage, she soon made the discovery that she did not like people sticking their tongues up her nose either. She pulled away violently, snorting for breath.

'Are you alright?' he looked concerned.

'It's – uh – fine. Uh.' She fumbled with a paper tissue. 'I'm just not used to – phew!'

She tried to appear as though the excitement was just too much for her.

'The excitement was just too much for me,' she said, in case her acting was not up to the job.

'Really?' he looked pleased. 'No-one's ever said that to me before.'

'No?' Paula blew her nose emphatically into her tissue. 'I can't believe that.'

He leaned forward eagerly. 'Shall we..?'

'No! I mean –' she was in the midst of blows, 'I think I need to – err – calm down. Err, outside. On my own.'

'Oh.' He sounded disappointed.

She put a hand on his arm. 'That was such an amazing experience we must never ever do it again.'

His face broke out into a boyish grin. 'Wow, you must've liked it. I wonder would you mind if I…' His eyes shuffled down shyly to her left hand.

'Oh, of course.' And she handed over the scrumpled tissue before bolting towards the exit…

Back out in the corridor, Paula stood with her back against the door, panting heavily. She had done it. Her first 'alternative' experience and it wasn't so bad. Ok, it hadn't done a whole lot for her in the arousal department but…

From the other side of the corridor, the woman in suspenders winked across. Paula felt her courage rising. She could do this. She *was* exciting. Not only that but she, Boring Paula, had an exciting nose!

Ready for her next adventure, she cast her eyes down the corridor, towards the soft, inviting curtains of the couples-only enclosed play area.

Her intrepid foot was just inching its way into this shrouded arena when she felt her feeble arm being locked in a hairy muscular one and herself being towed away with considerable force.

'But I only wanted to talk,' she protested, trying to wriggle out of Luda's grasp. But Luda was unstoppable, a charging rhinoceros in mini skirt and heels.

'Against club rules, honey,' she drawled. 'Couples only, or else you have to wait for an invite to join in, lover girl.'

'But I don't want to join in, I only want to ask a few questions… I'm sure nobody minds…' Paula protested, trying to slip out of Luda's grasp. She was answered with a swift headlock and a rapid march towards the bar, where she was then released and stared at in a menacing manner until she sat down.

Luda, who, until then had been bearing more of a resemblance to a combat wrestler than a Parisian lady, let out a long breath, fussed at her clothing and perched one bumcheek carefully upon a neighbouring stool, wrapping her long elegant legs around one another like necking swans. At least, this was the effect she was going for. In reality, thirteen years in the building trade had left Luda with a physique more brick shithouse than French cabaret artiste and Paula – half an eye on making her escape – looked on curiously as Luda's thick legs, hampered by a general lack of length and flexibility, failed to entwine themselves in a sufficiently swanlike manner; resembling instead two pugnacious pit bulls, squabbling over a scrap of meat.

Suitably wedged and balanced at last, Luda stuffed a cigarette brutally into the end of her cigarette holder, at which point she changed mode and pretended to inhale it, unlit, with a slow, deliberate and overweening elegance. This seemed to calm her down.

'So.' She gazed at her companion with designed objectivity. 'Are you a journalist?'

'No!' Paula was shocked. 'No,' she repeated, not sure what else to say.

'So, why are you nosing around, asking questions?'

Paula fidgeted uncomfortably. She suddenly felt the urge to pour out everything to this strange individual. About Alan. About Belinda. The spying. About being boring. About being boring in bed. Instead she said:

'I'm researching a play. Yes.' She chanced a quick smile. 'Research. Acting. Character research.'

'Character research?' Her companion unleashed a snaggle-toothed smile. 'How very interesting. And what kind of character are you researching?'

'Umm, someone a bit like me, I suppose,' Paula said, frowning, 'But maybe a little more adventurous. In bed. Or,' she continued, 'maybe not like me. Maybe more like someone else. Maybe a bit like me. If I was obsessed with designer clothes and very dominating in bed. Or maybe not dominating. I don't know if she's dominating or not... That's kind of the point... I mean – What does it take? To be exciting. Exciting in bed, I mean.'

Luda uncrossed and recrossed her legs, apparently struggling to maintain balance.

'Femininity,' she said with hauteur.

'Really?' Paula was not certain Luda was exactly the role model she was looking for, but suspended her pencil over her notebook nonetheless.

'There is nothing more exciting than the allure of the truly feminine woman.' Luda blew pretend smoke mysteriously into Paula's face. 'Of course it is rather out of fashion these days. Perhaps you wouldn't know,' she added, meanly.

Paula was too busy writing to take any notice. 'No, this is good, this is interesting. What do you mean by feminine? Breasts? Implants? What?'

Luda considered. Eventually she said, confidingly and with great significance, 'I cry a lot.'

Paula was confused. 'And that's exciting?'

'I suppose it's just the woman in me.' Warming to her theme, Luda leaned forward in sudden candour. 'Everyone has a male side and a female side – all of us. It just so happens that my female side is very developed.'

Her voice, which had fallen to a fragile whisper, fell away as she sat back in her seat. 'It is difficult sometimes to deal with the wealth of emotions I feel. I am a *very* feminine person.'

On the dance floor an overly amorous man slipped a stray arm around the hips of an unenthusiastic woman.

'Oi!' Luda roared gruffly rising up in her chair, a maggot-like vein popping out of her neck. 'WHAT PART OF FUCK OFF DO YOU NOT UNDERSTAND MATE?'

The offending man slunk off sheepishly and Luda gradually subsided back onto her seat, mirroring the vein subsiding back into her thick neck.

'See what I mean, no fucking sensitivity. Sorry where was I? Crying. Yes, I cry all the time. Anyone says a cross word to me and I'm just away, you know. I can't, just can't stand arguments...' She trailed off and rearranged her behind so that she was sitting on one buttock again.

Paula watched the figures on the dance floor, mesmerised. She had only ever been to a nightclub once before with Alan, years ago. Alan had refused to dance but sat at a table yelling at her about the joys of liquidation. She hadn't understood a thing he was saying and couldn't hear him anyway. Probably just as well.

Boring. Fine eight years. Nothing personal.

The music coiled about her mind, taking her to that other place, that other time, those months ago. She felt the despondency sweep over her again.

'So why are you *really* here?'

Paula was jolted back to the present to find Luda sitting staring at her, the one-buttock arrangement forgotten as she cast forward curiously.

'I told you.'

'Acting, research, of course, silly me. And the name of your play? I *adore* culture.'

'Oh, I don't think you'll have heard of it. It's just been translated from – from – a little known Brazilian piece.'

'Try me.'

'It's called…' Paula cast about for inspiration; an image of Belinda flashed into her mind. '*Bitchface*. Yes.'

Luda raised herself from her seat with grandeur. '*Bitchface*?'

'It sounds better in Brazilian.'

'Acting indeed!' Luda expostulated as soon as she was out of earshot, to anyone who would listen. 'Load of crap.'

'I think she's nice,' said Dave innocently, earning himself a poisonous look from the object of his affections. 'She's got a nice face.'

'Nice face, nice face!' Luda sputtered. 'Nice face? If your idea of nice is washed out, anaemic nothingness that is.'

'She's quite pretty. Well maybe not pretty exactly. Kind of pale and interesting.'

'Oh don't give me that pale and interesting shit.'

'Well she is.'

'Pale,' said Luda determinedly, looming her leathery orange face at Dave's, 'is never interesting. Otherwise we wouldn't spend half our lives in tanning salons. If pale was ever interesting there would be a word for it. Like "palteresting". Which there isn't! '

Dave who had never been to a tanning salon in his life, decided to change the subject.

'She's got a nice figure,' he tried. 'Very small and feminine.'

This was not a good ploy. Luda, anything but small and feminine herself, was particularly sensitive about anyone else being perceived as such.

'Feminine? *Feminine*? You think that *thing* over there is feminine?'

Dave weighed up his options, 'Yes?' (Wrong.)

'There is absolutely nothing feminine about that pale sliver of a person over there. Does she have dress sense, does she have style? DOES SHE EXFOLIATE?'

Dave, who had been reading a book about difficult people, decided to try out one of the techniques and started waving his hands slowly in front of Luda's face and crooning 'Luda, Luda,' in warm soothing tones. Luda ignored him.

'Does she get up and shave three times a day to keep her skin smooth as a baby's bottom? Does she glide across the room like a goddess? Does she command the attention of every man as soon as she walks into the room? Does she cry at *Lassie*?'

'We don't strictly speaking know the answer to that question,' said Dave.

'Of course she doesn't! Just look at her – hard as nails. Now myself on the other hand...'

But before Luda was given the chance to develop this favoured theme in too much detail, Gretchen jumped in.

'She must have an ulterior motive.'

The others looked at her.

'There must be more to this than meets the eye. A single suburban housewife coming to Liscious on her own, it's unheard of. She'll be from the council, I'll bet. Those old crowbags from the church will have put her onto us.'

They all peered across the room with growing suspicion. The object of this suspicion, unaware, was at that moment taking a breather from her research and sat self-consciously on a bar stool, negotiating a large and extraordinary cocktail, whose teaming array of umbrellas, sprays of foliage, floating olives and a flake was proving to be a considerable obstacle when it came to the practicalities of getting glass to mouth.

'Well, we'll just have to put her right back off us again,' said Luda ominously.

'What do you mean?' Gretchen asked.

'Give her something to really write about.'

The other two looked at her.

'What?' shouted Luda aggressively. 'What? What? What? What? What is your fucking problem? Have none of you got a fucking sense of humour?'

Dave put out a soothing hand, only to be abruptly shaken off again.

'Don't touch me!'

'Oh, this could be fun,' said Gretchen. 'Can we frighten her a little bit?'

Luda narrowed her eyes. 'She wants kink, let's give her fucking kink.'

*****

From her position at the bar, Paula surveyed the scene around her. *Would you look at that woman over there? Doesn't she know this is a fetish club? She could have made a bit more effort to look the part.*

The woman was treated to a pitying glance and Paula turned

her back and concentrated her attention on negotiating the thorny outcrops of her 'Liscious Lovehandle' and working out how to down it in sufficiently insouciant manner. The other woman turned her back likewise and, with a shock, Paula realised that it was herself.

Oh God, what had she been thinking? A smear of lipstick and an 'interesting' hairdo was never going to transform that sad drab individual into a trendy young mantrap.

A veil of depression drifted across her hunched shoulders as they began their resigned descent towards the floor. If Alan could see her now he would laugh. Nastily. The feeling of failure threatened to take her over and she peered into the dark exotic recesses of her drink, miserably. Alan's face floated past in the form of a bloated olive.

'You bore me,' said the apparition and laughed. 'Nothing personal.'

She paused over the Lovehandle for an instant, looked at the barman and downed it in one. 'Give us another of those, would you?' she braved. 'And put a double shot of whatyermecallit in – I can take it.'

The barman raised an eyebrow, curious at the pale woman all on her own in a place where women rarely came alone, and wondered momentarily about her story.

'Well, hello,' a deep voice murmured behind her.

She turned, slowly, and there he was. Tall and textbook handsome, wearing a fetching ensemble of Conan-the-Barbarian costume tastefully accessorised with blue Superman pants – no, Superman thong – muscle-bound in the way you only find in comic books and with a full head of hair. Best of all, he did not seem to have noticed that she was not supposed to be here.

Conan fixed her with an indefinable stare. Indefinable to Paula, that is. Anyone else would confidently have decoded it thus: 'Fancy a shag?'

'Let me introduce myself. You may call me –' He paused just long enough to lower his dark brooding brow, '– *The Master…*'

'Paula.'

Paula's small hand found itself whisked up into his gallant meaty fist, where it remained unshaken but ever so slightly stirred.

'Are you, indeed? Yes, I believe you are.' He unleashed the full force of his most mesmerising gaze upon her. 'But tell me – is that *really* who you are? Or perhaps you would prefer to be called something else? Provocative Paula, maybe, or Promiscuous Paula?'

'Umm. Just Paula's fine.'

Conan gave her a look, then with a shake of his virile mane and a snort of manly potent breath through his manly flaring nostrils, he said, 'I like it!'

'You do?' Paula was pleased. 'It's funny because there's quite an interesting history to it really. You see, my mother originally wanted to call me Veronica after my grandmother but then my great-aunt Pauline –'

'But enough small talk.'

His hand crushed hers determinedly in its potent manly grip and his gaze deepened into a whole new category of indefinableness.

'I know we are only at the beginning of our relationship but – we must be open with each other. I *want* you. Paula. Pouting Paula. Petulant Paula. Per-vy Pau-la. Can I call you 'Pervy', Paula?'

'I –'

'Pervypaula.'

'Well, I – '

'Pervy Paula!' He was breathing very heavily now.

'Just Paula, if it's all the same to you.'

'*Pervy, porny, horny Paula* –'The whites of his eyes were beginning to flicker. '*Pervy curvy nervy Paula… Porny horny tawny Paula.*'

With a groan his head fell onto the bar, the shiny surface of which he began to lick and caress, much to Paula's distress.

'Please, don't do that.' She found herself looking around nervously. 'That surface doesn't look very clean.'

But her companion took no notice. He continued to nuzzle the bar, issuing small fluttering cries of 'horny' and 'pervy', punctuated by a stray leg that suddenly hurled itself over the bar counter. 'Oh Paula!'

Bewildered, Paula looked about desperately for some means of distraction. From where she was sitting she watched a big woman in very scant attire sidling up to a muscular young man in a leotard, while a small man in a suit followed clutching a glass of orange juice. The unfriendly transvestite on the door had shut up shop and was leaning against the doorjamb talking to a man in a tartan dress. The girls on the dance floor were too busy admiring themselves in the floor-length mirror to notice her predicament. Nobody was looking, nobody was watching, it was perfectly safe.

'What's that?' she asked suddenly.

Bleary-eyed and with a disgruntled expression on his face, Conan rolled an eyeball in her direction, mid-lick. She nodded across and his eye swivelled around in the direction of the scary piece of apparatus in the corner.

'Oh that, that's the fucking machine.' The eyeball flicked round

ROSY BARNES

towards her once more. Unfortunately, this only had the effect of concentrating his attention more closely upon the object of his desire. Changing tack, he carefully extracted his leg from the bar-counter, and loomed seductively over her, instead.

'Why is it called that?' a suddenly fidgety Paula said.

'Because it fucks people, of course.'

Conan's hand, that had until now been caressing the surface of the bar, switched gear and began to creep conversationally up her leg. 'You bring the fittings…and away you go.'

The hand glided smoothly, upwards and onwards towards its goal.

Paula looked at the fucking machine, overcome with revulsion and awe. 'What? Here, in front of everyone?'

Conan, apparently irritated at these constant interruptions, said, 'Surely that's the whole point. For other people to know.'

'Know what?'

'That we're exciting… We're all exciting people, yes?'

Paula shifted awkwardly in her seat, resulting in a disappointing setback for the digit attempting to scale her leg. Undeterred, Conan resumed his attack, this time from above. His face ballooned towards her: mouth, slack-jawed and glistening in seductive pose; tongue quivering on the verge of his slug-like bottom lip, sending a distinct whiff of cheese and onion pasty in her direction.

Paula was just contemplating the general strangeness of being there, in such a situation, with a man in a thong who had a few hours before been eating a cheese and onion pasty – someone else entirely, in some other life she had no idea about…when the heavy realisation gradually dawned on her.

'*Oh god,*' she thought. '*He's going to kiss me.*'

As it prepared itself for action the mouth gave a quick lubricating smack of the lips and then, like a peregrine falcon that had been hovering elegantly over its prey, with sudden and deadly precision, it plunged.

However, his intentions were rudely thrown aside by the breathless arrival of a small bald man in a PVC thong and body harness who suddenly burst in upon the scene in an agony of terror.

'Oh lady! Lady! Save me! Quick, I must hide!'

And the bald man disappeared headfirst under Paula's chair, forcing its occupant to squirm to the side, leaving Conan to sail elegantly past and land face-first in a small dish of peanuts on the bar, behind.

'What are you doing?' Paula fussed, not knowing whether or not to feel relieved. (She did.)

'Hide me. Please!' the crouched figure wailed.

'Come now,' Paula said, trying to haul him out from between her legs and ignoring Conan's noisy attempts to remove himself from the peanut bowl.

'I've done it this time. Never seen her so angry. Oh Lady, you look kind. Please, help me?'

'Surely you can't have done anything that bad. Everyone quarrels sometimes. That's the nature of couples.'

'Oh, if only I could believe you,' gasped the cowering figure, tunnelling further in under her skirt and crushing himself between the legs of the barstool. 'But I know her and she is bound to enact a terrible TERRIBLE revenge…'

'Nonsense,' said Paula sensibly. 'You're over-reacting. What's she going to do to you? We're in a public place after all.'

She was about to go on to say something about allowing a bit of give and take, taking the rough with the smooth and how nothing was ever as bad as it seemed but – 'WHERE THE HELL IS THAT SNIVELLING LITTLE BASTARD!?' – interrupted her before she could go into any of that.

Paula's ears winced as the hairs on the back of her neck followed her shoulders.

The glassy-haired woman in the suit jacket and thigh-length boots was unlike anything she'd ever encountered before. Thin to the point of malnutrition and sporting a number of interesting piercings, including bolts through lip, cheek and eyebrow, with a large lump of metal thrust jaggedly through her navel. Most worrying of all, she brandished a riding crop above her head, with which she began to lay about Paula's feet. She was angry as hell.

'Come out, come out you pusillanimous worm, you snivelling toad, you spineless pooch. Get your pristine peaches out here at once! At once I say!'

'Oh please, please, don't hurt me, please…' came the wail. 'I did not mean to offend, I am abjectly sorry for the distress I have caused.' And he wiggled his way further underneath Paula's high stool.

His persecutor was having none of it. 'You lily-livered skunk!' she yelled, thrashing about again.

'Ow!' yelled Paula, whipping up her feet and wrapping her arms round her knees. 'Look out, would you?'

'You lily-livered excuse of a man. You sissy-skulled piece of pink frothiness. How DARE you disobey me? How DARE you? You know what this means, don't you?'

The figure under the stool wiggled wretchedly.

'I said YOU KNOW WHAT THIS MEANS, DON'T YOU?' she roared.

'Yes,' came the squeak.

'WHAT DOES IT MEAN?????'

'You are going to take your savage revenge on my puny body,' said the worm, meekly.

'I CAN'T HEAR YOU?'

'It means you're going to beat me,' piped up the sissy-skulled piece of pink frothiness obligingly, with a half-hearted attempt to bury himself further under Paula's feet.

Paula, by this time, had had enough. A faint memory came to her from one of her evening classes: 'Self-Defence is Con-fi-dence.' She stood up, swung round and faced the pierced fury who was still casting out randomly with her crop. Planting her feet stubbornly, she stuck out her arm so that its full determined length formed a forbidding distance between herself and the mad crop-wielder, raised one flat palm, took a moment to centre herself with a spot of yogic breathing, expanded her diaphragm as competently as any professional opera-singer and then bawled: 'STOP! STAY AWAY! DO NOT COME ANY NEARER!'

Even Paula was impressed with the volume her small frame managed to produce. The pierced apparition paused, riding crop hovering, mid-strike.

Buoyed up by her success, Paula shouted, 'Do not move!' rather unnecessarily and proceeded to edge, warily, eyes fixed on those of her opponent, around the seat. Keeping a careful watch, she leaned down slightly and said, 'It's alright, you can come out now.'

The crouching figure shook his shoulders and mumbled something inaudible to which Paula replied in soft gentling tones, 'It's alright, no one's going to hurt you. You can speak up now.'

He muttered something from under his armpit.

'What was that? Your voice is a bit indistinct.'

'Go away, I said. Go away!' he screamed, rather more distinctly.

Paula straightened up and nodded towards the red apparition who stood fidgeting in front of her shifting her weight impatiently from one booted leg to another.

'He says he would like you to go away now.' She eyeballed the woman with purpose. 'I think you should respect that, don't you?'

'Not her,' yelled the worm under the chair. 'You. I want *you* to go away.' He took his head out from under the stool. 'Go away!' An accusing finger jabbed his point home. 'I haven't paid good money to be dominated by a cruel mistress for it all to be ruined by the likes of you.'

And, to Paula's horrified amazement, he turned towards his tormentor and fell onto the floor in front of her.

'Please forgive me, Mistress,' he ingratiated. 'I prostrate myself before you. Crush my puny broken body under your heel. If you feel the need to whip my disobedient cheeks into totally abject submission…well…' He peered up hopefully from underneath his lashes. 'What can a mere nothing like me do to stop you?'

Paula was just about to butt in again, when events took yet another turn. Conan's mouth, which had – since exiting the peanut bowl – been quietly nursing its injured pride on Conan's face, decided to launch assault number two.

Like a heat-seeking missile (if missiles looked like rocket-propelled upholstery) the cushion-lips plunged and locked on course with Paula's anxiously-pinched portal which, tipped off by a chance movement at the corner of her eye, decided, in absolute panic, to take flight.

But Conan had no intention of allowing her a second escape. Seeing his quarry getting away, he grabbed both sides of her head in a vice-like clamp. 'Paula! Kiss me!'

Her head trembled with the struggle, her objecting mouth disappearing into a thin lipless line, clamped resolutely shut. 'Mmmm, Mmmmm,' she hummed desperately in the hope that he could understand her protest. But his wet moluskan mouth continued its inevitable descent like an amorous pink sea cucumber during sea cucumber mating season, that has spied a cute little female of the species in need of a bit of cucumber-on-cucumber action.

'Come on you guys, this has gone too far,' said a voice.

It was all too much. She just had time to see out of the corner of her eye a man, completely naked apart from a small black mask, standing over them, shaking a finger (it was not the only thing shaking), before she fell to the floor. As she passed out, she heard a voice say,

'Now, look what you've gone and done. We were all getting along just famously.'

And everything went dark.

*****

'Hello?'

Strange, she found herself thinking sleepily, how one can be with a man in a thong who, a few hours earlier, had been eating a cheese and onion pasty, someone else entirely, leading some other life…

'Hello?'

And strange how much a mouth could resemble a cheese and onion pasty, with its melting cheese tongue and pastryfleshy lips…

'Hello there?'

And strange too how the cheese and onion pasty has eyes and a nose and is calling to her, calling to her…

'Are you alright? Please say something. Hello.'

When she finally opened her eyes fully there were six pairs of eyes, masked, unmasked, anxious, concerned, inquisitive and still vaguely lustful, all peering back at her. She considered for a second not coming round, but decided in the end there was no choice, said, 'Where am I?' a few times and sat up.

She was ensconced, as they all were, on a rather comfortable velvet mattress, the one that she had observed earlier.

'Well thank god for that, luvvie,' said the pierced dominatrix, in friendly tones. 'You had us right worried there for a minute or two. It's all your fault,' she added to the crouching figure at her side, 'all that grovelling and whatnot, gets on yer nerves after a while.'

'Sorry Mistress.'

'Oh give over.'

'Will I get punished?' he added hopefully.

Gretchen tossed a cushion at him. 'God's sake. Give a girl a break, can't you? All this "dominate me, dominate me." Plain selfish, that's what I call it. Are you alright, love?'

Paula felt herself welling up at the motherly tones. Was this the woman who had seemed so terrifying just minutes before?

'Sorry about my friends,' the naked man said civilly.

Paula looked down. And quickly up again. Strange how conscious one becomes of keeping eye contact when faced with the prospect of copping an inadvertent eyeful of dangly bits. Paula's eyes clung onto his as limpets might cling to a couple of pebbles in the absence of a reassuringly clothed rock to cling to. This was not an easy task, in light of the two pebbles' habit of shifting about uneasily, in a shy attempt to avoid too much pebble-to-limpet contact.

'That's okay. I mean it wasn't your fault. I mean, if you hadn't come over, I mean –'

'Paula, is it? Or do you prefer Pervy Paula?' he added wickedly.

'Paula's fine.'

'Paula,' he said firmly. He held out his hand. 'Call me George.'

Still staring fixedly at his eyes, she groped about for his hand. 'Pleased to meet you. So you don't go about calling yourself The Hunk or Mr Nine-Inch or anything like that?'

The Man in the Mask laughed, an unexpected shocking noise. 'No.'

There was a pause, in which Paula looked everywhere but down. She looked at his hands. Nice hands.

'God's sake, Kevin, go and get her a cup of tea, would you? Make yourself a bit useful there!' said Gretchen.

Conan, who had been hovering guiltily in the background, reluctantly lugged himself to his feet. 'I don't see why I should be bossed about.'

'Just – do it.'

'Alright alright,' and he trundled off towards the bar area. Somehow the Conan the Barbarian costume did not look as imposing as she first thought, and the Superman thong was too big for him.

'You mustn't bother about Kevin. He's just a bit young that's all. Got carried away. He's a good lad really.'

Paula looked around the assembled cast shyly.

'I'm alright, you don't have to – I just –'

'Shhhhh!'

She 'shhhhed'. And sank back into the mattress again. It was very comfortable.

Conan returned with a nice cup of tea and Paula sat up again to sip it gently and shyly listen to the conversation around her.

'So,' said Gretchen after a while. 'What brings a girl like you to a place like this?'

Paula sat and sipped and thought. She wasn't quite sure what the answer was. Was she here to prove something? To find something? She finally settled on the simple truth and hoped that it did its own explaining. 'My boyfriend dumped me.' She thought for a minute. 'And I want him back.' She took a sip of tea and looked at Gretchen shyly. 'He said I'm boring in bed.'

'So you're here for love?' said Gretchen, croakily, 'Well isn't that lovely, and I think I would say a first too. Most people are here because they're frightened of love.'

Paula did not know what she meant but was too tired to ask.

'I think that's lovely,' said Gretchen loudly. 'I've all filled up, I really have.' She blew her nose loudly on a large handkerchief she managed to produce as if by magic from some part of her very small costume.

'Sounds more like revenge to me,' said The Man in the Mask.

'I don't know,' said Paula. 'I don't know what I'm doing here to be honest. I thought… I thought maybe…' And with that, to her surprise, she started to cry. This was embarrassing, out of character and completely unexpected. And it was messy full-on crying. Crying that spurted from her eyes and nose and guffawed full-throatedly out of her grotesque, grimacing mouth. The kind of crying that holds its breath for minutes at a time, only to explode forth in ugly frothy gulps.

Here she was, surrounded by exotic, semi-naked people, face-to-face with a fully naked man, and the only embarrassing thing in the room was herself.

*****

Later, lying on her bed, trying to master the swells of nausea that threatened to throw her retching over the side, Paula reflected miserably on her behaviour that evening, on men in general and Alan in particular. What was hardest to bear was the encroaching feeling of doubt that now licked at the edges of her memories like hungry gargoyles. The feeling, looking back, that nothing of what you thought at the time could be trusted. The good memories poisoned, the bad memories taking on a new and cruel significance, strutting triumphantly into the limelight. That they could have been laughing together over dinner, Alan half-up from his seat with excitement, flapping his arms about in some silly impression of a client at work, her clapping gleefully – when all the time his inner voice was murmuring 'Oh god, she is sooo boring!' What was really going through his mind when they had picnicked together on Hampstead Heath and he, in a rare fit of spontaneity, suddenly pounced and rolled her in the picnic-cloth and told her he loved her? Was he really thinking of her, or already imagining secret trysts? And what about when they had finished making love to lie damp and happy in each other's arms listening to the muffled rhythm of the city at night, his hand tangled idly in her hair whilst hers stroked his face, crumpled like a baby's, head on her chest, drifting and drowsy. Inside that head was there already forming, foetus-like, the plan to leave?

These were the thoughts that tormented, in the dark of the night, in those quiet moments of waking. That would catch her, breathless and unaware, at her office computer, in the supermarket, at her cake decoration class, anywhere and at anytime, hit 'n' run doubts that would punch her hard in the stomach and leave her reeling. She rolled over and clung to the mattress as she heaved over the side.

*****

Gretchen's slave crept forward slightly and touched Paula on the arm. 'We're all here for different reasons,' he said quietly. 'I'm here because my wife doesn't understand me. She thinks I'm away at a management training conference.'

'Don't worry,' Dave said, visibly moved by Paula's tale and casting a side-long glance at the object of his own unrequited affections. 'You're here now. Amongst friends. We'll help you. Won't we everyone? We'll help you with your quest!' He looked around feverishly.

SlaveBoy grinned, Conan shrugged doltishly, The Man in the Mask paused, then stuck a thumbs up.

'Oooooh, I like a good quest,' Gretchen said warmly.

It was left to Luda, to be the lone dissenting voice. 'What's got into you all? Pass me the fucking sick-bag. Some complete stranger barges in and starts passing out all over the place and suddenly everyone's clucking around and turning into *The Waltons*. Count me out!'

But nobody was listening to her.

Part Three: NOVEMBER

Chapter Nine | WEDDING PLANNER

Sometimes it seemed to Belinda as though she had been planning this wedding for months. This was because she *had* been planning it for months – ever since the whole disabled toilet incident, in fact, ever since she had decided Alan was the man for her just minutes before. Since then, however, things had not gone to plan and the wedding had to be put back three times, mainly due to her terrible luck with wedding planners.

Wedding Planner Number 1 was swiftly dispatched after the notorious cerise incident. Planner Number 2 came a cropper over that whole napkin fiasco (Belinda shuddered at the recollection). Whereas, when first Ashley in Accounts and Amanda, the department secretary, both got married – one in the very stately home Belinda planned to use, the other with Belinda's supposedly unique choice of table centrepieces – there was no way it wasn't an inside job: goodbye Planner Number 3. Planner Number 4, the strangest of all, just failed to turn up one day, later sending a short note (no return address) to the effect that she would be changing careers – and countries – due to stress.

Nearly a year of fevered planning and all Belinda had to show for it was a couple of draft seating plans and the bottom half of her honeymoon outfit.

Then there was her other problem. Alan.

Oh! If he would only lose some weight, wear trendier clothes and brush up on his knowledge of the arts, she was sure he would not be so easily overlooked. If only he would make some effort to be a bit more distinctive. It was not hard. Look at the ever attention-grabbing, wheelchair-bound Pat, for example. The woman could hardly move for Christ's sake and there everyone was, getting her special equipment and granting her extra privileges.

Nobody even stopped to consider the extra time she, Belinda, had to put in for Pat doing those little overlooked favours like… like…passing things, for example. Who would when there was Pat huffing and puffing around the office all 'no problem' this and 'don't worry about me' that? Ugh, it was enough to make you sick!

Perhaps she should start compiling a log to prove just how much time passing things to Pat took out of her working day. No wonder Pat was surging ahead with her productivity, because she was busily sucking the life-blood out of everyone around her, that's why. In fact, a percentage of Pat's productivity should really be apportioned to Belinda to take proper account of the whole *passing things* issue. Not to mention the fact that Pat now got to use the only disabled toilet, which the others were not allowed to use. Her own special toilet? That must surely give her the edge? Pat was never waylaid by small talk by the hand-driers, or whilst standing side-by-side grimacing into mirrors, touching up on one's lip-liner. Pat never had to queue. No, Pat was free to come and go as she chose. What kind of unfair advantage did that give her? She must save minutes every day, converting into hours every month. It might not look like much but if you added it all up over the course of a year, it was a considerable head-start on the rest of them.

But had Belinda complained, had she asked for a one-to-one with her line manager to air her concerns?

Well yes, she had as a matter of fact, but her line manager – stupid woman – rather than offering to do anything to allay Belinda's reasonable concerns, seemed blind, or should we say 'visually challenged', to the very real danger of provoking resentment amongst the staff at such favouritism, suggesting instead that Belinda attend a one-day disability training seminar to learn more about issues of disability in the workplace!

Belinda failed to see how this benefited her whatsoever. The only thing that had come out of that seminar was her meeting Alan, when they both hung back on a tour of the building's state-of-the-art facilities to test out the accessibility of the company's disabled toilet. Apart from that, it had been a perfect waste of time. All that fussing on. What difference did it make what politically correct term one used for the handicapped, disabled, people with disabilities – whatever the cripples were called these days?

A subtle cough behind her shocked her out of her reverie.

Belinda turned to face the elegant young woman behind her. Planner Number 5, folded into the armpit of one of the sleek cream leather sofas, hovered her pencil importantly over her loose-leaf book.

'And I want the bridesmaids in magenta – *magenta*, do you get that? *Not* fucking cerise,' Belinda warned.

'Very original,' intoned the other, her respectful head nodding time to the unseen goddess of marital detail.

'*Not* cerise! You see, I'm a very creative person and I want to express that.'

The planner watched as Belinda paced the room, necklace grating; a caged Gucci tigress in matching almond separates. She was nervous of this sharp-edged woman whose fearsome reputation went before her. In truth, the planner had only taken the job because no one else wanted it. As a recent college graduate, she badly needed the money. But she also knew she would have to come up with something special if she was to have a hope of being paid.

'*Creative person*. I'm writing that down. Would that creativity extend to the dress?' she asked helpfully.

Belinda clicked rapidly across to the microwave and back. 'The dress, oh the dress. Yes. I want it to express my 'out there' personality.'

'Out there personality,' monotoned the planner dutifully, wondering what on earth had happened to her dreams of becoming a children's book illustrator. 'Okay, I'm seeing sequin trouser suit –'

She flinched at the expression that shot her way.

'Bikini and stilettos? Elvis wig?'

Belinda's face looked in danger of corroding itself with its own acidity. 'I was thinking more in terms of a classic white dress,' she spat, less than pleasantly.

'*White* dress, right. I'm writing that down.'

'But going a bit mad with the posy, to express my outrageous personality.'

'Posy. Right. The detail is so important isn't it?' The planner's throwaway laugh faded in her throat.

Belinda continued her agitated staccato pacing.

'Overall I'm looking for strong classic lines –'

'Okay,' the planner piped up excitedly. 'I'm seeing feminine, Elizabeth Arden, I'm seeing English gardens, roses, carnations –'

'But with a unique, contemporary feel –'

'I'm seeing strong architectural forms – Japanese grasses'

'Picked up in the table decorations –'

'Bamboo! That's so in right now!'

'But with a spiky contemporary twist –'

'Cactus! This is fantastic. I can see it now!'

Belinda stopped her pacing to unleash her least pleasant expression upon the object of her derision.

'Nobody else will have cactus!' said the planner, faltering. '*Oh God*,' she whimpered inside, '*What am I doing here? What happened to the organic veg plot, the little house in the country, the pet goats…?*'

'The point is,' Belinda said clicking over to the window. 'Will my friends be jealous? Will my colleagues be impressed?'

The wedding planner, unable to believe her luck, relaxed and composed herself. Adopting her most serious professional tone she took a deep breath, 'I'm seeing a single classic cactus offset by one elegant stem of Japanese grass – it says contemporary modern woman with classic taste but with a hint of creativity and originality – Kate Moss on a bed of Catherine Zeta with a dollop of SJP. Trust me, they'll be drooling.'

Belinda looked at her for a second and then, much to the planner's relief, continued her pacing.

'Napkins!'

'Nap-kins...'

'I want them to say cutting edge but rooted in tradition.'

'You're not talking serviettes then?'

'I am NOT talking serviettes! I'm talking white, cotton, square...'

'Squa-are.'

'But with an original touch to express my unique and fun-loving personality.'

'Oh oh oh!' piped up the planner excitedly, 'What about an inscription? A quote? Groucho Marx, Stephen Fry?'

'I don't think we need to go mad, do you? I was thinking more in terms of a nice trim,' Belinda said icily.

'Trim. Okay. I'm writing that down.'

'In magenta. To pick up on the bridesmaids.'

'Oh I like that,' said the planner ingratiatingly, 'a witty touch.'

'Too much?'

'I think you'll get away with it.' The planner was growing in confidence now. 'Oh! What about this! Picture it – every napkin elegantly rolled and tied, beautifully, with one classic length of Japanese grass – picking up simultaneously on the bridesmaids *and* the posy.'

Belinda spun on her heel and the planner waited with trepidation.

'I like it!'

The wedding planner was stunned. 'You do?'

'Didn't I just say so?'

'I'm on fire now!' cried the planner in a surge of triumph. 'Okay, so we've got the dress, the bridesmaids, the posy, the table decorations, the napkins? Now what about the groom?'

'I want someone tall, classic but contemporary. Pierce Brosnan with a hint of Angus Deayton.'

The wedding planner paused in her scribbling. 'You don't have a bridegroom?'

'Of course I do!' snapped Belinda irritably. 'I just forgot about him momentarily in all the excitement, that's all! There he is.'

She nodded at a photograph of Alan on the mantelpiece, looking smug in an unbecoming pair of cycling shorts.

'Hmmm, bit more of your David Mellor than your Pierce Brosnan really, isn't he?' said the wedding planner.

Belinda's face, which in any circumstance was served well by a bit of distance, travelled rapidly across the room to be brought distressingly close to that of the wedding planner.

'Listen Missy.' She was so close, the planner could smell the Listerine on her breath. 'I have waited my whole life for this and – nothing – I repeat – nothing – is going to spoil my big day. Your job is to make sure my wedding is the wedding to end all weddings. Friends and colleagues smarting. Sister livid. Parents bust. Understand? You're the designer. When I say Pierce, I mean Pierce. Now sort it out or you won't get a fucking penny out of me.'

The wedding planner breathed hard. 'Pierce it is then!' she trilled.

'Good.' Slowly the face backed off.

Still keeping a suspicious eye on her victim, Belinda tripped towards the window and stood leaning on the sill. The planner eyed her nervously, but as Belinda looked out over the garden, her face illuminated by the low winter sun, she seemed lost in thought.

'You don't know a good tree surgeon, do you?' she said, unexpectedly.

The wedding planner thought about this. 'Wouldn't a plastic surgeon be more appropriate?' she suggested timidly.

Now, in common with most women, Belinda had a strong practical streak when it came to relationships. She had learnt about romance the hard way, had suffered her fair share of heartache, wept her share of unrequited tears. She too had slept with her friends' partners, had an affair with her married boss and seduced her sister's boyfriend. But she had learnt from her mistakes. (Not least in the case of her sister's boyfriend, who despite all her best efforts with blindfolds, handcuffs and various vibrating objects had insisted that he was still in love with the jellylike-one. To think that her own sister should be with such a spineless two-timer!)

However, when she had first met Alan, or rather, when her cool objective glance first took in Alan's ponderous form guffawing across at her at that fateful Disability Awareness Seminar, she had not been carried away. Rather, she viewed him as one might an old dilapidated property, seeing past the out-of-date décor, tired furnishings and cheapjack fixtures and fittings, through to his extension potential.

Dream man Alan was not, but Belinda saw something at his core – a wishy-washy mix of materialism, vanity, snobbery and lazy ambition: something she could *mould*.

Don't get the wrong idea, Belinda was not the kind of naïve woman who believed she could change her man. As one mature in the language of love, who knew the importance of give and take, live and let live, weathering the rough and spicing up the smooth; Belinda was a great believer in the maxim: 'You can't go changing him.' Indeed there was hardly an evening, dinner party or wedding summit where she could not be heard to declare as much, followed by a solemnly nodded, 'He must do it for himself.'

How to *make* him do it for himself, that was the problem…

Inside Belinda's head, at the moment the planner uttered the words, 'Wouldn't a plastic surgeon be more appropriate?', one floating handbag-obsessed neuron collided with another, idly dreaming about Pierce Brosnan, and they both toppled into another not averse to inflicting pain and torment on others for the sake of social advancement…and a whole chain reaction took place.

Of course, that was it! The answer. Why hadn't she thought of it before?… It all made sense…the perfect man…the *promotable* man… Pierce with a hint of… Yes!

Visions of a line of Brosnans queuing against a white medicinal wall. Faced by a line of Deaytons. Belinda, cool, fragrant, in a white pencil dress – very Audrey – and large fifties sunglasses, sauntering coolly, casually, debonairly amongst them. A lily in a field of irresistible alpha males – and Angus Deaytons.

'I'll have that one,' she says in her mind's eye, poking one Pierce in the chest with a nail so sharp it would be confiscated at an airport.

'With a bit of this one,' she adds condescendingly to one of the desperate-looking Anguses. 'I like that lived-in look.'

An embarrassed cough returned Belinda both to the present and the irritating sight of the wedding planner's face.

'You know, that's not such a bad idea,' Belinda said.

'Really?' The planner was not sure whether to be pleased.

'I've seen those make-over shows,' Belinda muttered. 'John Prescott – a few nips here, some tucks there and abracadabra – it's Angela Rippon. So why not David Mellor to Pierce Brosnan?'

The planner looked on nervously as her companion lost herself in thought for a second, before pulling herself together with a violent shiver.

'Only joking,' Belinda said. 'Where's your sense of humour?' The planner obliged with a nervous laugh. She had the vague feeling that she was missing something. And that something could turn out to be quite important.

'Right, so, where were we?' Belinda said.

Back on familiar territory, the planner consulted her notebook with relief. 'Centre-pieces, napkins, cactus... What about the cake? I was thinking white, iced - probably something involving raisins...'

'Whatever it is it has to be high, understand? With as many tiers as humanly possible. I want the Sears Tower of Cakes!'

The planner nodded gravely. 'Sears Tower of cakes - I'm writing that down.'

Chapter Ten | DAVE CALLS A CONFERENCE

'I think that it's because I have a very small penis. Sub-consciously, I want to expose it, present it for humiliation, so to speak. Invite people to laugh at it, you know?' The man gave her a straight look, threaded through with anxiety. 'I know no one would ever want it for real.'

Paula nodded sympathetically. After coming to the club for several weeks now, she had found a new use for her notebook. The stories, the hurts, the honest insights that could be gained from a man in a tutu sitting on a large yellow balloon were eye-opening, not to mention watering. Besides, she liked Graham even if, in her opinion, he did indulge in an over-analytical approach to fetishes.

The man gestured across. 'Like him over there, see. Tiny.' He seemed pleased. 'Smaller than mine, even.'

The object of his attention did not seem to mind, throwing back a hearty wave.

'We understand each other, see,' he said. 'We know we're not like other men. We dare to do what other men only fantasise about. Don't other men dream of everyone looking at their bodies? That's why we're so jealous of women. You can just put your tits on a tray and say, 'Look at these!'

Paula, who had never put her tits on a tray in her life, just smiled and nodded and made a note in her book.

SlaveBoy, who had read up extensively on the subject of fetish, preferred the Freudian explanation. According to that renowned expert on all things sexual and psychoanalytical, he told her, the boy looks up one day from where he is idling around under his mother's feet in search of her penis – just to check that she has one, you understand, like his own. Seeing she has none, he recoils in horror and disgust at her penisless state and as he averts his anguished eyes from the sight of her mutilated nether regions, whatever object strikes them in that moment – exotic or mundane – takes on the power of the missing phallus and becomes the new object of sexual potency.

Paula could see that this theory could make sense with SlaveBoy's particular fetish: feet. Or even certain items of clothing. Perhaps you could even go so far as to explain balloon fetishists – the result of that fateful averted glance after a recent birthday party, perhaps? But how the young innocent boy peeping out at the world from under his mother's skirts, managed to catch an eyeful of rubberised cyberdroid with platform roller-skates and inflatable PVC buttocks was anybody's guess.

No. In Paula's view it was all perfectly straightforward. After all, most women have, at some time or another, experienced the disconcerting feeling of being in competition with their own breasts. Particularly on those romantic occasions when for a brief second her partner peers lovingly into her eyes before disappearing for an extended session of sucking, shovelling and worse – wobbling – down below (most women don't care to be reminded of the less than perky condition of their mammaries, let alone to be faced by an enthusiastic partner playing Newton's cradle with them). Fetish, as far as Paula could ascertain, was merely an extension of this concept.

Just as the woman gets upstaged by her own breasts, so the sexual symbolism may radiate out from the usual suspects to settle on any manner of places along the way: the backs of the knees, the ankles, the feet. Or perhaps it travels the other way, up to the neck, ear, throat or, as Paula had found, nose.

But not everyone, Paula discovered, was into body parts. As the sexual symbolism radiates out further, the feet become shoes, the shoes become heels, the heels become fantasies about being stamped on by heels, the feel of the heel, the substance it is made of, the smell of the substance it is made of…

'Let's get this straight,' said another club goer – a well-built man in his forties and a pair of PVC shorts, 'I shag inflatable animals because I have a fetish for them, not because I'm desperate. What's the difference between shagging a woman or an inflatable zebra?' (Cue: another note in Paula's book.)

And then there was Marcus.

The first time Paula met Marcus she took him for a piece of funky designer furniture.

On her way to the toilets one evening, she tripped and stumbled into a large blue inflatable object that she had always assumed was part of the décor.

'Boo,' said a muffled voice. She nearly jumped out of her skin.

The voice was coming from a three times larger than life-size human-shaped blue inflatable, complete with gas mask and single large Wellington boot in which both legs terminated. It was propped against the wall adjacent to the dance floor.

Paula started edging away, and then said, because she wasn't thinking clearly, 'I didn't realise there was anyone in there.'

'I tried waving at you but you didn't pay any attention.'

She looked down to see an index finger, miraculously escaped from its confinement, was wiggling in friendly fashion somewhere around his right hip.

'Hello,' she said and wiggled an index finger back. 'Who are you?'

'Marcus.'

'Nice to meet you, Marcus.'

And she crooked her finger round his and shook it.

'Likewise.'

As his face was obscured by some complicated-looking breathing apparatus, it was hard to make out much of what Marcus said, which limited conversation somewhat. So the encounter pretty much ended there. Being incarcerated inside a giant blue inflatable bodysuit did not do much for his general mobility either; hence, Marcus spent most of his time leaning against the wall between the condom machine and the ladies loos. Paula was not sure what was so exciting about this. But Marcus seemed happy enough.

To many, the pale woman in her ill-fitting outfit became just another regular if curious fixture, never quite joining in, never quite part of things; they got used to her being there, like an isolated tribe of people, edging closer to the strange and eccentric anthropologist who has been patiently watching them, copying their gestures. Or an insular group of gorillas reaching out a trusting hand to the feebly gesturing Attenborough, pretending to pick ticks like the best of them.

They became used to her curious face slicing between their own and that of a petting partner with the cheery: 'You seem to be getting on. What would you say is the secret of sexual excitement?'

SlaveBoy liked to lecture her about the finer points of subordination; Gretchen taught her pearl and cross-stitch; and, although he said nothing, there was an energy radiating from The Man in the Mask that had not been there before.

Only Luda maintained a sniffy contempt for the newcomer, aggravated by Dave, whose irksome habit of waxing lyrical about Paula's general 'feminineness' had really begun to grate.

So when Dave and Gretchen, hopeless sentimentalists both, first mooted the idea of a brainstorming meeting to aid Paula on her Quest of Love (as Dave insisted on calling it) Luda initially refused to attend.

But after some cajoling, flattering and a bit of ego-massage (Dave: 'How will we cope without you?') and realising that everyone else was going, she reluctantly assented to come along, just to make sure 'things didn't get out of hand.'

They met on a rainy Saturday afternoon, in the back room of The Walnut Tree Café in Crouch End. The venue had been Luda's suggestion – a little more tranny-friendly than anything near Paula's place. Certainly the staff hardly turned a hair when Luda turned up in full make-up and what appeared to be a dark blue maternity dress with a wide cream corduroy collar that looked like it had been mouldering in some charity shop since the 70s.

It was the first time many of them had seen each other in the cold light of day. The cold light of day made absolutely no difference to Dave who looked just as Dave-like when wearing a nice dress or, as he was now, a Bolton Wanderers T-shirt and jeans. Gretchen, on the other hand, looked almost homely in her tie-dye skirt and green cardigan, busy scouring the menu for animal-friendly items.

'No thanks,' she said when the waiter proffered milk for her Earl Grey. 'I can't bear the thought of being the cause of suffering to any living thing.'

'Except me of course,' said SlaveBoy proudly who, dressed in an immaculate business suit and black tie, peered side-long at his mistress to see if she would take the bait.

Gretchen gave him a mildly irritated look to make it clear it was her day off. But he just said, 'Ooo do that again! It's a real turn-on,' which was even more annoying, so she went back to smiling vaguely.

They were all intrigued to see how The Man in the Mask would appear, and whether, at last, they would have the opportunity to see his face.

Strange, that a face should be such an object of excitement on a man who left so little to their collective imaginations. They were disappointed when he turned up — admittedly exotic in a long black cloak but with his face still safely obscured by that familiar mask. He could have been wearing the cloak commando, for all they knew, but it was the face that would have been the greater nakedness. (Besides, as Gretchen pointed out, he could easily have been wearing a warm pair of long johns underneath so it didn't really count as risqué.)

Nonetheless, he did attract a few funny glances from the Walnut Tree regulars who called out as he swished his way through to the back room.

'Hey Zorro – off to a fancy dress party are we?'

The Man in the Mask just smiled and ordered a glass of tap water and sat quietly sipping it on the sidelines.

'Just waiting for the lady herself now,' Dave informed them.

Luda, who was chewing an unlit cheroot in an attempt to give up smoking, jabbed at the table-leg with her toe. 'Lady, my arse,' she muttered to herself, but so loudly it might as well have been spoken aloud. 'I don't know what we are doing on this wild goose chase,' she said, louder still.

Dave snapped the top off his Coke. 'You don't have to be here.'

'Believe me. I have no interest in being here whatsoever. Just count me fucking out.'

At that moment, a small figure laden with several bulging carrier bags could be seen through the café's glass doors. She pushed her way in back-first. She looked round myopically before they were able to attract her attention with some energetic arm-waving and whistling (courtesy of SlaveBoy). The doorway of the backroom momentarily filled with a mountain of luggage as she bustled through.

'Been shopping?' Gretchen said, brightly.

Paula unburdened her bags, unloading three fat files, a pile of notebooks and a few A1 charts. 'Got any Blu-Tack?'

'Jesus bloody Christ,' said Luda, swallowing a large piece of cheroot, 'What the hell is that?'

'Information,' said a breathless Paula, pinning the charts to the wall. 'As you can see, I have been trailing the suspects for some time.'

'Suspects?'

'Objects of surveillance, whatever. Now, if you take for an example August 23rd – we can see from their movements –'

Gretchen leaned forwards. 'Shall we look at it afterwards, love. During the teabreak, maybe?'

'Yes let's put the creepy stuff away,' Luda said. 'No need to release the inner lunatic quite yet.'

Paula looked disappointed. 'But there is a lot of interesting data here.' She held up a second plastic bag full of folders.

Around the table, everyone could feel the collective non-stares of everyone else failing to bore into them.

'There's lots more where this came from,' Paula persisted.

Dave went over to her and gently prised the plastic bag from her anxious grip. 'We can refer to it if we need to. But for the moment let's just…?' He smiled encouragingly and nodded a few times. Paula reluctantly took her place next to The Man in the Mask.

Blowing out his cheeks with relief, Dave returned to the head of the table, took up the pointer and proceeded to do some ostentatious coughing, despite the fact that his audience were all sitting attentively, waiting for him to start. Apart from Luda, that is, who was absorbed in picking at the lumps of old nail polish on her long nails.

'Now, if I can have your attention, everyone. Attention!

Attention!'

They sat and looked at him. He did some more coughing.

'Okay, let's get this ball rolling, shall we? Get things up and running, the show on the road, the horse before the cart, the…'

'Oh get on with it,' Luda muttered, none too quietly.

Dave flushed. 'Alright. Ladies and gentlemen. So. To kick off. As you know I put myself forward to chair this meeting. If we could maybe take a vote on that…a show of hands?'

Luda made a face and took another munch on her cheroot.

'I think we can safely say that the motion is carried. Is anyone minuting this? Anyone like to volunteer…? Cheers Gretchen. Right. Now. First off. We must agree to a mission statement and aims. Preferably three. There are always at least three aims to any mission statement. Can anyone suggest the wording for the mission statement?'

'Jesus Christ.' Luda threw her eyes at the Artex ceiling.

'No? Ok. Well, let me start us off then. I propose we should start our mission statement with a definition of who we actually are, the target groups we are reaching out to and…err…an intention of the general direction, not specific but general, we want to aim toward.'

'How about northwest?' said Luda.

'Yes. Well,' said a flustered Dave, trying his best to ignore her.

'Oh get on with it!' Luda could hardly bear it any longer. It was quite obvious the lot of them couldn't organise themselves out of one of Paula's plastic bags without her own superior mental skills. And the meeting would never get off the ground whilst Dave insisted on hogging the limelight. But Luda wasn't going to give any ground. Let them learn, she thought.

'Right. Yes. Umm,' said Dave, stuffing his hands far into the pockets of his jeans. 'Okay. Well, today, as you know is about brainstorming. To help our new friend here. Now, first, if I may outline the situation –'

He picked up a piece of pink chalk from a 'specials' blackboard and drew three large concentric circles. Next, he wrote 'ALAN', 'BELINDA' and 'PAULA' in the middle of each in large pink letters. Not stopping there, he drew a large heart between Alan and Belinda and another with an arrow from Paula to Alan. He then began to delicately decorate this with geometric patterns of plants, birds and flowers.

Luda's drumming feet alerted him to his audience.

'Here's the situation: a classic love triangle, beloved of history and some of our most famous works of literature.' Slightly put-off by Luda's face-pulling, he continued shakily, 'In a nutshell: Paula loves Alan loves Belinda. We are gathered here today to see if there is any way we can help this – lovely young lady to win back her one true love.' He looked round the assembled group. 'So, let's have some brainstorming. Don't be shy. Think outside the box. That's what brainstorming is about. Just tell me the first thing that comes into your head. You never know where instinct might take you.' He turned to SlaveBoy with an encouraging smile, 'First thing that comes to mind, SlaveBoy?'

'Kill Belinda?' he shrugged.

'Kill Belinda. Now that's what I call out-of-the-box thinking! Have you got a note of that, Gretchen?'

'Err, yes, hold up a moment, love,' said Gretchen, casting about vaguely for something to write with.

'Anything else?' Dave said.

'Wait a minute.' Luda had gradually moved forward in her seat, the muscle in her cheek vibrating with excitement. 'That's not such a bad idea.'

'Thanks,' said SlaveBoy.

'Think about it. It's Simple. Clean. Effective. All Paula has to do is offer a sympathetic shoulder to cry on at the funeral and there you go. Problem solved. What?' Luda threw up her hands as they all turned in their seats to look at her.

'Well, it's a bit drastic, isn't it?' complained Gretchen. 'I mean, I know she's hateful and everything but I'm not sure cold-blooded murder fits in with my pacifist principles.'

'Hmmm,' Dave said, with a not-very-convincing appearance of thought. 'You're right, and we need to be democratic about this. Let's look at some more options.'

'That's right. Why don't you just ignore me? I'm not really here anyway.' Luda sat back again, cross-armed and scowling.

'Now,' said Dave, brightly. 'So far we've had killing. Anyone else got any suggestions?'

The pointy stick fell on the Masked Man.

'Ummm,' he said, unpromisingly. 'Ummm...' he said again.

Luda made a disgusting noise at the back of her throat. Everyone ignored her.

'It seems to me,' said The Man in the Mask slowly, 'that we have several problems to solve. We need to break the attachment that has formed between Alan and this Belinda character – discover her hold and diminish its power. Second, we need to see to it that the Belinda woman is unable to get her claws back into him again.'

'Looks like killing her is the only option, after all,' said Luda darkly.

'Third, we need to re-establish the relationship between Alan and Paula. We need to make him see her through new eyes, forget about past mistakes and preconceptions and allow him to see her as the fabulous, beautiful, desirable woman that she is.'

There was a short pause while Man in the Mask cleared his throat under the suspicious gaze of Luda, but his face – at least the portion of it visible below the mask – remained yet another mask.

'In short,' he looked round the assembled audience, 'We need to make Alan jealous.'

At that, a good deal of muttering broke out.

'I think we should at least give it a go,' said Gretchen. 'And it would certainly be less risky than the other plan…' adding a comforting, 'Although we always have the killing idea to fall back on,' as she caught sight of the disappointment on Luda's face. 'That can be our Plan B.'

The others agreed. A decision had been made.

Dave wrote a large 'MAKE ALAN JEALOUS' on the blackboard and they all shook hands and grinned at each other.

They had worked out the what; the how was a little trickier.

'Perhaps Paula could take an Advanced Accountancy Exam,' suggested SlaveBoy. 'That would make him jealous, particularly if she passed without doing any revision.'

'What about Paula becoming a celebrity?' Gretchen offered. 'It's all the rage these days. She could go on the telly, on that Big Brother and whatnot, come out, get her tits out all over the tabloids and make millions.'

'Brilliant,' said Luda.

'Really?' said Gretchen, looking pleased.

'No, not really,' said Luda, who was getting grumpier and grumpier at the way The Man in the Mask was looking at Paula. So annoyed, in fact, that she forgot momentarily that she was refusing to take part in proceedings. 'It's the most stupid idea I ever heard. He's hardly going to go for her after a stunt like that. Is it ladylike? Is it refined?'

'Here we go,' muttered SlaveBoy.

'Is it something Katherine Hepburn would do? Is it something Marlene would do?'

'Very probably,' said SlaveBoy.

'Of course she wouldn't. Those gals had style, those gals had class. Those gals were up there – untouchable – icons in our humble earth-bound hemisphere...'

She was ranting now and the others, sensing they were in for the long haul, started chatting amongst themselves. All, that is, except for The Man in the Mask, who quietly stood up and, with a dreamy look in his eye, said, 'That's it,' very softly – so softly, in fact, nobody heard him.

'They were role models to aspire to, goddesses sent to light up our sad pedestrian world...'

'Shut up and listen!'

Luda, put out, opened and shut her mouth a few times and fell silent.

Finally, The Man in the Mask had their attention. Taking up the mantle, he began to pace back and forth with his hands clutched behind his back. 'Paula *is* our goddess,' he said, barely audibly.

'Eh?' That was Luda.

'We make Paula into our goddess.' He quickly held up a silencing hand. 'I don't mean a cheap-jack celebrity like we have these days. I'm talking the real deal. A Marlene, a Marilyn, a –'

'Liza Minelli!' shouted Luda, excitedly.

'Liza Minelli, Judy Garland. Beautiful, tragic –'

'Feminine!' an excited Luda interrupted again.

'Feminine,' said The Man in the Mask. 'And totally, absolutely, knob-tinglingly unobtainable.'

'Ye-es,' the wind whistled through the gap in Luda's two front teeth as the idea sunk into her consciousness and resonated with the small boy who had, all those years ago, looked up at his Marilyn poster and mouthed that first, breathy halleluiah to the muse. 'It's brilliant,' she said. 'And completely counter-intuitive. You're saying that instead of making Paula accessible we make her completely out of bounds?'

'Exactly.'

They all peered intimidatingly at Paula who, true to form, shrunk away from their appraising stares.

It was down to Luda to voice what they were all thinking.

'It's going to be one helluva challenge.'

'What do you mean?' Paula said, defensively.

'I mean, darling, you ain't no Dietrich.' Luda cast a smug glance towards The Man in the Mask. 'And you ain't no Marilyn.'

Paula's shoulders attempted to stuff themselves into her ears. She appealed to the others. 'Is there no hope?' It was an honest question.

To everyone's surprise Dave was the one to answer. 'I don't know… I don't think it's beyond the realms of possibility.'

'Yes, well, look who's talking,' Luda shot back. 'What standards are we measuring this by?'

'No, but,' said Dave, sending a sly glance in Luda's direction.

'Remember Abigail?'

Luda remembered Abigail alright and pulled a face to prove it.

'Formerly Holland's own Mr Muscle turned Miss Transylvania 2004.'

'So?'

'There were others. Sid Carver? Robert Pigeon, *Simon Silliwell.*'

A small muscle threatened to explode out of the side of Luda's face.

'Your point being?'

'None of them were the greatest of raw material. Simon Silliwell impersonated his own sister. Sid Carver went out with a Brixton millionaire for over a year and a half before "Clarissa" was discovered. Robert Pigeon got through to the quarter-finals of the Crouch End Women's Bowling Championship.'

Something seemed to be dawning in Luda's face, and for once that something wasn't red and angry.

Dave pressed the point home. 'And if it wasn't for a bad case of food poisoning he'd have made the semis too!'

'Have you seen a member of the Crouch End Bowlers who doesn't look like a fella?' Gretchen pointed out, unhelpfully.

But Luda was nodding thoughtfully now. 'Yes,' she said slowly, 'Yes.'

'What did all those people have in common?'

Luda was nodding faster and faster. 'Yes,' she said, louder.

'What was the hidden secret of their success?'

'Duct-tape and falsies?' suggested Gretchen.

'Me!' shouted Luda, leaping to her feet, snatching the pointer off Dave and fixing them all with a steely-eyed stare.

'We have, in our midst, the greatest tranny coach you'll ever meet,' said Dave, excitedly. 'It's true. It was Luda who advised Sid on every move he made and, more importantly, every piece of undergarment engineering he wore on his dates with Carlos. It was Luda who taught Abigail how to style her wig to cover her bull neck and how to approach the judges in the diagonal plane to disguise the width of her pecs. As for Robert Pigeon…'

'Robert Pigeon,' murmured Luda with a sigh.

'The greatest transvestite bowler since…'

'Since…?'

'Since…?'

They lost themselves for a second in a breathless daydream at the particular wonders of Robert Pigeon.

'You're right,' Luda said. 'This is my destiny. My area of expertise. Besides,' she added meanly, 'You need me. No one else would be up to the job.'

'That's the spirit.'

'Who else has the foresight, the wisdom, to turn this piece of *nothingness* –'

'Hang on,' said a sensitive Paula, but nobody was listening to her.

' – into a bonafide goddess?' Luda put her hand dramatically to her chest. 'Fate has called upon me to do this thing and I will not shirk from the task. The road is long, the journey hard. We will be sore, tired, downcast – I have nothing to offer but blood, toil, tears and sweat. But one day in a thousand years men will say, "This was their finest hour."'

'Will we have to drink our own pee?' asked SlaveBoy, cheerfully.

'Ouch!'

Chapter Eleven | TRAINING

Training commenced the next day.

Wiping away the tears of sleep, Paula said, 'Luda what are you doing here?' a few times in an unfriendly tone of voice, hoping she might just take the hint and go away.

Luda, who never took hints on principle, proceeded to forge past and through to the small kitchen.

Hugging herself on the doorstep, Paula peered out into the dark wintry morning to see a white van parked at a jaunty angle against the kerb. But she was too sleepy to give it much thought.

She shut the door and followed the short burly figure through to the back of the house.

Luda had already filled the kettle and was busy hunting for cups in the bare cupboards. 'If you really want a thing you have to put the effort in,' she was saying briskly. Then, 'Bloody hell, does no-one else live in this place?' before finally finding two mugs hidden under the sink. She threw in some economy teabags she had miraculously located at the back of one of the empty cupboards, one for Paula, two for herself.

'It's five thirty in the morning,' Paula said.

'What's five thirty when you're desperate and in love?'

Paula felt desperate all right, but she eased the kitchen door closed and impressed on Luda the importance of not waking the other tenants or indeed the neighbours before tentatively sitting on the broken sofa next to the computer, her thin fingers twisting nervously in the material of her pyjamas. Luda looked different, but, Paula suspected, these were not her work clothes. She wore white cotton trousers and flip-flops and the kind of flowy top art teachers often wear. Her make-up, also, was more demure than usual.

Luda joined her with tea. Paula's cup had Peter Rabbit on it.

'Right,' Luda said, with worrying decisiveness. She started unpacking her bag to form an even-more worrying tower of DVDs beside them. 'We will commence on Lesson Number One. Emotional Literacy.'

Paula, eyeing the leaning tower sceptically, could not keep the lack of conviction from her voice. 'Emotional literacy?'

'Emotional literacy,' echoed her mentor. 'You've heard of *Men are from Mars, Women are from Venus*, I suppose?'

'I've heard of it...'

'Bit old-hat now but it cottons onto the basic idea. You know, man brooding in his cave, woman trying to engage him with her thoughts and feelings?'

Paula looked at Luda blankly.

'Not very in touch with your feminine side, are you? Surprised if you had one. Still, I've seen worse. *Simon Silliwell*...' Luda shook her head. 'For now, let's just concentrate on feelings.'

'Feelings. Right.'

'Go on then.'

'What?'

'Let's be having them.'

'Having them?'

'Your feelings. Pretend I'm Alan.'

Pause.

'I can't.'

'Why the hell not?'

'You don't look anything like Alan.'

'Oh for fuck's sake!'

Luda got up and stumped crossly over to the DVD player. 'I can't believe this. Even Robert Pigeon could do better. I'll just have to start with the basics. Let's see what this does to you.'

Luda inserted a DVD into the machine and settled back onto the sofa. Paula gingerly perched beside her. Sweeping music was unleashed into the room. It wasn't long before Paula heard the telltale snuffling from the hunched figure beside her. Then there was some snivelling, superseded by full-blown sobbing and wrenching of clothes.

Paula sat there, feeling awkward, conscientiously averting her gaze.

Luda, who had been observing her host angrily from under her hair, leapt out of her seat in tear-stained temper. 'Right, that's it!'

'What?' a shifty Paula responded guiltily.

'There is obviously something hideously wrong with you. How can you not feel moved by this film?'

'I'm sorry. I don't much like dogs.'

'What's that got to do with it? If you don't like the dog concentrate on the boy! There he is, missing his one companion in life…his only soulmate…'

'I suppose when you put it like that…' But Paula's tone was uncertain.

'Who has been taken away from him by the evil dognappers. Lassie didn't want to go. Lassie is yearning to get back home.'

'Yes,' said Paula.

'All the obstacles in their way and all they want to do is be together.'

'Together,' said Paula.

She tried to focus. She wondered where Alan was now. In bed probably, if he had any sense. Except he was not alone. Face facts, Paula. Belinda was part of the scene now, whether she liked it or not. She turned her attention back to Luda, who was shouting at her about the importance of emotion. What did Luda know about emotion? Why was she listening to her? She thought of Belinda and hardened her heart. If Luda could help her get Alan back, maybe it was worth a few early starts. She settled back into the sofa and observed her trainer as she gestured and pontificated about the importance of crying. She looked towards the television and let the emotive music wash over her. Yes, Alan was the boy and she was the dog. Time and space may separate them, but nothing could keep their love apart. If crying was what it took… Paula squeezed her eyes violently, okay it might take some practice but…

'Pass me that tissue,' she said, in a stronger voice.

Luda looked across at her approvingly. 'Good girl.'

For three weeks, training was intense. Two hours in the morning, two at night. They covered everything from what Luda called the physical aspects – deportment, crying, hair and nails, manicure, the art of wearing clothes (for indeed Luda believed it was an art), how to moisturise; beauty: both outer and inner (the former being down to the deportment, make-up and hair and nails etc, the latter, apparently, to do with drinking enough water. 'It's all about inner radiance, darling. After all, you're surrounded by water in the womb so…' Besides, Paula figured, she probably needed replenishing after all the crying she was doing) – to the emotional aspects: emotional literacy, multi-tasking, crying, how to laugh at men's jokes, crying again, how to walk only revealing one's best profile, how to eat, how not to eat, how to not eat…

'Where did you learn all this stuff?' Paula asked one day, sitting in her small bare bedroom, in front of the dressing table mirror, as Luda demonstrated how to create a 'day look'. The dressing table had been a recent acquisition at Luda's behest. She had found it in a sorry state, ridden with wormholes, the mirror cracked, sticking out of a skip in a neighbouring street and, when caught levering it out by its unfriendly owner, had been forced to part with a tenner for the ungainly thing. A tender rubdown, a coat of white bathroom paint, a drape of pink muslin and here it stood, a symbol of unabashed femininity, planted proudly in the window of Paula's bedroom.

'Oh observation mainly, it's amazing what you can pick up,' said Luda indistinctly, a cluster of hairpins protruding from her lips. She removed them with care one-by-one, fixing Paula's mousy hair back behind her ears.

'There's nothing like a woman getting ready to go out. The way she turns somewhere so ordinary – the bedroom, the bathroom – into a sacred space, an enchanted place full of mystery and glamour, where no man may enter. There she sits, like the high priestess, at her dressing table, setting out her magic wares – creams here, lipstick there, the potions and powders, tiny bottles shaped like miniature women's bodies, the brushes and colours. Her face, bare, naked – awaiting that final act of transformation – that magic spell. The dream. The fantasy. I love it all.'

She fell silent for a moment while Paula sat, hardly breathing, waiting for her to go on. But when she spoke next it was just a brisk, 'Close your eyes,' before changing tack completely by extolling the virtues of eyeliner pencils.

Paula dutifully closed her eyes. So there *had been a woman in Luda's life*. But whom and when she could not determine. She sat silently, concentrating on the smooth strokes rippling her lids. A mother? A sister? A lover?

Luda tugged at Paula's eyebrows to create a smoother canvas.

Paula felt the tickle of dust at the corners of her eyes as the feathery brush caressed her lids and thought of the little boy who would become the Luda she knew now, watching his mother putting on her make-up to go out. Had she been beautiful? Paula imagined Bette Davis in a diaphanous gown, draped peacock-like along the floor from her dressing table, with the little boy, behind, watching shyly from the doorway.

She opened her eyes and watched Luda in the mirror plastering on the buttery layers of foundation, much as one might ice a cake, and found herself considering her companion in detail for the first time. All that sound, all that fury. Yes, it was easy to laugh at her incongruity. The strong muscular figure, a little portly maybe, in a way that so cruelly belied her feminine yearnings; the beer belly; the stocky form; the pitted, pocketed face – the colour of weathered pine; the touches of grey at her temples; the dramatic red shoreline of her brillo-pad hair that curled proudly and pubically around her face, stubbornly refusing to soften that jutting jaw. Those cracked lines, the grizzled features. No dash of rouge could freshen those hard cheeks, no slash of red could plumpen that lipless mouth, no tongs or hair-straighteners could soften that infestation of wirewool. And what's more, from the odd sly glancing look she caught slipping out at her from under those creased, meagre-lashed yet so heavily burdened eyelids, she knew that Luda knew. Knew these facts only too painfully and too well. *Let's not speak of that*, the look said. *Do not draw attention*. It was a glance that invited complicity, but no RSVP.

Had that boy crept into his mother's room when she was out, to try on her feather boas and trip up and down in her satin-shiny stilettos? Did he dip a curious finger into her make-up box and smear his baby features with a clown's face of colour? Did he paint his eyelids and dance around the room in his mother's shoes?

She was dying to ask, but Luda said nothing more and Paula knew that any direct question would be met by silent hostility. *Let's not speak of it,* the twitching muscle in her cheek seemed to say. *Let it be our, very obvious, secret.*

This code of secrecy was in operation at all times and Paula got used to the routine of the doorbell ringing and Luda's arrival, sometimes in slacks, sometimes in high-waisted jeans and her departure a couple of hours later, after a quick visit to the toilet and a quick change of appearance.

Occasionally, Paula had almost been allowed to meet the other Luda, wearing the same slacks or jeans, subtly transformed by a shirt, a bulky jacket slung over her shoulder, a pair of wraparound sunglasses covering a face devoid of make-up.

At these moments, Paula would stand awkwardly by the door

and say, 'See you tomorrow,' receiving a curt nod for her pains, plus that look again. And Luda would cross the small tiled entranceway to her van. Even her walk was different at these times. Wider. More swaggering. Bandier.

Yet still, Paula was not allowed to witness the act of transformation. As if by denying her this, it could be pretended that the two Ludas were not in fact the same person at all.

Only once did Paula dare to follow her, when Luda left slightly later than normal one morning. Paula watched her pulling out into the street before grabbing a bike that belonged to one of the faceless tenants, leaning drunkenly against an old mattress in the inner hall. It was second nature to quickly pull on the old duffle coat hanging from the peg by the door, twist the woollen scarf once around her face and finish the look with the pair of skiing goggles poking out of one of the Wellington boots below.

She knew the way the van had turned, having watched it every morning for the past ten days. She pedalled swiftly in an attempt to catch up, which was not hard. The van moved slowly, almost uncertainly, earning more than one complaining beep as it trundled along.

After she had been tailing it for ten minutes or so, the van pulled down a lane into a run-down builder's yard. Paula dismounted and hovered at the end of the lane, feigning interest in the notices in the window of the small grubby launderette perched on the corner. She pushed the goggles up to her forehead in a vain effort to see what Luda was doing.

Finally Luda emerged. Traces of the old Luda were still there: the hair, of course, remained defiantly unaltered, but an attempt had been made to brush it back like a French footballer.

The rest of Luda's small squat body was encased in a pair of jeans that showed off the muscles in her thighs, a biker jacket that emphasised the broadness of her shoulders. His shoulders, Paula suddenly realised with a shock.

She expected him to turn away to the small prefab at the back of the yard, but to her surprise – and concern – he turned instead towards her (she shoved her goggles down her nose) and walked out of the yard and straight past her right shoulder. Paula held her breath before she looked round. Luda was already a block away, looking straight ahead and marching with some purpose.

Paula rewrapped her scarf tightly round her head and set off in her – or should she say 'his' – path.

Four blocks on and Luda dipped into a glass-fronted entrance. As she came nearer, Paula saw it was the window of a small greasy-spoon café. 'Builder's breakfast,' she thought, her stomach rumbling.

The windows were steamed up but Paula still managed to spy Luda's squat form as it crossed the other side of the café towards one of the tables.

A young man was sitting there reading a book – awkward, beautiful. He looked up as Luda sat down opposite. Paula could almost feel the tension. She could see it in the cut of Luda's back.

The young man was sitting, legs apart, hands on the table. He looked up and directly into Luda's eyes – with a fierce look – was it love? Or hate? Paula could see Luda was trembling. He (yes, it was definitely 'he' now) put out a hesitant arm.

Enough. Paula pulled back out of sight, heart beating. She leant back against the wall. Somehow she never felt guilty spying on

Alan. But this, this was different.

Let us not speak of it. The look had said.

And she didn't.

Instead, things continued as normal. Luda continued to appear, every morning like clockwork, and Paula never spied on her again.

Weekends, however, were different. Apart from every second Saturday, which was Liscious night, Luda had weekends off.

'Got to put the maintenance in,' she would say mysteriously.

Paula knew better than to ask her what this meant.

By the end of the second week, Luda declared her charge fit for public consumption and arranged for them to attend one of Luda's 'girls' nights out' together at a crusty but friendly little bar in Crouch End. Paula could hardly contain her excitement as she clipped along the chilly bus station at Finsbury Park to meet an unusually sophisticated Luda, who was attracting some unwelcome attention in a floor-sweeping evening dress and elbow-length gloves. As Paula approached, Luda was surveying the ground beneath her with irritation, and trying to remove something from the underside of her shoe. A sardonic wolf-whistle issued from one of the more permanent residents of the bus station.

'Good to know one can still break a few hearts,' she muttered icily, as she subjected Paula to a quick rotating inspection and pulled her blouse straight with quite unnecessary violence.

'Not bad.'

Paula's heart leapt.

'Not great, mind. But not bad.' She bared her yellowed teeth at her protégé. 'Not bad at all.'

As they hurried through the cold, Luda reeled off her final list of instructions.

'Remember the three *D*s: Deportment, Dress sense, Décolletage, the three *F*s: Feminine, Frivolous, Fashionable and the three *E*s: Emotional, Enigmatic and Elegant, not to mention the three *P*s: Posture, Profile and…'

They found Dave lurking under a lamp post on the corner adjacent to the pub, trying to look inconspicuous in a voluminous neon yellow plastic poncho and bicycle helmet, which succeeded in shielding the world from the sight of his V-neck cashmere twin-set and Marks and Spencer easy-iron grey skirt, but was less successful at distracting attention from either himself or his pink kitten heels.

'You look lovely,' he said to Paula, and the warmth in his eyes showed he meant it.

'So do you,' she returned the compliment with less certainty.

'If we can finish the love-in,' remarked Luda. 'What are you doing loitering here?' she asked Dave.

'Waiting for you,' he said. He lowered his voice, 'the full-timers are out in force.'

'Shit,' said Luda, looking for a moment like she was about to turn tail and leave.

'Full-timers?' Paula looked from one to the other, wide-eyed. But she might not have been there for all the attention they gave her.

'What about Paula? You know what they're like. They take no prisoners. Do you think she'll pass?' Dave asked Luda, anxiously.

Luda gave him a funny look.

'Come on,' said Luda. 'We're here now.' She pulled in her stomach and pushed out her chest. 'Onwards.'

Paula scuttled after them, shoulders aloft, clutching her new jacket to her for support. It took them a while to clatter down the street and Paula thought, not for the first time, how hard it was being a real woman, and wished she could go back to being the slightly ramshackle rubbish woman she used to be.

Luda entered the bar briskly and with purpose. Dave skulked by her side. She did not even acknowledge the turned heads at the table on her nearside. Not the usual turned heads she might have expected but the coiffed and permed heads of a group of elegantly dressed 'ladies' armed with synchronised bags and shoes.

Paula, scuttling in Luda's wake, felt their lash-logged eyes boring into her like knives, dissecting every fashion choice, deconstructing every label. Keeping her head well down, she heard the mutter of 'part-timer' and 'frill seeker' as she went past.

Luda bought a round and held them before her like an array of exotic-coloured weapons, before turning and facing her foe. 'Grace, how wonderful!'

'Well, if it isn't our friends the day-trippers, out for a jaunt.'

Paula took in a long aquiline figure, with elegant curve to the body and fine long-fingered hands. Even Paula could recognise this was a whole new ball park of alpha-femininity – particularly when contrasted with her own companions, whose exotic apparel suddenly seemed to have all the allure of costume jewellery next to bonafide diamonds. Here was a tranny who exuded femininity like a perfume. Who wore her feminine attributes with the elegance and confidence of a movie star. Here was a tranny who made *Paula* feel butch. Paula was fascinated by the complicated interplay between the 'yes' and 'no' of the figure in front of her: this was 'convincing' taken to another level. She found herself staring, scrutinising for flaws. When she found them it was an experience so subtle, as to be rendered unconscious. Two beautifully shaped and arching eyebrows belied the very slight lowering of her brow. The aquiline nose could be aristocratically female, but only just. A slight thickening of the wrists, a slight boniness in those glorious legs. A hint. Nothing more. It was the Adam's apple that really gave it away.

'And who is this?' Grace enquired, her eyes travelling the length of Paula, up and down, with undisguised disapproval, and a flicker of suspicion. 'Not another one of your "projects"?'

Luda bristled.

'Just what we need, another Simon Silliwell to lower the tone…'

Her table companions sniggered dutifully, although Paula detected a slight discomfiture.

'When will you get over the idea that you can *teach* someone how to be feminine, Luda? Being a woman isn't something you are taught, it is who you are. *I* should know.'

Paula looked at her mentor, Luda's cheek muscles were a scrum of activity. Dave looked plain terrified and had forgotten to remove his fluorescent poncho; a fact not lost on their adversary.

'Come on, girls,' Luda grunted and marched over to another table, leaving Dave and Paula vulnerable and exposed.

Dave shuffled from foot to foot passively and Paula knew it was up to her to get them out of this. To her great surprise, she bobbed a curtsey.

'Nice to meet you, Ma'am. Come on Dave.'

She took his arm and dragged him bodily across to the table opposite, where Luda was nonchalantly inspecting her face in her compact mirror.

Grace sat back in a gale of laughter.

'Fucking bitch,' said Luda waving aside a cloud of face powder. 'Thinks she's the mistress of the whole transuniverse.'

'Who is she?' Paula said.

'She looks down on us,' said Dave. 'Thinks we're not committed enough.'

'Committed enough, committed enough! What the hell does she know about my commitment?' said Luda, powdering furiously. 'What does she know of my suffering, my sacrifices? I tell you, this is not a walk in the park for me.'

'Shhh.' Dave comforted mildly.

'Some of us have jobs, some of us have…other considerations. Not all of us can afford to jeopardise our whole lives. Not all of us are left Daddy's little windfall to do all the necessary plumbing whilst wafting around all day looking down on everyone else!'

'She's not worth it.'

'Excuse me. Off to powder my nose,' Luda said, gathering her voluminous handbag to her side. She plunged off.

Dave hunched over his drink. 'She gets a bit upset,' he said. 'She's a passionate sort of person.'

'What did you mean when you said "full-timers"?' Paula asked.

'TSs – transsexuals,' said Dave, munching on an olive. 'According to Grace, we're just playing, getting off on it, you know. She's a *real* woman. Apparently.'

'A real woman?'

'That's the difference between TSs and TVs,' Dave said. 'Or at least, it is on paper. In reality it's never that simple.'

'So Grace has had an operation?' Paula pieced together, haltingly.

'She's saving up for it – on the hormones at the moment. Doesn't make any difference, though, according to her. She's a woman now, she says.'

'She's not very nice.'

Dave just shrugged.

'And Luda?' Paula was dying to ask.

Dave shot her a nervous look.

'What about her?'

'She's not transsexual? She doesn't consider herself to be a woman?'

Dave munched olives in silence.

'She talks a lot about crying,' Paula persisted.

The pretty gold bracelet dangling from Dave's wrist toyed with the foam on his pint. He looked at her, 'I know some people think she's a bit loud, a bit of a joke, even. All that stuff about crying and whatnot. But they don't really know her. She wants to be a better person. A good person. Not all men are very nice you know.' He searched her eyes for understanding

Paula wanted to ask so many questions, find out all about these strange new people she was spending so much of her time with. But all Dave would say was, 'Have you never wanted to be someone else?'

She looked at him then, and looked away.

By the time Grace and her girlfriends were leaving, Luda and

Dave were engaged in a heated discussion about what constituted a feminine car. Luda was arguing that the Nissan Micra was a 'BLATANTLY female car', whereas the MX5 was not only scrumptiously girlie but boasted rear wheel drive, sweet engine, and excellent handling. Meanwhile Dave was arguing for the Golf Cabriolet and the Mica Cx-7, but adding that the SO Merc C180K Coupé should also be considered for the fashionable girl about town as, being an automatic, it left one hand free to brush up on the hair and make-up while you drive.

Dave looked so animated, so happy, that Paula wondered, not for the first time, how Luda failed to notice how he lit up whenever she walked into the room.

Dave looked at his watch. 'Better get off,' he said dubiously.

'Okay, Dave, see you about,' said Luda.

He stood there uncertainly.

'Yes, okay, see you Dave.'

Dave hovered for a bit, then resignedly pulled on his poncho and headed for the door.

'Bye then.'

'Bye Dave.'

'Bye Dave.'

They sat in silence for a while.

'So, I'll be off then?' he said, standing by the door.

Luda glared at him. '*We're* not keeping you.'

'Right.'

And after a few more hovering seconds, he shrugged and slipped out into the drizzling night.

Paula watched him go. 'You will be – careful – of Dave, won't you?' she said.

Luda's expression was not a friendly one.

'The way he looks at you. Hangs on your every word. It's obvious to everyone.'

'I don't know what you're on about,' Luda said, unhelpfully. 'Anyway, it's nothing to do with me. He's got to sort himself out.'

Paula sighed.

They spent the next few minutes drinking in wary silence.

'Could you not cry…before?' Paula suddenly said. She hugged her cardigan to her for protection. 'As your other self I mean,' she added, awkwardly.

There was an unwritten rule at the club that you never referred to that other life, that other self. Luda was always, unquestionably 'she', no one asked The Man in the Mask's name. That was the deal. Unless invited. And Luda had not done any inviting. Not even when she stomped away from Paula's bathroom first thing every weekday morning.

'I don't know what you are talking about,' Luda said again.

The message was clear, but for some reason Paula battled on. She wanted to know what lay behind this extraordinary person. When had Luda – 'crossed' – was that the word? What was she in normal life? Who were her parents, her lovers, her friends?

'I meant, is that why? Why you feel the need to…?' she realised she was making a pig's ear of it. 'I just wondered why it was. When it was.'

Luda's face was a warning. '*Do not speak of it,*' it said. '*If we face it directly, the façade will crumble and where will we be then? And who?*'

'Why do you dress?' Paula asked. There. She had said it. That was the term they used in the club. To dress. Not 'cross-dress', not 'dress up', just 'dress'. Simple. She had not even realised the words were in her mouth, but she had asked it, the unasked question. She had broken the illusion, unconvincing though it was, what there was of it now lying in tatters between them.

Luda put her hand to her face in a momentary caress over her pitted cheek. It looked as though, for a few seconds, she was not going to answer.

'You don't mind if I have a fag?'

Paula wondered if she should point out it was illegal.

'Good.'

Luda unwrapped a pristine packet of cigarettes and pulled a slim roll from the box. She offered it to Paula, who shook her head.

'Good,' she said again, and stuffed it in her mouth and lit it, scowling in warning at a member of bar staff who looked as though he was going to say something, before thinking better of it and turning away to tea-towel dry some glasses. She pulled Paula's half-finished can towards her into which she delicately tapped some ash.

'The million dollar question. I don't know. How do you answer such a question?'

'When did you start?'

She looked at Paula as though sizing up her worth as a potential confidante, before another expression along the lines of 'What the hell?' overtook her reserve. She took the fag out of her mouth, smoke pluming after it like a train.

'I was seven years old or thereabouts. And I was at a party, my cousin's party.'

Luda looked up briefly to size-up Paula's expression. Paula

tried her best to look encouraging.

'She had this beautiful blue silk dress. It had lace round the neck and frills on the sleeves. And a bow. A large yellow ribbon round the waist – or a bit higher, little girls don't have waists do they? I can still remember it now, the feel of it, the exciting rustling noise it made when it moved, the layers of petticoats.

My aunt was one of those people who thought girls should be little girls. My cousin had long blonde hair, and my aunt used to curl it. All day I played with the girls, we had a tea party with little china cups and saucers all perfect and clean and small. All very civilised. I remember thinking I was much better off playing with the girls rather than rampaging around the garden with those nasty smelly boys. And all day I was eyeing that dress. Desperate to try it on.

Later in the day, I was going to the toilet and passed my cousin's room. The door was open and there it was, hanging on the wardrobe door – she was going to put it on at teatime for a special treat. I can remember the fear to this day. I edged a chair across and stood there, teetering, trying to hook it off. And then I had it in my hands. I remember the feel of it, the smoothness, the swish, the glamour – I can't even have understood that then – the feel of it against my face. That bow! I think everyone was in the kitchen, I don't know. But in a moment, without really thinking, I just carried it out of the house. I don't think I knew what I was going to do with it. I just carried it out and stopped. No plan of what to do next. And then I saw my father's golf bag, sitting next to the car. It did not feel like it was me doing it but I carried the dress over to the bag, unzipped it and folded the dress neatly inside. Then I zipped it up again and went back into the house as though nothing had happened.'

Luda tapped fag ash into the can and took another thoughtful drag.

'Anyway, we're in the kitchen, just as normal, and my cousin comes running in hysterical, tears streaming down her face. "My dress!" she kept saying. "My birthday dress!"

Of course everyone was up in arms. We were all sent to scour the house. My aunt was beside herself. Even Dad went looking in the garden in case "the dog had been at it". No trace to be found. My little cousin was inconsolable. I remember feeling very calm, tucking into the birthday cake in the kitchen. I think I felt a little sad for her, a little, but at the end of the day she would be alright. She would get another birthday dress. No one would buy a birthday dress for me.

We stayed late. And because my father had had a drink or two, my mother drove us home, which she didn't like doing. Thought it was unladylike. She was cross with him I think. Or perhaps I'm adding that in afterwards. She always hated it when he had been drinking. He would get all amorous, which never went down well, she'd say "not in front of the children" and "you've been drinking, your breath stinks" which would make him angry and then so on and so forth.

I thought about nothing else but my new dress all the way home, yet somehow I still managed to fall asleep in the car. I must have been carried into the house and put in my bed. I don't remember. All I know is that the next thing there was roaring and light and my father bursting into my room with my precious dress crushed in his hands. I remember wanting to tell him not to hold it that way, to hold it gently, remove it from him, but he already had a hand on me, hauling me up, the blue silk crushed under my nose. "What the fuck is this? You fucking faggot, fucking little thief. After all their hospitality you repay them like this. I'll teach you to take other people's things, you fucking sissy-prick."

Afterwards, I always thought it strange that he didn't think to take the dress with him. To him, it was just nothing I suppose. He didn't seem to see what I saw in it. He didn't see that it was a thing of beauty. I'm not sure my father saw any things of beauty. He was not that kind of man. He didn't see its elegance, its cleanliness, its purity. The rustling silk and the china teacups. He just saw something dirty, something shameful. And it was dirty and shameful, lying there on the floor where he dropped it. I was crying of course. I did then. Before I learnt boys didn't – couldn't. And I knelt down on the floor and picked it up. It was battered and bruised. A bit like me. But still beautiful. I remember crying and holding it against my face and the calming feeling of the silk against my skin. And then. And I don't know why I did this, but it just seemed like the thing to do. I put it on. The beautiful blue silk dress. Crumpled and torn. It was my dress. I can't even describe the feeling…it was wonderful. More than wonderful and less, it felt right, you know? Like the dress was…oh I don't know. But I knew, then, that I was me.'

The cigarette's long ashy tail fell off and scattered over the top of Luda's pint and the surrounding tabletop. Luda distractedly flicked it away.

'So what do you make of that?' she demanded. 'Early sexual excitement, associating women with care and empathy, running away from my maleness so as not to be like my father?'

She gave Paula a hard stare in case she threatened to go all mushy on her. 'But then Dave's Dad's a sweetie so how do you explain him?'

Paula looked away from Luda's red and bulging face and stared into her drink.

'Some men aren't very nice,' she said, echoing Dave's words of earlier. 'Doesn't really matter, really. Why, I mean. We just are, I suppose.' She had been trying to sound profound but it sounded to her ears more like an embarrassing line from a soap opera. She dipped her head in shame.

Luda squinted at her, as though looking for mockery then let out a breath. 'Come on,' she said. 'We can't sit around here all day – it's nearly eleven. We could fit another hour's training in, if we're quick.'

Chapter Twelve | THE KNIFE

In just a few short weeks, Planner Number 5 had put together a distillation of all Belinda's aspirations in plant, material and colour-chart form. Everything was pregnant with meaning – each detail a carefully coded manifesto, to any woman of fashionable discernment, of the taste, class and sophistication of its chooser.

Although she never expressed any pleasure about the way things were going, Belinda radiated a grim contentment with the formulation of this, her most important day. At last things were on track. Three months to go. The bridesmaids were sorted (magenta, outfits carefully crafted to add on an extra stone or two), the table decorations arranged (nobody was going to dream up that cactus idea), the stately home – larger and more stately than anything Amanda could afford – had been booked and an unflattering aubergine dress had been specially designed for her sister.

The stage was set for Belinda's day of rival-crushing superiority. Not everything was going completely her way, however.

'Have you heard?' Amanda had burst excitedly into the office that lunchtime.

Belinda had kept her composure. 'Shhhh Amanda, there is

no need for such unseemly excitement. There are people being liquidated all around us. Have some sensitivity.'

'Sorry. But I couldn't wait to tell you! Harry's standing down. Due to, oh something about family commitments or something. Dunno. Anyway, his job's up for grabs. And guess who's in the running?'

Belinda smoothed down her skirt and gazed levelly at Amanda. This was it. 'Naturally I would assume that I –'

'Both of you!' Amanda gasped, hardly able to draw breath in her agitation. 'You and Pat. You're going head to head.'

'Head to head?'

'Apparently they are very impressed with your portfolio, Belinda, and obviously you are the senior party, but they admire Pat's courage and commitment to the firm and reckon she could be real management material. How about that? Isn't that exciting?'

Belinda, unable to remove her rictus grin, was left with no choice but to widen it further. 'Yes, how exciting.'

'Obviously this is all highly confidential. I heard it in the ladies' loos. They will have to advertise it of course, for the sake of Equal Opportunities.'

'Yes. Of course. I wouldn't expect anything less,' Belinda said.

Belinda dug her fingernails into the sill, as she gazed sourly out of the sitting-room window at the tree, strangely stark and vulnerable now without its summer cloak of leaves. Surely they didn't really consider Pat to be on a par with herself? They must just be humouring the woman. They probably *had* to interview her for appearances sake. Part of all that Equal Opportunities rubbish Amanda was rabbiting on about.

The tree rattled its twigs provocatively in the breeze that gusted through the cracks in the windowpane and squeaked and groaned its way through the strangling cluster of modern jewellery around her neck – the kind that is made up of two smashed wing mirrors, bits of rusted fork and a diaphanous string of fisherman's netting – a demonstration of one's general modernness and artistic sensibility.

It was more important than ever that she got this wedding right. Be seen as the right sort of person marrying the right sort of person. Projecting an image of professional competence, neatness and tidiness, cool organisation and efficiency, exquisite and preferably stonkingly expensive taste and a ruthless, thrusting ambition. There was only one thing holding her back.

'I'm home!' called a fruity voice, accompanied by the sound of an expensive leather briefcase hitting the floor.

'Hallo darling.'

Alan planted a splodge of saliva on her right cheekbone, loosened his tie and plonked himself onto the sofa with a wheeze of white leather, where he began to grope about for the remote control.

'Don't suppose you've seen the remote?' He began the complicated business of dismantling sofa cushions. 'Bloody hell. What we want is a remote for the remote.' He was grunting now with the effort.

Belinda turned away from her nemesis waving and creaking at her through the window. She pulled a face. 'Don't know what you're waving and creaking about. You won't last long,' she muttered to herself as her heels tapped out their rhythm to the kitchen. Tap tap tap tap.

'Bumped into your sister today,' Alan called cheerfully from the living-room. He had found the remote and was settling down in front of a reality show about ten overweight individuals training for the female equivalent of the *Tour de France* with the inspirational title *Fatties go to the Frogs*.

'Look at her,' he scoffed. 'Lose a bit of weight, okay?' He guffawed to himself. 'Not a patch on you, darling.'

Belinda opened a drawer and looked at the range of Sabatier carving knives laid out in front of her.

'My sister?' she said. There was a warning in the voice for those who cared to hear it. Alan, busy sneering at the television, was not in careful listening mode.

'Yes, she's looking well.' (That was foolish.)

'Well? What do you mean well?'

'Well. Like – you know.'

'No, I don't. Enlighten me.'

Belinda returned to the living-room and stood behind the sofa staring down at the bald spot bobbing in front of her.

'She looked. Well, she looked happy for a start. Obviously this new fellow – Brad? Randy?'

'Brandon.'

'What like the pickle?'

'BRANDON!'

'Oh well, whatever his name is.'

'Brandon! Brandon! His name is bloody Brandon!'

Something about her tone alerted Alan to the fact that all was not as it should be. He tried to peer round at the razor-sharp image of tailored smoothness behind him but each time she nimbly sidestepped his gaze. Fighting the pressure from his shirt collar, he eventually gave up and collapsed back again.

'Well he obviously makes her happy.'

'If you say so.'

Alan mistook the iciness in her voice for distraction.

'Worth a bob or two, as well.'

Alan ignored the tidal wave of silence behind him.

'Handsome fella too. If you like that bronzed, muscular, broad-shouldered kind of thing.'

'Bit obvious for me.'

'Really?' He was pleased. He tried to reach round but she slipped out of his way again.

'You alright, love?'

There was no answer. Alan absorbed himself in the television once more, chortling smugly to himself.

'Wouldn't be surprised if there were a sparkly ring on her finger next time you see her. Mark my words. Come on chubby, put a bit of effort in, can't you? Honestly, how can people let themselves go like that?' He loosened his belt with a sigh. 'Ahhh!'

Belinda brooded behind the sofa. It seemed as though there was a danger that her wedding, which was to be the wedding to obliterate all weddings could, after all, turn out not to be the ultimate symbol of rival-crushing superiority she intended. It was so unfair, unfair! That her lard-tub of a sister was grabbing all the attention like this. She was the one getting married. She. Belinda. She was the one they all admired. The one with the glittering career, the hairdo, the accountant fiancé.

Why was this happening? Why did life always seem to punish

her – for following the rules, for doing the right thing? There she was killing herself with 5am exercise workouts and unseen overtime...for what? To find herself stuck in the shadow of a four-wheeled martyr and in a sprint to the altar against her elephantine sibling, neither of whom had ever tried to win in their lives? She began to jab the back of the sofa with her knife. So smooth. So sharp. So unfair. So fucking – jab – unfair.

Alan, from his position on the sofa, remained unaware of these activities and continued to point at the telly, spluttering in mirth. 'Go on fatty, get up the hill. Honestly! How can they humiliate themselves in that fashion?'

As Alan sat there, he contentedly reviewed his lot. Beautiful home, beautiful fiancée, good career prospects... A hi-fi system that had his friends orgasming with jealousy. No, nothing to complain of as far as he was concerned. Alright, there was the slight niggle that she had not slept with him for six weeks, ostensibly for the purpose of providing greater motivation for gaining promotion but...still. He could see her point, after all.

'By the way, I've been given the name of a tree surgeon,' she said suddenly from behind him and all Alan's good feelings were abruptly curtailed.

Alan looked up and straight into her eyes, boring into him from the mantelpiece mirror. Despite himself, Alan felt a shiver of fear run up his spine. 'Ah. I've been thinking about that...'

'Well, don't,' She leaned forward and flashed a grimace in his direction that might have approximated for amusement, if Belinda did amusement, which she didn't. 'Thinking really isn't your strong point, is it, darling?'

He licked his lips.

How can one describe the irrational fear that a man feels for a woman?

It has a primeval quality, dripping with the murky enigmatic power of ancient emotions that originated with our earliest and hairiest ancestors. She may be weaker than him, and shorter than him. And yet this fear has the power to keep him bound and gagged, weighed down by a multitude of silent terrors, faceless and formless.

Looking into Belinda's reflected eyes at that moment, Alan felt the fear and shame of centuries of male gynophobia. It was the same fear that Adam felt as Eve invited him to plunge into the abyss, fall into her, and with her, out of paradise, out of the protection of God's love into a world of sex and death.

When Belinda's contemptuous eyes looked back at him, they were the same contemptuous eyes that had looked down on Adam those many moons ago when he started blustering on about 'scout's honour' and doing things according to the 'rules'. They were the cold, ice-blue eyes that suggested to Lancelot he should do the dirty on his best friend, 'He'll never know, he's a bit past it anyway – you'll be doing *him* a favour.' And they were those same black treacly eyes that gazed unrelenting upon Mark Anthony as he wavered about taking over the empire with a 'Maybe we should think about it some more,' and 'What about a year next Tuesday?'

There is nothing, *nothing*, as terrifying as a woman's scornful gaze. *Do you not love me?* those terrible eyes seemed to say. Not a plea but a challenge, a declaration of war. *Without me you are lost. Without pleasing me, you are a Failure, Worthless. Nothing.*

That was the fear. The fear of being useless, purposeless. Surplus to requirement. The deep buried fear of the baby boy needing the mother-love mixes explosively with the grown man's desire and desire to be desired. The fear of being unwanted, unaccepted, unlovable. The fear that, in the end, it might turn out *not* to be all about his penis.

(No, that last thought was patently ridiculous; Alan pushed it roughly from his mind.)

That fear, Alan felt now crippling his whole being, weighing down upon his oesophagus. (He hiccupped.) Yet, somehow, despite himself, despite the terror he felt looking into those pitiless hawk-like eyes, something small, deep inside him, flickered with rebellion, and that small deep rebellious something refused to go away.

Go on, it whispered. *You can do it. Don't be pushed about. Do it. Tell her. Be a man.*

For once, it added, a bit meanly.

Alan took a deep shuddering breath and opened his mouth…

'About the tree…' Alan started and paused, too scared to go on.

Belinda upped the stakes with an unpleasant contortion of her facial features, so much so that Alan was relieved that the resultant expression came to him mediated by the mantelpiece mirror. She shifted uncomfortably, as though screening something from him.

'What have you got there?' He tried to turn round but she moved nimbly out of eyeshot.

'Nothing.'

She said no more and waited for him to continue, which he presently did, without much conviction.

'I want to keep it.' There he had said it.

'What?' The single bullet of a word shot out of her mouth,

ricocheted off the mantelpiece mirror, straight into his right temple.

Alan rubbed his head, unsure.

'I like it, it's a nice tree. I don't like the idea of taking it down just for the sake of it. The way the light plays through its summer leaves, the way the branches wave in the wind. It cheers me up,' he said defiantly. *What was he doing? Where had those words come from, he did not even know he carried such sentiments.* He sat there, on the sofa, a slightly startled look overtaking his usually complacent features.

Belinda was speechless with rage. That state of affairs did not last long.

'What's *wrong* with it?' she yelled. 'What's wrong with you? It's horrible, ugly, that's what it is. Look at it — messy, large, chaotic — I don't understand you sometimes, Alan. I don't know why you're so obsessed with the old unfashionable thing.'

'*I'm* an old unfashionable thing,' Alan blustered. (*Go on!* said the voice. *Tell her. Give her what's for.*)

Belinda drew in a breath and narrowed her eyes.

'Yes, it's interesting that you should mention that. I've been meaning to have a word with you on that very subject.'

'You have?'

The eyes were merciless. 'What would you say to plastic surgery?'

'Oh darling, you are fine the way you are!'

'It was you I was thinking of.'

'What? Then I'd say bugger off, quite frankly.' He spoke half in jest, but the mirror confirmed the joke was only on one side.

He turned round fully in his seat then, and his expression changed…

However one describes the fear that a man feels towards a woman; it is as nothing to the fear a man feels towards a woman holding a knife.

The feeling of being worthless, useless, purposeless. Surplus to requirement. The need to be wanted, accepted, completed. The fear that it might turn out not to be, in the end, all about his penis – all this pales into insignificance next to the fear of being maimed, mutilated and killed.

Everything's relative.

'Umm. What are you doing, darling?' Alan swallowed. His mouth felt as dry as mouldy biscuits and twice as nasty-tasting.

Belinda sighed and ran the knife along the edge of the sofa where he was sitting and continued to trace a deadly and seductive path up around his right ear around his bald patch and down again. Alan felt his body stiffen to the cold steel at his ear. Much to his surprise, it was not the only thing to stiffen.

'You want me to be proud of you, don't you, when I see you standing waiting for me to walk down the aisle?' She fluttered a breathy mouth around his ear that was quivering like an antenna at her touch.

'What's wrong with a bit of self-improvement? A few nips here, some tucks there?'

'Nips!' Alan squeaked. 'You want me to go under the knife?'

'Under the knife? Do you have to be so melodramatic?'

The Sabatier slicer crept along his neck and began to play dangerously with his left lobe.

'Well how else, may I ask, am I going to be nipped?'

She had moved round in front of the sofa now and was leaning over him so that he could see her protruding collarbones and a suggestion of where those small neat breasts might be. He shivered

191

and felt his resolve weakening.

'Okay. So there's a bit of pain involved –' And she leaned forward and nipped his ear, playfully, thrusting those small neat breasts in his face.

'Pain? Ouch! Mmmm.'

'But so what? It'd be no more than I do for you wearing these every day,' she pushed a viciously pointed shoe into his leg as she straddled him bodily.

'I never asked you to wear those.'

'Of course I wear them for you – who else would I bloody wear them for?'

'I thought you liked wearing them.'

'Oh darling.' A hollow laugh. 'How innocent you are. You think it is nature that leaves me looking this good? It's dedication darling. Discipline. Blood, sweat and tears.'

Alan looked at her then with genuine fear. Reaching tremblingly for her hand, the one not wielding the 8-inch blade, Alan tried cosseting it in his. The gesture was a little too desperate.

'Belinda,' he said huskily. 'What's happened to us? We never just sit and talk like we used to. We never discuss how crap everyone else is and how great we are in comparison anymore. What happened? Don't you love me still?'

'Of course I do darling,' she said, impatiently, 'But I want the outside to reflect the amazing, dynamic, alluring man I know on the inside…'

A tongue had got to work on the ear now and Alan felt the night-watchmen of longing igniting the fires of passion along the wall of his resistance. 'Mmmmm, that's nice. Keep doing that.'

'I want to be able to show you off.'

Alan was torn. He had not had a shag for six weeks, remember. That is a powerful motivation for putting up with a moderate amount of psychopathic behaviour, as long as things didn't get out of hand. (Although two terrified eyeballs followed every movement of the sparkling blade.)

Bringing the knife to Alan's throat, Belinda adopted her little kitten voice. 'Can't you do it? An ickle nip and ickler tuck, for itsy-bitsy me?'

She revealed a breast.

Gasping, Alan nodded slowly, the sweat pouring from his body.

She put the breast away, replaced his roving hand onto his own leg, caressing it briefly with her steel, then, 'Good good,' she said and got up. 'The florists will be calling in a minute.' She clipped off to the kitchen.

Wrung out and sweating, Alan lay back into the cushions of the sofa. What a woman! He laughed out loud.

'And the tree can go?' she called from the kitchen.

'Anything, darling. Anything.'

But as he lay back in the cushions giggling hysterically, he could not help his gaze creeping out to rest upon the tree, arms waving, branches creaking, moaning slightly in the wind.

You let me down, it seemed to howl. Alan slid beneath the line of vision of the window onto the floor out of sight of the wailing apparition outside.

You betrayed me! Betrayed me! Betrayed me!

Part Four: JANUARY

Chapter Thirteen | MENTAL PROGRAMMING

Apart from club nights, Fred's days varied little.

Each morning he would emerge from the futon under his bedsit sink, grimace at himself whilst brushing his teeth in the mirror and proceed to track the least smelly of his socks through the jumbled undergrowth of dirty clothes and old newspapers that formed the leaf-litter of his room. Then, he would pick a T-shirt that reflected his mood of the day – *Star Wars,* Lego or, if he was feeling particularly adventurous – *Star Wars* Lego. If he was lucky there might be a curling slice of bread to stuff into the toaster, parked next to the single kettle and single fork, knife and spoon, on the floor next to the single plug socket. If not, he would rinse out the unwashed and slimy single cup and make black tea. Thus primed, he would set out across the little park towards the bus that took him to the small silent office in Camden, where he would lose himself in whatever it was he did there; that other peculiar universe inhabited by vectors, floating-point algorithms and bilinear equations that could seem more real than the keyboard under your fingers, the chair you were sitting on, more crucial to your existence than your family or friends. Not that Fred had any friends.

As autumn eased into winter, his habits remained pretty much the same. Even the annual arrival of Christmas and New Year failed to interrupt his daily routine as he took advantage of the empty office to work through both.

But today things were different.

As Fred ducked shyly through the door of the small silent office and headed awkwardly for his desk, head well-down to avoid the embarrassment of any inadvertent eye-contact, he hardly dared to take a brief hopeful peer around the room lest he feel embarrassed by the sight of the congratulatory banners and balloons lining the walls; the streamers festooned across his familiar grey terminal; the sight of his colleagues leaping to their feet and presenting him with a bottle of wine and a comedy card that said, '40 Today' with the '40' crossed out and replaced with a 31 in shaky ballpoint pen.

He need not have worried.

There were no cards and banners. There were no streamers. His familiar grey terminal faced him as usual, unadorned. And as usual, the ten long-haired figures, hunched over their monitors, appeared not to have noticed his unspectacular entrance. They continued not to notice as Fred, self-consciously, sat down. This would have been the ideal moment for everyone to have leapt to their feet, shouting 'surprise' and doing all those festive things mentioned earlier. Fred waited a few hopeful seconds, before this chance, too, faded away.

The small silent office was silent because it was crammed full of other computer programmers, who put a lot of effort into keeping it that way.

Fred rebooted his computer and hardly acknowledged

the forms of Simon, Sanjay and the indeterminate number of Andrews hunched over their monitors. Why were so many computer programmers called Andrew he wondered? Almost as though their parents were setting them up from birth for a life of shy obscurity.

That Fred was not even sure about the total Andrew quotient was yet further proof of the silence of the small silent office. Of course, being a computer programmer himself, Fred's preferred solution to this problem was rigorous avoidance of any interaction that would require him to identify any of the Andrews and non-Andrews around him.

So far he had succeeded; he had worked there eight years.

Thirty-one. He was thirty-one years old today.

The computer having finished doing its thing, Fred opened up his email to see if there were any surprise messages – wishing him a happy birthday perhaps.

There were three.

'*U got Horny Cutie Baby and No Erection?*' was the title of one, but as Fred did not have a Horny Cutie Baby, this was not really a big problem for him. And one other:

'*Dear Sir. You may be wondering why I am writing to you. My husband, the Vice Presedent of the National Bank of Nigeria, was trajeckly killed in an aircrash leaving $1,600,000 dollars.*'

Delete.

He yawned. It was almost 2.30pm. He was not used to getting up this early, but had been keen to see if he had any emails. Being left to the discretion of each individual, working hours could be anything from five in the morning to – well, five in the morning. Fred couldn't swear to it that some of the keener Andrews were not squatting on the premises; certainly one couldn't tell from their general state of hygiene.

He briefly considered doing some work.

The kind of programming Fred was involved in was so mind-bogglingly dull that to dwell on it here would be to risk those readers with a genetic disposition towards boredom-induced disease dropping dead. Suffice to say, his particular area of expertise was so specialised that even other computer programmers were uninterested in it, leading to his being even more isolated, socially dysfunctional and all-out weird than his professional peers - a considerable achievement.

Fred was uncool even for a computer programmer. Whilst most of the silent geeky guys where he worked experimented with various unattractive straggly ponytails and beards and wore T-shirts with slogans such as 'Geek Power' and 'Make Code not War'; the best Fred could produce on the beard-front was something that resembled a couple of pieces of dental floss sprouting asymmetrically from his chin, whilst he still winced to think of the time he had crept into the office sporting his 'Code Name: Code' T-shirt and heard a faint snort of derision from the direction of one of the hunched Andrews. Since then he had stuck to his regular *Star Wars* and *Empire Strikes Back* T-Shirts. And when they were in the wash − 'I ♥ Lego'. It was a uniform that he knew would never elevate him to the dizzying heights of Geek SuperStardom, but at least, he reasoned, they would know he had soul.

Thirty-one. Thirty-one today. And what did he have to show for it?

He stared at a particularly knotty piece of code and found himself dwelling heavily on the contours and dimensions of

Paula's breasts, something he immediately felt bad about.

He decided to try expressing them as an equation, in order to feel less bad about it.

He was just considering whether this should be a polynomial equation or a series of bezier patches (of which you would need a number rather than creating a perfect single equation which would be displeasing – no he definitely favoured the polynomial option, with differential equations to sort out the movement), when the guilty badness overwhelmed him once more.

He decided to take a look at the internal wiki to take his mind off things.

The internal wiki was the company's communication system. As the office was full of shy silent sociophobes, an unofficial no talking policy was in operation. This was in operation to such an extent that, on the odd occasion that the phone went, ten rigid bodies would stiffen in anticipation of somebody else taking the call, that somebody usually being the answer-machine. If any hapless individual ever came to the door, ten silent heads would swivel round and stare at them in a collective effort to intimidate them into leaving. If this failed, someone – usually Andrew – would flick his head coolly towards the inner sanctum where the Uber-programmer resided, also called Andrew. Probably. This Andrew was almost certainly their boss, but as nobody cared to admit to this and, as he never talked to them, this fact had never been officially verified.

Being a computer programming company, set up by computer programmers for computer programmers, the ethos of ComPro: *Computer Programming for Computer Programmers* (comprocompro.com) was naturally averse to anything computer programmers are normally naturally averse to: namely talking, short hair, clean clothes and hierarchies.

Computer programmers are naturally averse to hierarchies because this would involve people having to talk to each other, which is the main thing they are averse to. Whereas clean clothes and short hair demonstrate attachment to status, to what other people think, and therefore ultimately to hierarchy (to which they are averse). Besides which, sprucing up a bit might inadvertently attract the attention of some member of the opposite sex which would be too terrifying for words, and – as we know – computer programmers are not fond of words. This is why many computer programmers form intense emotional attachments to cartoon characters with impossible breasts. Because, at the end of the day, however outrageously large her breasts, a cartoon character can never take you away from your mother and, as it is mandatory for all programmers to live with their mothers until they are at least forty, until then, the barrage of dirty clothes, straggly unwashed hair and all-over pong acts as a very effective deterrent. (A fact of which the mothers are well aware, of course.)

But however strong the culture of silence, it has to be admitted it is hard to run a company with no interchange whatsoever and there had been various attempts, over the years, to devise a low-stress non-talking form of communication in the office. Most of these attempts favoured variations of semaphore or Morse code. Unfortunately, as the instigator could never pluck up enough courage to let the others know what system they were using, none of these methods ever actually worked, usually ending up with one person waving and tapping feebly in the corner whilst the others sat staring at their screens, iPods blasting away, completely oblivious to their gesticulating colleague. Eventually one or other of them had realised the only way to communicate was through the screen itself. And so had implemented an internal wiki system which would allow a form of indirect communication that most of them could handle.

The internal wiki contained loads of useful information, from what to do in case of a fire (**'Shout "fire!" and run'**) to today's optimistic report on phone answering.

> **When somebody answers the phone** (stated the wiki, helpfully), **it is customary to introduce yourself – 'Hello, I'm Andrew,' can be a good way to do this, followed by an enquiry as to the identity of the speaker. After this there are several possibilities as to how the exchange may go. The speaker may:**
>   **a) Ask to speak to Andrew**
>   **b) Ask to speak to somebody else**
>   **c) Ask for further information**
>   **d) Other**
>
> **If a) Say 'Andrew is busy right now, can I take a message?'**
> **If b) Say 'Person other than Andrew is busy right now, can I take a message?'**
> **If c) Take an email address and say you will send it on to the speaker.**
> **If d) Make a strange electronic noise in the back of your throat and quickly replace the handset.**

As the compiler of this information was, no doubt, totally incapable of executing any of his own advice, Fred knew that this, like so many of ComPro's internal documents, was completely theoretical. However, adding to it was a useful way of filling in time so he decided to write a section on door answering for those unsure what to do in the unlikely event of someone actually putting their head around it.

What to do in the case of someone coming to the door, he started confidently.

1) Stand up.

2) Put out your hand.

3) Introduce yourself. Suggestion: 'Hello I'm Andrew/person other than Andrew'.

4) Shake hand.

5) Enquire as to purpose of said visit. (Suggestion: 'What do you want?')

6) Listen attentively. (Suggestion: try nodding at frequent intervals to give impression of interest)

7) Say 'Andrew's not available right now.'

8) Make small talk. This is a form of speaking where people fill in awkward silences by talking about inconsequential matters that will not cause any dispute such as the weather. Suggestion: 'Terrible weather we've been having.' Important to gauge relevance of assessment prior to making statement. If in doubt look out of the window. A good alternative: 'Great weather we've been having lately'.

Fred felt he was doing well, but got rather stuck at the theory of getting rid of the customer again and sat staring long and hard at the screen, chewing his fingernails. He checked his emails again, but there was nothing but a couple of penis extensions and the news that he had won a lottery in Spain.

Paula's breasts zoomed back into focus.

Okay, he thought, he had to get on top of this. Take control. He needed to look at the Paula problem coldly and rationally and apply his programmer's mind.

His thought process went something like this:

```
(* Package: PaulaOutAsk Asking Paula Out *)

MODULE
    PaulaOutAsk
TYPE
    Class: female;
BEGIN
    Phone her up;
    Say 'Hello';
    Say 'Are you doing anything tonight. Do you
    like Chinese food?';
    IF Paula: 'fuck off' THEN
    replace the handset; EXIT;
    IF Paula: 'yes' THEN
    Say 'How about I pick you up
    tonight at 8 o'clock?'; EXIT;
END
```

Fred then ran the programme through the hardware of his brain and received the following message:

> **ERROR 342: PANIC!!**
>
> **Too many variables and risk of rejection.**
> **Press any key to start again.**

Fred's mind was racing: why should she be interested in him? What if she thought he was an idiot? What if she recognised his voice? She was already attached to someone else – what was he thinking? How could he admit to her his dirty secret? She knew him as the cool masked avenger, how could he bring himself to tell her that he was really a computer nerd? If he introduced himself as a computer nerd – how could he admit that he went to a fetish club at the weekends?

Calming himself down he took a few deep breaths. All he needed to do was think clearly and calmly and assess the variables. He started again.

```
MODULE
    PaulaOutAsk;
IMPORT
    Vital statistics on Paula,
    Past pain and rejection;
TYPE
    Female = POINTER TO
```

```
        otherfemalesofpastexperience;i.e.mother;
CONST
    PaulaNicePerson = TRUE;
VAR
    (*variable:affection-objects
    list of affection-objects we currently need values
for*)
    Affection-objects:
            Alan;OthersPerhapsYetUnidentified;
VAR
    PaulaInterestInFred: (Yes, No);
VAR
    PaulaInterestInFredAsFredorFredAsNakedMan:
            (FredAsFred, FredAsNakedMan);
PROCEDURE
    AskPaulaOut;
BEGIN
    AskHerOutNaked;
    Fred: 'Would you go out with me?'
    IF Paula: 'Ugh, you're naked!'
            THEN
            Ask her out clothed
            ClothedFred: 'Would you go out
            with me?'
            IF Paula: 'Ugh, you're a computer
            programmer!'
                    THEN
                    ClothedLyingFred: 'Would you
                    go out with me – I'm not naked
```

> **and I'm not a programmer?'**
> **ENDIF**
> **ENDIF**
> **END AskPaulaOut;**

Fred sat back satisfied and took a moment before pressing the Return key of his mind. The message came back straight away: it was the blue screen of death.

ERROR 400067: TOTAL TERROR OF ALL MEMBERS OF THE OPPOSITE SEX.

A FATAL EXCEPTION HAS OCCURRED. THIS PROGRAM IS SHUTTING DOWN. ANY UNSAVED INFORMATION WILL BE LOST. PLEASE CONTACT YOUR LOCAL MENTAL ASYLUM FOR ASSISTANCE.

There are few advantages to being a computer programmer, but one of them is the ability to switch off any thought that requires a level of emotional response. Fred proceeded to do this, switching his mind onto auto-pilot and putting it into hibernation mode. He lowered his chair, back, back and further back until his praying mantis body was levitating almost parallel to the floor below.

To his left and his right he felt the collective protective stance of a couple of Andrews as they sliced their bodies between his line of vision and the porn sites they were presently perusing. Fred did not have that problem: he had put a lot of effort into the positioning of his screen so that the others would not be able to see what he was doing. He was too ashamed.

Here, in the position of greatest efficiency, he had to move nothing but one knuckly digit to hit his keyboard. He hit. And a tit flashed up on the screen. Fred sighed with relief and sunk down even lower in his swivel chair. He indulged himself in a few more photographs. Great tit. Coal tit. And his personal favourite, the blue tit. None of this 'great crested' exotica for him, he liked the ordinary birds best.

There he stayed, practically immobile, until, some hours later, he put out his digit again, logged off and slunk out of the office.

Chapter Fourteen | **SOURNESS AND SIDFOBS**

Belinda sat at her desk in the vast concrete and glass excrescence that was the Smith, Smith-Brown and Smith building, fiddling with her SecurId fob (or 'Sidfob' as Belinda called it) and sourly contemplating the question of whether plastic surgery leads to promotion.

You might have thought it incestuous to work in the same company as one's fiancé. Not to mention said fiancé's ex. But the Smith, Smith-Brown and Smith building was so vast and labyrinthine, its far-flung corners home to so many different departments, that the fact that Alan worked in Insolvency and Liquidation – three floors and several miles of corridor from the Auditing department – guaranteed that Belinda had never even set eyes on him until that fateful disability training seminar. And was of his acquaintance barely an hour before the rendezvous in the disabled toilets.

Cast, as it was now, in a pale and sickly green by the overhead fluorescents, Belinda's face was a picture of sourness. Sour in the manner of one who has encountered something sour. Sour milk for example. Or sour oranges. Or, in Belinda's case, the sourness of her own thoughts rippling sourly between her ears with a frightening and sour regularity; the changing subject matter of her contemplations impacting little upon the set of her features due to the unchanging nature of their interpretation. Benevolent thoughts were objects of great suspicion. Occasionally, just occasionally, it had been known for a more sanguine reverie to pass inadvertently across her neural pathways, for it to be bundled off sharpish by the overzealous and bureaucratic thought police that patrolled her mind twenty-four hours a day. It is when one has a benevolent thought that one is most vulnerable – to manipulation, to losing power, to *getting on with people*.

You can't get on with people if you want to get on.

A message flashed up on her screen.

PAT_RAWLEY: You alright, Linds?

Oh why did the woman insist on forever trying to *befriend* her?

Belinda swung her eyes across the office to be greeted by Pat's waving probe. Fuck. Wasn't it bad enough that she was being continually upstaged by Pat's oppressive positive attitude without her thinking they could do the whole *chatting* thing? Anyway, what was she suggesting? That she, Belinda, was not coping? Could not cope? Just because she, Pat, was coping so bloody magnificently? How dare she! Being paralysed had obviously gone to her head.

In the circumstances, however, Belinda knew it was important to hold her fire. She smiled a magnanimous smile. 'Fine, thanks, Pat.'

Pat returned her probe to the keyboard.

PAT_RAWLEY: Glad to hear it. Wondered if you'd like to look over the proposals I sent to David. Would appreciate your input.

Belinda smiled and nodded. What was the manipulative cow up to now? Trying to butter up David before the interview, eh? She was not going to give her special dispensation just because she was paralysed. Quality was quality. Totally objective. Pat would not welcome being patronised by lenient attitudes in the work place.

PAT_RAWLEY: It's just a discussion document – I'd really value your thoughts.

Oh, what a pain in the arse the woman was. Belinda smiled and nodded in the special way she reserved for the very young or the senile. Nonetheless, she found herself oddly disarmed.

'I see,' she said, stiffly, and, 'well in that case,' before brusquely snatching the document from Pat's outstretched head-pincer.

(The woman was even accessorising now! Where the fuck had she got that from – Ebay? Hmmm, obviously she needed to have a word with her about surfing the net during office hours…)

Belinda's eyes flashed side-to-side over the page, hunting as a pig for truffles amongst dead leaves. At first she could not find what she was looking for and her heart lurched with panic as the cold sense of potential inferiority chilled her insides. She felt a faint fizzing across her cheeks as Pat's quizzical face politely watched her own. A wave of radioactive heat: the combined force of all the faces in the room – all two of them – swelled over her. She felt on the brink of exposure, like a figure in a dream, suddenly looking down and realising that she was wearing nothing but one of Alan's old cricketing jock-straps. Her eyelids fluttered feebly as a moth fighting the surface of a cold cup of tea. Rather like the moth presently struggling on the cup of tea sitting forgotten on her desk.

Belinda stood clutching the report, trying to collect the scattered troops of her mind.

'Look who's talking,' she heard a familiar voice say, somewhere under the eaves of her consciousness, 'Hark at her, thinks she bloody knows it all – little Miss Feminism over there – Don't you know I'm a powerful respected figure? Oh why was I denied a son! Why? Who now can I look upon to pick up my silver salver?'

(This, of course, was a reference to the silver-plated serving dish, presented to her father by the Frozen Food Society in recognition of a lifetime of achievement in summer pudding manufacturing, uttered from behind a creaseless copy of the *Daily Telegraph* – ironed by her mother, with the setting on delicate.)

It could be, at this point, you are beginning to feel some vague stirrings of pity for Belinda. Bad childhood. Neglected by her father. Perhaps she is starting to pass worryingly from out-and-out villain, to a rather more sympathetic character. A *Victim* even. Is the relentless egotism, selfishness and general meanness towards Pat about to give way to more earnest ramblings about Belinda's inner life: her needs, wants and emotions? Could she be reclaimed as a Feminist icon? The overlooked martyr, whose man-eating ways may be viewed as a political statement in this 'man-munch-man' world.

The simple answer is no.

Feel free to write discursive essays if you wish, but for the record, let it be revealed, through the omniscience of fiction, that Belinda was destined to be a nasty piece of work from the moment the meanest and most competitive of her mother's eggs made that beautiful union with the smuggest, shallowest and most handbag obsessed of her father's sperm. (No sexism here.) Rest assured that the whole 'disappointed father' thing is just an unconvincing attempt to contextualise and give motivation for some innately mean behaviour that, no doubt, would have presented itself in other unpleasant evil ways given another upbringing.

'Are you alright? Do you want a glass of water?'

'I'm fine!' Belinda snapped in alarm.

'So, what do you think of the proposals?'

The page seemed to bulge in Belinda's trembling hands. And then she saw it. Why didn't she notice before? Her eyes settled happily on the text as a butterfly quivering upon a beautiful flower.

'Oh what a pity,' she sighed, angrily waving away the proffered glass.

'Is there a problem?'

'I take it you haven't sent this out in advance of the meeting?'

'Yes, I did.'

Belinda presented her evidence with sorrowful triumph.

'I think you'll find that the company font is Helvetica 11, *not* Arial 12.'

Belinda was gratified to note Pat's probe quiver with consternation as Belinda joyfully scoured her pen across the page and wrote 'Rewrite in Helvetica 11' in large blood-red, lacerating letters. She looked up sweetly, back on form.

'Perhaps if you are not confident of the house style you might like to consult me *first* in future?'

Belinda returned to her desk, where she fished the dead moth out of her tea and sighed back into her seat in satisfaction. Pat could do her worst, she, Belinda, could handle it.

You can't get on with people if you want to get on.

*****

Meanwhile, three floors up and several intestinal miles of corridor along, in the Insolvency and Liquidation department, Alan sat at his desk, listless and despondent, pondering his fate and that of the tree.

It seemed that they were both – to varying extents – in for the chop.

He related to the tree. But it wasn't even that simple. It wasn't something he cared to admit to, but the tree had started talking to him.

It had started with the odd emotive word – 'Help' or 'Save me', that sort of thing. That he could live with. Evidence of a guilty conscience on his part, or too much identification with the out-of-date, about-to-be-disposed-of leaf-laden one? Perhaps. But increasingly, the tree had become more ambitious with its monologues, extemporising on the subject of the rationalisation of its own existence.

'Do you realise,' it riffed one morning over Alan's jug of weak coffee, 'that I am not just a tree, not just one single organic life-form, one more greenhouse effect rectifying ed-I-face. I AM the environment.'

Or later over a mid-morning iced bun: 'I am the life, I am the power, I am the healer, I am the giver. There are over 500,000 lives depend-ent on my ex-ist-ence – what do you think of that, brother? Hey man, give me life, oh give me life. Raise your hands, man. Look at the sun! I am the past, I am the future, look over your shoulder brother, look out for the reaper, brother, look for the reaper, yeah man.'

Alan tried his best to ignore this invasion of the relatively empty space that was normally the inside of his head. At the best of times, all he had rattling about in there were a few serial numbers of gadgets he was interested in, some names and places with which to strategically pepper his conversation, and an altogether understandable obsession with iced buns.

Now the newcomer, finding the flat empty, had moved in, possessions and all, and had assumed squatting rights. Why it had such an annoying, hippyish way of talking, Alan could not fathom. He simply did not believe his subconscious was capable of coming up with such an idiom.

But it would not go away.

'Yo bro!' it yelled one morning, in a friendly fashion.

'Leave me alone,' said Alan, trying to disappear into his coffee cup.

'Look at my branches man!' crooned the tree, waving them around a bit. Alan looked up and was momentarily lost in the dappled patches of winter sun.

'I don't know why you're picking on me,' Alan complained. 'I'm not the least bit interested in horticulture and have never pretended to be environmentally friendly in my life.'

'Feel my ox-y-gen. Breathe me in, *compadre*, breathe me fucking in!'

Alan breathed.

'What are you drinking that muck for anyhow?' asked the tree, disapprovingly.

'What, this?' Alan raised his jug.

'Think of all that nasty brown yuck on your insides man. You don't need caffeine. You need the soothing hand of Mother Nature, man. Have you ever thought about getting away for a bit?'

Now Alan, sofa-lubber that he was, was not the kind of guy who generally considered the soothing anything of Mother Nature. So he assumed, rationally enough, that he was going mad. You might have thought this a natural assumption to make in the circumstances of a large be-twigged organic life-form suddenly striking up a conversation about your summer hols. What he didn't realise was that he was not going mad at all, but was experiencing an exciting hitherto undiscovered phenomenon of reverse-meditative telepathy: something the tree just chanced upon as a by-product of its recent conversion to Buddhism. Had he known this, Alan could have become a very rich man. But he didn't. So he couldn't.

Instead, he told himself he was being silly, irrational, *sentimental* even. Perhaps he needed a break from work. From life.

Thinking about it now as he looked around his office at the other strained blue shirts, the unnatural lighting, the unnaturally controlled air conditioning, Malcolm and Anthony giggling over something or other on Anthony's screensaver.

He looked out the window, straight into another office window – my God when had he last noticed the sterility of his existence?

And he thought of Paula, only for the briefest of seconds. But in that briefest of seconds he felt just the tiniest hint of regret.

He got up from his desk.

This couldn't be it. Couldn't be all there was. Could it?

Staggering like a drunk man, he lurched out into the striplit eternity of the Liquidation corridor and set off, slaloming his way past the regular water coolers that punctuated the corridor at standard intervals, until he crashed into one. For a beautiful moment, it looked as though Alan and the cooler had fallen in love as the two swayed perilously for a while, in close embrace. Finally, they disentangled and stood on their own feet, looking at each other, breathing heavily. He was so busy staring at the cooler breathing heavily that he hadn't noticed where he was. He heard the click of the disabled toilet opening and a low electronic hum. Alan stood, transfixed by the sight of the wheelchair.

He looked up, his eyes locked in Pat's appraising gaze.

Beautiful woman. Disabled toilet. It all felt strangely familiar.

Chapter Fifteen | THE INSPECTION

'I'm not sure it's very me,' a dubious Paula addressed the be-sequinned, feather-draped vision in powder blue before her in the dressing-table mirror. 'Isn't it a bit...' she struggled hard to be tactful, '...drag queen?'

'Nonsense,' said Luda briskly. 'You're just unaccustomed to true style, that's all.'

When they saw her the others agreed.

'I can't believe it. It's Robert Pigeon all over again!' cried Dave, looking visibly moved.

They were in one of the club's private playrooms where Luda had rushed them all excitedly to display her protégé.

Paula would hardly have recognised Gretchen in her leather miniskirt, metal-spiked bustier and cruelly studded knuckleduster as the same tie-dyed hippy preaching peace and love at The Walnut Tree Café, had not closer attention revealed the separation in her cocktail glass and the creaking of her miniskirt: tell-tale signs of soya milk and leather-effect plastic.

Paula had never actually set foot in one of the club playrooms before and couldn't keep the look of wonder from her face. This room had a padded theme with peculiar upholstered PVC walls and a red rubber floor which made her head swim. Rubber and PVC were both popular fetish materials – the look, the smell – plus the added convenience of being wipeable, which was always a bonus. At the centre of the ceiling the now-expected glitterball spun slowly, a leftover from a job lot that had been ordered in – Betsy and Ron had a deep fondness for glitterballs. Arranged around the centre of the room were various scary-looking items of equipment: a strange insectile table, with wrist and ankle restraints built in, reminiscent of the one upon which she had gone through her nose ravishing ordeal, and at the back of the room, a large revolving wheel to which, much to Paula's consternation, an inhabitant remained strapped upside-down with a hood over his face and a couple of savage-looking nipple clamps attached to his chest.

'We seem to have company,' Paula pointed out shyly, sitting down on a pink plastic-covered, machine-washable PVC pouffe.

'Oh that's just SlaveBoy,' Gretchen said. 'We were in the middle of – well, never mind. We had stopped for a break, anyway.' And she extracted an ice cube from her soya drink and ran it down SlaveBoy's inner thigh.

'Agghhhhhh!'

'Just to keep him happy,' she smiled.

'Enough of that. Show them your décolletage!' said Luda excitedly, clawing at Paula's cleavage. 'You wouldn't believe the difficulty I've had convincing her of the importance of a lady's décolletage.'

'Oh you look lovely,' sighed Gretchen, wistfully. 'Reminds me of a young Danny La Rue.'

The others 'oohed' and 'ahhed' excitedly.

It remained for The Masked Man to break the spell. Resplendent in his habitual black mask and birthday suit, he stepped forward.

'Am I missing the point here? I thought we said *femme fatale*? I thought we were going for the unobtainable goddess, the woman of mystery. Since when has Danny La Rue been considered a suitable role model for such a person?'

There was a brief confused pause.

Dave put a restraining hand on Luda's bulging tensed arm.

The Masked Man continued relentlessly. 'I think you've got the wrong end of the stick. Before us we have a beautiful woman, demanding to be satisfied, calling out to be worshipped. Paula doesn't have to *pretend* to be a woman. She *is* a woman. We need to release her. The inner woman. Her inner sexuality. That's all.'

Paula caught herself leaning forward slightly as though floating on the force of his words, which hung in the air between them. As he finished speaking she realised her mouth too was swinging open and shut it with a snap.

The club members looked at each other in thought.

Luda carefully unfolded her right hook and let it drop feebly by her side before turning to her charge and giving her the critical once-over.

'I can see where you're coming from…' she conceded. 'But, there's only so much you can do with the raw material.'

The Masked Man walked towards Paula. 'I don't think you could improve upon the raw material.'

Paula felt a shiver ripple across her raised shoulders. She was good raw material. She, *Paula*, was good raw material.

'She doesn't need all this stuff,' he said gently, taking a baby wet-wipe from Luda's bag and, with some difficulty, attempting to excavate a small port-hole in the layer of thick orange putty obscuring her face.

Paula felt her knees tremble. She was not used to this level of attention.

'Luda,' The Man in the Mask continued. 'This isn't Robert Pigeon. You don't need to hide anything. Look at her skin. Clear, smooth...'

He continued to chip away at the foundation that had solidified like volcanic crust on her face. She could not bring herself to look at him. She knew she was blushing.

'Okay, okay!' Luda quickly interjected her short thick body between Paula and The Man in the Mask. 'She's my pupil not yours okay? Alright, so maybe she needs a bit of toning down.' (She said 'toning down' as one might utter the name of a kitten-murdering paedophile.) 'But give us a fucking chance. It's all in the fine-tuning. We can sort it out in the edit.'

The Man in the Mask stood back, his eyes holding Paula's, and let the baby wet-wipe fall from his hand. She could not bear it any longer, and let her gaze fall – she forgot he was wearing no clothes – then quickly raised her eyes again to settle on his hands. Nice hands.

'I have faith!' cried Dave, needlessly and dramatically.

Luda sent him an irritated look (the kind of look that secretly made Dave squirm with joy).

'And I think she looks lovely,' said Gretchen, pinging one of SlaveBoy's nipple clamps. ('Agghhh!') 'But perhaps you're right and Danny La Rue isn't quite the right vibe.'

'We need to test her out,' said Dave. 'We need to try her out with an objective party. To see if she passes.' He was breathless and pleased with himself. Besides, Luda's attention was making him bold.

'We did that already,' said Luda.

'Passes? As what exactly? A drag queen?' said The Man in the Mask. 'Extra marks if she actually gets mistaken for a man? She IS a woman. Why do you lot have such difficulty with that concept?'

'You don't have to be so withering,' Dave said, hurt.

The Man in the Mask, who had puffed his cheeks out in annoyance, released them in a wheeze of resignation. 'Look, we're losing sight of our goal here,' he said. 'Try and keep in mind why we are doing this.'

'To bring out Paula's femininity,' said Luda.

'To turn her into a woman,' Dave said.

'To make Alan jealous!' said The Man in the Mask in frustration.

'Oh yeah,' Dave said. 'I forgot about that part.'

Paula looked from one face to another.

'We're trying to get them back together,' said The Man in the Mask. 'Not coach a finalist for a Tranny of the Year competition.'

Luda chewed her cheek while Dave examined his chipped nail varnish.

It was up to Gretchen to take up the mantle of peacemaker once more, from where she was sitting on her haunches, attaching some disturbing-looking electrical equipment to SlaveBoy's nipple-clamps. 'Now, now, give over chucks –'

'Agghh!' The sweat trickled down SlaveBoy's upside-down neck.'

'– let's not fight.'

'Ow ow ow!'

'You're both right.'

They stared at her, ignoring SlaveBoy's shrieks: *What was she talking about?*

'George here is quite right, obviously. But our Dave's also onto something. You gotta ask yourself, what better way of making Alan jealous than Paula stepping out with another man?'

They continued to stare at her, but with their expressions morphing from irritation to inspiration.

'There's nowt like someone else wanting a thing to make you want the same. It's human nature. Besides, Paula could do with a bit of spoiling. She's looking right pale and peaky.'

They all looked at Paula to check this fact for themselves, but as Paula presently resembled a radioactive tangerine, they had to take Gretchen's word for it.

'Do you know anyone?' Gretchen asked Paula. 'Who'd be prepared to go out with you for an evening? Take you out for a bit of a road test? Any exes?' she prompted, as Paula continued to stare at her.

Luda turned to the assembled company. 'See. Of course there isn't. Or else why would she need our services?'

Luda hastily brushed past their uncertainty at this question. 'Well, anyway, there's no one who'd go out with her.'

Paula looked at her feet, breathing hard.

The Man in the Mask, who had retreated to the other side of the room and was now sat, legs swinging, on the insectile table, looked up. Sparkles from the glitterball played across his face. He looked naked and vulnerable all of a sudden, and not just in the usual way. He opened his mouth.

'Perhaps I – I – I m-m-might…' He stopped, appearing to be fighting something at the back of his throat.

'There *is* someone,' said a small voice.

They turned to look at the speaker. The speaker was still scrutinising her feet as if unaware of their attention bearing down upon her, but her shoulders, in their usual and by this time expected response, gave her away by flying at once to her ears, causing Luda to purse her mouth in disapproval. The Man in the Mask stopped fighting whatever it was at the back of his throat and swallowed hard.

'Who? Who?' the words flew out of Luda's grim mouth like fighter jets.

'Anthony,' Paula said.

Luda threw up her arms and turned towards the others in a gesture that said something along the lines of, 'Well, she could have bloody said, what was the point of all that hard work I've been putting in if she's got a sodding boyfriend already, eh? Eh? EH?'

'He's a colleague of Alan's,' said Paula. 'From work,' she added, unnecessarily.

'Even better!' cried Luda, 'If we get his bloody workmate interested − that's going to make you EVEN MORE unattainable, make Alan EVEN MORE jealous.'

'If you pass with his work colleague…' said Dave, knowingly. They waited for him to finish the sentence but he just continued to nod wisely and then added a couple of *Mmm*s for good measure.

'How did you meet this person?'

Paula was too busy feeling awkward to hear the sad note in the Masked Man's voice.

'Umm.' She thought about the question and realised it was a tricky one to answer. 'We − err… We met at − an art installation,' she said, in a sudden burst of inspiration.

Thankfully Luda was causing such a rumpus stumping up and down complaining that no one seemed to notice Paula's prior hesitation.

'How nice,' said Gretchen. SlaveBoy gurgled up happily from his headlock.

Paula smiled, tiredly. She had been up since 5.30am, after all.

'Okay,' said Luda. 'We're going to have to put some more work into this.'

Paula winced internally.

'We might as well think big, aim for the top. After all, what have we got to lose?'

Pride? Thought Paula. *Confidence? Self-esteem?*

'I think you should go the whole hog.'

'And what's that?' asked Gretchen.

'Get him to propose.'

'What?' said Paula, for no other reason than to remind her faint body that she was still there.

'Why not? That's sure to piss off Alan.'

'I hardly know him.'

'Even better,' said Luda. 'He'd never propose once he got to know you.'

'It'd take months – years.'

'Don't you believe it,' Luda said, grimly, 'I thought this might come in handy one day.' And she extracted a book called *How to Get That Sparkly Ring on Your Third Finger on the First Date* from her bag.

'Remember, you are a *femme fatale* now – this is the kind of thing *femme fatales* do.'

Paula hid her eyes with her fingers.

'It's up to you to spin the magic,' Luda said. 'Well, what are you waiting for?' she demanded. 'Get your finger out. Give him a call.'

Chapter Sixteen | THE DATE

The others did not know where Luda had managed to find the van or what clue the words 'James McKay Builders' spelt out on the side held to her other life. Neither did they dare to ask as the large rolling side-door was opened with a belligerent scowl, as if daring them to speak. They all knew better.

In they bundled: Dave, looking very fetching in an A-line green skirt and blouse; Gretchen in one of what she liked to call her 'customised second-hand originals' – a shapeless garment of no fixed colour, material or purpose; Conan, in jeans and a T-shirt that read, 'I'm not a lesbian but my girlfriend is,' ('Subverting from within,' he clarified mysteriously, their polite smiles giving way to mystified eyebrow exchanges as soon as he disappeared into the back of the van), and lastly Luda herself in a glamorous silver dress and shoes: 'Just in case.'

'We're missing someone,' she said, drilling her heels on the metal floor like a timpani-player. She squinted at her watch through contact-lenseless eyes. 'Well, ladies and gentlemen, we have a deadline to meet. So –' she jumped through to the front of the van, 'Hit it, Dave!'

Dave threw his stiletto to the floor and the car took off.

'There he is,' shouted Gretchen, as a small grey figure appeared at the mouth of the cobbled lane.

'Run SlaveBoy, run!'

The small figure cascaded down the street after them. Conan and Gretchen threw open the double doors followed by suppliant arms. SlaveBoy, his body wondering if it should throw a spanner in the works by having a heart attack there and then, hurled his briefcase into the van with a roar, or at least a whimper, and himself after, like a small be-suited Jackie Chan – if Chan were very unfit and knew nothing about martial arts.

They all cheered.

'Wait! We've forgotten someone!'

With a squeak of the brakes the small van came to a halt and rapidly reversed up the cobbled street again. Gretchen, SlaveBoy and Dave jumped out.

'You alright there, Marcus?' croaked Luda, as the three lugged the inflatable blue form past the bins, over the cobbles and in through the sliding door. Marcus wiggled a finger.

'We're in,' SlaveBoy gasped.

'Then hit it, Dave!' cried Luda excitedly, as she had enjoyed saying it so much the first time. And with that, the white van careered out of the cobbled street with a squeal of wheels and a parting puff of black exhaust.

After they had been sitting at their final destination for at least forty minutes, the initial excitement of pretending they were in the car chase sequence of an action-adventure movie began to wear off. Things in the back of the van began to get less than friendly.

'Can't I have a go?' said Gretchen.

'Shhhhhh!' hissed Luda. 'Do you think I can tell what's going on with you gas-bagging on?'

'We've been here ages!'

'You have to be prepared. If there's one thing I learned from scouts it was that,' said Dave.

'Ow! You stood on me!' (That was Gretchen.)

'Can't we get any heat in the back here, Dave? I'm freezing.' (And SlaveBoy.)

'Well, why don't you put your fucking suit back on then?'

'I am relaxing! Ooh I feel a spot of naughtiness coming on.'

'Day off, SlaveBoy.' (Gretchen again.)

'Oh come on, it's me you're talking to. You could at least try jamming me in the door.'

'Someone would see!'

'A spot of foot worship?'

'Leave her alone, SlaveBoy!' (Luda)

'I'm bored!' (Conan)

'Put a fucking sock in it back there!' (Guess.)

(Dave): 'Anyone want a bite of tuna sandwich?'

Things were threatening to get out of hand, when Luda, who had spent the last forty minutes bent over some impressive-looking audio apparatus, furiously hitting buttons and twiddling knobs, held up a hairy hand.

'Shhhhhhhhhhhhhhhhhhhhhhhhhhh! I think I'm getting something!'

The others subsided into muted mutterings and cellophane crumplings (that was the sandwich), straining to make sense of the ghostly whirrings and shushings of Luda's machine.

'What are we listening for?' Conan asked. Luda shhed him with her hand.

'Ooo,' Gretchen said, happily, putting down her knitting. She had relented and was allowing her foot to be worshipped out of hours by SlaveBoy. 'This reminds me of the last séance I went to. We had to listen to this crackling tape for hours hoping to catch voices from the spirit world. You can hear them chattering in the white noise, you see.'

'Mmmmmfff,' said SlaveBoy, getting to work on her second metatarsal.

'I couldn't hear anything at first, and then after five hours and a couple of glasses of this special drink that helps amplify your aura I definitely heard someone say, Shhhhh-shhhhhhhhhhhh-Shhhhhhhhhh'

'Shhhhhhhhh?'

'I know! I was very excited.' Gretchen's voice dropped to a menacing hush. 'The medium suggested that what they were actually saying was "six" as in "six six six."'

'Maybe they were playing bingo and they wanted you to zip it,' Conan said.

'That's right, laugh if you want to, if that makes you feel better,' she said. 'But I tell you, the spirits are out there. And if we are going to meddle in the portals of the supernatural, then we can't be surprised when –'

'Shut up you lot,' interjected Luda rudely. 'I think I have something.'

They paused again, straining to hear something, anything, amidst the cackles and crackles of Luda's radio waves. They all sat completely still, their carefully arranged expressions masking the chill that passed across them like a Mexican wave at the thought of Beelzebub suddenly tuning in for a gossip.

The cackles and hisses rose and fell, and for a moment they heard a million lost souls chattering in that other sphere, before the hissing and crackling coalesced into a nasty crescendo of babbling. Then loud and clear they heard a terrible laugh, a laugh of the devil, a terrible braying devilish laugh, a laugh that conjured images of donkeys disappearing round U-bends...

They all looked at each other.

Paula had not seen Anthony since what she now thought of as The Fateful Wall Day. She had spoken to him on the phone on a couple of occasions, fending off invitations to dinner and an exhibition called, 'Soft Art: A History of the Semi-pornographic Nude in Western Civilisation.' The nature of the Smith-Brown building being as it was, their paths had never actually crossed at work, although she had caught sight of him once in the office canteen, when he had failed to acknowledge her.

As far as Anthony was concerned he had never set eyes on Paula either before or since the Fateful Wall Day. In fact, unbeknownst to Anthony, his retinae had received Paula's image on many occasions: the drab ghost flitting down the office corridors, the instantly forgettable figure hidden at the back of meetings, the pale form hesitating over a tuna wrap in the office canteen. But these images made little impression on him at the time. Indeed, so little impression was made, that the journey from the optic nerve to the primary visual cortex was never even completed. At least, not until the Fateful Wall Day when not only did Paula's image successfully reach its destination, but overshot it by a mile

– straight to the groin.

Paula did not strictly-speaking know this last point, but was beginning to get a pretty good idea from the way Antony was leering at her.

'I was pleased you called,' he said, massaging a breadstick seductively between his thumb and forefinger. 'You look different somehow, I can't put my finger on it.'

'Is it the clothes, maybe?' Paula turned in her chair to better show off Luda's latest recommendation.

'Of course! You weren't wearing any last time, were you? Better off, I'd say.'

'Spaghetti Carbonara. Linguini Marinara,' said a harsh voice.

The waitress, who apart from the black hair was a dead ringer for Barbra Streisand, plonked their food down between them with perfunctory grace and stood aside indifferently, brandishing a large pepper mill.

Paula nodded. The condiment was briskly dispatched with a couple of ruthless crunches on the grinder.

The waitress turned her back on them with Latin contempt and left them to their meal.

Anthony shovelled up a forkful of the Linguini. 'So what's next in the pipeline?'

'Sorry?'

'Art-wise.'

'Art, yes. Of course. Umm. The next project is currently in development.'

'Will it involve nudity?' he asked excitedly.

'I don't think so.'

'Oh.' He sounded disappointed. 'But it could?'

'I – '

'It could be your motif, your signature style.'

Paula had never realised being an artist could be such hard work. She gave up trying and smiled faintly instead.

'Listen, I had an idea for you, bear with me – you'll like this. I thought you could get all these takeaway foods – you know, Chinese, Indian…spagboll – then you get naked and smear them all over your smooth, sexy body. What do you think?'

'Sorry?'

'As a comment on multi-culturalism.'

'Oh.'

'Alan told me you do a lot of wall-work,' Anthony said, sucking up his Linguini Marinara in a fountain of tomato.

'Alan talks about me?' Paula's heart skipped a beat.

'Not much.'

And regained it again.

'Said you met at the Tate Modern.'

'Oh.'

'And you agreed to do some work for him.'

'Oh. Right.'

So eight years of cohabitation didn't get a mention, then.

Anthony looked up at her from under his eyebrows. 'To be honest, I was probably being a bit heavy-handed, pumping him for info. I was trying to get your number, see? Man Wolf says you should grasp the moment if you meet a SHBB6.5.'

'SHBB6.5?'

'Super Hot Bunny Babe.'

'What does the 6.5 stand for?'

'Out of ten'

'Oh.'

'6.5's pretty good!'

'Right.'

Anthony continued to stare into her eyes. 'Anyway, Alan said he didn't know you that well and you were probably a lesbian. But I'm not the sort of bloke who is easily put off by that sort of thing.'

Paula hid her face in her spaghetti. That Alan should so casually brush aside the life they had lived together as if it had never been... As if he had always worn pinstripes. As if his flat had always been taupe. She tried to pull herself together and concentrate her mind on the task in hand. Whatever she was supposed to be doing, she was pretty sure a long succession of '*oh*'s wasn't it. She was supposed to be feeding Anthony information to make Alan jealous. She tried to think of all the things going well in her life that she could boast about.

The long and oppressive silence was finally broken by Anthony who said, 'You alright, old girl?'

Paula looked down at her serviette lying surrendered on her lap.

'I'm sorry, I'm not very good at this sort of thing.'

He stared deep into her eyes, 'That's alright. I'm used to taking a lead in these situations,' before launching into a no-holds-barred, lose-the-will-to-live monologue on the subject of...himself. Confusingly, he kept mentioning this 'Man Wolf' character. Paula was not too sure who 'Man Wolf' was, but nodded and smiled as seemed appropriate.

In the van, Luda took everyone by surprise by kicking out at one of the metal doors in frustration. 'She's forgotten everything I taught her, everything.' (Dave's comforting hand on her forearm was thrown off.) 'He's never going to propose to her at this rate.'

'He seems pretty keen.'

'Bah!' Luda said. 'He won't be as soon as he realises he's sitting opposite the most boring woman since…since…whoever she is, she is so boring I can't even think who she could possibly be.'

'I expect you are wondering what a guy like me is doing still single?' Anthony said suddenly, leaning back and wiping his mouth, leaving a long trail of tomato on his serviette.

Paula had not really been wondering this but nodded politely.

To her horror, he took this as his cue for an excruciatingly detailed account of his love life and the succession of ungrateful and misguided women he had *never* been out with.

The trouble was, Paula thought, the more time she spent with Anthony, the more she ended up thinking of Alan. Silly things. The way what hair he had left stood up on end in the morning, two knobbly legs sticking out of a pair of boxer shorts, padding to the bathroom, the dog-like snuffles that he insisted were NOT snores, the annoying way he declared 'Home James' every time they got in the car, even if they were not going home. That's what Luda didn't understand about love, she thought to herself. It was not about heroes and heroines, *femme fatales* and movie stars. It wasn't about sweeping generalities – dark brooding heroes with flashing eyes and strong chiselled countenances. It was about the small eccentric specifics: the particular feel of somebody's familiar buttocks shuffling back into yours in the morning. It was about tug'o'wars with the duvet, shoving each other out of bed, squabbling over who got the last of the coffee and who was relegated to the business section of the newspaper; pouring over sudokus and crosswords together (her doing the anagrams and anything requiring knowledge of the periodic table, him remembering the odd bit of useful Latin from school), it was about being able to share someone else's toothbrush, chat to them on the toilet, attempt to pick their spots while they are lying in the bath and getting angrily chased out of the bathroom for your pains. It was about the precise feel, the sound, the warm sleeping smell of a body so familiar to you that you could shut your eyes and almost feel their breath on your face. Paula closed her eyes. Was she going mad?

('She is mad, that one, no?' said Barbra Streisand, from where she stood in the doorway, blowing a nonchalant plume of smoke out onto the street – her husband bouncing beside her out of sheer restless Italianness on his new airsoled trainers.

'It will all end in tragedy, tragedy. Someone will die. I feel it in my –' she banged on her chest passionately. 'Here, I feel it.'

Fabio looked at her sideways through thick black eyelashes. He looked back at the strange woman sitting silently at the window, staring vacantly past her animated colleague. So odd, so eccentric the English, with their strange little understated ways. All that small-scale idiosyncratic peculiarity reigned in under a brittle veneer of unimpassioned politeness. No wonder they were all perverts and paedophiles.

'Bah! She needs a good fuck,' he said simply, then 'Oof!' as the packet of Camel Lights hit him in the chest.)

…Then let her be mad, if to love is mad, to feel is mad!

She opened her eyes again. Really, Anthony was not a bad-looking man, if you liked that louche, floppy-haired, buggered-

235

at–Rugby sort of thing. She looked at his mouth. Incredibly, it was still moving.

'I mean – alright – it was an office dress-down day, but it's still important to demonstrate taste and moderation and attention to detail. The whole point of dress-down day is to show how serious you are about your work even on your day off. I don't go in for it myself. I might loosen my tie a bit but that's about as far as I'll go. But red braces and polka dot shorts? Horrible mistake. Horrible. Seemed to think it was funny, but what decent accountancy firm can trust his judgement after that? Bang went his promotion. Tragic, really.'

It was the first time she had been out on a date since that day all those years ago when Alan, just an ordinary bespectacled accountant, as he was then, tripped up with his tray in the Smith-Brown cafeteria and landed face-first in Paula's bosom (aided by a little helpful anticipation from Paula herself).

But Paula was no longer that same quiet yet determinedly manipulative twenty-eight-year-old of nearly a decade before. It was all she could do to try and keep her objective for the evening in view. Her mentor's voice karate-kicked into her mind:

'Be enigmatic about your past, present and future.'

'If he asks anything personal, turn away with a faraway look in your eyes so he gets the impression you are a woman hiding a wealth of emotion.'

'Only let him see you in left profile, your nose is fucked on the right.'

She tried presenting her left profile with the faraway look in her eyes of a woman hiding a wealth of emotion, but unfortunately Anthony seemed too engrossed in relaying the details of his first promotion, to notice either her attempts at enigmatic melancholia or how handsome her nose appeared from that particular angle.

So, instead, she concentrated on nodding. A lot. And touching her hair: the last refuge of the *femme fatale*.

'Alan and Belinda are doing well,' said Anthony suddenly, filling his mouth with wine. 'Looks like there might be some news on that front soon.' And he winked.

'What do you mean?' she asked slightly more sharply than she intended. She did not like the look of that wink. Not at all.

'*A-ha*!' Anthony touched his nose in an irritating manner. He had been doing this a lot, Paula had noticed. She had thought maybe he had a spot.

'*A-ha*?'

'*A-ha*!' He sat back looking chuffed and disappeared importantly behind the wine list. 'Waiter!' he called, grandly, 'Another bottle of house red for the lady if you please.'

'What kind of answer is *a-ha*?' Paula was meanwhile saying, forgetting about hiding a wealth of emotion in her annoyance. He really was getting on her nerves now.

Anthony peered over the top of his menu with some surprise.

'You like it really,' he said, in crestfallen tones. 'All women do. Man Wolf would say…' He stopped.

Paula stared at him, annoyed. 'Who is this Man Wolf you keep mentioning?'

Anthony shifted in his seat. An attempt to take refuge behind the wine list was cut short by Paula's snatching it from his hand.

'Sorry, can't divulge that particular piece of information,' he said. 'Need-to-know basis, only.'

'*I* need to know,' said Paula, giving him a hard stare.

Anthony looked about him for some means of escape. But there was none. 'But I swore, a pledge. We all have to… If we divulge the secrets of the brotherhood…'

Paula's glare prompted him.

'We forfeit all right to call ourselves…' he trailed off miserably.

Idly curious as she was, Paula was not that concerned with the laddish ramblings of Anthony's macho Internet chums. But the terror on his face exposed an opportunity to find out what she really wanted to know.

'Tell me about Alan, then,' she said.

'What?'

'Tell me about Alan or else I will tell every woman I know about your dating guru.'

'My…my… But you can't possibly know…' He goggled at her.

'Can you take that chance?' She nodded meaningfully.

'You're bluffing, you must be.'

Of course she was, but seeing the fear in his eyes, Paula pressed home her advantage.

'I'll tell every woman in your acquaintance. I'll circulate it round your office. You think any advance to any woman is going anywhere after that?'

'You wouldn't! Why? Why would you do that?'

Paula was suddenly intensely distracted by her own nails.

'Oh I don't know. Jealousy maybe?'

He perked up, then.

'Unable to control my animalistic lust?'

'Really?'

She looked at him. 'Not really.'

'Oh.' He dropped his head, crestfallen.

'But you never know…' she mused, idly doodling with her

fork. 'Feelings are complicated things…'

He was leaning so far forward now he looked as though he was about to fall face-first in the entrails of his dinner. Instead, he dug into his breast pocket and produced a small card, which he held out, starry-eyed. 'Don't say anything.' He looked round furtively. 'This…fell…out of Alan's desk.'

Paula flicked the card over in her fingers.

Dr Marshall Addams.

——

Younger, tighter, tauter, bigger.

Paula frowned. 'I don't understand. Is it prostitution?'

'Good God no! Do you think anyone's going to worry about a bit of good old wholesome professional hanky-panky? No, Paula. This is hardcore.'

Ever since the wall incident, it had been clear that Anthony was not the sharpest tool in the box. But Paula completely failed to see what he was hinting at.

'It's a plastic surgeon.'

'I still don't understand.'

'Don't you see? She must be preggers. That's how they do it these days. Pop the puppy out and get rid of the spare tyre at the same time. Jolly efficient way to do it too, if you ask me.'

Paula was too deep in thought to answer him. This was a blow.

A big blow. It was one thing taking back what was rightfully hers; it was quite another wrenching a father from his own flesh and blood.

'You better not tell anyone or there'll be all hell to pay. Belinda's not the kind of woman I'd want knowing that I was the one to spill the beans before her big day. Mind you, she'd better get on with it. She's not the kind of woman to take advantage of the wonderful range of maternity brideswear they have on offer these days either – size 16-32, all colours and styles.'

Paula did not think to wonder how Anthony should know such information, but sat turning the card over and over in her hands.

Reaching for her pocket, she found none. (Nothing Luda put her in ever had pockets ('interferes with your figure, dahrling – quickest way I know of putting on half a stone'). So she carefully stowed the card away in her handbag ('*Pochette*! Oh get it right!').

She looked up straight into the cornflower blue eyes of Anthony Hossier.

'God, you're a fascinating woman,' he said, evidently struck.

('Now! Here's your chance!' yelled Luda over the whirr of the van heater.)

'I'm not,' said Paula sadly. 'That's the trouble.'

'Men,' says Luda's book, authoritatively, 'want you to be vulnerable, helpless, weak, the sort of woman they can look after, will make them feel the size of their muscles and their general all-round potency. But no man really wants a woman who is vulnerable helpless, weak. So cry over the slightest thing, but make sure it IS the slightest thing, and not a real problem, or he may start to worry that you are indeed vulnerable, helpless, weak, the sort of

woman that he will have to put a lot of effort into looking after — the last thing any normal bloke wants to do. Alternatively, be the kind of woman who shouts and threatens to leave, and then initiates sex.' (from How to Get that Sparkly Ring on Your Third Finger on the First Date *by Lorin L'Amour.)*

'I cry at Lassie,' said Paula.

Winded, Anthony sat back in his seat. 'Steady on,' he said. He narrowed his eyes. 'You're not one of those women looking for the old sparkly rock for the old third finger are you?'

Paula laughed nervously.

He lifted his glass and crashed it chummily against hers. 'Thank God for that. Because, I tell you, no one's tying this playboy down. I don't cry easily, myself,' he added, taking a sip. 'Boarding school hardens one to life's knocks. I cried when we lost the Ashes, mind. That was a toughie.' His bottom lip trembled. 'I like to think of it as a character building experience…'

Whether this beautiful moment of connection could have been the start of a whole new beautifully connected kind of relationship, we shall never know, as the possibility was wiped out, once and for all, by the arrival of Luda who chose that moment to crash into the room much as a charging rhinoceros might crash through the doors of a small quiet Italian restaurant.

It was the reference to Lassie that did it.

'Oh for Christ's sake!' Luda had cried. And, with that, she was struggling out of her headphones and reaching for the van doors.

'What are you doing?' said a panicky Dave, trying to stop her.

'Femme fatale my fucking arse!'

With a parting cry of, 'If you want to do a thing properly you have to do it your bloody self!' the doors were wrenched open and Luda was gone.

'Oh no, oh no,' Dave panicked quietly to himself. He flustered about the van for a bit, tidying crisp packets and half a tuna fish sandwich into an old carrier bag, tying the corners neatly together. Then he could not think what to do next. So he closed up the van doors and decided to listen to his iPod for a while instead.

'Dave?'

'Yeah.'

'Can we go and get something to eat?'

He turned towards the group of bored faces behind him.

'It's cold in here.'

'We're hungry,' added Conan.

'I'm not,' said SlaveBoy, through a mouthful of toe.

Having crashed into the restaurant with such spectacular force, it presently dawned on Luda that every pair of eyes in the room was trained expectantly upon her. She quickly composed herself, drawing in her portly carriage and tripping delicately towards a table in the centre of the room, where she proceeded to position herself daintily on the edge of a chair.

'Have you a menu please?' she cooed in a voice that contained more than a hint of Southern Belle. She retired behind it modestly and, using it as a fan, peeked surreptitiously over the top at Paula and Anthony who ruined the effect somewhat by staring directly at her. Rumbled, Luda slapped down her menu with a sigh.

'Paula!' she cried, as though Paula's presence had only just impinged on her consciousness. 'How wonderful! What are you doing here?' She gave a little hop and was on her feet again, teetering sweetly towards them. Paula's blood flew to her cheeks, her shoulders close behind.

Luda was unmoved. 'So dear, are you going to introduce us to your boyfriend?' she said, dipping slightly over their table and giving them both the full benefit of her 52doubleE chest.

'Dear?'

Luda shot Paula an irritated glance before leaning across – her short barrel-like body attempting to ingratiate itself with Anthony.

'You wouldn't believe she was the fruit of my loins sometimes would you?' Luda said. 'Isn't "dear" what mothers always call their daughters?' She turned her face full on towards Paula, who was goggling at her in horror. 'Look at her face, poor pet. Teenagers, they're all the same. Always embarrassed by their old Mum. Now, young lady, where are your manners? Are you not going to introduce me to this handsome young man?'

Realising she was goggling, Paula attempted to swallow her general horror at the whole situation and awkwardly extended an introductory arm. 'This is Anthony. Anthony this is –'

But Luda had already shot out one large hairy hand in excited anticipation of intimate contact with Anthony's, upon receipt of which she dipped at the knees and cooed, 'Very pleased to meet you. Oh, I am – You are tall, aren't you?'

Anthony flopped his fringe over to his other eye and puffed out his chest. 'Do you think so?'

'Oh yes,' Luda purred. 'I feel all small and feminine just standing here next to you… I can't imagine what it would feel like if you were standing up.'

Paula tried to send a look Anthony's way. But to her amazement his gaze was lost to her.

Without taking his eyes from Luda's, Anthony gallantly whipped out a chair. Luda was thrilled.

'Well thank you, young man. What a lovely young man.' She sat down and pulled her chair alongside his and, to Paula's embarrassment, squeezed his leg.

Anthony did not seem to mind, however. 'I can see the family likeness.'

'Ah, but without her youth and beauty,' Luda said, coyly.

'I've always been a bit partial to the older bird,' Anthony said, gallantly. 'Tougher to chew but more than makes up for it on the flavour. Don't worry, though – I don't bite,' he murmured, eyes brimming with 52DoubleE. 'That is, unless you want me to, of course.'

Luda bent her head coquettishly.

Could this have been a beautiful moment of connection shared by three lonely and slightly inadequate people on the road to love? Well, probably not. But, whatever strange connections were going on, again we shall never really know as the moment was shattered forever by the arrival of Dave crashing through the restaurant doors rather as a charging rhinoceros might crash, if it were a slightly put-out mild-mannered transvestite.

It was the mention of chewy older birds that did it.

'Right, that's it,' cried Dave, sweating as he struggled ineffectually with the van doors.

'Here,' said SlaveBoy, leaping out and opening them for him from the other side.

Dave was too angry to do more than nod. Which he did, before determinedly setting off towards the restaurant.

'Can we come?' yelled Conan after his resolute back. 'I'm starving!'

But he received no answer.

Dave sat down at table two and glowered at them from behind his menu. Luda twittered on at Anthony as though she had never before set eyes on the bloke in the skirt sending them dirty looks from his seat beside the cake display. Anthony, who had hardly raised his eyes from his new object of desire, continued to gaze adoringly at Luda's cleavage.

Paula quickly realised her *femme fatale* was no competition for Luda's *femmer fatale* on her right. If Paula was trying to give the impression of a woman hiding a wealth of emotion, Luda resembled a Celia Johnston impersonator who had lost her entire family in a forest fire, but still somehow found the composure to apply a full face of make-up and set her hair.

'One Tiramisu and one Black Forest Gateau.'

Paula hardly looked up as Barbra Streisand plonked the deserts down in front of them.

'You want something?' Streisand demanded of Luda, who was eyeing up Anthony's Tiramisu greedily.

'Oh, just a tap water for me,' said Luda modestly. 'I'm on a diet you see. Typical woman,' she said to Anthony.

'Nothing wrong with a bit of meat,' said Anthony appreciatively. 'More to get your teeth into.'

'More to chew!' said Luda.

They collapsed towards each other, tittering.

A smash of broken crockery sounded behind them. Paula swivelled round to see Dave's baleful face glaring at Anthony, his glass in pieces by his feet.

She turned back just in time to witness Gretchen entering the restaurant, followed by SlaveBoy and Conan, carrying Marcus like a battering ram between them. Gretchen offered up an airy wave to Paula along with a heavily mouthed: '*Just pretend we're not here*,' before pulling a 'What-you-looking-at?' face at the dozen or so customers, all of whom had let their knives and forks fall and were sat gawping at Marcus.

Paula shut her eyes – Anthony: 'That blue chap. It isn't... David Blaine, is it?' – and put her head in her hands.

It was the reference to Tiramisu that did it.

'*Right, that's it!*' *cried Conan, throwing open the van doors and racing for the restaurant, the others in hot pursuit.*

They came to a halt on the restaurant threshold.

'*Bugger. Marcus.*'

And rapidly retraced their steps.

It was clear the date was at an end.

'I think I'll be off now,' Paula said loudly, in the middle of Luda's now-so-familiar assertion that the Nissan Micra was the *only* car for a girl about town.

'Bye,' said Anthony not looking up.

Luda, locked in an eyeball embrace with Anthony, raised a hand.

Paula stood for a while waiting for something, but as she was not sure what that something was and as – whatever it was – that something was not forthcoming, she gave up and started heading for the door.

'Bye,' hissed the David Blaine contingent.

Paula collected her coat and rucksack from the door and turned for one last wave before she left. Nobody noticed. As she pushed out into the damp evening air, Paula's lasting image was of Luda and Anthony, like two stone figures petrified by love, staring into one another's eyes, against the backdrop of Dave's livid face.

Chapter Seventeen | FIRE AND CANDLE WAX

Paula ran out into the night. Actually, she did nothing of the sort, that was not her style. Rather, hunched against the rain she scurried along the side of the street in her usual unmemorable way. A woman with a buggy saw her hurrying past and thought 'woman' before moving on.

Paula did not know where she was going, just that she needed to get away. She felt strangely comforted by the falling rain. Luda's betrayal washed from her shoulders. Alan, Luda, what difference did it make? She was getting used to it by now. Betrayal. Was it even that strong a word? She was beginning to get the sense that people betrayed her less out of malice, and more out of a failure to remember she was there. A proper betrayal might be preferable to being treated as a constant oversight.

Even as a child Paula remembered her father peering into her upturned face and saying, 'Knock knock, anyone at home?' before turning back to a guffawing crowd of Christmas relatives. 'You wouldn't credit it, would you?' he would say, 'That a child of mine could be so *dull*?'

But she was not thinking about any of this as she scuttled along.

Instead images of Alan played before her eyes: Alan, leaning over a cot oozing paternal warmth; Alan as a bare-chested hunk from an Athena poster, cradling Baby Prugg against his puffy chest; Alan striding through a park with toddler Prugg laughing on his shoulders; Alan collapsing and clutching his heart as Prugg Junior zips a ball past him into the goal behind; an old grizzled, yet still noble Alan standing next to a young, pudgy, yet virile version of his younger self – clapping him manfully on the shoulder; generations of young pudgy versions of Alan standing in a line beside him, stretching into the mists of time…

So, Belinda was pregnant. Of course she was. Paula let the full weight of the inevitable fall across her hunched shoulders.

This changed everything.

Paula had never wasted a second's compunction on Belinda. As far as she was concerned, Belinda had forfeited all rights to be treated as a human being the moment she hurled herself at Alan after the Disability Awareness Seminar. (Paula did not know that the hurling had not, in fact, happened after the seminar, but during it – on a tour of the office disabled toilet facilities – in one particular facility outside the canteen. She didn't, strictly speaking, know that it was Belinda who had done the hurling either, but knew enough about Alan in that regard to have made an educated – and in this case wildly accurate – guess.)

A child, however, was a totally different proposition. It could not be blamed for the behaviour of its parents. And, tempted as she was to embark on a kind of genetic persecution down the generations worthy of spurned lover Heathcliff in *Wuthering Heights,* she knew she lacked the requisite theatricality to keep it up. Not for generations anyway.

As the rain deepened, painting the streets gloss-black, Paula wondered if she even felt a sense of relief. To be able to give up the fight with honour. To be handed a suitably noble get-out clause.

She hurriedly swept the rain – or was it tears? – from her face. Her feet knew where she was going before she did, carrying her down a familiar cobbled street and towards a familiar red painted door. As she thought of Alan, Belinda, Luda, Anthony, her father, the woman she had just passed in the street, everyone, her feet were taking her to the one place, and the one person, where she knew she was *seen*.

She let her body fall back and be held gently by the blush-red drapes and breathed in the familiarity of it all. The pulsing music, the exotically dressed clientele strutting their stuff on the dance floor, the dim shapes disappearing into the playrooms, the dungeon-style decorations; all seemed almost cosy to her now. She looked round, but she could not see him. He must be here somewhere. She paused, trembling against a padded red leather wall, heart beating.

Feeling exposed, Paula retreated to one of the seating booths – specially designed for that feeling of privacy. From the safety of its tall padded cocoon she could watch the club revolving around her: the dancers on the floor, the couples in the corners, Trevor the nose fetishist demonstrating his ten sexiest sneezes to an enthusiastic novice in the art of nose-blowing. She watched as Betsy disappeared into one of the private rooms hand-in-hand with a large shaven-headed bloke encrusted with body piercings, Ron trotting behind obediently like a small, fiercely loyal dog. She pressed her back against the seat absorbing its comforting squoodge. Just when you thought you were getting on top of things… She sighed her neck into the padding for a moment, before straightening up. Where was he? It suddenly seemed very important. He was the only person who noticed. She paused. Paula was not used to the idea of being noticed, she was more comfortable with being rubbed easily from people's memory, by the next event or person they met, blank wall, whatever. Perhaps this hadn't been such a good idea, after all.

And then she saw him, exiting one of the playrooms. He was accompanied by an unknown lady in a PVC catsuit, with long red hair. Not wanting to be seen to pry, Paula ducked down quickly out of sight. Getting onto her seat in a kneeling position, Paula inched her eyes over the padded back of her booth. They were obviously taking their leave of one another. She watched as The Man in the Mask held the woman's hand just a second too long, then broke off as both went their separate ways.

'Ready to order?'

Paula was so distracted she had not noticed the waitress, despite the eye-catching combination of leopard-print hot pants and diamante dog collar.

'Anything,' she said, not looking round.

'You want to choose from the menu?'

Paula snatched the cocktail menu from the waitress's insistent hand.

'Give me one of those blue things,' she said, eventually, having surveyed the exciting range of raunchy drinks on offer.

'The Blue Orgy, The Blue Bumfiddle or the Blue Nun's Lesbian Night of Passion?'

'I don't care. Just the blue stuff. Neat.'

'True Blue?'

'Make it a pint,' she added, handing back the menu and returning to her sentry duty once more.

'I don't think she means that,' said a voice.

Paula jumped to find The Man in the Mask installed next to her in her padded booth. His eyes were twinkling.

'Do you mind if I sit here?'

As he was already sitting there, the question seemed redundant. Paula shrugged and tried to look as though she always preferred kneeling on seats the wrong way round. She tried to brush unwelcome thoughts of red-haired catwomen from her mind.

'You ok?'

She said nothing. Oh this was childish. What was she – jealous – of some anonymous encounter in a nightclub? Of him and some – some – *Batman* movie reject doing whatever it was they were doing in that playroom?

Just what were *they doing in the playroom?*

'You sure about the pint?' the waitress asked

'You can make it a half if you like,' Paula conceded.

'What about a vodka and tonic?' said The Man in the Mask.

'Don't patronise me!' Paula swung herself round in her seat. 'What about *my* fantasies, eh? Mine. Me. What about ME?'

The Man in the Mask's eyes glittered in the half-light. 'Hey. You go ahead, fantasise about blue pints if you want to. Whatever floats your boat. We're a tolerant bunch here.'

The waitress retreated hastily to the bar.

They sat in glum silence.

'Who was that woman you were talking to earlier?' Paula tried to sound conversational, but could not quite dampen the edge in her voice.

'Who?' He could not keep the guilt out of his.

'Miss Pussy Galore over there.'

'Oh – her. That's…err…Pussy Galore.'

'You're not serious.'

' 'fraid so.'

What was it with these people, Paula thought crossly. Did they not have an original thought in their heads? Was there no escaping the bad make-up, ill-fitting costumes and unimaginative film references?

'It's nothing,' he said then, looking at his hands.

Nice hands.

'Whatever *that* means.'

'It means it's not a relationship, okay? It's just what we do here. It means, what the hell are we here for? It means if you have a problem with that what the hell are *you* here for? You say you want to be exciting but it's all words. You don't actually *do* anything. What are you anyway? A voyeur? Spying on the rest of us? Is that your bag?'

'Sorry.' He returned to studying his hands.

They sat like that for a while. Neither quite hiding the fact that they were both still sitting there, despite their dispute.

'How was the date?' asked The Man in the Mask eventually, in an almost-nearly-but-not-quite-casual tone of voice.

'Terrible,' Paula said. 'I am a failure.'

The waitress returned with their drinks and Paula reached out to clasp the glass of radiant blue and took an urgent gulp. For a moment she could not breathe. The silent battle raged for some seconds.

The Man in the Mask put out an uncertain hand – ('I'm fine!' she said with force) – hesitated, and withdrew it again. 'Right.'

They stayed like that for a while, two figures painted red and blue like two dancers in front of a projection screen. The story flickered around them and across them; it did not seem so relevant, then.

'You must think I'm very stupid,' she said.

The Masked Man looked at her in surprise. 'The thought never occurred.'

She swallowed another mouthful and peered at him curiously through a head-full of blue. She could not read the expression behind that mask, but his glittering eyes seemed to deepen and she imagined she felt his gaze boring into her, dissecting every thought. She turned to him then.

'All I wanted was a man who could do sums.'

'You don't have to tell me.'

'I want to tell you.'

The Man in the Mask said nothing, waiting for her to go on.

'He was always the strong one, you know. The exciting one. The one who booked the hire car, treated me at restaurants. Sorted the electricity, that sort of thing. He was always the one who –' She took another gulp. 'I thought that was the way… I *assumed* things I suppose. You shouldn't do that, you know. I read up about it. You have to keep the romance alive. Scented baths, body massage, scissors position – that never really worked for me.'

Paula stared dully into her drink. The blue reflection rippled weirdly across her face. 'I obviously didn't do enough scented baths.' Her voice trailed off. 'No wonder Alan thought I was unexciting. That's why I came here. To learn.'

'How to do scented baths?'

She smiled. 'No.'

The Man in the Mask sounded husky. 'There's more to relationships than being exciting.' It was an unexpected remark for a naked man in an eye mask to come out with.

'Like what?'

'Like love and loyalty and trust.' He sounded embarrassed. 'Like dependability. Companionship. Acceptance.'

She realised she was staring at his hands again, hands that were fastidiously shredding the napkin that had accompanied her olive bowl into tiny, tiny square pieces – fastidiously, but with great agitation.

'Not very passionate-sounding,' she said.

'Passionate?'

She watched the small mound building up on the table in front of him.

'Oh well, if passion is a set of prescribed actions. What are we supposed to do? Swoon over fourteen year old models and orgasm over face cream? Has it ever struck you that passion is a personal thing? If I was to describe my passions...' He stopped. The pieces were no longer squares, but small screwed up shapes of an indeterminate nature.

'I didn't think men did personal. I thought it was all tits 'n' ass, love 'em and leave 'em,' Paula said, not entirely without bitterness.

'Oh tits 'n' ass. Well yes...but it's personal tits 'n' ass. I like your tits for example.'

There was a pause, then the nice hands resumed shredding again. Paula listened to the booming in her ears and waited for him to continue. But the booming died long before the silence did.

'Can I ask you something?' he said, at last.

'Yes – oh – Hang on.' She signalled to the waitress and jabbed and nodded at something pink on the menu. She wanted to make sure she was prepared.'Yes?' She was breathless.

'It's just that I wondered, wondered if – if you k-knew anything about – penguins.'

She was slightly disappointed with the change of direction the conversation had taken; she wanted more compliments about her tits.

'What kind of thing?'

'Like – like – where they live for example.'

Paula thought about this.'You have a pen-guin fetish?' she said slowly.

'No!' He seemed agitated.

'Here you go,' said the waitress, placing an exotic pink cocktail before her. It did not seem quite so appropriate now and Paula felt almost embarrassed at what it signalled about her intentions.

'You were talking about penguins.'

The Man in the Mask shook his head as though it was waterlogged and smiled, 'No, it's just… I'm sorry. It's nothing. Forget it.'

They sat in silence for a while. These silences were becoming a painful habit. Paula wished he would return to the subject of her breasts. Not sure what to do, she picked up her glass.

The exotic pink cocktail was not called The Mound of Venus for nothing and certainly lived up to its reputation. Flaming like a flamingo-coloured tornado through her larynx, hurtling past her oesophagus and blazing like a burning meteorite of girliness into her stomach; it plunged into the volatile blue lagoon already sizzling therein. Inebriation flooded her body like water on a rice paddy.

Instantly The Man in the Mask became irresistibly attractive. Paula forgot her composure and grabbed his arm.

'Ouch,' he said.

'Please?' she implored him, swinging heavily off his trapped limb.

He looked at her. She smiled back, sloshedly.

'Perhaps you've had enough?' he suggested.

'Just one more.' She winked rakishly at him and fell off her chair.

'Water,' The Man in the Mask called to the waitress, dropping to her side. 'Lots of water.'

'You know, you are very attractive,' she said, from under the table.

'Yes, right. Let's get you up.'

'You look very good from down here. The red lighting really does something for you from this angle. Okay, so the naked thing is a bit weird…'

He pushed a pint of water to her lips. 'Drink this.'

'But you know, live and let live, each to his own, I say. I mean it wouldn't do if we were all the same, now, would it?'

'No, it wouldn't. Now, drink this.'

She struggled to take in the water.

'More!' he ordered, practically pouring water into her. She struggled and gasped, flapping about the floor like a grounded fish. He sat back and straightened his mask which had gone askew in all the excitement.

Paula lay on the floor and stared at the ceiling lights – shaped like large pink-nippled breasts. She looked at them through one eye, then the other and felt strangely comforted. She rolled her head round towards her saviour. She knew she should feel ashamed of her embarrassing antics, but right now she really did not give a buggery. She thought for a moment and then said, 'Can I do anything for you?'

He looked down at her where she lay, spread-eagled on the floor.

'No, you're alright.'

'I'm very broad-minded. Miss Pussy over there has nothing on me.'

'That's nice.'

'I mean Alan said I was boring. Boring in bed. But I'm very flexible. My mother used to say I was double-jointed.'

The Man in the Mask clutched his head, tufts of hair stuck up between his fingers. Nice hands.

'I don't think I am really though,' she added sadly. 'Do you want to call me your bitch?'

'No!'

Paula rolled her head miserably back to the ceiling. What an utter abject failure she was. In the space of one evening she had comprehensively failed to seduce a man so anxious to be seduced he had run off with a middle-aged builder in a dress and now she could not even pull a naked man in a fetish club. What kind of excuse for a member of the female sex was she?

A sick one, her stomach abruptly told her.

She struggled up from the ground just as The Man in the Mask turned towards her, eyes vivid.

'Actually, there *is* something you could do for me,' he said.

'Hang on,' she said with some urgency, 'I'll be back.'

By the time she had ejected the pink contents of her stomach into the toilet bowl, splashed water over her face and stumbled out into the cool of the foyer she was beginning to feel slightly better.

'Can I have one of those please?' she indicated to the Gothic totty standing next to the clothes rack. 'And, err, one of those… And – that. Oh, and while we're about it, what about one of those? And –'

Ten minutes later, a woman in thigh-length leather boots and a skin-tight PVC mini skirt emerged from the ladies toilets and stalked stiffly (it wasn't easy to walk in those boots) into the heart of the club. On her top-half, a black PVC bustier grasped her breasts tightly and invitingly whilst thin straps of leather criss-crossed her otherwise bare back. Around her neck a studded collar shone in the overhead nipple lights. A regulation riding whip was clutched in one hand. She strode, with difficulty, up to the naked man sitting at the bar.

'You look different.'

'Yeah well. I needed a change.'

'You look good.'

'Yeah well.' She looked straight at him. 'So, tell me what I can do for you.'

*****

Desire flickered like the match in his hand. The flame leapt up from the candle, dancing in eyes that were wide, wild and too too bright. He gently closed the door and leant back against it, smiling. They looked at each other. She wanted to ask him how many people he had been in that room with. A part of her wanted to ask if she was different to the others. A part of her wanted to ask if she was the same.

She hesitated, suddenly shy. Suddenly conscious of her ridiculous outfit. Suddenly feeling naked. Seeing his nakedness. How could she assent to such a request? With a man she hardly knew?

'What's that?' she said, jumping at a sound behind them.

'Oh don't worry,' he said. 'That's just Bill.'

'Who the hell is Bill?' She looked round in alarm but could see nothing, except a strange box-type construction in the corner – a cross between the Tardis and somewhere birdwatchers might hang out.

'Bill the voyeur. Don't tell me you haven't met Bill?'

'I haven't met Bill.'

'Well, he doesn't tend to get out much. Don't worry. He won't disturb us. That's not his bag. You'll forget about him after a while. Come here...'

Trying (and failing) to put all thoughts of Bill to one side, Paula concentrated on the moment in hand...

'You know I've never done this before. I'll probably be no good.'

'Please,' he urged. 'Or are you too – boring?'

He was teasing her, of course he was.

She was not sure why she felt so shocked. She could, if she wished, remain completely aloof, removed, icily unengaged. And yet, in some way, she felt she might have been more comfortable if he had just asked her for sex.

But the mild jest was enough to prick her pride. She grabbed the candle off him with violence and brandished it over him in a menacing fashion.

'Okay, whip it out.'

'Whoooaaaa!' he said, with some concern.

ROSY BARNES

'I thought that's what you wanted me to do? I thought you wanted me to take control,' she said crossly.

'Yes, but…' He dropped his voice. 'Gently. Tenderly.' He looked at her insistently. 'I have to trust you.'

She was silenced by the look in his eyes. At once intense and intensely vulnerable.

'I don't want to hurt you.'

'Please.'

'Alright,' she said quietly. 'Alright.'

So, this is the secret every woman of experience shares, she thought in wonder. No amount of phallic skyscrapers or cars or towers or other invincible symbols can hide the fact that it is we who hold them trembling in our hands, able to crush with a look or a word. Now that is real power.

She let the hot wax fall onto him, trembling. He cried out, before tangibly stiffening and closing his eyes with the pain.

And she felt, despite herself, profoundly moved. She leaned over and kissed him gently on the forehead.

'South Pole,' she murmured, without really knowing why.

He said nothing, but inclined his head once amidst his tears.

261

Part Five: **APRIL**

Chapter Eighteen | NOCTURNE

All across the city the lights shimmer. The summer air expands and condenses to fill small dark rooms with the snatched sounds of the city asleep, the slumbering sounds of shrieks and drunks, the fights and screams, a few snatched bars of 'The Road to Mandalay'. There they stand, each at their respective windows, looking out across the city. Three lonely minds reaching out into the night air. Three disparate souls connected by that faint thread of consciousness, twisting out and shimmering over the night streets that spread between them. Tendrils of longing curl out holding, gentle as a flower, the budding fruit of their longing, shyly opening its petals to release their night-heavy scent into the pregnant air. There they stand, each thinking their respective thoughts.

Fred thinks of Paula. Paula thinks of Alan. Alan thinks of Alan.

Slowly, each turns away from the window to switch on a light and back again towards their own lonely reflection in the dark glass.

'What is "Woman"?' thinks Paula sadly, wiping the last traces of make-up away from her blanched face.

'Who is Paula, and who am I?' thinks Fred, removing his mask and covering his nakedness with a dressing gown. 'H-h-h-how could sh-she ever? H-h-how could she…?'

'Shit,' thinks Alan. 'It's really not very Pierce at all. More David Mellor with Botox. Bloody hell!'

Chapter Nineteen | **PLASTIC SURGERY**

When he finally came face-to-face with the blue ballooning mess that had once been his face, Alan observed how like it was to a country undergoing painful reconstruction after a long and bloody war.

Tramlines of stitches redrew the borders of his mouth, his cheeks, his ears and, most painfully, his eyelids which now had been divided amongst the various quarrelsome groups belonging to the agony tribe. His lips had been commandeered by the black and blues; his eyes by the red-raw seepage society; whilst his ears, resembling the results of a crude 19th century experiment, were being conquered and reconquered minute by minute by the combined forces of pain and pus.

Having spent just two days in hospital, doing his best impersonation of the Invisible Man, the one *with* the bandages, Alan was duly discharged and sent back home. The strong blood supply to the face, he was told, meant that wounds heal quicker than in other places. But still, he should not expect too much too soon. There would, he was warned, be some swelling.

He moved his head – *Aaagh!* – to the left and – *Aggghh!* – right.

It wasn't a bad nose, he supposed, inspecting the sheer upturned slice that remained of his once proud proboscis. More Michael Jackson than Pierce Brosnan, but still.

Trembling, he put a hand out to touch the jagged railway line crisscrossing his hairline, surrounded by mottled patches of greens and blues that disappeared somewhere over the top of his right ear. His new youthful forehead, so smooth you could play billiards on it, stared blankly back at him.

He raised his eyebrows sardonically. At least he would have done had he not found them raised already. Indeed, now, it seemed, they could no longer descend. He tried frowning but found his face would not allow him so antisocial an expression. Smiling was out too. Instead, expressively, his face operated in the strictly defined region of the mildly surprised. It did mildly surprised. And, with a lot of effort, mildly surprised.

Belinda flashed past in her designer suit, and leant over to inspect her lipstick in the bathroom mirror before turning to inspect her husband-to-be.

'Hmm, not bad,' she said, swivelling his face this way and that between her red-tipped talons. 'Did we ask for a Michael Jackson nose? I know they couldn't do a Pierce but I thought we compromised on the Jeremy Paxman in the end. *Hmmm*, perhaps we can get some money off,' before turning tail once more to the soundtrack of their roaming phone, tinnily insisting on Beethoven's 5th.

Alan returned to the mirror, this time to look at the neatly planted rows of new hair sprouting like some unspecified genetically modified crop in clustered bunches across the top of his head. A searing pain in his newly-lifted posterior reminded him of yet more surgical indignity. The painful immobility of his helium balloon buttocks was masked by their youthful image of buoyant perkiness and cheery optimism: a perfect synergy of uplift in form and spirit.

But still Belinda had not slept with him. Well, to be fair, he had only been out of hospital a week and for the first few days he couldn't move at all, let alone indulge in other forms of activity. He frowned; at least, he frowned inside. Still, give him another fortnight and...after all how could she resist him with this nose? Those eyes? Those helium-lifted buttocks?

A howl of rage came through from the other room.

Alan felt a thrilling shiver overtake him.

Like most men, Alan knew, somewhere deep in his secret chauvinist heart, there was a fine line between a household nag and a psychopath. At what point Belinda crossed this line, her hold over him mutating from a conventional case of female control-freakery, with its traditional terrain of unreplaced toothpaste caps and toilet seats, into something altogether more sinister, was hard to determine.

But, by the time the wedding plans were galloping headlong through their penultimate furlong, just the mere sound of her voice sent him into a state of terrified anticipation.

She appeared to him as a distorted goddess, feeding him on the succour of her milky regard, yet brutally demanding her due in human sacrifice.

Just because his secret heart was perfectly well aware of all this, however, does not mean that Alan cared to inform *himself* of the information. No, despite the odd flutter of misgiving from his aorta major, Alan still firmly believed Belinda was an incredible woman: the envy of his friends and love of his life (when he was getting some). Even her withheld desire just added to her allure, keeping him hanging on, desperate and needy, magnifying current attributes and retouching memories of past triumphs with Technicolor glory.

'The wedding's coming forward,' Belinda snapped re-entering the room at speed.

Alan's new hair seemed to stand on end; as if in question.

'What's happened?'

'My sodding sister has got engaged.'

'To Branston?'

'Brandon!'

'That's good isn't it?' asked Alan innocently.

Belinda was flabbergasted. 'What's remotely good about it?'

'They're in love.' He stroked her shoulder, nervously. 'Like us.'

'Love? Love? What does she know about love? She hasn't been out with one man who hasn't slept with me first! Or second,' she added. 'Whatever. That's not the point. The bitch is blatantly trying to nip in there first. She's getting married in two months. One month before us. Can't wait, apparently. Too much in love! Isn't that marvellous? And to a man with such wonderful teeth! Mummy's having orgasms over it already.'

'Does seem a bit hasty,' Alan said, unsure.

'Months of planning down the toilet, to be upstaged by a blancmange in a dress. I want to claw the bitch's eyes out. I really should have followed through on that noose incident when we were toddlers. Why did I ever let the adults talk me out of it?'

Mesmerised by her impassioned face – the bead of sweat sizzling fiercely upon her angry brow, the vicious curl of her red mouth – Alan felt himself overtaken by a flush of emotion and made a rash grab for her jabbing hand.

'Belinda, Bella, Baby, Honey, Baby.' She looked at him as though he were mad. 'Why don't we just escape? Just the two of us. A romantic getaway. Just go somewhere, get married on a beach.' He gazed doggily up into her eyes.

She stared back as though he was a pile of something the dog had just produced.

'Have you lost your mind? I'm not getting married on a sodding beach! What are you thinking of? You think I'm going to have my cellulite on show to the world? Sometimes you really are the most insensitive –'

'It's our day. About us. All I want. You and me. What does it matter about other people, as long as we're together?'

She was brisk. 'Look Alan. I'm really not in the mood for this romantic crap. I can't believe even you are trying to do me out of my big day. Of course it matters. It doesn't count if nobody SEES me!'

'It's supposed to be the happiest day of your life,' Alan said, not sounding convincing, even to himself.

'Yes, well, if we move it forward about six weeks it will be,' she retorted. 'Enough time for the swelling to go down a bit.' She patted him on the cheek, turning tail as he slowly folded onto the floor with pain.

Dizzy with agony and exhausted with the apparent impossibility of ever pleasing the woman of his dreams, Alan slid back down the tiles under the toilet bowl. His shoulders began to heave with small shuddering, painful gasps.

'What a fuss men make,' said Belinda's head, popping back round the door. 'Try giving birth. The day you squeeze something the size of a melon out the end of your penis, *then* you can start complaining,' and she disappeared again.

Something welled up from deep inside him, pressing at his throat, punching through his lungs and forcing its way between his protesting tonsils.

'*Aaaaaaaaaaaaaaaaaaaaaggggggggggggggggggghhhhhhhhh*!' he screamed.

But he made sure the front door had already slammed before he did.

Wrung out and anxious he lay very still, listening, in case he had miscalculated. But the flat remained lifeless. He stared up at the cold underside of the sink. No sympathy there. He looked at his pathetic reflection on the underside of their new stainless steel toilet.

Conjuring up all his remaining energy he fished into his back pocket for his mobile phone. It did not mean anything. A friendly phonecall, that's all. Friend to friend. He gazed for a second at Belinda's face glaring back at him from the small cell screen, before eradicating it with the contacts menu.

A. B. D.J.L.M.N…

There was a shocked silence at the other end of the phone. Then, 'Alan?'

Then, 'You phoned me.'

Then silence.

'I was…err…just thought I'd…see how you… How are you getting on with your bills?' he enquired authoritatively.

'My bills?'

'I just thought maybe you could do with a bit of advice. I am an accountant, after all, and you've never been very capable in that particular arena…'

'No. Thank you.'

It was his turn to be stumped. 'Well, if you're sure.'

'If I have any strenuous adding up to do, I'll let you know.'

Alan was taken aback at the stiffness in her voice.

'I suppose I should say congratulations,' she said, then, surprisingly.

Alan was perplexed at this and attempted a corresponding eyebrow raise. But they stayed exactly where they were – nestled in his hairline. 'Goodness, news travels quick, I only got back from the hospital on Friday.'

Paula's turn for surprise. 'I had no idea it was so far on. I thought you'd have months to go yet.'

'Oh we thought there was no point in hanging around – might as well get it over with before the wedding.'

The other end of the phone seemed to be thinking about this. 'Are you going to spill the beans – boy or girl?'

Alan's turn to be confused. What did she think, that he was having a sex change or something?

'Well boy, obviously.'

'And who does it look like?'

Alan stared at himself in the underside of the toilet and marvelled at the black rings around his eyes. 'Pierce Brosnan,' he said with confidence, and as an afterthought, 'Plus Michael Jackson's nose. Belinda's not too happy about that.'

'Pierce Brosnan? That's unusual. Most people say Kojack. Or Winston Churchill, if they're being honest.'

Alan frowned, or at least he tried to.

'Why would *anyone* choose Winston Churchill?'

'He's bald and fat I suppose,' came the intriguing reply.

Alan felt the tears pricking at his eyes. To think that she seriously believed that anyone would pay money to look like *him*. Even Alan could not kid himself on that score.

'You shouldn't still – be thinking about me…' he sniffed.

'I'm not thinking about you.'

'You aren't?'

'There's no point is there? Not now. Wouldn't be right.'

'No, no, it wouldn't be right.' Belinda would never have shown such scruples, he thought.

'You're a new man now, with new responsibilities.'

'Yes, yes I suppose I am.' Alan felt a tear running down his mildly surprised face.

'Paula?'

'Yes, Alan.'

'I wonder…'

'….?'

'Do you ever..?'

'Ever…?'

'Wonder… whether…' He petered off. '*I* do, you know.'

'Alan, is there something wrong?'

'I…well…I…Belinda, she's really…an incredible woman. She's really improved me, made me a better man.'

'That's – nice.'

'You wouldn't recognise me now. I'm much improved.'

'I…kind of liked you the way you were.'

'Really?'

'Goodbye Alan.'

'Goodbye Paula.'

Alan made no attempt to stem the tears.

Chapter Twenty | COLDLY AND RATIONALLY

PROGRAMME: FRED'S HEAD
   AUTHOR: FRED
   FILENAME: LOVE
   AUTHOREDIT

Fred threw himself back from his terminal and put his head in his hands. He did not understand what was wrong with him. A hand strayed out to grab the cup of lukewarm coffee at his side. It was no good, he could not concentrate. The incredibly complex and boring computer programming seemed too incredibly boring and complex, even to him.

A quick flick of the fingers for a perusal of 'Need to Know', but somehow its collection of web typos and techie cock-ups were neither as amusing nor as ego-building as he expected.

Even a selection of new and unusual bird-sites was not enough to take his mind off his obsession.

He was not used to the strange and urgent feelings coursing through his body. The agitation of his stomach, the singing in his veins. In fact he was not used to feeling much going on with his body at all. The odd surge of excitement generated by the sight of a naked pickled egg, perhaps? The cloak of calm that descended on his undressed self as the small black mask went over his eyes?

A being that took virtually no exercise (what exercise he did take tending to be of the virtual variety), Fred could not have even sworn he had veins. But today they were practically jumping out of his body. They were not just singing, they were a full deafening dawn chorus of chirping, tweeting and warbling: 'Paula! Paula! Paula!' abundant and glorious. 'Paula! Paula! Paula!'

Hell, what was he thinking of? A woman like Paula would never look at him twice.

But she had, she *had* looked twice at him. She fell off her chair looking at him. She had told him he looked attractive from underneath the bar-counter.

But that wasn't *him*. She did not mean him, Fred. She meant George. George was attractive. Not Fred. She wouldn't give Fred a second glance.

But she had told George he looked attractive; surely that counted for something? If George looked attractive surely it followed, by objective reasoning, that Fred, sharing George's physical attributes, should also look attractive. After all, George and Fred could not look totally unlike one another.

But it's all in the mind with women, everyone knew that. They don't care what you look like. They fancy an idea, a perception. That's what she liked. The *perception* of George. Not Fred. Fred was dead. Dead in the water. Fred.

But she had…together, alone. *They* had… He could not think of it without his mind clenching shut with terror.

What was the problem? It's not like it was the first time for him.

That's why he went to the club. For unpressurised unemotional interaction.

But he wasn't unemotional. It was a disaster. Mask or no mask she had seen him. He knew she had, for a second, a brief moment. There were no hiding places anymore.

'Paula! Paula! Paula!' sang the chorus. 'Paula! Paula! Paula!'

Love, he thought.

He had never thought about love before. Breasts, yes. Sex, when he dared…and breasts. But love?

The partridges were no company to him anymore. Nothing, nothing was what it was. *Star Wars*, penguins, his favourite fungi. That was the transformative power of love, he supposed sadly. Nothing was what it was and nothing could ever be as it was. No longer was he satisfied with his simple life, no longer was it enough to dream about programming and aviaries. Something subtle had shifted. And something not so subtle.

He felt a chill run through his body. It was a disaster. She was a woman. She was bound to be domineering. She would insist he tidy his bedsit. Get rid of the stuffed birds, or move. Move somewhere womanly. Somewhere *clean*. Somewhere he would feel out of place, like a visitor at an art gallery, frightened of touching anything.

An internal email flashed up on his screen. It was from one of the Probably Andrews, two feet to his left. It said,

You can never be depressed with Doom Metal in the world.

Fred looked sideways. The Probably Andrew did not acknowledge his glance but continued to stare straight ahead, banging his head to the unidentified medley of doom metal hits beating out of his earphones.

She would demand he buy a house. That's what women did. And get a better job and brush his hair and gargle. A tremble rippled across the back of his neck, not pleasurably. She would *insist* that he gargle!

And she would buy him clothes. Trendy clothes with words on, but not words like *Star Wars* but words like 'Babe' or 'Fuckbuddy'. And he would grow designer stubble and one of those almost-bald cuts that tough people had, with a fake parting shaved into it. She would demand he tattoo 'I love Paula' on his buttock and wear one earring and a gold chain and a watch encrusted with diamonds! No no no. That wasn't Paula. That's why he liked her. Paula was like no other woman he'd ever met. She was different.

He tried to calm himself down and think rationally.

It was obvious, once he had done this, that his previous thoughts had been mistaken. Alan was hardly some shaven-headed gold-chain-wearing rapper. He thought about it some more. Oh god, she would demand he carry a briefcase, put on some weight and develop a bald patch. She would push him into qualifying as an accountant and make him eat muesli, for the good of his heart. She would insist he read the Sunday papers, listen to 'Yesterday in Parliament', fancy women with proper hairdos, watch sport, collect mobile phones. No no no no no no no! It could not happen. He could not let this excess of…excess of…irrational feeling take over his life. He had it all worked out, he was happy as he was. He had his routine.

The pickled eggs would have to go. Oh God!

Hot and sweating, Fred charged into the ComPro: *Computer Programming for Computer Programmers'* toilets and locked himself, still shaking, into a cubicle. There he sat on the toilet, meditating on a small but disturbingly vivid Japanese animé sticker stuck to the handle of the bog-brush in an effort to calm down.

But if love was such torture, why did so many people *go on* about it, he wondered. Not that anyone had ever mentioned it to him. Men didn't. Not computer programmers anyway. Except for one of the Andrews, who had quietly confided in him one day that he was saving himself for an Eastern European supermodel who was a member of MENSA. He seemed to view this as a serious possibility.

I'm not fussy, he had messaged electronically one lunchtime. *She'd do for example.*

He nodded over a bag of cheese and onion crisps, towards his screen where platinum 'Natascha' gyrated over a profile that read, 'I just LOVE for you to jiggle my titties.'

You can tell she's intelligent.

How do you figure that? Fred typed, head on one side.

She's studying medicine.

Just because she's wearing a nurse's outfit doesn't mean she's a medical student.

How do you explain the stethoscope, then?

Alright, maybe computer geeks did not tend to talk about love. Computer programmers notoriously didn't need love, they just lived with their mothers into their forties before, if they 'made it', hitching up with a former Miss Bolivia. And if they didn't make it? Well then they'd shack up with an electronic cyberdoll with enormous breasts, state-of-the-art private parts and a selection of greetings such as 'Do it to me, big boy' and 'My god, you are hung like a hippopotamus' and live happily ever after. In fact the ones who married the former Miss Bolivia probably had the worst deal.

But other people talked of love. In the media. Arty-types, he thought to himself. They were into it. Poets. Writers. Journalists – not journalists. Pop singers.

He put his head in his hands again. What was he going to do? Oh this was just silly. He should come straight out with it. March up to her and tell her how he felt about her, like a man. He would be bold, for once, take a risk. Yes.

Hardly daring to hope, he turned the idea over in his mind.

---

500 Internal Error: Fear of Closeness

Try replacing memory card, personality and other features. If not try rebooting and drunkenly blaming mother and all the other bitches.

It was no good. He could not let a woman into his life. What had he been thinking of?

Buoyed up with the imperative of avoiding a relationship at all costs, Fred considered his options.

She loved Alan. Of course she did. It was only natural from what he had been told. Fine figure of a man who could do sums...

He distractedly spun the toilet roll dispenser and sent a streamer of tissue cascading towards the floor with himself diving ineffectually after it.

Damn. Damn. Damn. Damn.

Why did she like George? For she did seem to. Like him, that is. And what had got into George, come to think of it? He had dabbled around with many women in his time. Nameless anonymous women, safe in the dark privacy of the playrooms. It was no big deal. Just two grown people, enjoying each other in an adult environment...

Shit. Shit. Shit. Shit. Shit.

He leant back against the cistern.

His love for Paula could never be allowed to flourish. No, he must turn it to another purpose, to help her, help her get Alan back. She did not want *him* (*but she wanted George, a small voice said rather too loudly – to be quickly stifled*). She wanted Alan: paunch, briefcase and all. And he, Fred, was the man to help her. It was quite selfless really; he would turn his love for her into a non-possessive, pure, altruistic force that would help her achieve her wants and dreams whilst allowing him to maintain everything exactly as it was. Yes.

If Paula and Alan didn't get back together themselves, he would have to crowbar them back together – through force.

Feeling better, he reached round for a piece of bogroll to blow his nose and, suddenly inspired, took a biro out of his pocket and scrawled, 'Love is a non-possessive, pure, altruistic force,' on the wall next to the holder. He sat back and admired it.

By that evening his graffiti had been joined by the words 'No, it's not' scrawled mysteriously underneath, but, by this time, Fred was busy collecting his paper-parcelled pickled egg.

Silently, the anonymous Andrew illustrated this sentiment with a pair of fastidiously drawn mammaries and added a tattooed 'MENSA' on one for good measure.

Chapter Twenty-One | **BACK TO THE DRAWING BOARD**

'Threesomes, threesomes? Yawn. Come back when you've thought of something *really* sordid. We're smearing each other with vegan ice-cream in here – you can't get more sordid than that, ugh!'

With that, Luda ejected a protesting couple and their 'friend' from one of the club playrooms and slammed the door in their faces.

She turned back into the room and looked at the dejected outfit before her: The Man in the Mask sat hunched at the back. Paula sat at the front, shoulders poised as though about to take flight and beside her Dave, staring at the wall, which – in keeping with the room's general dungeon-theme – was stark, grey and exposed. The medieval style equipment, in this case, some solid-looking leg-irons and a peculiar metal and wood contraption that Gretchen referred to as 'the stocks' had been pushed to one side. (The only pair acting like their normal selves was Gretchen and SlaveBoy. Gretchen, who, on occasions like this could not decide if she was 'on' or not, had decided to play it ambiguous by indulging in a spot of crochet, whilst pausing every now and then to stick SlaveBoy, hanging happily upside-down from the ceiling, in the ribs with her hook.)

'What's got into everyone?' Luda was in belligerent mode.

The remark was greeted with silence and despondency. Luda was just about to let fly with a comment about lack of grit and commitment when there was a soft knock at the door.

'What is it about the words "fuck" and "off" you don't understand mate?' she hollered, only to be answered by the quizzical head of Anthony Hossier, questing round the edge.

'Any room in here for an old Etonian?'

Luda changed tone without a beat. 'Oh! My! Oh!' she said, clasping her hands and deftly presenting him with her right profile. 'You don't mind, everyone, do you?' She looked round at the hostile faces.

'Everyone this is Anthony. Anthony, this is Everyone.'

Anthony gave Everyone a hearty wave. Everyone, less than enthusiastic, gazed darkly back at him. Everyone, that is, except Dave, whose normally contented face was overtaken with an expression of murderous hatred.

'I hope you don't mind,' said Anthony. 'But I took the liberty of inviting along a friend.'

A slim red-faced youth, looking rather fetching in a thick sheepskin jacket, sidled in, hands rammed in his pockets, his thinning fair hair pasted to the top of his head. He nodded shyly at the assembled company.

'Malcolm, meet – Everyone.'

Malcolm ducked his head and gave a slight flicker of his hand in greeting.

'Budge up, old girl,' Anthony said, comfortably bumping his bottom into Paula's. She shifted, reluctantly.

Malcolm slid in next to Dave.

'No hard feelings, eh?' Anthony said to Paula, in a deafening whisper.

Paula looked at him bitterly.

'You're a cracker, you know,' Anthony said, generously. 'A total 6.5.'

'So you said.'

'Don't be like that, old girl.' He patted her arm and leaned in to shout conspiratorially down her ear. 'None of us can avert the hand of fate. I mean, it was pretty long odds – there you were, a decent 6.5. To be completely eclipsed by a total SHBB-10, walking – nay gliding! – into the room. I mean, what were the chances?'

He gazed across at Luda, starry-eyed, who rose to the occasion magnificently, losing centimetres off her waist and adding them to her chest with one single in-breath. Paula flicked a sympathetic look towards Dave, but he refused to catch her eye. Instead, he gave the impression of someone looking at something infinitely more fascinating than the rather boring wall he was scrutinising with such immense concentration.

Paula stole a glance over her shoulder at The Man in the Mask. But he too seemed suddenly taken with the partition next to him. Was this the same person from the night before? Could those be the same eyes that had flickered in the darkness, eyes that had seen her, that had devoured her and that now appeared to be gazing with that same desirous zeal at a piece of grey breezeblock?

'Are we going to have group sex now?' Malcolm whispered to wall-staring Dave. Dave continued to stare at the wall.

'Shall we start?' Luda said.

Paula coughed meaningfully in the direction of Anthony and Malcolm.

'Oh of course,' said Luda. She turned towards Anthony. 'Quick run-down: Paula's obsessed with Alan, who I think you're acquainted with, and who dumped her for being boring. She came here to learn how to be exciting. We taught her how to be a real woman and…err…that's where you came in. Now we have to come up with a plan to get him back. That's all you need to know really. What's wrong?' she protested to Paula whose head was in her hands. 'Didn't miss anything out, did I?'

Paula shook her head with shame.

Anthony leant into Paula. 'You dark horse,' he said, saucily. 'Alan, eh? Well I never. Lucky bastard.'

Paula smiled weakly.

'Don't know what you see in him, though,' Anthony added. 'A decent 6.5 like you. What's so special about Alan?'

Paula pulled her face out of her hands. It was possibly the first time she had considered this question. What *was* so special about Alan? She could not think of anything particularly spectacular about the love of her life. She saw everything, all his faults, all his weaknesses, blazing before her.

She opened her mouth, caught sight of The Man in the Mask, changed her mind and shut it again.

'I know him, I suppose,' she said at last. It was not much as declarations of love go, but it seemed to satisfy her audience, who smiled and nodded and took the opportunity of squeezing her thigh.

'Right, so,' announced Luda, determined to get everything under her control again. 'What's the plan?'

Dave, SlaveBoy, Gretchen, Conan, Malcolm, Anthony and

Paula all returned the question with blank faces, and then turned, as one, towards The Man in the Mask. By this time they all knew there was only one man in that room with any ideas at all.

'Or,' said Luda crossly, jealous of the fact that this man was someone other than her. 'We could go back to Plan B.'

'What's Plan B?' asked Anthony, getting into the spirit of things.

'Doing away with the evil bitch, that's what!' said Luda, forgetting to be ladylike in her excitement.

'We could – have group sex,' said a small voice excitedly.

'Not now, Malcolm,' said Anthony, with an apologetic grimace to the others, before leaning across Paula and hissing, 'I said, if the opportunity presented itself, *opportunity presented itself*, got it?'

'Look,' said Gretchen, in motherly tones. 'We can't just go around murdering people. I absolutely draw the line at that. All this talk is one thing but we're not in fantasy land now.' She ground her crotchet needle into SlaveBoy's shoulder, who shuddered and grunted in ecstasy whilst Malcolm watched with interest.

Luda paused for a second. 'So much for the view of the animal rights lobby. But –' And she bared her snaggle-toothed smile at Dave. 'I like to think we are living in a democracy. What does everyone else think?'

The remainder of the group looked round at each other blankly, apart from Dave who looked blankly at everyone but Luda. And The Man in the Mask, who looked blankly at everyone but Paula.

Luda clapped her hands together. 'Right. Plan B it is then.'

'You seriously think we should consider killing the woman?' an incredulous Gretchen cried. 'I'm sorry but as far as I'm concerned this discussion ends right here. Come on SlaveBoy.'

She stood up, unclipped him – 'Aarghh!' (as he fell to the ground with a bump) – and started folding away the shawl she had been crocheting.

'No,' he said, petulantly, wiggling his legs in the air.

'DO AS YOU'RE TOLD!'

SlaveBoy paused before sticking out his bottom lip. 'Make me. And then maybe punish me extremely severely for my naughtiness.'

Gretchen threw up her hands causing him to shut his eyes with a premature wince of excitement.

'Sometimes,' she shouted, 'You can be so – *selfish*!' before storming out of the room.

SlaveBoy looked round at the others with an expression of wounded innocence on his face. 'What did I do?' he implored. 'What?' He pleaded with Paula. 'What did I do?'

Paula puffed her cheeks out tiredly. 'I think, perhaps, Gretchen sometimes feels a bit…dominated by your submissiveness.'

SlaveBoy went red. 'That's just ridiculous. Gretchen is my *mistress*. She doesn't let me get away with anything. Not a thing. Got that?'

And he too was gone, leaving nothing but a muted padded slam in his wake.

Luda rolled her shadow-encrusted eyes. 'Bloody vegans!'

She looked across to Dave for support but found, to her surprise, that his eyes were still staring steadfastedly at the wall beside him and there was nothing she could do to persuade them to catch her own.

'So,' said Luda with a shrug, but there was no satisfaction in it this time. 'Plan B it is.'

'No,' said a voice.

And out of the shadows emerged The Man in the Mask, striding manfully to the front of the room. 'Gretchen is wrong.'

'Yes, like I said. Plan B.'

'No, not that.' He turned to face his audience. 'When she said we weren't in fantasy land.'

Not an inkling of animation on those blank faces. Nobody could remember what it was Gretchen had said and they were not that interested anyway.

'Don't you see?' He was getting carried away again. His arms outstretched, messianic; face uplifted to some unseen spiritual inspirer. 'This *is* fantasy land!'

In the time it took for Dave to glance up from the piece of crumbling cement he was now so intimately acquainted with, the room had turned electric. *Fantasy land*. They liked that. Images of that exotic sounding place flashed before all of their eyes, although differently for each individual.

For Luda it was Oz, complete with a green-faced Paula as the Wicked Witch of the West whilst a pigtailed version of herself skipped nimbly down the yellow-brick road, a loyal Lassie taking Toto's place at her heel; Dave, sneaking a resentful glance at his beloved, pictured himself and Luda side-by-side in enormous white wedding dresses with large pink bows round their middles and matching shoes; Conan envisaged himself in a prehistoric swamp wrestling naked with a Tyrannosaurus Rex watched by an adoring crowd of sexy Neanderthal maidens in loincloths. Only Paula, who had always been lacking in imagination, could not think of anything, so she thought miserably of Alan instead.

'Don't you get it?' said The Man in the Mask. He was on a roll now. 'Fantasy is what we deal in, fantasy is what we know about. Fantasies are what we are good at!'

They took a collective in-breath.

Then, for the first time that day, The Man in the Mask turned and looked directly at Paula. Then, even more surprisingly and to her great embarrassment, he knelt down in front of her and gently took her hand.

'What is Alan's fantasy?' he asked her, searching her eyes.

'I – I don't know.'

'You don't *know*!' (That was Luda.) 'You don't know?' (To the others.) 'She doesn't *know*. She doesn't know. You were with him for years. How can you not *know*?'

Paula looked at The Man in the Mask's hands. Nice hands.

She heard Luda's voice continue to berate her in the background. 'You must have *some* idea? Even the most *mundane* relationships – Don't you *read* any magazines? I mean, what is it? Uniforms? Come on. Doctors and Nurses? Teacher and pupil?'

'Queen and Beefeater?' offered Dave with a shy look towards Luda.

'Don't even go there,' the love of his life warned. 'Master and slave, headmistress and pupil, vicar and tart – what? What is it? What? What? What?'

'What?' asked The Man in the Mask, gently.

'He quite likes James Bond,' Paula said in a small voice.

'He quite likes James Bond. He quite – likes - James – Bond. *Every* man likes James Bond!'

'No,' said The Man in the Mask, waving Luda to silence. 'This is the key. Every man does indeed like James Bond. The super-smooth masculine secret agent. Saving his woman from the villain. Yes.' He still had hold of Paula's hand.

Paula, who had been fidgeting ever since the resurrection of Plan B, nervously pulling apart the end of her sleeve, shook her head, silently. She shifted awkwardly in her seat, knowing that she was about to let them all down.

'Oh bloody what now?' said Luda, throwing her eyes about dramatically.

A long piece of thread unravelled from Paula's sleeve. She twisted it round her fingers. 'I don't want Plan B,' Paula said. 'I don't want Plan A either. Or C, D or E.'

'What do you mean?' Luda said, Southern Belle twang and waistline collapsing simultaneously.

'It's over.'

'WHAT DO YOU MEAN?'

'It's no good.' She twisted the thread savagely and snapped it off her sleeve. 'I realised…'

Paula looked intensely up at The Man in the Mask, willing him to understand. Those eyes, *those kind eyes, the eyes that saw her, the flame jumping up*…

'Alan is gone. I have to face facts. He's with Belinda now.' She spoke as if the two of them were the only people in the room. Not a flicker from behind that black mask. She wanted to add something dramatic about honour, decency and sacrificing herself for the sake of Alan's unborn child, but it was not her style. She could not think of the words.

'It's over,' she repeated, simply. Nothing flashy, but the effect was dramatic enough all the same.

Luda was apoplectic.

'After all the work I put in?' She appealed to Dave, 'After all the work I put in, Dave?', to The Man in the Mask, 'After all the work I put in!!'; but he was staring at Paula. She did not even bother with Conan. 'After all the work I put in, Anthony?' she said.

Anthony grinned back goofily. 'I don't know what's going on.'

Luda clicked her teeth crossly and, with something of an anti-climax, sat down next to Anthony with a feminine sigh.

'Well that's lovely that is,' she muttered to herself. 'After all the work I've put in.'

'It's the right thing to do,' Paula said, through clenched shoulders.

She watched as The Man in the Mask, who had, up until her announcement, been staring hypnotically into her eyes, suddenly stood up.

'You love Alan,' he said.

What was this?

'You and Alan are obviously made for each other.' Those eyes – the eyes that saw her, *wanted* her – twinkled now, not as they had done, but with a cold hardness.

'Love is a non-possessive, pure, altruistic force,' he said diffidently.

What was he talking about?

For an unaccountable second, she wanted to hit him.

'See,' Luda, impatient with this exhausting subtext of looks and avoidance of looks, tried to take back control. 'Plan B.'

'I said it's no good!' said Paula, surprisingly loudly. 'Sorry. Sorry…' And she too was gone, stumbling out the door.

'Well!' said Luda, looking round at what was left of the party.

'That's gratitude for you.'

She tried Dave again but he crossed his arms and turned to stare at another equally fascinating wall in the other direction. *What the hell was up with everyone?*

The Man in the Mask collapsed onto one of the machine-washable PVC pouffes (in black this time, to match the medieval torture chamber vibe) and stared at the door.

'Are we going to have group sex now?' said a small voice, from somewhere next to Dave. 'Anthony told me you – indulged.'

'I don't want to be referred to as Anthony anymore,' Anthony said suddenly. 'From now on I want to be known as – Conundrum.' He rolled his mouth around the word with pleasure. 'Connn-unnn-drrrum. Meaning Mysterious. Enigmatic…get it? Conundrum: exciting, never humdrum.'

'I find you anything but humdrum,' Luda said.

This was the final straw for Dave who lurched across the room and pushed past Luda as though pursued by a hoard of marauding hornets.

'Great,' said Luda. 'Bloody wonderful.' She felt suddenly weary and wondered, not for the first time, how she had managed to surround herself with such a bunch of lunatics.

But she was saved from this particular line of thought by a soft knock on the door.

'That'll be Mr and Mrs Threesome again.' She swung open the door and stuck her head belligerently into the gap, 'Will you just fu – ! Oh it's you.'

'Did I hear something about threesomes?' Betsy said, gracefully entering the room. The gurgle in her voice that always suggested laughter, like the birth of a giggle in her throat, bounced like a wriggling puppy across the room to Malcolm, who sat, saucer-eyed with wonder at this inviting woman, twinkling across at him, twin chins wobbling in welcome. She was followed in by the familiar small dapper figure. Business-like nods were exchanged.

'Ron.'

'Luda.'

'Is the room free?'

Luda peered round from where she was jamming the door with her body. 'I think we've finished up. Come on, people.'

Anthony got up to leave.

'Umm. I think I might just stay here a while,' said Malcolm in a voice that could have convinced as a young Aled Jones. 'If I'm not getting in anybody's way.' He flickered a glance at Betsy, who smiled back in encouragement.

Luda was short. 'Fine by me.' Then, to The Man in the Mask, 'You staying here too?'

The Man in the Mask, still slumped over the machine-washable pouffe, appeared rather too emotional for Luda's liking. She started to wonder if he were ill. She did not like the way the tone in his voice went up a scale or two as he said, 'It's up to us to help her. We have to. We have to, don't you see?' And she liked even less the way his eyes flickered behind his mask like two crazed tadpoles as he cried aloud, 'We have to get them back together. For our own good! Our own good! What would people think? I can't live in a museum or wear T-shirts saying "Fuckbuddy" or "I love Muesli"!' His voice petered out and he slumped back onto the pouffe once more.

Luda was overwhelmed by a surge of weariness and closed

her eyes.

Then, she said to The Man in the Mask, 'Okay, okay, I'll help. You can count on me.' And to herself, 'Honestly, all this talk about love. The sooner this place can go back to being a good old-fashioned cesspit of sleaze, the better for all of us.'

Part Six: MAY

Chapter Twenty-Two | THE LETTER

What was wrong with him?

What was wrong with him? What was this…emotion?

Alan clutched at his chest and felt as though he was falling.

It was a tree for Christ's sake. A tree.

He rushed to the cabinet and poured himself a scotch. But the fire trickling down his throat, into his chest and tearing at his heart did not bring the comfort he expected. He clutched the edge of the cabinet as though sure his thumping heart was about to pull apart his plump chest and thrust hotly into the room demanding to be appeased.

'Save me, save me brother! Get your arse out here, how hard can it be? Do it for me, do it for the planet, do it for yourself!'

Alan returned to the window, carefully obscured by the tasteful cream curtains (a recent addition to Belinda's minimal white-on-white design) and watched as a man in a white jumpsuit and goggles powered up his chainsaw, whilst his spotty youth of an assistant stood by gormlessly. He felt a wince flicker across his face, at least he would have done if wincing had been physically possible, and instinctively shut his eyes, or would have if his sutured eyelids had allowed.

'Save me! Oh please! Don't do this to me, brother. Have you *seen* the blades on those things?'

From the outside, all that could be seen was a trembling hand holding back the white drapes. But this was enough for Sam Spade (a trade-name, his real name was Stephen Ludlow, but somehow this worked less well on the side of his white transit van accompanied by the tagline 'Call a spade a spade. Call Sam Spade.')

'Mr. Prugg!' he hollered, waving a roaring chainsaw over his head in jovial manner.

'Call me Alan!' Alan yelled back. 'And be a bit more bloody careful with that chainsaw, would you?'

Insulated by his layers of Perspex goggles, ear protectors, balaclava and Manchester city scarf, Spade heard nothing. Instead he took the saw, rumbling angrily in his hands like a nest of wasps, and launched it roaring at the tree, relieving it of a low branch.

'No!' To his surprise Alan found himself clawing at the window as the tree deafened him with a piercing scream: 'I'm being murdered!'

'Stop!' cried Alan, as another branch met the saw's wrath. He turned from the window. 'Killer!' he cried as he plunged down the stair and, 'Ow ow ow ow ow!' as the buttocks kicked in.

Sam Spade unpeeled his scarf, removed his ear protectors and pushed up his goggles to confront the bandaged and broken figure, who now stood shaking before him, brandishing the connection lead.

'Problem, is there?' he asked, looking at the plug swinging to and fro in the other's trembling hands.

'The problem is, I want you to leave.'

Spade scratched his head and raised his eyes at his assistant, who was standing well back and looking scared. 'We agreed – four days work.'

'It's cancelled.' Alan looked at his watch. 'You should be packing up now anyway. It's nearly 6 o'clock.'

Sam Spade looked at him. 'Oh there's a couple of hours of daylight yet,' he said comfortably. 'Might as well make the most of it now the weather's cleared.' He indicated the grass shining with rain. 'Not my fault the whole afternoon's been a washout. Just bad luck, that's all.'

'A quick check of the weather forecast might have helped,' Alan couldn't help observing, sarcastically.

'Look, if you're trying to say something here…I charge by the hour. Come rain or shine. I made that clear before we even started.'

Alan pulled himself up to his full height and instantly wished he hadn't as he winced with pain. 'I'm sure you did. So, let me pay you for the valuable time you've already put into this project and you can be on your way.'

Sam Spade shook his head. 'Sorry, no can do. Four days, that's a lot of work for us. I've got to get this tree out before I can put those patio stones in. Not to mention the garden lights, automatic body-activated sound-system and state-of-the-art water feature. I can't cancel at this short notice.'

'Of course you can cancel, it is my garden, I can change my mind if I want to.'

'Mmm, interesting one, that,' said Spade, unhelpfully. 'Sure about that, are you? He took out a packet of chewing gum and extracted a sheet, very slowly. 'If I recollect correctly Mr – err – Mr – err…'

'Prugg.'

'Now I'm sure I have it here somewhere…'

'Prugg, the name's Prugg.'

'Now let me just check my pockets…'

'Alan Prugg! What the hell does it matter?'

'Ah, here we are.'

Sam Spade took an absurdly deep inhalation of breath. He held it for some time. Alan held his too, not trusting his rebellious body not to use the next puff to fuel some murderous action. Slowly, ever so slowly, like a fizzy drink bottle being opened inch by inch, Alan's breath began to fit and start through his clenched lips.

'Ahhhh!' said Spade, breathing out evenly. Then he said, 'No,' in a decisive voice and calmly replaced the small piece of folded paper into his overall pocket. He continued to stand, leisurely munching on his gum.

'What do you mean "No?"' Alan exploded, doubling over to gasp for breath and gasping in pain instead.

'No Prugg here,' Spade said. 'The name of my client is Belinda Cartwright. Is that your name?'

'Do I look like a Belinda?!'

'Parents can be cruel.'

'She's my fiancée.'

'Oh well in that case…' Sam 'Call-a-Spade-a-Spade' Spade turned back and began powering up his chainsaw with evident relish. Alan looked at the plug in his hand and realised it belonged to the lawnmower, which was lying abandoned next to the stack of decking, waiting to be laid. He threw it aside in disgust.

'What are you doing?' he yelled into the din, to no apparent avail.

Indulging himself in a couple of flashy-sounding motorcycle revs Spade held the saw upright before him like a Samurai sword in noisy salute before sweeping it round towards another branch.

'Nooo!!' yelled Alan as the leafy plume phlumphed to the ground. 'Murderer! Killer! I'll take you to court, I'll sue the arse off you – you – you –'

Spade turned off his machine and pulled his goggles up a second time.

'Tell you what,' he said, in a sudden flash of reasonableness. 'I will agree to temporarily suspend operations, *temporarily.*' He shot Alan a warning look from under his goggles. 'Meanwhile I'll have a quick cuppa whilst you phone my client for confirmation.'

'It's not a proper teabreak, mind,' he added in more threatening tones, 'I will have to be paid for my time. Milk and two sugars, ta. Coming, Ter?' And he wandered across the lawn, plonked himself down on one of the deckchairs, pulled his hard hat down over his eyes and fell asleep.

'Ter' stood awkwardly, balancing on one leg before making up his mind. 'Three sugars here,' he said before trotting across the lawn after his boss.

'Just black for me,' said the tree. But for once, Alan wasn't listening.

Alan wandered into the kitchen, filled the kettle, flicked the switch, and went over to the fridge, that was lurking, along with the other white goods, behind a black granite façade. He extracted the milk – *skimmed, ugh* – and with it, the mobile phone – *so that's where it was* – and pressed a few buttons.

'Belinda Cartwright, please? Yes it is rather urgent.'

Nothing but skimmed. Bugger. A cursory look out of the window revealed Sam Spade's assistant having a quick fag next to Belinda's new patio stones.

'She's in a meeting? No problem.'

He switched off the phone with some relief and peered into the fridge, deftly compiling a text message, one-handed, as he did so:

Grdnrs here. Keeping tree. Luv U. Alan.

He nervously hit the send button before peering anxiously out of the window again at the two workmen who, jackets off, were making themselves comfortable with a couple of beers (where had they come from?) and tapping their fag-ash into one of Belinda's new potted Japanese Acers. The metallic sound of Beethoven's 5th yo-yoed his head back into the room.

Assuming it was Belinda returning his call, Alan toyed with the idea of not answering it, before deciding that the repercussions could be too terrible to contemplate.

'Hello,' he said. But it wasn't the mobile that was ringing. That's odd. Why was she phoning the landline?

Being the latest state-of-the-art cordless variety, the phone took a while to locate, but was eventually ambushed underneath the newspaper he had been reading in the toilet. Shutting the seat, Alan sat down heavily with an involuntary wince at his protesting buttocks. He lifted the phone to his painful cheek. Wincing again, he removed it to a safe distance.

'Hello?'

'Hello,' said a gravelly voice. 'Is this Mr Prugg? We have it on good authority that a Mr Prugg resides at this residence.'

The phone being several feet from his ear, Alan could not hear too well. The voice yelling in his head did not help either: 'Hey brother, give us a chance, man! Don't do it, man! Don't just leave me, brother.'

'I am Mr Prugg,' Alan said, simply. He saw no reason not to.

'I have a piece of information for you, Mr Prugg, that you might find interesting,' said the gravelly voice.

Alan suddenly felt very tired. 'Look, I don't want to buy life insurance, I am not interested in any mobile phone deals and I am double glazed up to my eyeballs.'

'I think you should listen, Mr Prugg. If you care about the safety of a little friend of yours.'

Despite the pain, the screaming and the buttock–ache, Alan sat up.

'Go on,' he said.

'I trust you got our note,' said the sinister voice, authoritatively.

'What note?'

'You didn't get it? But we sent it on Monday, first class.'

'Hang on, wait there.' Alan padded down the hall to the front door. There was an envelope there, under his briefcase. Belinda must have missed it on her way out. He turned it over in his hands.

'To: whomever it may concern' was written mysteriously on the front, followed by 'Alan Prugg Esquire, 11 Elmtree Avenue, London.' The writing was spiky and naïve, with the kind of aggressive lack of control suggestive of the hand of a thirteen year old delinquent. However, despite himself, Alan nodded with approval at the attention to polite formalities. He returned with the envelope to the bathroom and plonked himself down on the toilet seat to peruse its contexts.

DEAR MR PRUGG (Nice polite start)

WE HAVE YOUR GIRLFRIEND. WE ARE THE ONES WOT DONE IT. IF YOU WANT TO SEE YOUR GIRLFRIEND ALIVE AND WITHOUT LOTS OF DISFIGERING AND HIDEOUS MUTILATIONS YOU WILL HAVE TO RESCUE HER FROM OUR SADISTIC CLUTCHES. IF YOU TELL THE POLICE WE WILL CUT HER NOSE OFF AND FEED IT TO THE PIDGINS OF TRAFALGAR SQUARE. WE WILL PHONE YOU AT 6 O'CLOCK TODAY, SHARP. MAKE SURE YOU'RE IN WITH A NOTEBOOK HANDY.

YOURS SINCERELY

THE KIDNAPPERS xxx

For a split second Alan felt a twinge of relief. Not that he wanted any harm to come to Belinda of *course* – he worshipped both her and the stiletto-speared ground she stamped on: she was the love of his life! But…

It is funny how the mind works in situations of extreme stress. The anxious housewife whose husband is late home from work, whose children are staying with their grandparents, mind a-frenzy with the possibilities of danger: *What if? What if? What if? Whatifheishavinganaffair? Whatifhehasbeenrunoverbyabus? Whatifthelittledarlingsfelloutofanaeroplane?*

WhatifGranaccidentallyleftthegasonandthehouseexplodedsending thelittledarlingsupintothesky? What if? What if? What if?

And whilst the head races with all the appalling possibilities of familial breakdown and imminent demise, whilst the heart palpitates and a trickle of sweat runs down your face, there is a little voice (however small, however almost-undetectably tiny) saying, 'Life insurance policy, no kids, everyone sorry for me. At last I'll be able to move to Australia and pursue my interest in online bingo. *Fan-fucking-tastic!*'

'You read it yet?' said the sinister voice, agitatedly.

'Yes, yes I have.'

'A certain young lady named Paula Wocziac.'

Alan stood up, trembling. 'No. Not Paula.'

'I take it you know the young lady?'

'Of course I do. You know I do. If you harm one hair on her head I'll –'

'What? What will you do, Mr Prugg?'

Alan fell silent. Even the tree stopped shouting. What would he do? Alan had always fancied himself as a bit of a hero, bit of a rescuer, with a strong emphasis on the 'bit of a' part. He was not one for dangerous energetics, or even for prising himself off the sofa, usually.

If Alan had been paying proper attention he might have noticed that the gravelly voice on the other end of the phone had raised a couple of decibels and was sounding slightly too keen to find out his thoughts and feelings about the whole affair. But he was too taken up with his unexpectedly overwhelming reaction to the idea that Paula might be in trouble in some way. Paula. Paula. He had not given her a thought since he had phoned her and they had that nice chat about his plastic surgery. The searing pain in his chest, the beating of his heart – okay all that had been going on before – but he wasn't expecting to feel so…so…protective. He paced around the toilet cubicle, picking up the power shower and giving it a couple of blasts for no particular reason. It felt real. Manly. He inflated his chest in full pigeon glory – Ouch! – It felt *good*.

'What do you want?' he said manfully.

'What do most kidnappers want?' asked the kidnapper sarcastically. 'Money. Fame. Name in the papers.'

'Really? Wouldn't that be counter-productive?'

The kidnapper thought for a moment before resuming, *Gravel voce*, 'Perhaps you're right. Perhaps we don't want anything.' There was a pause.

Alan thought he heard a sneeze.

'Yeah, there's nothing we want from you, nothing. There's nothing you can do. She's a gonner.'

Alan clutched at the phone. 'But you must want *something*?'

'No, nothing.'

'But that's not – rational.'

'This is the 20th century mate, the world is a messy, irrational place.' There was a muffled sound, followed by some coughing, followed by, 'This is the 21st century mate, the world is a messy, irrational place.'

'I see.'

Alan tried to think. But his head was a mess. Plus it was throbbing unbearably. He put a hand to his forehead and screamed in pain.

'Who are you?' he said at last.

'Who are we? Who are we?' said the voice, menacingly. 'Who are we?' it said in a slightly different tone of voice. There was some undefined mumbling. The voice returned, sounding confident.

'We are a small radical terrorist cell with undivulged purposes and allegiances who will, for legal reasons, remain nameless.'

'Oh.' Alan thought about this. 'And the name of your outfit?'

'I cannot divulge that information for legal reasons. Data Protection Act.'

Alan scratched his nose thoughtfully and dropped to the floor in agony.

'I don't understand,' he gasped. 'If you don't want money, fame, fortune, a spot on the telly or furtherance of your cause, why did you phone me up in the first place?'

It was a good question. One that the caller obviously had not considered before.

'That's a good question,' the caller said, slowly. There was the sound of some rustling and shuffling, followed by a low but definite, 'Just fuck off, Dave.'

'Do you mind if I take a moment to confer with my – err – confederates?' said the voice, awkwardly.

'Confer away,' Alan said generously.

When it came back, the voice not only sounded more sure of itself but had fallen to a whole new level of menacingness.

'We thought you might like to know that unless you do something, your little friend is due to be exterminated in the most debilitating and painful manner at nine o'clock this evening exactly.'

'What? What? What?' Alan clutched his head, ears and nose in quick succession, and collapsed in agony again. (He was a slow learner.) 'Do something? What the hell do you expect me to do?'

'We just thought you'd like to know in case you might be interested in – I don't know – launching a rescue attempt or something.'

'Rescue attempt?' stammered Alan. If a man could be described as looking ashen, Alan, at that moment, was that man. 'Me?'

'Do you want directions?' asked the voice on the phone, civilly.

'No, I do not!'

'So you are prepared to let this young lady – Paula Wocziac – endure unimaginable suffering and you are prepared to go to your grave knowing that it was in your power to do something about it?'

Alan clutched his head again. 'Aaaghh!' he screamed, as his nerve-endings reminded him, agonisingly, of his recent facelift. 'No. NO! Look, can't we discuss this sensibly and reasonably?'

'What is there to discuss, Mr Prugg?' asked the voice, reasonably enough.

'You must want *something*? Money, err…possessions. I have a state-of-the-art MP3 player. It is rather good…No, hang on...' He hesitated for a second. Or more. 'You can take the reproduction regency chandelier. It was extremely expensive, you know. The opera season tickets.' He closed his eyes. 'The Bang and Olufsens.'

Alan waited with baited breath, hoping against hope that somehow the Bang and Olufsens would be saved.

'I am not interested in your bloody speakers!' said the voice, losing its temper. 'Don't you have any guts? Are you a man at all? Give me fucking strength!'

There was more muttering and rustling.

'Look, if you're interested, your girlfriend's going to meet her end at 9pm precisely this evening. If you want to consider rescuing her, the address is…' The address was reeled off. 'So fucking sort yourself out and get your arse down here and don't tell the police or she's dead. Now, I don't want to be having to phone you again.'

And suddenly Alan was alone with nothing but the sad drone of the dialling tone for company.

If Alan had been a more astute individual and, perhaps, if he had not been suffering the effects of extensive plastic surgery and its associated pain-alleviating medication, he might have worked out that there was something a bit odd about this phone call. As it was, he flung himself painfully to the bathroom floor, sweating copiously and feeling very put upon.

What had he done to deserve this? Here he was, shuddering on the handcrafted Italian tiled floor of his bathroom, an ordinary accountant – nay a man even, just a man. Trying to get along in the world. And now someone bloody expected him to act like James Bond. At any other time, *any* other time, he would have been delighted to oblige. But he had just undergone extensive surgery. He was in no fit state to mount any sort of rescue attempt. No, it was no good, he would have to phone them back and say, thanks very much but it's absolutely impossible. *Any other time…*

'Prugg here,' Alan stated in his most overbearing tones. It was the only way to deal with these people.

'Who?'

'Alan Prugg, we were talking a few minutes ago.'

'How did you get this number?'

'I dialled 1471 of course. I know you people are a bit backward, but it really would be worth your while brushing up on your telephone technology.'

'What do you want?' the voice asked icily.

'Look, my man, about what we were discussing earlier, whilst under normal circumstances I would – naturally – be leaping into my nice little classic MG Roadster and coming round to give you what for, today is just not convenient and I won't be able to make it. So thank you very much for your offer and everything but...'

Most receptionists, telephonists, supermarket checkout people, bank managers and shop assistants tended to respond to Alan's special commanding tone: the gravelly voice didn't.

'Okay, like that is it? We'll send the car round at eight. Don't be late.' And he hung up.

Shit. What was he going to do now?

Chapter Twenty-Three | **A SPOT OF SURVEILLANCE**

The letter was lying unfolded on Pat's desk. Its virgin-whiteness belied the terrible news contained therein. Belinda stood over it, pretending that she was examining the wall-chart monitoring holiday leave pinned at eye-level behind. She squinted down. The letters swum and bulged beneath her eyes. They looked unreal, as though written in a foreign language.

'Dear Patricia Rawley,

We are delighted to inform you that you were successful in your application...'

That's what it should have said, anyway. In reality, some stupid idiot in Human Resources had messed up the mail-merge again and the letter instead commiserated with the successful applicant, offering its 'regret' at having to inform her of the happy news. Belinda's own letter, now lying scrumpled on top of the black granite breakfast bar at home, had read,

'Dear Belinda Cartwright,

We are delighted to inform you that you have been unsuccessful on this occasion.'

Not exactly complimentary to either party, but the message

was clear enough. Pat had won.

In full, Belinda's letter said rather more.

Belinda Cartwright
11 Elmtree Avenue
Clapham

15th May

Dear Belinda Cartwright,

We are delighted to inform you that your application has been unsuccessful on this occasion.

Whilst the panel were extremely impressed with your portfolio and experience, the other was an exceptional candidate, who has shown flair, skill and an admirable courage and commitment to the firm. We know this will come as an inevitable disappointment but we hope the knowledge that you lost out to a truly excellent candidate may lessen the blow somewhat.

We wish you every success in the future whether here at Smith, Smith-Brown and Smith, or elsewhere.

Yours sincerely
Paula Wocziac
pp Sir Alan Smith-Brown

'…courage and commitment to the firm. Exceptional candidate who has shown flair and skill.'

After everything Belinda had done. All those extra hours. All that fawning. And for what? A kick in the teeth. Courage and commitment? What courage and commitment? Just because Pat was one of those dreadful smiley, coping individuals that everyone loved to pity so much. 'Oh isn't she marvellous?' they would say when she was out of earshot, 'the way she copes.' The woman was having a field-day. Why couldn't anybody else see? Special probe, special toilet. Who wouldn't blossom in the face of such favouritism? As for 'exceptional candidate' – exceptional? Attention-seeking more like.

It was ridiculous! Did they want to encourage people to be having accidents all over the place, just so that they too could enjoy the privilege of a head-probe, their own personal toilet and a leg-up the greasy pole? It was a slippery slope. Before you knew it, there would be people trapping themselves under the wheels of moving vehicles simply to get ahead. And could we blame them? Admirable? What was there to admire? After all, having an accident was hardly rocket science. Anyone could have an accident.

The sound of Pat's chair creaking down the corridor back from enjoying the luxurious facility of the disabled toilet was enough to drive Belinda back to her desk, where she sat, staring at her monitor in stony silence. She had not exchanged a word with Pat all day. This in itself was not unusual, but now Pat had no choice in the matter, as Belinda had set up her instant messenger to say that she was currently abroad. As they shared an office, Pat must have known this to be a lie, but Belinda didn't care. Without the instant messenger on, she didn't have to know, or care, what Pat thought about it one way or the other.

Pat entered the office and headed towards her desk. Amanda, opposite, was sitting bolt upright and staring ahead with strangely flushed cheeks. Belinda could almost feel her suppressed amusement.

'Amanda – can you photocopy fifteen copies of the report I put in your in-tray, please?' *Yes, not sniggering now, are you?*

'But, it's four hundred and fifty pages long.'

'Well counted.'

'The feeder is broken.'

'What a pity. You'll just have to do it by hand then, won't you?'

Amanda fell silent.

Belinda leaned back in her chair and fell to brooding again, her fractious heart somewhat soothed by the sound of the photocopier whirring into action.

Meanwhile, over in Human Resources, Tanya had given up pretending to have any real work to do and was perched on Sonya's desk regaling her on the benefits of having a food guru.

'It's all about knowing your blood-line descendency, Sonya,' she was saying. 'You see, we're all descended from different apes. She tests to find out whether you are an orangutan, gorilla or chimpanzee, and works out your food groups to match. I'm an orangutan.'

'*Rea-lly?*'

Paula sat, unnoticed as usual, tapping her automatic pencil. She gazed tiredly at 'Social Inclusion: The Inclusion Zone: A Policy Statement'.

She hesitated... No.

No.

Her hand started the inexorable drift towards the activation key again, almost without her permission. Almost.

'It's amazing what they know these days, isn't it, Tanya?'

Instantly, the dreaded policy document disappeared from her screen, to be replaced by the back of a head, in front of another screen. Paula sighed happily and sank her face into her hands.

'Does she take your blood? I hate that. I'd just die!'

'Oh no, she can tell just by studying your earlobes.'

'*Rea-lly*? That's amazing, Tanya.'

The hair was brownish: not curly, not straight. There was a flat part in the middle like a squashed piece of lawn after a picnic and a strange tufty bit to the left, perhaps a refugee from the last visit to the hairdresser. Some time ago by the looks of things.

She switched to Camera 2 which presented a good view of the north-west face of her subject: his body, almost parallel to the ground, his face tantalisingly obscured by the long-haired bespectacled and headphoned youth beside him – whose suspiciously unnatural position suggested he was hiding something on his monitor.

She returned to the target of her surveillance. His straggly jeans, his insectile posture, his – Was that a *Star Wars* T-shirt? So washed out it was hard to tell, but she was certain that that brown blob was Chewbacca's hairy face staring out from his left breast, either that or lunch. No. Further scrutiny confirmed it was definitely Chewbacca.

She returned to Camera 1 and gazed fondly at the hairs on the nape of his neck, silhouetted against a screen that was filled with the cruel black eyes, vicious yellow beak and take-no-prisoner talons of an osprey in full flight. She tried to read the text but couldn't make it out, something to do with a breeding programme in Scotland. Was it Scotland? She knew it was an osprey anyway.

She had to admit when she first started observing him in his native environment it had not been quite what she had expected. But then what did one expect to be the secret life of The Man in the Mask? That he should live in a castle and be employed in some romantic swash-buckling occupation like – like – ? Real life was always going to be more mundane. But then Paula quite liked mundane.

Spying on Fred was never that eventful; movement tended to be the exception rather the norm. As for conversation, she had, as yet, witnessed not one word exchanged in that small and dingy office. But, nevertheless, there was something comforting about watching him sitting there. Existing. She was happy enough with what drama there was – a tightening of hands around a coffee-cup, maybe; she lived for the excitement of a lunchbreak or a trip to the toilet.

So far, to her great disgruntlement, she had not even witnessed him getting up from his chair, let alone going to the toilet. He didn't seem to eat, either – perhaps due to the risk of then needing to go the toilet. Not that she was desperate to become overly acquainted with his bowel movements (although she had met some club members who were into that sort of thing). No, her continuing frustration was that, despite having seen every part of him, his body, his skin, the mole on his back, the hairs on his toes; despite having done things with him that she would not have dreamt of doing with any other man – she had yet to see his face.

This should not have presented much of a challenge to Paula, for whom espionage was a walk in the park: rather like the one through which she tailed him after the club one dark night. Thankfully, the office, to which she followed him the next afternoon, did not appear to harbour any security whatsoever and posed no problem to entry, or the subsequent installation of cameras and microphone.

That she had managed to avoid his face throughout the entire journey was a wonder in itself. She considered whether she might be stalling, reluctant to confront his true features, to finally come face-to-face with his day-to-day reality.

Perhaps they were all wearing masks, Paula thought sadly – Fred, herself, Alan. Perhaps she had been wearing a mask with Alan all those years. Perhaps they had never really known each other: playing out roles prescribed by others, not knowing what they wanted, so going for what they thought other people wanted instead. Looking for permission to want. To be wanted.

But something had changed in that small dark room, where no one was watching. (Well, apart from Bill.) She thought of the eyes glittering behind his black mask. Eyes that looked at her, wanted her, saw her. Eyes that had flickered in the darkness, like the candle flame between them. Thinking about it now, she was surprised at the violence of her reaction when he had offered her the candle, asked her to take control – anger, sharp painful anger like the burn of the candle wax dropping on her skin. It felt like a betrayal, an abuse, what he was asking from her. He asked her to take on a role – a mask – and with it came the ultimate exposure, not of body, of personality, of thought, feeling, who you thought you were; but an exposure of *her* desire. Never before had that been asked of her. *Desire me*, he said. *Want me, hurt me, desire me. Show me who you are.*

'You know she's sooo right about me. She said, 'Orangutans don't eat junk food. You don't see an orangutan sitting in a tree or whatever, scoffing a pizza or helping themselves to chocolate chip ice-cream, now do you?'

'That makes so much sense. So your system can't cope?'

'Exactly, Sonya.'

She was fooling herself. He did not see her. She was just another conquest for him. Another woman, another encounter. Perhaps, after all, he also considered her boring.

The full horror of this thought slapped her in the face and Paula leapt up and stood quivering by her chair.

The twin heads of Sonya and Tanya swivelled blankly in her direction, then swivelled back again, where Tanya, undeterred, continued from where she left off about her orangutan-related food intolerances.

'It's not about dieting, I can eat what I want. I've lost a stone without even trying. As long as I stick to twigs and leaves, I'm fine.'

'Wow, it's amazing what knowing a bit of science can do, isn't it Tanya?'

'I'd recommend it to everyone.'

Unknown to Sonya and Tanya, just a few feet away from them, standing by her chair and clutching tightly onto her automatic pencil, Paula was undergoing an epiphany. The myriad of thoughts and feelings she was experiencing is far too complicated to describe here, and in any case, would be too profound and poetic for a book such as this. Fleeting feelings, memories, snatches of words, tugs of regret, moments of kindness, pictures of past experiences: it all boiled down to the same thing. *She had to throw away the mask. She, too, had to be naked. Take the risk. Of being naked. Being seen. Take off the mask, Paula... take off the mask... And he had to take his mask off too...*

She trembled at the sheer profundity of it all.

'You're probably a gorilla,' Tanya was saying, examining Sonya's earlobes critically.

'Do you really think so?'

'Well you're quite hairy, aren't you?'

'So what kind of food can my blood cope with then?'

'Hmmm. I'd say, bananas really. And that's about it.'

'And I can eat as much as I like?'

'You never have to diet again.'

They did not notice that Paula had already left the office. Hurrying down the street, she rehearsed her actions in her mind. She would just ring the bell and ask if he wanted to go out for lunch. Well, strictly speaking it would be dinner, she supposed. But as Fred's working day only started in the afternoon, it would be lunch for him. 'Do you want to come for lunch?' she would say outright like that. So simple.

It started to rain, and she pulled her fleece tightly around herself as she fled along the pavement, scattering kids and shoppers, leaving a wave of market researchers, one-off make-up consultants and *Big Issue* sellers in her anxious wake.

'Do you want to come for lunch?' That's all.

*****

Anyone could have an accident. Anyone could have an accident. Anyone…

Belinda leant her head in her hands, she couldn't keep track of all the people she was competing with anymore: Pat, her sister, Amanda, her colleagues and friends. And yet still they crept ahead, inexorably, laughingly, crossing the finishing line before her one by one.

Equal Opportunities. Those seven poisoned syllables, the thorn in Belinda's side for so long.

It seemed clear now, what was going on.

She, Belinda, was being unfairly penalised for *not* having had an accident.

She brooded on the problem, oblivious to the pressure of her sharp nails digging into her perfect scalp. So preoccupied was she that she did not even notice when a bead of blood ran down her forehead and ski-jumped off the end of her nose, meeting an explosive end on the financial modelling report lying quietly on her desk.

If Pat was to be given an unfair advantage through her own clumsiness in failing to avoid that milk float, then what was to stop Belinda reaping those same advantages?

But how?

As devoted as she was to the cause of her own personal advancement, the idea of throwing herself under a slow-moving delivery vehicle did not exactly appeal.

She glanced across at Amanda who had been standing over the photocopier for two hours now. It came as something of a relief for Belinda to discover that these small abuses of power still provoked a flicker of pleasure even at times like this.

The vibration of her left breast pocket, however, heralded the fact that things were about to get a whole lot worse.

Belinda read Alan's text without expression.

What?-what?-what?-what?-what? Rage steamed heavily in her stomach like boil-in-the-bag haggis.

What was wrong with the man? She had given him chance after chance. And here he was, involved in some petty rebellion against the ONLY person interested in his improvement. All she had done, everything she had pushed him to do, was merely for his own benefit. Where would he be without her? Achieving nothing! Why couldn't he bloody see that? (And what the hell did 'Grdnrs' mean?)

And then it happened. Not exactly a light-bulb going off in her brain, but an extraordinary epiphany nonetheless. (They must have put something in the Smith, Smith-Brown and Smith drinking water that day.)

Anyone could have an accident…

Unbidden, a sudden vivid vision flashed into her mind.

Herself and Alan at their wedding. She in a simple parchment dress: coy, modest, self-sacrificing. He in a wheelchair. Whispers in the congregation:

'How coy and modest she is,' said one.

'Such courage and commitment to the firm,' added another. 'Do you know she hasn't taken a single day's sick-leave? That's the kind of attitude that can't remain unrewarded for long.

'That simple parchment dress looks really expensive,' added somebody else.

Anyone could have an accident.

The words rang out, sweet and bell-like, full of new meaning. How had she not *seen* before? Equal Opportunities was one thing; Equal Opportunities by proxy? Even better. It was time to level the playing field.

She rose stiffly to her feet.

Amanda looked up hopefully from the photocopier then stared at her forehead. Belinda passed her hand across her face and was surprised at the red blood blooming on her fingers.

'What are you looking at?' she snapped. 'I want those copies on my table first thing tomorrow morning.'

'But –' Amanda's face reddened and turned back to the machine.

'You staying on, Pat?'

Pat waved her probe angelically before bowing to the keyboard.

'Of course you are,' Belinda said. She smiled a beatific smile and looked at her watch. 6.30pm. She frowned. 'As you know I would have stayed on, any other time. But…there's something I have to do.'

Trying not to be dragged down to Pat's level, Belinda carefully collected up her bag, packing her mobile and her Sidfob and exited the office. All that showed of her inner purpose: a straightening of her back and the vigour of her stride.

She did not hear the explosion of laughter straight away, at least not until she had passed the water cooler and was coming up to the lifts. She would recognise Amanda's snorting wheeze anywhere. Pat, of course, remained silent. Was she there, sitting angelically in her chair pretending not to hear Amanda's catty comment? Or was she, too, internally punching the air in paralysed glee? Whatever the case, Belinda was impervious to their ridicule. She had seen a vision of the future. And it was glorious.

Chapter Twenty-Four | KIDNAP

'So, Alan, do you want to tell me what the *fuck* is going on?'

Alan had been deep in discussion with Sam Spade about the possibility of installing a mini Al–Hambra fountain adjacent to the decking, when Belinda's cold voice hit him between the shoulder blades like a freezing jet of water.

The familiar feeling of fear prickled across the back of his neck and trickled pathetically down the gutter of his somewhat fleshy spine. He took a fortifying gulp of cold tea.

Contained within the timbre of that voice was all that kept him pinned, froglike, upon the dissection table. The sliding sound of contempt and disapproval along with all the terror and thrill that conjured: the connotations with headmistress, mother (let's not go there) and a host of other unnamed authority figures. In the shrill of her voice, the singing chorus of all the teenage girls who had laughed and sneered at him in his pimply youth; the gasps of a myriad older married women he'd lusted after in his twenties; the leer of a thousand white miniskirts prancing provocatively before him as a student, a thousand tiny wiggling bottoms, laughing... *Oh God, now bottoms were talking to him.* This had to stop.

Steeling himself for the inevitable, slowly, oh so slowly, Alan turned. This was partly for effect and partly due to his newly stuffed and stitched posterior. What he saw made him immediately want to turn away again.

Belinda stood, gripping her handbag for emotional support rather as a psychopath might cling to a sawn-off shotgun. Alan tried to look into her eyes but found that he didn't have the stomach, his disobedient pupils flickering off weakly at the last minute. The savagery of her stare was shocking.

'This is the famous Belinda Cartwright, I take it,' said Sam Spade cheerfully, stubbing out his fag on the side of the stone lion and rubbing his hands on his radioactive yellow jacket. 'Well, I must say, Missus, the name looks better on you.'

She completely ignored the offer of his smudgy hand and shot straight at Alan, 'What's this about the tree?'

He knew in that moment, preternaturally, supernaturally, he never knew how, that the woman before him was no longer the Belinda he had fallen in love with – bitchy, nasty, ungenerous and great in the sack. Here was another creature altogether – bitchy, nasty, ungenerous and to all extents and purposes frigid. He hardly recognised her.

'Ah, the tree...' he said, non-committally, biding his time.

'Is there something you want to tell me?'

He looked at her, standing his ground, although his legs were slightly flexed in anticipation. 'The tree stays. I like it. It's – pretty.'

For Belinda, this was the final straw. Her sister's wedding, Pat's promotion, the Michael Jackson nose, all her disappointments and bitternesses bubbled up inside her and finally, at last, her boil-in-the-bag rage exploded.

'Everything! You undermine everything. Everything I try to do!'

She stood forward and snatched the chainsaw out of Sam Spade's hand.

'Everything I force you to do. I do it for you! Do you hear? I do it for you!' she screamed, unaware of this possible infringement of Brian Adams' copyright. 'Where do you think you're fucking going?' The words were ripped out of her mouth by the screeching saw.

'I'm getting the hell out of here,' yelled Alan as he pelted for the garden door.

'Alan, come right back here. We're getting fucking married!'

He struggled with the door and then he was gone.

'Come back here at once!' Belinda was hysterical now. With a wailing ululation of war, she raised the whirring saw high above her head and took off after him.

Sam Spade sat down on the head of a terracotta figurine and sucked his breath through his front teeth. 'Time for another teabreak.' He said to 'Ter'. 'This is not going to be cheap,' he added with satisfaction.

Paula cut down a side street. He was bound to wonder how she knew where he worked. She lowered her head guiltily. This was maybe not the best time to admit to her predilection for spying. She would say that she had found out from a friend. A friend of a friend. Where he worked. And as she was passing, she just thought...she was just dropping in to – to –

That she was just passing by and...

How would she recognise him? She would know those eyes anywhere. Even without the mask. Those eyes. Those eyes flickering in the darkness... Now, where to get a bus? Bus bus bus. Oh – and what was that dark-windowed car doing there? And who were those two men in balaclavas leaping out of it and heading her way?

*****

Panting and perspiring heavily, Alan negotiated three bicycles, a hedge trimmer, one of the neighbour's cats and some spare pieces of leg-mutilating cast iron furniture on the communal stair before finally arriving at and hauling open the heavy, treacle-black front door.

Laughing hysterically, he emerged out onto the street. At last, he was taking control. He had taken charge, told his woman what for. The tree was staying and there was nothing she could do about it. He looked up at the blue sky, clear after the slight shower. A flock of starlings gossiped overhead. Oh the beauty of it, the sheer wonder of it! He laughed out loud. Why had he never noticed the sensuous shapes of the trees on this road, the shine on the paving stones after the rain, the rustic collage of leaves across the ground, the ordinary things: families carrying their shopping, turned in towards one another, two small children in red Wellington boots jumping in puddles, the couriers on their bicycles racing the wind, the rainbow spray fountaining up from under the wheels of a passing white van out of which two men in balaclavas were merrily leaping. You never know, he might even get a shag out of it. He could tell she was responding to his manly approach…

'Is this something to do with refuse collection?' was the last thing the small children in Wellingtons heard the slightly tubby balding man say as he was bundled into the van.

*****

'No, you don't understand!'

Paula struggled as the two men in balaclavas grabbed her by the arms and manhandled her into the dark car.

'I've got to rescue someone.'

'I think you're the one needs rescuing, Miss,' said a deep voice.

*****

Belinda and chainsaw, both howling with rage, exploded out onto the street in time to see Alan disappearing into a white van and racing off down the road.

'Bloody coward! You're not getting out of the wedding that easily!' she yelled. She turned to see two terrified faces, watching her. 'What are you bloody looking at?' – the Wellington boots instantly stopped and turned to carry their owners off screaming in the opposite direction – then, chainsaw brandished above her head, 'Taxi! Taxi!'

*****

Paula felt herself roughly (not too roughly) bound and blindfolded, and harshly (not too harshly) pushed out of the van onto a cobbled street.

That, at least, she could tell. Plus it was not the best-fitting of blindfolds and she could see, through the gap where it failed to meet her nose, not only the cobbles under her feet but the arm of her aggressor with its familiar tattoo, as it hauled her roughly (but not too roughly) along.

Paula opened her mouth to say something. But before she could, the arms let her go and she was shoved forward to stand, blind and swaying.

She felt his presence in front of her before he spoke. Someone else. Someone new. She was being delivered into the hands of goodness knew who. But she felt his gaze burning into her, looking her up and down, assessing her.

Before she could say anything her arms were grabbed and held behind her back and she was propelled forward towards a building.

'What are you doing?' Paula protested, struggling with the bonds on her wrists.

'Shhhh.' It sounded familiar, but it was hard to tell from just a 'Shhhh'.

'Is that you?' she opened her mouth to say. But before she could do so something strange occurred. Fear caressed her head and neck, sweat beaded at her temples and excitement licked up her back and round her breasts. Trepidation nibbled at her toes while anxiety crowed like a hyena from her shoulders. It was thrilling! After all, she thought to herself, deliciously, she could be mistaken.

What if it wasn't his familiar candle-licked 'Shhh'? Many people could 'shhh' like that, after all. What if she was wrong and the arm next to hers did not bear the telltale mole on the forearm? Many potential assailants may have the very same mole… Maybe, she could not quite see it properly, blurring behind her fearful eyes.

Paula closed her mouth again and let his hands shove her roughly through the doorway of some unknown building. Nice hands.

'I tell you, I will be complaining to the council about this,' Alan was saying crossly, as his masked assailants dragged him bodily out of the van, across the cobbles and shoved him roughly, slightly too roughly – ('Ow! Be careful, my man. I'm recovering from an operation. And I'll have you know it was extremely expensive!') – through some large red double-doors.

*****

'In here,' said the voice.

Maybe she didn't recognise that voice. Maybe it was the rough gruff unemotional voice of a man who did not care whether she lived or died. Her fate was in his hands. And there was nothing she could do about it!

Paula closed her eyes, dropping her shoulders, hyena and all, and, for the first time in her life, decided, thrillingly, to go with the flow.

*****

Alan looked around in bewilderment. A kaleidoscope of coloured lights in front of which unidentified shadows and shapes moved indefinably. His head hurt, his face hurt, his buttocks hurt, his eyes swam.

'Hello, Mr Prugg,' said a figure.

'Welcome Mr Prugg.'

'Welcome to our headquarters, Mr Prugg.'

'Ah! Prugg. Mr Prugg. Welcome.'

Chapter Twenty-Five | SEQUINS AND CHAINSAWS

Whether it was the effects of the surgery and its associated medication, the stress of meeting a band of lunatic terrorists, or the pressures of achieving good garden design, Alan was beginning to feel distinctly worse for wear. Faint, dizzy, sick, his eyes and his buttocks were beginning to ache unbearably: all in all it had been a really *really* awful day.

The interior of the building into which he was rudely bundled was unlike anywhere he had ever seen. Coloured spinning lights rotated across the black rubber floor; cool car crash sequences and explosions were projected across the walls. It seemed to him that everywhere he looked were beautiful exotic people, dressed to kill (in fact as it was only eight-thirty in the evening, there was only a handful). Women in the tightest of tight black leather shimmied on a dance floor under bulbous lights which resembled giant pink breasts. Men in strange garments involving complicated constructions made of straps and pulleys, or else in pin-striped suits, leant against the walls and watched him with interest. What was even stranger was that they all seemed to know him.

'Mr Prugg.'

'Hello Mr Prugg.'

'Welcome Mr Prugg.'

He moved slowly forward as though in a dream, not even glancing back at his balaclava-ed assailants, further and further into the heart of this strange new world.

'Good evening Mr Prugg. Or can I call you Al?'

Alan spun round to be faced by a thin woman, painted gold from head to toe. She had a variety of exotic-looking piercings and a thick Manchester accent. 'Good evening, Mr Prugg,' she breathed. 'I am Honey Von Trapp.'

Alan goggled at her.

'And I am Bunny O'Juicebox,' said the half-naked shaven-headed figure crouched by her side. He bared his teeth to reveal a solid gold smile.

Honey Von Trapp moseyed over to Alan and draped herself across him.

'We have heard a lot about you, Mr Prugg. Your razor-sharp intelligence, your ready wit and your ruthless manliness.'

'Your prowess with a calculator,' said Bunny.

Back to Honey: 'Your popularity with the ladies. You are a man to be reckoned with, Mr Prugg.'

'*Mr Pru-ugg*,' whined Bunny, disturbingly.

A small piece of Alan's brain questioned how Honey was party to this intelligence; an even smaller piece questioned its findings. Both, however, were overruled by the much larger piece of Alan's brain that liked what it heard.

'Your reputation goes before you, Mr Prugg,' said Bunny O'Juicebox, flashing his disconcerting golden grin.

Alan could not help indulging a quick inflation of pride.

'I take it you've heard of my work at Smith, Smith-Brown and Smith. I am certainly renowned for my prowess with the spreadsheet.'

'And between the spreadsheets too, I'm told,' breathed Honey.

Alan felt a ripple of pleasure course across his painful buttocks.

'Well,' he said coyly, 'I don't like to brag…'

'Would you like to join us for a drink, Mr Prugg?'

'*Mr Pru-ugg*,' echoed her companion, nasally, followed by a dazzling smile.

The small part of Alan's brain that had been a little cynical about the spreadsheet comment, tried to remind him of his doctor's instructions not to mix alcohol with the powerful painkillers presently keeping the agony of his wounds at bay; but the much larger part of his brain, still chuffed about the 'prowess with the ladies' comment, was having none of it.

'That would be very nice, thank you.'

They led him, as in a dream, across the dance floor towards the small bar area and Alan found himself drifting pleasurably off into a medicated daydream of possibilities. *Who were these people? Where was he? Was he dreaming? Did he give a shit?* At least they appreciated him for his talents. He nestled his aching bumcheeks into the comforting scoop of a rotating upholstered cherry pink bar stool and ordered a 'Vodka martini, shaken not stirred,' without turning a hair.

Honey Von Trapp, in a nimble manoeuvre, perched herself up on the bar counter whilst Bunny O'JuiceBox crouched between her dangling legs.

'Ahh! Mr Prugg, I believe,' said a voice at Alan's shoulder.

Alan looked up and straight into the breasts of one of the most beautiful woman he had ever seen, standing resplendent in the dappled disco lights. She stood like a mountain before him, a fountain of auburn hair sprouting abundantly from the crown of her head, her mouth the red of the true sexual predator. Her teeth whiter than lilies, her voluptuous form shimmering with sequins. Granted, she was not his usual type, Alan being drawn neither to voluptuousness nor bosoms. Never would he normally have been so transfixed by her twin symbols of womanliness. But, remember, this was a whole new context for him and he had not had a shag in months. (Besides, the swelling from his plastic surgery prevented him from raising his head any further.)

'If I may introduce myself,' said the lusty beauty in an alluring voice. 'My name is Bermuda Triangle.'

Alan took her hand and kissed it. What had come over him?

'The pleasure is all mine.'

'But you may call me Betsy,' she added warmly.

'And I'm Ron,' said a small sparrow-like man who had mysteriously materialised from somewhere amidst her shimmering bulk.

Bermuda stood for a second, fixing Alan with her violet-lidded eyes, then she took her seat next to him and ordered herself a Liscious Lovehandle.

'Your reputation goes before you, Mr Prugg,' she rasped.

Alan wondered dreamily how his accountancy skills could be the subject of so much rumour; meanwhile the Martini slipped happily down, mingling toxically with both medication and post-operative trauma, so that he could no longer tell left from right, up from down: a group of friendly crossdressers from a bunch of lunatic terrorists.

'Ah, my reputation,' he said, expansively, as the septic brew burst into his veins. 'Well, I have to admit, although I say so myself, that I am quite nimble with the old financial modelling. And if you need someone to negotiate their way round the labyrinth of Sage, I don't like to blow my own trumpet but –'

Bermuda Triangle let her spanking paddle linger on Alan's arm.

'We know all about your legendary potency,' she breathed. 'We have our sources.' And she nodded toward two figures sat across the other side of the bar.

Alan blinked. His head was whirling with Martini and pain, and something close to euphoria.

'Good God, it's Anthony and Malcolm!' he exploded with joy.

'Yes,' Bermuda said. 'We captured 008 and 009 some time ago.'

Alan did not pause to wonder at her words, but stumbled round to clap his colleagues on the shoulder: both looking debonair in their freshly pressed dinner jackets, Malcolm was even wearing a bow-tie – not a dead sheep in sight.

'*Conundrum*,' corrected Anthony sternly. '*Exciting, never humdrum.* And you, I presume, are going under the name of *Enigma*?'

'Oh, yes,' said Alan, uncertainly. 'I forgot.'

'And I'm not called Malcolm anymore,' Malcolm chipped in eagerly. 'Anthony's – sorry – *Conundrum*'s given me a new pulling name. Just call me The Dong.'

Malcolm's eyes had wandered and were gazing adoringly over Alan's right shoulder. Alan craned behind him. Bermuda blew a kiss. He turned back again to catch Malcolm flushing proudly.

Alan frowned.

'You look – different,' Malcolm said shyly.

Alan had forgotten his change of face since they last saw him.

'Rather good, isn't it?' he said. 'Wanted the Pierce Brosnan nose, of course, rather than the Michael Jackson, but still… What can you expect? Levels of service aren't what they used to be. Country's going to the dogs.'

Alan noticed Malcolm smiling at Bermuda again, it was starting to irritate him. Couldn't he leave the poor woman alone? He turned his back on Malcolm crossly and turned to Anthony.

'Tell me, what is this place?'

Anthony, or *Conundrum*, smiled into his gin and tonic.

'I believe we are in heaven,' he said, softly. 'We only discovered it a fortnight ago. Great, isn't it?'

Alan looked around him with wonder and awe.

'My God, yes. Why have I never been here before?'

******

Paula felt her hands pulled roughly behind her back until her shoulders ached. Ripples of excitement xylophoned down her spine at the knowledge that her diminutive chest thrust outwards in so brazen a fashion. Hands pulled her roughly forward and then shoved her back against a large lumpen object, smooth and hard under her bound hands. The acrid tang assaulted her nostrils. The rope cut savagely into her wrists as she was tied to something hard, unyielding. Her hands were getting crushed. She gasped.

'Sorry,' said her attacker.

'You're tying me so hard,' she said. 'How do you know I won't escape your bonds?'

'I'll tie you harder,' said the savage voice.

'Please no, don't hurt me.'

The ropes burned into her arms, her chest thrust out.

Forced at a cruel angle, Paula's back ached with the discomfort.

'I am going to take the blindfold off now,' said the voice quietly. 'You must remain quiet, or else I will have to kill you.'

She gasped.

'Do you understand?'

She nodded, vehemently.

Hands crept around the back of her head, her neck shivering in delight, and gently released the blindfold.

'You!' she gasped.

'Yes,' said The Man in the Mask. 'Don't make a noise. Not yet anyway.'

They were in the club. It was still quite early but some people had started drifting in, the odd brave soul taking to the near-empty dance floor, apparently unperturbed by the dreadful scene being enacted before them.

Paula wriggled ecstatically. 'Set me free, at once!'

'No,' said the Masked Man. There was something odd and intense about the way he looked at her. *Was he about to ravish her? Against her will? Here on the dance floor?*

'Why are you doing this?' she moaned, melodramatically. 'Why are you treating me so cruelly?'

The Man in the Mask frowned slightly. Then, to her great surprise, he leaned forward, took her by the shoulder and shook her. Then he said something strange and not very in keeping with the whole ravishing fantasy she had been hopefully imagining in her head.

'Look Paula. I *can't*. Okay? I can't. I'm not who you want me to be. I'm not *able* to be who you want me to be. Do you understand?'

He stared at her intensely. She shook her head, slowly.

'You are supposed to be with Alan. *Alan*, remember?'

Paula stared at him.

'Alan is here. To rescue you.'

'Me?'

'Yes. You.'

'But he can't – I mean – There's something I need to tell you –'

He placed a hand over her mouth.

'Don't say it,' he said softly, 'Whatever it is. I can't bear it.'

Her eyes widened over the side of his index finger.

'This is your moment,' he whispered, and he kissed her forehead tenderly. 'No more boring Paula.' And he let her go.

She gazed up at him, transfixed. The searing noise of the duct tape shocked her back to reality.

'It'll be okay,' he whispered and stuck it over her mouth.

*****

Bermuda Triangle squeezed herself in next to Alan and stroked his cheek. 'There is someone who wishes to meet you, Mr Prugg,' she breathed.

Alan scrunched his face into his neck in order to view her caress. 'Is there?'

'Follow me.' She took hold of his hand and propelled him into the centre of the dance floor. All around, a sea of gyrating figures, a soft swell of sensuous bodies lazily moving and grooving to the music, or, at least, so it seemed to Alan. Actually there were only five, but the drink, medication and general stress were taking their toll.

'*Aha*! Mr Prugg you have deigned to join us, I see...'

Alan felt like Charlton Heston in *The Ten Commandments*, as the waves of dancing figures (all five of them) parted to reveal a seated figure on a black swivel chair, sensuously stroking a white cat on his knee.

'Good evening, Mr Prugg.'

Alan opened and shut his mouth a couple of times. Nothing came out.

'My name is Beerbelly Von Tripplehoffen. I take it you know why you are here?'

All Alan's previous excitement at the situation drained away along with the colour in his face.

'I've no idea. I'm sure you've got the wrong man. Okay – glad that's established. So let's just forget this ever happened and –' He turned quickly and started heading for the door, for it to be smoothly blocked by a succession of be-suited, scantily-clad or gold-painted people.

'Not so fast, Mr Prugg.'

His escape barred, Alan turned slowly back towards Beerbelly Von Tripplehoffen.

Beerbelly Von Tripplehoffen stood, cat in his arms, and paced dominantly up and down for a bit.

'Now then, don't be shy. I'm sure there will be things you'll want to ask me.'

Alan racked his brain for a question. He really didn't want to know anything. The less he knew the better. He just wanted to get out alive, go home and forget about the whole thing.

'That's okay. I'm not a very curious person. I'm happy not to know.'

Beerbelly Von Tripplehoffen was not impressed.

'Fucking hell! We have gone to a lot of effort for you, Mr Prugg. The least you could do is to pay us the courtesy of asking a fucking question. Is that really too much to ask?'

Alan felt the blood rush back into his face. His eyes hurt, his nose throbbed. He felt faint and flushed.

'Who *are* you?' he said, finally.

'*Aha*, I thought you might ask that!'

His interrogator paused and leaned forwards eagerly, before apparently changing his mind (and direction) and leaning back again and off to the left. A lone figure emerged from the crowd and whispered in his ear. Beerbelly turned back towards Alan.

'We are,' it was stated grandly, 'an unidentified terrorist outfit that intends to take over the entire world through an innovative non-hierarchically-structured approach.'

Alan was too busy staring at the unidentified minion taking up position beside Beerbelly, who, apart from a small, black eye-mask, appeared to be completely nude.

'What?' said Alan, faintly.

'We are an unidentified terrorist outfit that intends –'

'No, the last bit.'

'Oh you mean the non-hierarchically-structured bit?'

'Yes.'

'Ah, we're particularly proud of that. Nicked the idea from shareware.'

'I don't understand.'

Alan, still staring at the naked man, wondered if naturism was conventional amongst unidentified terrorist circles.

The other said, 'You know – like Linux.'

Alan transferred his blank stare to Beerbelly and continued to stare – just as blankly.

Beerbelly sighed. 'Never mind. Anything else you wish to know?'

Knowing he was not going to get away with 'No', Alan considered carefully. 'What do you want?'

'Want? Want?' The other paced up and down importantly, occasionally pausing to maul the white cat in his arms.

'How very 20th century of you, Mr Prugg. Terrorist cells do not have such old-fashioned things as concrete "wants" these days! That would be too easy. Oh no, no! No, no, no, no, no!'

'Why not?' Alan haltered.

The white-felined figure sat down. 'That's enough questions out of you! All you need to know is that we will take over the world. Yes, yes, whatever our aims, the world is well and truly going to be taken over. And then! And then, Mr Prugg, we're going to sell it!'

'Sell it?'

'That's right. All the money's in real estate these days. Anyway,' continued Beerbelly Von Tripplehoffen, quickly, before Alan got a chance to further this line of enquiry. 'I expect you would like to know why we brought you here?' He sat down.

Alan did not want to know this at all.

'Oh that's alright,' he said, warily, 'Too much knowledge and all that...' and he started edging his way towards the exit.

'Look,' said Beerbelly, standing up again. 'As we are here

enjoying ourselves having this little chat and I have a bit of time on my hands - I am now going to outline my whole fiendish, horrible plan, before killing you slowly, very very slowly, and very painfully. Along with your accomplice. I think you are familiar with our friend, Mzzz Wocziac?'

The crowds parted and Alan was faced with the most horrible vision yet. There, before him, strapped to an immense and terrifying piece of metal machinery, was Paula, bound and gagged, her arms pulled cruelly and tied behind her back. He felt like swooning with the horror of it all.

'In precisely fifteen minutes, you and Mzz Wocziac will be lowered into a pit of flesh-eating glowworms. Unless, that is, you manage to find a way of escaping…'

Alan was not listening. He was too busy still swooning at the horror of it all.

'Did you hear me, Mr Prugg? I said, *unless you find a way of escaping.*'

But Alan was not paying attention. He checked Paula, her eyes yearned back, pleadingly. He asked himself what a proper hero would do in the circumstances, what a real man would do. What James Bond would do… And immediately decided against it.

'Oh *please, please, please, please* don't kill me! *Please, please, please, please, please.* You can have her. It's fine. Do anything you like to her. I won't tell anyone. Just let me go, I beg you. Don't kill me. I will do anything, *anything.*'

'Mr Prugg, please get up off the floor.'

'I'm too young to die!'

'This is unseemly.'

Alan, practically eating the ground, felt equally overwhelmed by the situation, the throbbing of his nose and buttocks, and the strong rubbery smell wafting up from the floor.

'Don't you want to hear how I'm going to kill you?'

Alan's shuddering form wriggled further into the hard rubber floor.

'I am going to tell you, anyway. Because you see, Mr Prugg, I am not worried about you telling your superiors. Because you see –' Beerbelly got up and strolled nonchalantly over to where Paula was struggling, '– after I have attached you to Mzzz Wocziac like this –' he produced a pair of fluffy handcuffs with a flourish and attached them to Paula and himself,' – activated the laser, which is, by the way, on a ten minute timer, and left the room. I will return and find that two have become four.'

This was too much for Alan, who promptly fainted on the spot.

'Fucksake, somebody, bring him round,' said Luda crossly, throwing the toy cat to one side. 'And I hadn't even got to the crocodile bit yet,' she added sadly, indicating the plastic crocodile, nestled against the paddling pool, which was standing in for the pit of flesh-eating glowworms.

'This isn't working,' she said to The Man in the Mask. 'He just won't play ball.'

Gretchen and Anthony knelt over Alan, slapping him round the face and loosening his collar. They pulled him to the side of the dance floor and propped him against the mattress, where Alan lay, rolling his head from side to side and moaning gently.

The Man in the Mask shook his head. 'I don't know what's the matter with him. I thought he was supposed to *like* James Bond?'

'He certainly doesn't seem to be enjoying himself much,' Dave said. 'I thought this was supposed to be his dream come true.'

'Ungrateful bastard,' said Luda. 'After all the trouble we've gone to. I tell you, that stuffed cat wasn't cheap.'

She gave Paula, who was issuing some frantic noises from behind the duct-tape, a friendly pat and stood up from the fucking machine.

'Shit.'

'What?'

'I've gone and handcuffed myself to the machine.'

'Don't be silly.'

'Fuck-ing hell!' Luda struggled to loosen herself from the handcuffs as Paula watched wide-eyed. 'Well, that's just brilliant!' She collapsed back against the fucking machine. 'Now what?'

'Perhaps he doesn't realise what's happening?' Dave said, finally.

Luda did not hold back on what she thought of this statement. 'Dave, I know you are not renowned for your powers of deduction, but that really is the most ridiculous thing I've ever heard.' Then, picking up the stuffed cat with her unrestricted hand from where it lay abandoned by her feet, 'Miaow, Miaow, Miaow. Does this look realistic to you?'

'It was only a thought.'

'Miaow Miaow,' Luda persisted, waving the cat.

Dave turned away.

'Wait a minute, Dave might have a point there, Luda,' said the Masked Man. 'Did anyone think to issue Alan with a "safe word"?' He looked round the assembled company, who all stared back at him blankly. He put his head in his hands. 'How could we overlook something so fundamental? No wonder he's feeling uncomfortable.'

They looked down at the moaning figure at their feet. It was up to Dave to voice their thoughts.

'He really doesn't look too good.'

'Nonsense!' said Luda, not sounding convinced. 'Anthony – Gretchen – throw a bit of water over him. He'll be fine. Come on, get him up.'

*****

The bucket of freezing water hit Alan's face like a bucket of freezing water.

'Brrmmm, grrrrrggg,' he gurgled, half-opening his eyes and looking into the blurred face of Anthony Hossier.

The tiny part of Alan's brain that had been questioning events all along suddenly wondered what Anthony Hossier was doing loitering about with a bunch of crazed terrorists. It came to the only rational conclusion: that this was not, in fact, the real Anthony Hossier as he had previously thought, but some crazed terrorist Anthony Hossier body double. Why hadn't he realised before?

'Look – ' the Hossier-doppelganger leaned in. 'It's me.'

Alan's watering eyes blinked a few times and he wondered why the Anthony Hossier lookalike was saying, 'Look, it's me.' It seemed an odd thing to say in the circumstances.

'Pull yourself together, old boy. It's perfectly possible for you to escape. You can escape and win the girl and everything. Come on, have a bit of fun.' Clap on the shoulder. 'There's a good man.'

With that, Anthony whirled out of view to be replaced by the gold-covered woman from earlier. 'The word is Andalucia.

Andalucia, remember?' she breathed, seductively.

It was all too much.

Alan cast about him in terror. He felt Paula's eyes burning into him like the laser he was about to be dissected with, but could not bring himself to raise his gaze to hers. He knew he had let her down in her hour of need. But he was under no illusions. His days of reckless heroics were over. (Not that they'd ever really begun.) After all, he was almost a married man now; he had responsibilities. And first amongst those was to stay alive. He scanned round quickly, judging the distance between himself and the doorway.

'*Aha*, Mr Prugg,' Beerbelly started up again, from where he was standing rather cosily close to Paula. 'You thought you could trick us. Distract our attention with the old "pretend fainting" routine… But, of course, we know you are far too manly for such swooning fits to be genuine.'

At that moment, Alan couldn't give a stuff what Beerbelly thought of his general manliness. As far as he was concerned, all ideas of manliness had flown out the window the moment slow painful deaths were mentioned.

With a loud, blood-curdling cry he managed to surprise everyone, including himself, by launching himself up from the floor and plummeting through the crowd.

'Come back here!' yelled Beerbelly, struggling against the fluffy pink handcuffs. 'Stop him!'

Several menacing individuals tried to block his path, but Alan skilfully managed to dodge them, slaloming desperately between the gold-painted henchmen, PVC outfits and areas of exposed flesh. A brightly smiling feathered individual tried to block his path with outstretched arms and the warm rejoinder to, 'Have a hug', but Alan was not fooled. Ducking under her arms he careered into some tassled drapes and fell against what appeared to be a voluminous blue mummy, propped up against the wall next to a potted palm.

'Arggh!' cried Alan in terror.

'Hello,' the mummy mumbled back in muffled tones.

'Argggh! Arggh!' Alan yelped again, bouncing off the mummy and tangling himself up in the curtains, through which, at last, he glimpsed the stone foyer and the entrance beyond. He couldn't believe it: he'd made it!

Throwing a terrified glance over his shoulder he captured a last frozen image of the grim outfit of unidentified terrorists all standing placidly watching him – some of them had even started dancing again: *trying to lull him into a false sense of security, eh?* Alan turned back to his goal, careered towards the double doors, and, with great effort, hauled one open. *Thank God Thank God Thank God.* The light streaked down the side of the door and burst into the room – *Thankyou Thankyou Thankyou* – along with the terrifying vision of Belinda, spinning chainsaw in hand, her face suffused with something beyond irritation, beyond unpleasant. As he stood there, caught in the forcefield of Belinda's wrath, for the first time in their relationship the veil of idealism fell from Alan's eyes and he could finally see the love of his life as she really was. The woman was a bloody maniac.

'Sorry I'm late,' she said. 'Traffic was murder.'

And she took up the saw and whirled it round her head a couple of times with a throaty cry.

The club goers gazed at the new intruder with horror and not a little excitement.

'Bloody hell, who the fuck is that?' muttered Luda, giving up on her battle to free herself from the handcuffs and sitting back heavily on the fucking machine.

Dave and The Man in the Mask took hypnotised steps forward in unison, then hastily back again. Malcolm peeked out curiously from under Betsy's crippling bulk. Gretchen felt a lump of disappointment in her throat and turned away.

But it was SlaveBoy, lying prone at her feet, who found the words to express their collective awe, as he leaned towards the doorway, face alight, in rapture.

'Now *that's* what I call a Dominatrix!'

Belinda lowered her saw and stepped into the room.

'So this is where you've been, you fucking pervert,' she said nastily. 'What a squalid little man you are. A sex club. Jesus Christ. And look at it − cerise everywhere. If you have to be squalid do you have to be so tasteless too?'

Alan's brain tried desperately to faint again, but his adrenalin-fuelled body was having none of it.

'It's not what you think,' he stammered. 'I can explain, explain everything.' But he knew that he would never be able to explain what had happened that night. Apart from anything, he had not the faintest idea what *had* happened that night.

Belinda prowled across the dance floor, using her chainsaw to cut through the crowd that had been steadily dribbling into the club since Alan's arrival.

'You come to a place like this − a dirty cerise dump like this,' she held her saw up to a trembling bunny boy. 'And yet you won't do one little thing for me?' She gazed round at Alan.

'I'll do anything,' said Alan. But to his horror found he could no longer speak and nothing emerged from his mouth save a muffled yelp.

'Put out your arm.'

'What?'

'Put out your arm.'

Transfixed, Alan moved towards her. 'What are you going to do?'

'You have left me with no choice.' She sounded calm, rational. 'I've tried everything with you. Everything. I have no alternative. I must dismember you.'

'Dis-*what* me?'

'Disable you. They can't not promote you then.' She was not sounding quite so rational now. 'Like Pat. Taking everything. Stealing my promotion!'

The horror in Alan's head was fit to burst.

'Put out your arm.'

The eyes of everyone in the room fled to Alan's face to see his reaction... only to be disappointed. Alan remained completely expressionless.

Perhaps it was the effects of extensive plastic surgery and its associated medicines mingling with copious amounts of alcohol; the pressure of his upcoming marriage; a freak hallucination...whatever the reason, inside Alan's head things weren't going so well.

'Human kind cannot bear very much reality,' wrote the poet, TS Eliot.

Even a little reality was too much for Alan's mind. It decided to jettison reality altogether and began to indulge itself, instead, in the drunken, traumatised and heavily medicated imaginings of a drunken, traumatised, heavily medicated accountant in fear of his life. (Not to mention his fiancée.)

He saw the phantom Belinda moving limitlessly and inexorably towards him, her thirteen-toned, ironed hair flapping like two slices of paper at the sides of her head. He saw himself (he was in the realm of pure fantasy now), pectoral muscles waxed and shining, his rippling shoulders – well – rippling with abandon, reclining as if on the very air itself in the style of a Bollywood heroine.

From the outside, none of this was visible. All that could be seen by the now thirty or so onlookers was Alan swaying slightly and looking about to pass out.

Inside Alan's head things were altogether more lively.

The karate-chopping whirlwind continued her approach. It no longer appeared human: the whirling arms spinning faster and faster, merging and multiplying into some designer-clad octopus. The creature's face was no longer visible, just a precise curtain of hair, impervious to the chaos all around. Alan stared into the faceless horror before him and shuddered.

After this, the inside of Alan's head went really weird.

The whole scene started to split, everything: women, men, Paula, Beerbelly, everything was sucked into the whirling vortex where once had been his wife-to-be. Alan felt himself scream as – in his fevered mind – his body underwent the same process: gasping as first one then the other of his new buttocks flew off, followed closely by his new lips and new nose; looking down in horror as, one-by-one, the stitches round his middle started to come undone reopening his wounds; staring in amazement as the rippling muscles rippled off his body onto the floor where they continued like undulating caterpillars before – like the rest – being sucked away into nothingness. One-by-one the neatly planted bunches of hair plucked themselves out of his skull and fled into the wind. The ears released themselves, flying forward in the wind tunnel, the jowls were loosened to float free in front of his face, and, finally, at long last, the stitches across the top of his head and along his eyelids were unpicked. 'Aaaaaaaaaaaaaaaaaaaaggggggggggggggggghhhhhhhhhhhhhhhhhh!' screamed Alan as his face flapped like a piece of corrugated sheeting in the force of Belinda's wrath.

And with one more birth pang of 'AAAAAgggggggggggggghhh!' away flew the final stitch and with it the face of mild surprise...

Back in the real world, to his army of onlookers, Alan just looked – well – mildly surprised. He appeared quite serene, as though in total ignorance of the angry woman with a chainsaw in front of him. His face even broke out into a goofy smile. Then, slowly, carefully, Alan rolled up one sleeve and – proffered an arm.

With a whoop of triumph, Belinda swashed the chainsaw around in front of her – the crowd muttering backwards – before steering it like a nest of hornets, in Alan's direction.

'Don't you think this is taking social advancement a little too far?' said a voice.

Alan looked up, watery-eyed, to see a small vital figure leaping over his head and charging at Belinda, plastic crocodile aloft.

'Paula,' he said, 'My Paula'.

'Back off bitch!' yelled Paula the Pale jabbing at Belinda the Homicidal Maniac with her crocodile. Belinda recoiled momentarily in surprise.

*****

Paula, who had been watching the scene unfolding with horror from her captive position on the fucking machine, knew it was up to her to do something.

'Mmmm-mmm,' she indicated to Luda, with wild eyes.

'It's no good Mmmm-mmming at me, I can't understand a word you're saying,' said Luda irritably, still wrestling with the handcuffs.

'Mmmm-mmmmmm!' Paula opened her eyes as wide as she could and rolled them dramatically downwards towards her duct-tape gag.

'Oh, you want me to ungag you?'

Paula nodded violently.

'Well why didn't you say so?'

Luda duly ungagged her.

'Not that it's going to do any good, we're still stuck.'

'Untie the ropes.'

'What?'

'With your other hand, untie my ropes. They're tied with a double-bow.'

'Oh.'

Luda did what she was told and the ropes fell away from her companion, who quickly leaned across and undid the handcuffs. Luda was stunned.

'How the hell did you do that? Who are you, Houdini or something?'

Paula threw the cuffs at Luda.

'The fluffy pink ones always have a safety catch.'

Luda looked at the cuffs. 'Hell's teeth, you're right!'

Paula grabbed the forgotten crocodile from its resting place beside the paddling pool. 'There may be a role for this yet...' She put a hand on Luda's shoulder. 'I've gotta go now. But I want you to know, just in case…'

Luda's voice was croaky. 'Don't even say it. You'll be back.'

*****

'Who the hell are you?' spluttered Belinda, stumbling backwards in surprise.

'Who am I? Who am I?' Paula mused, advancing, crocodile at the ready.

'Catch!' yelled The Man in the Mask, throwing her a whip.

Paula turned and caught it deftly by the handle, briefly locking eyes with his.

'Thanks,' she said grimly and swung round to snap it with relish at Belinda's feet.

CRACK.

'You need a hand?' asked The Man in the Mask, anxiously.

'That's okay,' Paula's eyes were now locked on those of her opponent. 'This is my battle.' She moved towards Belinda. 'The name's Paula.'

Belinda frowned.

'I am surprised you haven't heard of me. I would have thought you might even have told your friends about me. Had the odd joke at my expense?'

'I don't know what you're talking about.'

'Paula. Remember. The boring one.'

Recognition dawned slowly over Belinda's angry features. 'Oh my god, it's the stalker!' And she laughed. She actually bent over and laughed. 'I didn't recognise you! My God! Boring Paula. *Boring* Paula.'

'Yes, enough of that,' Paula said, with another crack of the whip.

'The thing is you see,' Belinda pointed out reasonably. 'However flashy you have become, Miss Boring Paula, a bit of string on a stick and a – a –' she sized up the crocodile '– large toy reptile isn't really a match for this.' And she revved up the chainsaw with a deafening roar.

Paula looked at the chainsaw. Then she looked at Alan, who was now inexplicably kneeling on the floor with his eyes shut – what was he doing? Then she looked at the pressed and powdered bitch in front of her. What Belinda had said was true enough.

'You know what?' she said, 'I don't care.' And holding the crocodile up like a shield in front of her, she advanced menacingly.

Whooping with rage, Belinda raised her saw above her head and with a vicious swipe lopped the left leg off the plastic crocodile.

Paula continued her advance. She lifted the whip.

CRACK!

Behind her, Alan, on his hands and knees, began to crawl away.

Belinda raised the saw again, whirled it once around her head and brought it spinning down in Paula's direction. Ducking deftly, Paula straightened up to see the crocodile's head crashing to the floor. She continued her advance.

CRACK!

Belinda raised her head. The look in Paula's eyes was a challenge she had never encountered before; a novelty she was not at all sure how to deal with.

'Look,' she said 'You don't need to fight me. We're the same you and I, both strong women. I have no quarrel with you. All I'm asking for is Alan's arm. Let me have it and we'll call it quits.' She continued to wave her saw, yet there was a tinge of respect in her voice that had not been there before.

But Paula did not care to earn Belinda's respect. Lowering her head, she pressed forward, holding what remained of the plastic reptile in front of her and raising her whip again.

CRACK!

With a howl of rage, Belinda brought her chainsaw crashing down to slice through what was left of the crocodile in Paula's hands and narrowly missing Paula herself.

In that next moment, a number of things happened. Paula, in an effort to avoid the saw slicing through her abdomen, lurched back violently, tripping over SlaveBoy (who had crept forward for a better view of the action) and fell to the ground; Alan, seeing his chance to escape, shot across the floor towards the ladies loos and tried to squeeze his terrified body in behind Marcus. Meanwhile, The Man in the Mask, seeing Paula in trouble, suddenly turned to Betsy and plunged his arm down her top.

'Hey!' said Betsy. 'Cold hands.'

'Sorry.'

'Well,' she giggled. 'As it's you…'

The Man in the Mask winked gallantly, then, armed with

nothing but Betsy's spanking paddle charged towards Belinda, who, seeing her foe at a disadvantage on the floor before her, was lifting the chainsaw high above her head with a maniacal gleam in her eye.

But Paula wasn't done yet. With a heave, she hauled herself up on her elbows and gave a last yank of the whip. The lash curled elegantly behind her like the cast line of a fishing rod, hovered for a moment, then flew forward, snaking around Belinda's ankle. As Belinda brought the chainsaw crashing down, Paula pulled as hard as she could. A horrified Belinda glanced down at her feet before mouthing 'Bitch' and cascading to the floor in an explosion of hair, burring saw and naked man – who had chosen that very moment to hurl himself bodily on top of her.

Belinda and The Man in the Mask rolled along the floor, coming to a rest just outside the door to the ladies loos, where they both lay, winded. They took a while to disentangle themselves, then the fight was back on. The Man in the Mask grappled for his spanking paddle, which had somehow become detached from him in the struggle. While Belinda sat up to find herself cheek-to-cheek with Alan's terrified bottom, which was attempting to follow the rest of him hiding behind what looked like a giant blue Michelin Man, propped against the wall.

'Oh for goodness sake,' Belinda said impatiently and she leant forward and lopped off one of Alan's arms.

After this, things got a bit confused.

The force of the chainsaw sent the arm flying behind the bar, knocking out Dave, who had been attempting to diffuse the tension in the room by mixing up a few Liscious Lovehandles. Alan fell immediately unconscious (probably the kindest thing for him), while Belinda, eyes cast with the fanatical glaze of one who has had her first taste of bloodlust, got to her feet somewhat unsteadily and, chainsaw in hand, addressed the small crowd of aghast onlookers.

'It was an accident! An accident, okay? You saw that, didn't you? You saw it! Okay, fine, go ahead, *judge* me! But you have no idea what I've been through, no idea! You don't know me. How I was driven to this, driven to it, I tell you.'

The crowd quailed at her.

'I've been psychologically abused by this man! I have had to do everything, *everything* for that bloody wedding. Has he done one thing, one thing? One last tiny damn thing? Apart from the plastic surgery. And he couldn't even get that right, could he? Does that look like a Pierce Brosnan nose to you? I don't think so!'

What Belinda had failed to notice in all the excitement was that, when she had sliced off Alan's arm, she had inadvertently punctured Marcus's inflatable body suit at the same time.

At the very moment Belinda yelled, 'It was an accident. An accident, okay?' behind her, Marcus, issuing a noise that was music to the ears of the scatological fetishists in the room, took off.

During the ensuing speech, the blue inflatable man wheezed and squeaked its way around the room like a burst balloon. On past the pink nipple ceiling lights he plunged: past Luda, in her spectator's seat on the fucking machine, skimming the top of Paula's head, as she sat up on her elbows with the whip clutched to her chest and puttering gently over the inert form of Alan, lying unconscious in a pool of blood. The balloon man sailed past

The Man in the Mask who was standing motionless in the middle of the dance floor, spanking paddle lying forgotten in his hand, and rose up like a voluminous blue shadow behind the frenzied figure with a chainsaw. accosting the crowd. Finally, it floated for a moment, like some magnificent totem of sexual freedom, before taking a nose-dive straight for her.

Of course Belinda, deafened by the chainsaw, heard nothing. 'How dare you judge me, you perverts!' she was screaming at anyone who cared to listen, waving her saw around randomly. *'You're* the perverts! Not me!'

But at that moment, with a splutter and a putter, her weapon died out.

'Useless thing,' she muttered, throwing it to one side, catching, as she did so, a glimpse of the vast and shapeless homunculus hurtling towards her.

'Shit!' was all she managed to say before disappearing beneath its blue, billowing form.

'Out of the way, out of the way,' cried a voice and SlaveBoy ran forwards out of the crowd. Starry-eyed, he plunged himself to the ground before the crash-site. Breathing heavily, he closed his eyes and held out a sacrificial arm.

'I would be honoured if you would accept this gift. This token of my esteem, oh mistress!'

But there was no answer from beneath the ballooning blue PVC.

Anthony walked over to Paula and helped her to her feet. 'You artists,' he said amiably. 'Mad lot. Totally mad. I must say, though,

Alan's arm flying through the air like that was very effective. Still can't see how you managed to get the blood gushing out of the stump like that. Horribly realistic. I think he really got into it by the end. Look, he's still playing dead. My word, that fake blood is convincing, isn't it?'

'I think we'd better call an ambulance,' Paula said.

To the casual observer in a helicopter, the scene below might resemble a messianic tableau: a bleeding man on a stretcher being carried out of the building towards the first of three waiting ambulances, a bright splash of blood across his right side shining suddenly under the yellow streetlamps, as though energetically splatted across the canvas of his body by some passing abstract expressionist. A second stretcher, this time with a woman still gripping a chainsaw tightly to her chest. A crowd of figures gather, making phonecalls, getting in the way of the paramedics. Yet another unconscious figure is hurried out, this time a rather nice-looking man in a dress, followed by two more stretchers: the first bearing a vast blue billowing form; the second, designed for a child, carries a single bloody arm.

The ambulance doors close and they race away into the night, sirens blaring into the distance. A shimmering cloud of leaves caresses the central image, branches rustling gently, a lattice of twigs obscuring the scene as the helicopter moves away.

Back in Alan's flat, Sam Spade looks up from his fifth cup of tea out of the window at the starry sky. He yawns and stretches from his position on the cream leather sofa and points the remote control at the television.

'Home time,' he says to Ter, who is snoozing on the floor, his head resting on a pile of wedding brochures.

Spade 'tut-tuts' contentedly. 'This is not going to be cheap, my friend. Not cheap at all.'

Outside the window, the tree, forgotten, creaks in the slight breeze.

Is that a sigh of relief or just the sound of the wind whispering in its branches?

Part Seven: **SEPTEMBER**

Chapter Twenty-Six | WEDDING

St John's had not seen much change since the last Harvest Festival.

The remains of yet another vegetable offering mouldered gently on top of the upright piano, the folding picnic tables with their chequered cloths had been packed up and stacked at the back of the room, whilst the old lady in the pleated skirt beloved of old ladies and Scottish country dancers was wearing a different, but basically the same, pleated garment equally irresistible to both of the groups just mentioned.

At the entrance to the church, the friendly painted sign still offering 'R&B, Funky Grooves and Garage Beats', had been taken down (where it remained hopeful of notice beside a free-standing flower display) and replaced with another, of less friendly bent: 'Follow arrows to wedding. No gatecrashers.'

A quick glance at the congregation reveals some familiar faces. There are Luda and Dave, on either side of Paula, in the fourth row from the back. Dave is looking at Luda who is looking at Anthony, in full black-tie next to Malcolm in the third row from the front. The respective families, hers and his, take up the first two rows on either side of the aisle.

'This way, this way.' The old lady in the pleated skirt ushers people to their seats, graciously offering shortbread to all and stabbing any accepting hands with a stamp that reads, 'Matrimony is cool!'

Thankfully, one of the volunteer flower-arrangers notices the putrid pumpkin and bunch of semi-fossilised carrots just in time to remove them, along with all unsavoury traces with a hearty squirt of air freshener, as from somewhere deep in the bowels of the building the rumbling groan of the organ starts up. The volunteer flower-arranger waves at the organist wildly and the drone of the instrument drains away into silence once more.

All seated, they look towards the arched entrance. There is a breeze, a rustle of hymn-sheets, and the silhouette of a figure in a pleated skirt comes forward to stand in front of a stained glass window. There is a cough.

'Now, as you know, St John's is presently collecting for an expensive refurbishment programme. So if you and your friends feel you have enjoyed this wedding, please feel free to make a donation as a token of your satisfaction. We suggest a minimum contribution of £50 per person. Think about it.'

The colonic rumble of the organ starts up once more. Everyone turns as one to look towards the front entrance. And there she is.

The old man at her side walks with nobility and arthritis. The vision in parchment beside him is so cool, so fragrant, offset by the dumpy woman behind in a shapeless aubergine dress. The procession moves slowly down the aisle.

'How beautiful she looks,' gasps one onlooker.

'How brave…to take him on…in spite of everything,' says another.

'I heard that parchment dress cost a bomb,' adds a third.

All turn their collective heads to the front to the sound of the electric wheelchair humming down the aisle. The bride takes her place beside the groom. The groom, a pink flush of love and expectation on his face, looks round briefly and squeezes her hand with the one he has left.

Paula felt a nudge from Dave, who was sitting prettily beside her in a peach satin dress.

'Don't they look happy?' he said, his cheeks shining with a sentimental glow.

'Well, they say she's up for another promotion and she'll be worth at least £100,000 a year, so he can't go far wrong,' Paula whispered. 'But what's *she* getting out of it?'

'You're just jealous,' whispered Dave. 'I think it's true love.'

And he returned to the scene in front of him, enthusiastically mouthing along to the drone of the service and shooting the odd sly glance at Luda who sat to the other side of Paula, looking cheesed off.

'What's wrong with you?' Paula said.

'Fucking weddings,' Luda said, darkly. 'Bring back bad memories.'

Paula turned round in her seat to look at Luda. 'I didn't know you had been married!'

'Still am,' Luda said, with a frown. 'What the hell do you think this is?' And she brandished one meaty hand under Paula's nose.

On it was a small, subtle band – nothing flashy, nothing pretentious – but a wedding band nonetheless. Paula was amazed. How had she never noticed it before?

'But, I don't understand…' she started, flicking her eyes at Anthony Hossier's dinner-jacketed back.

Luda followed Paula's gaze, face in question, saw Anthony, and frowned. 'Jesus Christ. I'm not a fucking poof!'

'You're not?'

'Fucksake!'

A lady in the row in front turned round in disapproval.

'What you looking at?' Luda roared.

Paula sat back in her uncomfortable wooden seat and faced the ceremony once more. She turned back.

'But I thought…'

'I like standing next to him – *standing next to him* – alright?'

'Shhhhhhhhhhhhh!'

Luda glared at the lady in front, but lowered her voice nonetheless. 'You can't feel very ladylike standing next to the wife, she's only 5ft 1. Anyway, she isn't keen on my "little habit" as she calls it. She's picking me up later outside the newsagents on the corner. In case her *friends* see.' Luda subsided back in her chair, muttering, 'Me? A poof? *Fucksake*.'

Paula looked across at Dave, but his eyes slipped from hers like jellied eels. So he had known all along. What was it with these people?

Paula suddenly remembered the greasy-spoon café, the beautiful youth, Luda's trembling hand…

'But I saw you…' Paula trailed off. 'With…'

'With who?' Luda's eyes bore into her. Then she zipped her

breath in between her teeth. 'I don't believe it – have you been spying on me?'

'No!' said Paula. 'Once,' she admitted, 'but only that one time. I saw you with…he was very beautiful. But I went away again – didn't like to intrude.'

'How very considerate of you,' Luda said. ' Well, if you have to know, that was my son.' She shifted in her seat. 'Things are not easy at the moment. Not that it's any of your business.' She turned back to the front. 'I can't believe you, I really can't. After all I've done.'

'Shhh! Shhh!' said Dave excitedly, bobbing up and down in his seat. 'Here comes the bit when they ask if there's any reason…'

The vicar peered out into the seated crowd. 'I must now turn to the congregation and ask, does anyone here present know of any reason that this couple should not be wed? Speak now or forever hold your peace…'

Everyone looked at each other, egging each other to do it. The vicar waited and then breathed a sigh of relief.

'In that case…'

But his relief was short-lived as a commotion broke out at the back of the church.

'I am not a gatecrasher,' said a shrill voice. 'I am a friend of the bride!' And the front doors were flung open to admit a figure who stood, breathing hard on the threshold.

Paula grabbed Dave's arm. 'Look who it is!'

Dave grabbed her back and mouthed 'Shit'.

They had all been in court the day Belinda had received her sentence. From the beginning the case had been an unusually complex one. The charge that was brought against her – of G.B.H. with intent – was a crime that if found guilty carried with it a lengthy prison sentence. It all rested on that tiny word 'intent'.

Whilst it could be argued (and was) that the bearing of a dangerous weapon to the scene of the crime in a taxi had a distinct whiff of intent about it, the defence's position was that Belinda had already suffered more than her fair share of provocation by this point ('I mean, M'Lud, does an Alhambra waterfeature go with Japanese acers? – what was he thinking?'), the chainsaw's acquisition was a spur of the moment thing and its subsequent journey was a simple misunderstanding.

According to the defence, following the altercation over water-features, Mr Prugg had said his goodbyes and set off to his secret S&M hideaway, followed closely by Miss Cartwright who, mistaking the chainsaw's ownership, had picked it up, brandished it ululating above her head and hailed a taxi with it merely in an attempt to reunite her partner with his beloved power tool.

Discovering, upon entry to the club, her husband-to-be engaged in all sorts of deviant sexual pursuits, Miss Cartwright, under extreme provocation, cracked, and – in a moment of madness – cut off Mr Prugg's arm.

'And, given his obvious sexual predilections,' the defence smirked. 'Who's to say he didn't even *enjoy* the experience?'

This had led to howls of protest from the gallery from the clubgoers who gathered next day outside the court with placards reading:

'Spanking for justice!'
'He was completely "armless!"'

ROSY BARNES

'We Demand Pain with Consent, not the Unauthorised Removal of Limbs'.

In the end, the judge sentenced Belinda to eight years.

Paula felt a pinch at her side.

'I wish they'd get on with it,' Dave said, in a rustle of peach silk. 'The interruption's completely ruining the sense of occasion for me.'

Paula looked towards the door of the church where the vengeful figure stood glaring murderously at the bride and groom. The groom looked, frankly, terrified but Pat faced down her opponent with tangible relish.

'Belinda!' she called merrily, or as merrily as her new electronic voice-box would allow. 'So glad you could make it! I didn't realise that overcrowding in prisons had got so bad lately that they let homicidal maniacs attend their victim's weddings. Tell me, what did you have to do to wangle it?' She looked pointedly at the prison officer.

The prison officer took a step forward but Belinda put a restraining hand on her arm. 'Leave it sweetcheeks. Her voice, rusty from misuse, sounded like a bag of old nails. 'Let's just say it was a case of good behaviour,' Belinda said, exchanging a glance with the officer.

Alan moaned and hid behind the wheelchair.

'I see,' said Pat. 'Well, do invite your...*friend*...to make herself at home.'

'Much as I hate to interrupt this touching reunion,' the vicar said sweetly, 'if you could tell us the nature of your objection –'

'What?'

'Your objection. To the marriage. I know it is terribly bureaucratic of me but I really need to have a reason, you see. For the paperwork. Otherwise, if I could impress upon you to take a seat...'

Belinda looked at him sourly.

'Objection?' she said slowly. 'Objection? I have an objection alright. That this –' she pointed dramatically at Pat, '*thing* stole my fiancé while I was...otherwise indisposed.'

There were gasps from the audience. Paula, Luda and Dave all gasped along happily.

'She *poisoned* him towards me. She,' Belinda lowered her voice, 'won him with promises of a *sexual nature.*'

They all gasped again.

'For months she sowed the seeds of doubt in his mind as they bonded together at their PHYSIOTHERAPY class.'

'How did you know that?' came Alan's voice from behind Pat's chair.

'I have my sources,' was the dark reply.

('You didn't!' said Dave, aghast.

'Of course not,' said Paula, shoulders leaping guiltily to her ears.)

'And then,' Belinda continued, 'for her *fait accompli* – she *seduced* him!'

(Gasp.)

'In the office disabled toilets.'

(Gasp.)

'So, Ladies and Gentlemen, I put it to you: not only a

poisonous snake in the grass, a betrayer of trust, of friendship, of the accountants' code of conduct and of The Sisterhood – but not even original to boot!'

('Oooooo!' the audience turned their accusatory stares on the happy couple.)

'Well this is all very unfortunate,' said the vicar, consulting his watch tactfully, 'but none of this constitutes any solid reason why these persons should not be wed.'

'Well, what kind of reasons ARE you looking for?' Belinda demanded.

'Oh I don't know,' the vicar said, 'That they are married to other people. That Pat is short for Patrick…'

'No, none of those things.'

'Then, may I ask you to sit down please, madam?'

Belinda stood for a second, then, warden in tow, angrily pushed her way into the crowd and sat down beside a delighted-looking SlaveBoy, who, with a beady eye on their handcuffs, wasted no time in introducing himself to both.

'I, Alan James Francis Prugg.'

'I, Alan James Francis Prugg.'

'Do hereby take Patricia Charlotte Rosemary Rawley.'

'Do hereby take Patricia Charlotte Rosemary Rawley.'

'To be my lawful wedded wife.'

'To be my lawful wedded wife.'

He slipped the ring onto her lovingly outstretched probe and the congregation let out its collective breath.

'You may now kiss the bride.'

*****

Paula shoved aside an annoying old lady with a shortbread tin who was inviting her to think of herself as 'the baking of The Lord' and pushed through the champagne-swilling crowd.

Where was he?

She had been sure he would be here. She had not seen him for weeks. Not in the flesh anyway (although she continued to spy on his uneventful life from afar).

Even after the club had reopened (once the police, forensics and then the Health and Safety people had had their say), The Man in the Mask was nowhere to be found. She had begun to wonder if he was avoiding the place. Then, she had started worrying that he was avoiding *her.*

She had thought of dropping by his office, she'd *thought* about it. But it had never seemed the right time what with Alan's arm, getting his shopping in, helping him into the taxi for his physio sessions...

She looked around anxiously for that familiar mop of brown hair. Alan had definitely invited him, surely? After what had happened, Alan considered all the club-members his personal saviours. The blood loss coupled with severe concussion had wiped all recollection of 'unidentified terrorist' outfits from his mind and he instead credited them all with having saved his life. Asked how it was he found himself in the club in the first place, he would answer proudly, 'Oh, I've never been one to swim with the crowd,' leaving the puzzled enquirer with rather more questions than answers.

Paula pushed through to where Alan was regaling a group of

admiring financial administrators with the story of how he lost his arm. He swooped down on Paula and clasped, or more accurately hooked, her to him.

'Paula, Paula, Paula,' he said warmly. 'Come and meet my lovely Pat.'

'I was looking for someone,' Paula said.

'I want you to meet her,' Alan said, bustling her across the room. 'She really is the most wonderful woman.' He paused and looked into her eyes. 'We have so much in common. Like –'

'Accountancy for instance?'

'How did you know?'

'A lucky guess.'

They approached Pat's chair, its occupant a picture of silk resplendence.

'You must be?'

'Paula.'

'How lovely.'

Alan planted himself next to his bride and draped a fond arm – the one he had left – over her shoulders.

'Meet Pat,' he said simply. 'She really is the most –' he turned and stared doggily into her eyes, ' – wonderful woman.'

Pat's eyes laughed up into his before returning to Paula with an appraising stare.

'I'll leave you girls to it.' He planted a kiss on the top of Pat's head, cried, 'Geoffrey, how marvellous to see you!' and bowled off into the crowd.

Pat motored her chair closer to Paula.

'So you are the famous Paula?'

'Famous?'

'He talks of you very warmly.'

Paula searched Pat's face for mockery, but found none.

'Alan said you worked with Belinda.'

'Oh that poor woman!' said Pat with feeling. Or, at least, as much feeling as her robotic voice allowed. 'We used to work in the same office, you know? We weren't friends exactly… I always say, you can't afford to get on with people if you want to get on.' She laughed, charmingly. Or, at least, Paula decided it might have been charming had it not sounded so much like a crazed automaton.

'And all that stuff at the ceremony…'

'Oh goodness, what was all that about? Obviously a case of projected guilt, don't you agree? The woman needs help. I mean, I felt very bad about what happened between Alan and I but…well, you can't stop true love, can you?'

Paula got the distinct impression she was being eyeballed into submission.

'No,' she said uncertainly. A vision of twinkling eyes behind a lively black mask flashed before her. 'No,' she said a bit louder. 'You're right. Life's just so short, isn't it? If you feel it you should… well grab it! With both hands! Or one hand, even.' She clasped one of Pat's. 'Thank you. That's really…that's really helped. I hope you and Alan are very happy together,' she said suddenly. And to her surprise she actually meant it.

Pat's voicebox crackled like an untuned radio.

'I think where Belinda went wrong was in thinking she could change him. The secret of a good marriage is acceptance, understanding. Having some give and take, accepting the rough with the smooth. You mustn't go into it thinking you can change your man.'

Paula nodded vigorously. So wise.

'He must be *forced* to do it for himself.'

Paula returned to the chattering guests, searching through the forest of fancy hats for that familiar masked face. She wondered, not for the first time, what his face looked like behind the mask. She passed Anthony who sent her a hearty wave from where he was dutifully looming over Luda, past the happily chattering Betsy, Ron and Malcolm – both men sheltering contentedly under the eaves of Betsy's munificent bust – and caught an airborn kiss from Gretchen, standing slightly apart from SlaveBoy, who was handcuffed happily to Belinda's personal guard.

'Hi Marcus.'

Paula patted the now fuchsia balloon-man presently leant against an upright piano and being fed fairy-cakes by the lady in the pleated skirt. ('Have you ever considered being inflated and immobilised by the love of our Lord? No? Think about it.')

But it was no good, there was no sign of The Man in the Mask anywhere. Seeing Alan propping up one of the drinks' tables, Paula rushed towards him and clutched his stump. He turned in surprise.

'Where's Fred?'

Alan looked at her blankly.

'You did invite him, didn't you?'

'Who's Fred?'

'You know. From the club. George. The Man in the Mask.'

Alan frowned.

'The naked fellow?'

'Yes.'

'Oh he couldn't make it.'

'Couldn't make it?'

'Something cropped up. I don't know. Don't worry about it. Have a glass of champagne.'

'I think I love him.'

Alan paused over his champagne glass. After all, it was not as though he wanted Paula himself, but he was not sure he was ready to let go of her adoration completely, not just yet.

'I see.'

'No, no you don't see. You have *never* seen,' she cried, casting around wildly.

Alan felt very put upon suddenly. He set down his *vol au vont*.

'What is it with you women? Always pushing, always complaining. Nothing's ever bloody good enough. Us blokes must strive to be better, but still always in your control. If we don't want you, we're uncaring bastards; if we do want you, we're sexist arseholes. If we chase you, we're desperate and pushy, if we don't chase you, we're uptight and unemotional. We're supposed to pick up endless bloody hints about what you want for birthdays or Christmases to show we really care, yet dare to have an idea of our own and we get nothing but abuse. You say you want spontaneous romance, but only at certain times, when you're not having your hair done, or going to the gym or having a smear test. We are never *ever* good enough. Why can't you just accept things as they are? Simple. Straightforward. Why do you women always have to *complicate* everything?'

Paula stared at him.

'You're right,' she said.

'I am?'

'Yes,' she said. 'Here, take this.'

'Oh right,' he said, staring after her hunched back with two glasses in his hand. 'Well done, Alan. Brownie point to you, then.'

Epilogue | UBER-PROGRAMMER

COMPRO: COMPUTER PROGRAMMING
FOR COMPUTER PROGRAMMERS
www.comprocompro.com

UPSTAIRS, SECOND DOOR
ON THE RIGHT,
PAST THE PHOTOCOPIER.
DON'T COME IN!

Paula looked at the curling A4 laminated sign. It was Blu-Tacked prominently to a heavy door next to a rundown newsagent. The door had seen better days and was prevented from imminent collapse only by a complex network of thin rope and string. She skirted it dubiously, traversed an unpleasant-smelling puddle and headed for the stairs.

This is it, she thought. *This is it.*

She tentatively pushed open the second door on the right past the photocopier and walked in.

Ten pair of eyes looked up at her. Ten pairs of eyes stared at her for one, two...six, seven, eight long seconds. Then nine pairs of eyes returned to their screens and the silence was replaced by the sound of industrious fingers tapping away. One pair of eyes remained.

She knew it was him straight away. She saw the kind eyes. The tufty hair. And she saw his face. She would know that face anywhere, whether masked by a small piece of black material or, as it was now, by a rictus of terror. He did not look too happy to see her.

They stayed like that for a while, staring at each other to the calm and rhythmic soundtrack of tapping fingers. No one else made a move. They could have stayed like that all day had not a miraculous thing happened. An unheard-of thing. There was a noise from behind them and a small, unnoticed door behind the rows of grey terminals slowly creaked open.

Ten pairs of eyes swivelled stealthily in the direction of the noise, desperate to get a glance, at last, at long last, of the hitherto mythical figure. Until this point, nobody had been quite sure of his existence. They had heard rumours, yes. But not hard scientific evidence. And hard scientific evidence was what they dealt in.

As the door inched open, it seemed to Paula and Fred that from the opening emanated a strange golden light, shafting through into the rest of the room and deep into their hidden souls. A chorus of angels sang and light burst forth into the room, while the air was full of the smell of rose petals...and at last, finally, at long long last, the Uber-programmer emerged.

Eight feet tall, with flowing hair clasped in a ponytail and glasses like cinema screens, wearing a T-shirt that read simply

'*Code*' (they gasped at the audacious simplicity of this statement) he stood amongst them like a colossus, eyes two flashing tadpoles, blinking uncertainly in the light.

The Uber-programmer looked at Paula and smiled. At least, she *felt* he did. Programmers never smile. Most have lost the capacity for all welcoming facial expressions by the time they hit puberty. But, nevertheless, Paula felt such an extraordinary feeling of fogeyish benevolence radiating towards her, that she was certain that was his intention.

'Sorry for barging in,' she said in a rush. 'I was just dropping in on − a friend of mine.'

Nine pairs of eyes swivelled in Fred's direction. He felt the hot accusations of desertion in the eyes of the Probably-Andrews and blushed.

'I didn't mean to disturb your office.'

The Uber-programmer stared at Paula from behind the panes of his enormous spectacles. Had he heard her? Did he understand what she had just said? They stayed like that for some minutes. It was beginning to get embarrassing. She opened her mouth to repeat her explanation.

In a delayed reflex, he put out a hand. She held it non-plussed and then, as it wasn't doing anything, shook it up and down a couple of times as was the done thing. He continued to stare at her.

'Paula,' she said, eventually, desperately, as it did not seem as though he was ever going to say anything.

Several minutes went by, so that she felt forced to shake his hand again. Twice. With gaps. She looked past him at the posters of *Kill Bill*, Jordan, the Millennium Falcon, she took in the reams of paper covered in streams of incomprehensible letters, the unwashed mugs: *Star Wars*, Lego, and, curiously, My Little Pony. She observed the ladder of shelves against the wall, almost completely empty aside from a lone spider plant, drooping unhappily towards the floor. Having exhausted the contents of the room she looked hopefully towards the one window, to find it was obscured by a layer of grime so thick that she could see nothing but the grime.

And then the Uber-programmer spoke.

'Andrew,' he said in the soft ethereal prepubescent voice of one who is not from this world. And with that he dropped her hand abruptly and headed back towards his office door. On the cusp of his inner sanctum he hesitated, turned slightly and said thoughtfully, 'At least I think so.'

The door closed and the light, the singing, the chorus of angels, and the scent of rose petals disappeared with him.

Eleven pairs of eyes exchanged one-sided glances of awe (they weren't quite brave enough for the two-sided glance just yet).

Then, gradually, nine pairs returned to their screens and the small office returned to quiet tapping normality.

Two pairs of eyes remained. The emergence of the Uber-programmer had removed all signs of terror from Fred's face, replacing it instead with surprise, awe, spiritual grace, and finally, calm. Paula smiled at him. To their mutual amazement, he smiled back.

'I came by to see if you wanted to get some lunch,' she said.

Acknowledgments

Writing a book takes so long that nearly everyone I've met during the course of writing this has helped in some way or another. But I want to give a special thanks to the following:

Leticia Agudo and fellow-writer Lisa Glass (lisaglass.co.uk) for reading far more versions of this than is healthy and peeling me off the floor every time I was having a nervous breakdown; my agent Adrian Weston at Raft for all his help and support; Catheryn, Rebecca, Kit and Alice at Marion Boyars for their hard work, vision and having the faith – thank you; Lucy Luck for her incredible attention to detail; Jessica Houghton for her help with a particular passage; Alistair for helping me work out the 'programming thoughts' and Mum and Andrew (for too many things to mention).

I also want to thank Margaret, Leena, all my various internet chums for their encouragement (particularly the lovely 'Whingers and Fuckers' in WF: you know who you are) and thanks to Pru Rowlandson and everyone at the Debut Authors' Festival in Edinburgh for giving me the confidence to finish the damn thing – particularly Sam Kelly, whose kindness was invaluable.

Thanks, also, to Robert; to Stephen and Brian, who patiently answered my detailed questions about the finer points of accountancy life; and to a tree surgeon I phoned in Edinburgh. Plus all the staff at Leith Victoria Swimming Pool, Edinburgh.

A special thank you to Sheila Moore who sadly died before I knew the book was going to be published. The best friend anyone could have.